SHERRYL WOODS

TEXAS
EVER AFTER

The Pint-Sized Secret and
Marrying a Delacourt

mira

mira™

Recycling programs
for this product may
not exist in your area.

ISBN-13: 978-0-7783-6949-3

Texas Ever After

Copyright © 2024 by Harlequin Enterprises ULC

The Pint-Sized Secret
First published in 2000. This edition published in 2024.
Copyright © 2000 by Sherryl Woods

Marrying a Delacourt
First published in 2000. This edition published in 2024.
Copyright © 2000 by Sherryl Woods

For questions and comments about the quality of this book, please contact us
at CustomerService@Harlequin.com.

TM is a trademark of Harlequin Enterprises ULC.

Mira
22 Adelaide St. West, 41st Floor
Toronto, Ontario M5H 4E3, Canada
www.Harlequin.com

Printed in U.S.A.

CONTENTS

THE PINT-SIZED SECRET

One

"Blast it, Dad, you have to do something about this. If you don't stop it now, one of these days you'll wake up and the whole company will have been eaten up by your competitors." Jeb barely resisted the desire to slam his fist into the wall in frustration.

Bryce Delacourt thought he controlled the universe, and maybe he did.

At least he'd always had a pretty tight grip on Delacourt Oil and on his family. One by one, though, his children were easing away. Trish—the youngest—had married a ranch hand across the state in Los Piños, and only a few months later Dylan had fallen for a pediatrician in the same city while conducting a search for her missing son.

More than miles separated them, though. As huge as Texas was, it was nothing compared to the gulf filled with hurt feelings and unyielding pride.

That left thirty-three-year-old Jeb and two younger brothers still in the family business, still trying to juggle their own independence and their father's need to control everything and everyone around him.

Unlike his big brother, Jeb's only form of rebellion was to try to carve out a niche for himself that would allow him to do the sort of undercover investigative work he loved, but within the world of Delacourt Oil.

Sometimes—like now—he regretted not bolting as Dylan had. His brother would have welcomed him as a partner.

Over the past couple of months, though, there had been evidence of trouble inside the company. Jeb thought he'd finally found the perfect opportunity to prove to his father just how important it could be to have an insider staying on top of corporate leaks.

So far, however, his father hadn't seen it his way. If anything, Bryce Delacourt was more determined than ever to keep all of his remaining sons bound to their desks—"paying their dues," as he put it. He was also blind as a bat when it came to the possibility that someone was stealing the company's oil exploration test results and feeding them to rival oil corporations.

Twice in recent months Delacourt Oil had lost potential new sites for drilling just as bids for the land were being formulated. To Jeb, that all but shouted that an insider was betraying them. To his father, it appeared to be no more than a minor annoyance.

"You don't understand business, son. This sort of thing happens from time to time."

"Twice? Back-to-back?" Jeb questioned.

"Sometimes. We'll get the next one," Bryce insisted with surprising equanimity for a man who had a well-earned reputation for ruthlessness. "I'm convinced this is nothing more than coincidence."

"I wish I shared your optimism. Maybe I'd buy your theory—if the timing hadn't coincided with the arrival of your new geologist," Jeb said, doing exactly what he'd sworn to himself he wouldn't do—tipping his hand and making an accusation that he had no evidence to prove.

Brianna O'Ryan's possible involvement had been nagging at him for weeks now, but he'd managed to keep silent. He'd wanted his father's permission before he went digging any further for the truth. Obviously, judging from his father's shocked expression, he should have handled this in reverse. He should have found the proof first.

"Brianna? You think she's selling us out? Don't be ridiculous. She's as loyal as they come," his father declared with passionate conviction. "She's grateful to have the job here. Why, she hasn't even turned thirty. She knows no other oil company would have moved her into a job with so much responsibility. Besides…" His voice trailed off.

Jeb caught something in his father's expression. "Besides…what?"

"Nothing," he mumbled, and suddenly developed an uncharacteristic fascination with straightening things on his desk. His pens had never been aligned so neatly.

"Dad, what are you not telling me?"

"Nothing," Bryce insisted, his expression setting stubbornly.

"Let me check into her background at least," Jeb pleaded.

"Absolutely not."

"Why?"

"Because you're in no position to question my judgment. Don't you think I know what I'm doing when it comes to hiring someone in such a critical position?"

There was no answer to that that was going to please

his father and Jeb knew it. He searched for a way to suggest that even the great Bryce Delacourt could occasionally be duped by someone intent on deceiving him.

"Spies tend to be clever at concealing things, Dad. That's their nature," he ventured cautiously. "If we're up against a pro, not even your well-honed instincts would kick in. Why not let me look into it? If you're so sure she's innocent, what's the harm?"

"The harm is that you could damage an innocent woman's reputation."

"I don't intend to broadcast my suspicions," Jeb countered. "Give me a little credit."

"Forget it," Bryce said again. "I don't care how careful you think you're being, word will leak out. Brianna's good name will be forever tarnished."

Jeb studied his father. He was missing something. Was there more going on between him and Brianna than Jeb had guessed? She was a beautiful woman, after all. He'd noticed that long before he'd had any cause to be suspicious of her. In fact, it was because of his own attraction to Brianna that he'd forced himself to try to examine objectively what little evidence he had. To his regret, no matter how he looked at the facts, he still thought everything pointed to Brianna being involved in the leaks to their competitors. The problems hadn't arisen until after her arrival, and now they were being repeated.

Maybe his father was incapable of such objectivity. After all, his father wouldn't be the first man to let his libido overrule his common sense.

Maybe he had noticed the same drop-dead gorgeous body that Jeb had seen, though in a company the size of Delacourt Oil, surely there would have been rampant rumors if there had been anything personal going on between the president and his top geologist, a woman nearly thirty years younger than he.

Still, Jeb couldn't deny that his father was a handsome, vital man, to say nothing of being a very wealthy one. There was little gray in his black hair, just enough to make him look even more distinguished. He jogged daily, used his home gym regularly. He could easily have passed for a man ten years younger. And if Brianna was deceitful enough to sell corporate secrets, why not make a play for the married CEO, as well?

Now in their late fifties, Bryce and Helen Delacourt had been married a long time. The road hadn't always been smooth, despite the united front they tried to present to the world. Even so, Jeb didn't think there had been affairs on either side. He simply didn't want to believe that his father's reasons for defending Brianna were personal. He was sure his father had too much integrity to engage in a tawdry office romance.

But despite his conviction, he felt compelled to broach the subject. If his dad was wearing blinders when it came to the beautiful Brianna, Jeb needed to know it. He could rally his brothers to his side, then together they could present a united front. His father would have to listen to reason and allow the investigation to go forward.

"Dad," he began cautiously, "is there something going on here I don't know about? Are you and Brianna—?"

"Stop right now!" In a way that demonstrated just how angry he really was, his father set his coffee cup down very carefully, very precisely, then leaned forward. "Don't even go there, Jeb. Don't insult me or Brianna O'Ryan. This is about the fact that *I* am still in charge of this company. It's about who decides if and when we have a problem, nothing more or less," he said in a cool, measured tone. "I won't have so much as a hint that our top geologist is anything other than loyal. I sure as hell don't want my own son suggesting that there's something going on between the two of us. Are we clear?"

Only marginally reassured, Jeb knew when he was defeated. He sighed, but murmured dutifully, "We're clear."

"Good. That's that then." His father's expression turned neutral. "So," he inquired casually, "how was Dylan when you saw him? And Trish?"

Jeb wanted to protest the shift in topic but knew better. Any further discussion of Brianna would have to wait until his father's temper cooled. Besides, maybe this new subject was an area in which he could actually engineer some progress. If so, the meeting wouldn't have been a total waste of his time.

"Happy," he told his father. "They both wish you'd break down and come to Los Piños to see them. They want to show off your grandkids."

"They know where I live if they want to see me," Bryce said stiffly.

Uneasy at being cast in the unfamiliar role of peacemaker usually played by Trish, Jeb tried to cut through to his father's weak spot: family. "Dad, I know you were hurt that they settled somewhere else, that they're out from under your thumb, but don't you think it's time to make peace, bring this family back together?"

"It's not up to me. They're the ones who left."

Jeb shook his head. "This hard line is Mom talking, not you. You've always known when to cut your losses. Family has always meant the world to you. You miss them both. I know you do. You're dying to spend time with your granddaughter and with Dylan's new stepson. Plus Dylan has Shane one weekend a month now. Why can't you just pop over there one day and surprise them? Mend some fences."

This time it was his father who sighed. "Your mother…"

"Doesn't know what she's missing," Jeb said. "She'll come around if you do. She's always overreacted when anyone hurts you. She thinks she's being loyal and protective. I think you're both cutting off your noses to spite your faces. We're talking about Dylan and Trish here, not a couple of strangers who've offended you and can be excised from your lives without leaving a scar."

His father didn't respond, but when Jeb casually tossed a package of snapshots onto his desk, there was no mistaking the eagerness in his father's expression as he reached for them. Jeb left him scanning each one as thoroughly as if they were geological survey maps.

Stubborn as a mule, he thought with a mix of affection and frustration as he left. It was a trait they'd all inherited, often to his father's very sincere regret.

But because the stubbornness was as ingrained as breathing, Jeb had every intention of learning everything he could about Brianna O'Ryan, despite his father's forceful edict to stay away from her. Because she was a smart, intriguing, beautiful woman, he figured it would be a pleasure, even if she turned out to be as honest as the day was long.

Which he doubted with every instinct he possessed.

The last thing Brianna wanted to do after a long day at the office was to drive clear across town in rush-hour traffic, but she never missed spending an evening with Emma when she was in Houston. There were too many nights she had to miss when she was on the road for Delacourt Oil. Besides, once she got to the residential treatment facility where Emma had been living for the past year, her day always brightened. All it took was one of her daughter's shy smiles or some tiny hint of improvement in her movements.

Fourteen months ago Brianna hadn't even been sure her little girl would live. Emma had been in the car with her dad when Larry had lost his temper at being cut off by another driver. In less time than it took to mutter an oath, he had been caught up in a full-blown incident of road rage. His car had been forced off the road into a culvert, where it had rolled over and over.

Miraculously, he had walked away with barely a scratch, but just about every bone in Emma's fragile four-year-old body had been shattered.

For days, united by grief and fear, they had sat by Emma's bedside, uncertain if she could possibly pull through, but God had spared her life. Then they had been faced with the long ordeal of healing and the very real threat that she would never walk again.

That had been more than Larry could bear. Consumed by guilt, he had walked away from the hospital one night and never looked back.

Until that moment, Brianna had thought she had a solid marriage. She had respected her husband, a man she had known most of her life, a man she had loved with every fiber of her being. She kept thinking he would come to his senses and come home, and for a long time she had been prepared to forgive him.

When the divorce papers had arrived in the mail a

few weeks later, Brianna had been shocked. Filled with anger and pain at the betrayal, she had signed them with little regret. Or so she had told herself. Looking back, she could see now that Larry's selfish act had left her with a heart filled with resentment and bitterness. She doubted she would ever trust another man. If a man as honorable as she had thought Larry to be could show such weakness in the face of adversity, how could she possibly risk her heart with anyone else?

Not that she had time for a personal life now, anyway. Her days began at dawn and stretched until midnight. As exhausting as they were, she was grateful to have her baby alive and a job that not only paid the exorbitant medical bills, but was totally challenging and fulfilling. For a time after the accident she had been terrified she might never find work in her chosen profession again.

During those first weeks of Emma's recovery, Brianna had taken so much time off from work that she had lost her job. Stunned, she had been devastated as much by the loss of her insurance as by the blow to her career.

How could Emma possibly recover if her mother couldn't afford the best possible care? Brianna had needed to find a new job in a hurry. In a highly competitive field, that was easier said than done, and she was approaching the job search with more than the usual baggage that might daunt a prospective employer.

To her amazement, Bryce Delacourt had overlooked the firing and the demands of her daughter's recovery when she'd applied for the top geologist's position at his company. With astounding compassion, he had also seen to it that her insurance kicked in for Emma's treatment, running roughshod over his carrier to make it happen. He would have her undying loyalty forever because of that.

They had made a deal, though, that no one at work would know about Emma. She didn't want their pity, but more important she didn't want special treatment because of her situation. She needed to have the people she worked with respect her as a professional. She was being brought in to supervise people who were older than she, people who had been there longer. She desperately needed to have credibility, to gain their trust. She knew all too well that no matter what their credentials, too often single moms weren't taken seriously in the workforce. Because of that, Brianna threw herself into her work 150 percent and still found time for her daughter at the end of the day.

Running late tonight, she dashed inside the treatment facility with its brightly lit, sterile interior, and as always she was struck by the fact that there was no mistaking that this was just one step removed from a hospital. Only in the pediatric wing had an attempt been made to create an atmosphere that was both more cheerful and more like home. Here colorful murals had been painted on the corridor walls, the small area of the cafeteria reserved for children had been decorated in brilliant shades of blues, yellows and reds, and toys were strewn about as carelessly as they might be in a child's bedroom at home.

"Hi, Gretchen," Brianna whispered to the evening supervisor, waving as she passed the desk where the young woman was on the phone.

Gretchen glanced up, then covered the phone's mouthpiece and called out to her. "Hey, Mrs. O'Ryan, wait a sec, okay?"

Brianna's heart thudded dully as she waited for the nurse to finish her call. Had something happened today? Was Emma regressing? Her progress had come in fits and starts, in frustratingly slow little bursts, followed by weeks of status quo. All too often there were twice as many steps backward as forward. Brianna grinned ruefully at the mental pun. In Emma's case, there had been no "steps" at all.

Gretchen, tall, blond and athletic, strode out from behind the desk, a smile forming. "Don't look so worried," she said, giving Brianna's suddenly icy hand a warm squeeze. "I didn't mean to scare you. Emma's fine. I just wanted to be with you when you saw her."

"Why?" Brianna asked, still not entirely reassured.

"You'll see. She's in the sunroom, watching TV."

Brianna followed her down the hall, her mind whirling. It wasn't something bad. Gretchen wouldn't torture her if it was—she'd say so straight out. She was the most direct person Brianna had dealt with at the facility, always telling Brianna the unvarnished truth, even when the doctors danced around it, even when it was painful to hear. And because Gretchen was on in the evenings when treatments were over and the facility was settling into a quieter rhythm, she had more time to spend with anxious parents like Brianna.

In the sunroom, which was mostly glass, she spotted Emma at once with her halo of strawberry-blond curls, watching reruns of a favorite sitcom. For a moment, just the sight of her daughter was enough to clog Brianna's throat with tears. She was so blessed to still have her baby. Everything else in her life was just window dressing.

"Emma," Gretchen called out. "Your mom's here."

The wheelchair slowly rotated as Emma struggled with the mechanized controls she had finally mastered only a few days earlier. A frown of concentration knit her brow. She didn't look up until she'd stopped in front of Brianna. Then that shy little smile stole across her face.

"Hi, Mama."

Brianna leaned down and kissed her, resisting the desire to linger, to cling. Even at five, even under the circumstances, Emma craved her independence.

"Hey, baby. What's up? Gretchen has been hinting you have a surprise for me."

Emma nodded, clearly bursting with excitement. "Watch."

Ever so slowly, with an effort that was almost painful to see, she slid to the edge of the seat, then placed her feet gingerly on the floor. Her knees wobbled uncertainly for a heartbeat, then stiffened. Finally she released her hold on the wheelchair and stood. All alone. Not quite upright, but completely, amazingly, on her own. Tears filled Brianna's eyes and spilled down her cheeks.

"Oh, baby, that's *wonderful.*"

"I'm gonna walk, Mama. I am," Emma said with fierce determination.

Overcome with emotion, Brianna knelt and gathered her in a fierce hug that for once Emma didn't resist. For the longest time words wouldn't come.

Then she leaned back, dabbed at her eyes and beamed at Emma. She stroked her baby's cheek.

"Sweetie, I am so proud of you. You are going to be walking in no time at all. I never doubted it for a minute," she said, even though she had. Late at night and all alone, she had worried and wondered if Emma would ever run and play like other kids again, if she would have the friends and the adventures she deserved.

This sweet, poignant moment was the reason she worked herself to exhaustion. It made all the sacrifices, the loneliness and the single-minded focus of her life worthwhile. Emma *was* going to walk again.

Two

Jeb was a big believer in the direct approach, especially when it came to his social life. There were plenty of people in Houston who thought of him as a scoundrel, nothing more than a rich playboy who thought he had a right to use women, but the truth was actually very different.

For all his carefree ways, he felt things deeply. Once he had wanted nothing more than to marry and have a family, but now he doubted he ever would. He wasn't sure that he'd ever again trust a woman deeply enough to risk his heart. The one time he had, he'd been burned badly. He'd been engaged to a woman his senior year in college, a woman who'd stolen his heart during a freshman English class and never let go.

Everyone said they were a perfect match. His parents adored Gloria Ann. Her parents welcomed him into their lives as if he were a son. Only Dylan had expressed doubts, but because they were nebulous, instinctive doubts, rather than fact-based, Jeb had ignored him.

Too late he'd discovered that Dylan had been right. Gloria Ann was more fascinated with the Delacourt fortune than she was with him specifically. She had actually made a play for his younger brother, Michael, the one who was most clearly destined to become president of Delacourt.

Turned down flat, she had attempted to smooth things over with Jeb, but his eyes were open by then. He'd walked away, filled with hurt and disillusionment.

After that, he'd made a conscious decision to keep his relationships casual and his intentions direct. There would be no promises of happily-ever-after, not on his part, anyway. He couldn't see himself getting past his now ingrained suspicions. Of course, Dylan and Trish had felt exactly the same way before they'd met their current matches. Given the family track record, it probably would be wise never to say never, but he knew himself well enough to say it with conviction.

In the meantime, there was Brianna. The very beautiful, very brilliant Brianna. There was no question of falling for her. He already had very valid reasons for distrusting her. Getting close to her would be a little like going into a foreign country without all the necessary inoculations very much up-to-date. That didn't mean he couldn't appreciate the journey.

After a restless night during which he considered, then again dismissed, his father's warning to steer clear of the geologist, Jeb concluded that the simplest way to discover just what kind of person Brianna was would be to ask her out, get to know her outside the office, see what her lifestyle was like and if there was any chance she might be spending income that outdistanced her Delacourt Oil salary.

He knew she was single. Divorced, according to the rumor mill, though no one seemed to know much about the circumstances. He also knew she'd turned down dates with half a dozen of their colleagues. Her social life—if she had one—was a mystery. He considered such discretion to be admirable, as well as wise. He also considered it a challenge.

And that was what brought him to the fourth floor at Delacourt Oil just after seven in the morning. Although he knew very little about Brianna's habits, he did know that she was an early riser. A morning person himself, on several occasions he'd spotted her car already in the parking lot when he arrived. Obviously neither of them had the sort of exciting nightlife that others probably thought they did.

As he walked toward her office, Jeb wasn't the least bit surprised to find Brianna's lights on and her head bent over a huge geological map spread across her desk. Her computer was booted up, and all sorts of mysterious calculations were on the screen.

Since she was totally absorbed, he took a moment simply to stand there and appreciate the auburn highlights in her no-muss, no-fuss short hair. If her hairstyle was almost boyish, the graceful curve of her neck was contrastingly feminine. She was wearing an outfit with simple lines, in natural fabrics—linen and silk. Her short-sleeved blouse was the same deep teal shade as her eyes. Her only jewelry was a simple gold cross. From the look of it, he guessed it was an antique. A family heirloom, perhaps? At any rate, she wasn't adorned with expensive diamonds, which might be telltale bounty from any ill-gotten gains.

"Find anything interesting?" he asked eventually, trying to tame hormones that seemed inclined to run amok at the mere sight of her.

Her head shot up, and startled blue-green eyes stared

at him guiltily…or so he thought. Was she trying to pinpoint a new site she could pass on to the competition? When she made no attempt to hide the map, he told himself he was being ridiculous. Any investigator worth the title should think more rationally and behave more objectively than he was at this moment. So far, he had suspicions and coincidence and not much else, yet he'd already all but tried and convicted her.

"You," she said, as if he were a particularly annoying interruption, despite the fact that they probably hadn't exchanged more than a few dozen words since she'd been hired.

"Now is that any way to greet a man who's come bearing coffee and pastry?"

"No thanks," she said, pointedly going back to her study of the map.

Ignoring the blatant dismissal, Jeb crossed the room and perched on the corner of her desk, close enough to be impossible for her to ignore. He opened the bag he'd brought, removed two cups of coffee and two warm cheese Danishes. He wafted one, then another under her nose. Though she didn't look up, there was no mistaking her subtle sniff of the aroma.

"Tempting, aren't they?"

She heaved a resigned sigh, then sat back. "You're not going to go away, are you?" Despite the exasperation in her tone, there was a faint hint of a smile on her lips.

He beamed at her. "Nope." He held out the coffee. She accepted it with exaggerated reluctance, took a quick sip, then another slow, appreciative swallow.

"You didn't get this here," she said. "Not even the executive dining room makes coffee like this."

"Nope. I made a stop at a bakery."

She regarded him warily. "Why?"

"No special reason."

"Of course not," she said with blatant skepticism. "This is something you make a habit of doing for everyone around here. Sort of an executive welcoming committee, a way to let the troops know that management cares. Today just happens to be my turn."

"Exactly."

Her unflinching gaze met his. "Bull, Mr. Delacourt."

Startled by the direct hit, he laughed. This was going to be more fun than he'd anticipated. "You don't mince words, do you, Mrs. O'Ryan?"

"Not enough time in the day as it is. Why waste it searching for polite phrases when the direct approach is quicker?"

"A woman after my own heart," Jeb concluded. "Okay, then. I'll be direct, too. I have a charity ball to attend on Friday. It's for a good cause. The food and wine promise to be excellent. How about going with me?"

"Thanks, but no thanks."

Vaguely insulted by the quick, unequivocal—if not unexpected—refusal, Jeb pulled out his trump card. "Max Coleman will be there," he said innocently, watching closely for a reaction. Other than a slight narrowing of her lips, there was nothing to give away the fact that the name meant anything at all to her. He pressed harder. "Might be interesting to see how he reacts to knowing just how well you're doing at Delacourt Oil, don't you think?"

"Max Coleman is slime," she said at once. "I don't care what he thinks."

"Sure you do, sweetheart. It wouldn't be human not to want a little revenge against a man who fired you." He let his gaze travel slowly over her, waited until he saw the color rise in her cheeks before adding, "You look very human to me." He winked. "Pick you up at six-thirty."

He headed for the door, anticipating all the way that she might contradict him, might refuse even more emphatically, though he knew he'd found her Achilles' heel.

Instead, she said softly, "Formal?"

He turned back, feigning confusion. "What was that?"

She frowned at him. "I asked if it was formal?"

"Definitely black tie," he said. "Wear something sexy. You'll bring him to his knees."

Amusement seemed to flit across her face at that. "And you, Mr. Delacourt? Will it bring you to your knees?"

"Could be. I guess we'll just have to wait and see." To his sincere regret, in the past couple of minutes he'd discovered it was definitely possible. That alone should have been warning enough to induce him to abandon his investigation before it went wildly awry. Instead, it merely increased his anticipation.

Agreeing to go to a charity ball with Jeb Delacourt was quite possibly the dumbest thing she'd ever done, Brianna told herself as she raced around with her assistant during their lunch hour on Friday trying to find an appropriate gown that wouldn't destroy her budget for the next six months. She had waited until the last minute as if to prove to herself that the evening didn't matter.

And of course it didn't mean anything. How could it? She barely knew Jeb Delacourt. They'd exchanged a few polite words on occasion, but that was it. She knew he had a reputation as a charming rogue, and she'd certainly seen evidence of that when he'd shown up in her office. He'd known just what to say to entice her into breaking her rule against dating coworkers. She would have to stay on her guard constantly.

But this ball wasn't about spending an evening with Jeb at all. Not really. As he had guessed, it was about seeing Max Coleman again, maybe even forcing him to eat crow over his cruel, unsympathetic treatment of her during the worst weeks of her life. The opportunity to slap him in the face with her new success at Delacourt Oil had been too irresistible to pass up, just as Jeb had guessed it would be.

That was her reason for accepting. It remained to be seen what Jeb's motives had been for seeking her out and asking her to share the evening with him. She sincerely doubted it had been some altruistic inclination to help her get even with her old boss. She also couldn't help wondering just how much Jeb knew about her firing. The dismissal itself was common knowledge. The reasons behind it were less so. Even back then, she had worked very hard to keep her private life private.

Whatever Jeb's motives, she was determined to avoid "sexy" at all costs. She'd seen the glint of masculine appreciation in his eyes. She figured his imagination was working overtime as it was. There was no point in giving him anything blatantly provocative to work with. She intended to keep Friday night all-business or die trying.

"What about this one?" Carly Winthrop asked, calling Brianna's attention to a slender sheath of shimmery bronze. "It would be devastating with your coloring."

Carly had picked the consignment shop for their lunch-hour excursion, declaring that the bargains were incredible. "All those rich biddies who can't bear to be seen in the same dress twice take their castoffs there," she had explained. "It's like walking into designer heaven for all us poor folks."

"How much?" Brianna asked, her gaze fixed on the bronze dress. She'd never owned anything like it and, to her amazement, she discovered she very much wanted to. She stiffened her resolve. "I'm not going bankrupt for this event."

"Just try it on," her assistant urged. "Then we'll see about the price."

"There's a tag right on it," Brianna pointed out. "What does it say?"

"It says it was made for you," Carly responded, removing it and tucking it into her pocket. "Try it on."

The dress really was a dream. Slinky and elegant at the same time, provocative but not daring. Brianna itched to reach out and run her fingers over the luxurious fabric. But a glimpse of the label told her that the dress had probably cost in the thousands when new. She doubted it had been reduced enough for her wallet.

"I'm sure I'll find something else," she said, unable to mask the regret in her voice.

"You want this dress," Carly countered with the unerring conviction of a woman who'd learned to read her boss well. "I can see it in your eyes."

"It doesn't matter what I want. I'm not going to pay a fortune for a dress I'll wear one time and that's that."

"Think of it as an investment. You're going out with one of Houston's wealthiest, most eligible bachelors. Reel him in and you can have a closet filled with dresses like this one."

"I have no intention of reeling in Jeb Delacourt or anyone else," Brianna replied firmly. "I don't have time for a social life."

"Then what do you call this date?"

"Lunacy."

Carly blinked. "I beg your pardon."

"It was a mistake, an impulse, a desire for revenge."

"You have something against Mr. Delacourt?"

Brianna shook her head. "No, my battle is with someone else. Jeb is just giving me a chance to claim a very sweet victory."

"Does he know that? Isn't he going to be ticked off when he figures out you're using him?"

"He knows," Brianna assured her. "That's how he got me to agree to go in the first place."

Carly sank down on a delicate Queen Anne chair, the dress cascading over her lap in waves of bronze. "This is way too complicated for me. I like the kind of date where the guy who asks actually wants to spend time with me and vice versa."

"In a perfect world, that's what we all want. My world has veered sharply off course."

"I don't get it. You're beautiful. You're single. You have an incredible career. What's off course?"

Carly's incredulity was the price Brianna had to pay for keeping Emma a secret. "It's not important," she assured the young woman, who was fingering the fabric of the bronze dress longingly.

Brianna sighed. "Hand it over," she said, gesturing for the dress. "It can't hurt to try it on."

"Isn't that what I've been telling you?" Carly replied, beaming her approval. "You will knock them all dead in this dress."

"Now there's a goal to aspire to," Brianna said wryly as she went into the dressing room.

She slipped off her shoes, then her blouse and skirt.

A glance at the dress also assured her she'd have to ditch her bra, too. When she was ready, she slid the dress over her head and felt the soft glide of silky fabric caress her skin as it fell into place. She zipped it up before daring a look in the mirror. When she finally looked, her mouth fell open.

She looked…incredible. Sophisticated and ultrachic. Dazzling. Those were definitely words that had never been ascribed to her in the past. She was more inclined toward tailored clothes in the office and rugged outdoor wear for on-site explorations. This dress turned an inveterate tomboy into a sleek, desirable woman. She wanted to strip it off before she got too used to the image.

She wanted to wear it forever. That was such a dangerous desire that she reached quickly for the zipper, but it was stuck. She poked her head out of the dressing room and called for Carly.

"Let me see," her assistant commanded.

Brianna shook her head. "Just help me get the zipper unstuck. It's all wrong for me."

Carly yanked open the dressing room curtain, then gaped. "*Wrong?* You think this is all wrong? Either you're blind or you've been staying out in the sun way too long and it's fried your brain. This dress is *perfect*. It's devastating."

Wear something sexy. You'll bring him to his knees.

Jeb's words came back to taunt her. Was that what she wanted? Did she want to see Max Coleman's mouth drop open as hers and Carly's had? Did she want him to regret the day he'd dismissed her? Yes, but not because she looked so darned good in a dress. She wanted him to regret it because she was great at what she did and he was a mean-spirited fool.

Still, it wouldn't hurt to go to that ball armed and dangerous, so to speak. Temptation overruled logic. As Carly freed the zipper, Brianna made up her mind.

"I'll take it."

"Way to go, girl. Mr. Delacourt won't know what hit him."

Jeb? For just a moment, Brianna had been so intent on revenge, she'd almost forgotten her date. Sweet heaven, this was no dress to be wearing on a date with her boss. She needed something simple, a basic little black dress that could last for years, even if it did spend most of the time in the back of her closet. She swallowed hard and carefully replaced the bronze dress on its hanger.

"Carly, remember that black dress I was looking at?"

Carly's nose wrinkled in distaste. "The one that looked as if it would suit your grandmother?"

"Yes, that one," Brianna said firmly. "Get it for me, please."

"Don't tell me—"

"Just get it, okay? No lectures."

"You're going to regret this," her assistant warned.

"No," she said with a determined shake of her head. "No, I won't." The black dress, with its long sleeves and white satin cuffs and collar, was sophisticated, too, she told herself. Even if she did look a little like a nun in it, she conceded, studying her reflection in the dressing room mirror. It was perfect for an evening with a man known far and wide as a scoundrel. It would send a very definite message that she wasn't available, that this evening was all about business. Dignified and prim, it was the perfect solution.

She marched out to buy it, feeling reassured that there would be no contradictory messages being sent later that evening. But even as she stood at the counter to pay for it, her gaze kept straying around the consignment shop for one last glimpse of that spectacular bronze dress.

"Looking for something?" Carly inquired innocently.

"No," she insisted.

"Well, it's gone," her assistant said. "In case you were interested, after all."

Brianna felt some vague little spark inside her die. For a few minutes in that dress, she had felt like a sexy, totally alive female again, instead of a responsible professional, a single mom with no illusions about the lack of romance in her life. She'd had no idea a dress could transform the way a person felt about herself.

"Somebody bought it?" she asked, trying to mask her disappointment.

"Obviously somebody recognized a knockout dress when they saw one," Carly declared pointedly. "Snatched it right up without even trying it on."

"Good for them," Brianna said without much enthusiasm. She signed the credit card receipt for her basic black dress, accepted the package and left the store without a backward glance. "Let's get back to the office. We have a lot of work to do. And Mrs. Hanover will be wondering what on earth happened to us."

"Work?" Carly echoed incredulously. "You should be at home pampering yourself, taking a nice long bubble bath. I'm sure your secretary will cover for you, if anyone calls. And I can handle any emergencies that crop up. Not that there are a lot of emergencies with rocks that have been around forever."

"Indulging in bubble baths is for people who don't have a mountain of paperwork on their desks."

"You really are going to give women a bad name," her

assistant grumbled when they arrived back at the office. "Mr. Delacourt is used to going out with society women who have nothing but time on their hands. You're not even going for a manicure, am I right?"

Brianna grinned at her despondent tone. "You're right."

Carly shook her head. "Pitiful." A moment later her expression brightened. "I know. I'll give you a manicure, while you're doing that all-important paperwork."

"Manicures are not in your job description," Brianna protested as she tossed her new dress onto the couch in her office and settled behind her desk.

"I'll do it on my coffee break."

"You don't get a coffee break."

"I do now." She bounced out of Brianna's office, then returned with three shades of nail polish. She held them up for Brianna's inspection. "Which one?"

"Carly—"

Ignoring her, Carly pulled up a chair, chose the shade herself and began shaking the bottle. "This one, I think. Hold out your hand."

Despite her very strong instinct to refuse, Brianna couldn't seem to stop herself from doing as Carly instructed. She watched in fascination as the dark polish with its hint of bronze was applied. The younger woman glanced up and caught her expression.

"Haven't you ever had a manicure before?"

"Not really. When you spend your life playing with rocks and digging around for soil samples, it doesn't make a lot of sense. I'm lucky I even have nails."

"Pitiful," Carly decreed for the second time that day.

A few minutes later, when all the nails had been painted, she leaned back and studied them with satisfaction. "Perfect."

"I'm glad you're pleased," Brianna said wryly, but she couldn't tear her own gaze away, either. Her hands no longer looked like a workman's. In fact, they looked almost as if they might belong to a lady.

"Maybe I will go home and take that bubble bath after all," she said.

Carly grinned. "All right! Remember to take notes tonight. I'll want to hear every last detail on Monday."

"I'm not going on this date for your vicarious enjoyment," Brianna pointed out.

"I thought you said that it wasn't a date, it was business. I am your assistant, aren't I? If it's business, we should have something on record."

"You have a very twisted mind," Brianna proclaimed.

"Will I get the details or not?"

A faint stirring of excitement fluttered in Brianna's stomach. It had been a long time since she'd felt anything like it. Because she owed at least some of that to her assistant, she nodded.

"You'll get details. I'll make it a point to remember what everyone is wearing and what food was served."

"Forget all that. I just want to know what kind of a kisser Mr. Delacourt is."

Brianna gulped. "Forget it. No kissing. No telling."

Maybe if she repeated that often enough between now and six-thirty, she wouldn't even be tempted. But something told her it was going to be a wasted effort, especially if Jeb Delacourt had other ideas.

Three

Brianna soaked in her hyacinth-scented bubble bath for a half hour, which was more feminine self-indulgence than she'd experienced in years. She fiddled with her hair and managed to coax a little curl into the short style, then added one of those fancy rhinestone-studded hair clips shaped like a butterfly. Emma had given it to her last Christmas. She'd had one of the nurses at the rehab center pick it out, then had wrapped it in paper she'd colored herself with swirls of holiday red and green.

At six o'clock Brianna slipped on the black dress and lost a little of the sparkle in her eyes. It was a lovely gown, but compared to the one she hadn't bought, it was boring. It did nothing for her figure or her coloring. It just covered her body—most of her body, she noted glumly.

Which was exactly what she'd wanted, she reminded herself. She might want to make an impression on Max Coleman, but she needed to keep Jeb Delacourt's mind strictly on business.

She turned away from the mirror just as the doorbell rang. Since it was barely six-ten, she doubted it was Jeb.

She padded to the door in her stockinged feet and found a stranger on the doorstep.

"Yes?"

The man glanced down at a slip. "Brianna O'Ryan? That you?"

"Yes."

He held out a large box and a form.

Brianna noted despondently that he didn't even give her a second glance in her boring black gown. "Yes, but I'm not expecting—"

"Your name and address are on here. That's what I go by," he countered, and waited for her to sign.

She signed his form, accepted the box and went to get him a tip. When he had left, she stared at the box, then recognized the name of the consignment shop in discreet gold letters in the lower corner.

"What on earth?" she murmured, pulling off the lid, then unfolding layers of tissue paper. Her eyes widened when she saw the bronze dress nestled inside, along with a note.

Clutching the dress, she ripped open the note.

"I figured you'd be suffering pangs of regret about now and, if you aren't, you should be," Carly had written. "Enjoy."

"I'm going to fire her," Brianna muttered, even as she raced back to her room and changed into the killer dress. She sighed as she twirled in front of her mirror. "Then again, anyone who dares to defy the boss when she's wrong ought to get a raise." She took another excited survey of her image. "A really big raise."

The charity ball turned out to be a masterstroke, Jeb concluded as he held Brianna in his arms and whirled her around the dance floor. She was concentrating so hard on looking for her ex-boss, she was paying little attention to the questions Jeb was asking. Her responses, for once, were uncensored, if not particularly illuminating.

Unfortunately, he was having an equally difficult time concentrating. He had been ever since he'd arrived on her doorstep and caught his first glimpse of her in a dress that even Cinderella would have envied. His mouth had gone dry, and he'd been having difficulty swallowing ever since. Why had he never suspected that the beautiful Brianna was capable of bringing a man's heart slamming to a halt? Because of his taunt, he'd fully expected her to be covered from head to toe in black, something discreet, something that wouldn't have every male head in the room swiveling for another, longer look. Unless he was very careful, he was going to forget what this evening was all about.

In fact, he'd been so dumbstruck when she opened her door that he hadn't even taken note of what little he could see of the interior of her small town house. His surprise at the modest community in which she lived had vanished in a sea of purely masculine appreciation.

Now he caught the speculative glances of some of his oldest and dearest bachelor friends and tightened his grip on Brianna possessively. This reaction was a very bad sign, he noted, forcing himself to take a step back and look Brianna directly in the eyes. Another mistake, he realized, when his throat went dry again.

"Having fun?" he managed to ask finally.

"I didn't come to have fun," she murmured, avoiding his gaze.

"What the heck," he countered. "Have some, anyway. It's free."

Her gaze swept the room again. "Where is Max Coleman? Shouldn't he be here by now?"

"There are a thousand people crushed into this ballroom. I'm sure he's here somewhere. If we keep dancing, we're bound to bump into him."

Brianna regarded him suspiciously. "He is going to be here, though, right? You're sure of it."

"That's what I was told. Maybe we should take a break, get some champagne and you can tell me why he fired you."

Even as she studied the crowd, she waved off his inquiry. "I'm sure you've seen the personnel records. It's no big secret," she said dismissively.

Actually Jeb *had* read the personnel file. It was almost as vague as Brianna herself was being now. "It wasn't working out. I believe that's what the file states. Was that it?"

She shrugged. "That about sums it up."

"Max Coleman doesn't strike me as a man prone to whims."

For a fleeting moment her attention returned to him. "You'd have to ask him about that. One day I was working there, the next day, I wasn't."

"If your firing was that capricious, why didn't you sue him?"

"Not my nature," she said. "All I cared about was getting another job." Her attention drifted yet again.

Jeb struggled to accept her response. It was so deliberately disingenuous, he almost wondered if Max hadn't staged the firing just so she could be hired by his competitor, making her a well-placed spy for her old boss.

So far, though, Coleman hadn't been involved in any of the soured deals.

Besides which, Brianna genuinely seemed to despise the man. She might not have wanted to waste time and money taking him to court for wrongful dismissal, but she resented his actions just the same. That much was clear from the venom in her voice whenever she mentioned his name. Unless she was a better actress than Jeb imagined, her hatred was sincere.

"How about a little fresh air?" Jeb suggested when they had their champagne.

She cast one last, disappointed look around the room, then nodded. "Fine."

Outside on the terrace, there was a soft breeze. The sky was brilliant with stars, competing with the lights of downtown Houston. But none of the scenery could hold a candle to the woman beside him. Jeb found himself wishing for the hundredth time that this were a real date, that he could take her in his arms and kiss her the way he'd been wanting to ever since he'd picked her up. Aware of just how inappropriate that would be on any number of levels, he held back. For a man reputed to have no scruples, now was a fine time for his to be kicking in.

He leaned back against the railing and sipped his champagne. "Tell me about your marriage," he suggested idly.

Without the distraction of looking for Max, she was instantly suspicious. "Why?" she asked bluntly.

"Just making small talk, sweetheart. That's what men and women do at these things."

She shrugged off the explanation. "I wouldn't know. I don't spend a lot of time at charity balls."

"Well, let me explain the rules, then. We eat a little, drink a little, dance when the mood strikes us, exchange pleasantries with people we know, chitchat with those we'd like to know better, gossip about the bad guys, network with business associates. Then we go home and crash, so we can do it all again tomorrow."

"Two balls in one weekend?"

"Downright decadent, isn't it?"

"Tedious."

"Depends on your companion. Now something tells me you could relieve the tedium, if you'd just relax a little."

"I am relaxed," she protested.

She didn't look it. She'd started looking uptight the instant he mentioned her ex-husband. In fact, she looked so thoroughly uncomfortable, so totally wary, that he couldn't help himself. He forgot all about his resolve of moments ago and leaned forward and kissed her.

It was meant to be no more than a quick peck, something to startle her, maybe put a little color in her cheeks. But when she gasped softly, when her lips seemed to heat instantaneously, Jeb was lost. He dipped his head and kissed her again, longer this time, deeper, savoring the taste of cool champagne and hot Brianna. He lifted his hand, curved his fingers around her neck and felt the wild beating of her pulse beneath his thumb.

When he leaned back at last, she looked dazed. He felt as if he'd been sucker punched. The kiss wasn't supposed to happen, but he'd kissed plenty of women without having his insides turn to mush. His reaction told him that this informal, unauthorized investigation of his had just gotten a whole lot more complicated.

Distance, that's what he needed. Not physical, but emotional. He knew a surefire way to get it, too.

"Let's try that again," he suggested innocently, and caught the flare of color in her cheeks. Before her protest could form, he grinned. "Tell me about your marriage."

Just as he'd anticipated, her expression closed down. "It didn't work out," she said evasively.

"Sort of like the job," he countered, deliberately trying to provoke her with innuendo. "Are there a lot of things in your life that just don't work out?"

"No more than the average person," she retorted. "I just know when to cut my losses." She gave him a hard once-over. "This seems like a good time to do that to-night."

The suddenness and depth of her anger took him by surprise. She moved before he could stop her. Jeb watched her cross the terrace, spine stiff, shoulders square. The effect was lost a little when his gaze drifted lower and he saw the sway of slim hips encased in bronze. Damn, but she was something.

He followed her inside at a leisurely pace, so leisurely that he might have risked losing her in the throng if Max Coleman hadn't chosen that moment to put in an appearance. Brianna was frozen in place, her face pale.

"You okay?" Jeb asked, moving up beside her.

Apparently she counted Jeb as the lesser of two evils, because she linked her arm through his and plastered a smile on her face. "Just peachy," she announced. "I've been waiting for this chance for a long time. Since it's the only reason I'm here tonight, let's make the most of it."

Jeb could have chosen to be insulted by the role he'd been cast in second fiddle to revenge—but if it brought her back to his side, he was more than willing to go along with her. He wanted to see how she interacted with her old boss, see if he could glean any relevant information from their exchange.

Max Coleman had scrambled his way to the presidency of a small Houston-based oil conglomerate. He'd started in the fields, studied hard and been driven by blind ambition to reach the top. He wasn't as polished as Bryce Delacourt, nor as handsome, but he presented a commanding figure, especially in a well-tailored tuxedo. His gaze settled on Brianna, then moved to Jeb.

If seeing her made Max uncomfortable, spotting his rival's son made him downright nervous, but he covered both reactions quickly with a smile that only a close observer would recognize as fake.

"Brianna, my dear, you're looking lovely tonight. How nice to see you here. Things must be going well for you." He glanced pointedly at Jeb, as if to imply that he now knew why she was succeeding in the aftermath of his dismissal. "I had no idea that you and Jeb were so close."

"First date," Jeb retorted. "I needed the most beautiful woman in Houston on my arm tonight, so naturally I thought of Brianna. She's become a very valuable asset to Delacourt Oil." He hesitated ever so slightly. "And to me."

Her startled gaze shot to his, as if she couldn't believe the audacity of the remark. He winked at her, drawing her into the game.

"Yes, Brianna was always as interested in corporate benefits as she was in the challenges of her work," Max said, then gave them both a curt nod and walked away.

Jeb stared after him, puzzling over the comment. It

sounded like the embittered response of a man who'd
been wronged in some way, but how? Had he made ad-
vances toward her and been spurned? Was her firing as
simple as that, a sexual harassment case that she hadn't
had the will to fight?

Glancing down, he caught the bright red patches of
color in her cheeks and realized that, whatever the man
had meant, his comment had hit its mark.

"What was that all about?" Jeb asked.

"Just Max getting in the last blow," she said. "I'd like
to leave now, if you don't mind."

"I do mind," he said, catching her off guard. "You
can't walk away in defeat. You need to show the man
he can't get to you."

"How am I supposed to do that? Being here with you
certainly backfired."

"Darlin', that was just the first volley." He beckoned
her toward the dance floor. "Now let's show the man
what you're made of."

A fast tune had just started, and Brianna stared at
Jeb as if she'd never been on a dance floor before in
her life. "I can't."

"You don't know how? You don't want to? Or what?"

"Dancing is not going to prove anything to Max
Coleman," she said, as if she pitied Jeb for being fool-
ish enough to think otherwise.

For the moment Jeb forgot all about his secret mission
for the evening and concentrated on hers. She looked
vulnerable and defeated, and he was too much of a gentleman to let that continue.

"Then you're not doing it right," he assured her,
sweeping her into a dip that clearly left her dizzy. She
was laughing by the time he brought her upright.

"Okay," she said, the sparkle returning to her eyes. "Let's do it."

For the next three dances, they ruled the floor. The crowd parted to observe, cheering the intricate steps, applauding and begging for an encore when each song ended. Jeb caught Max's expression as they whirled by him in one tempestuous sweep of the room. He looked as if he'd swallowed something particularly nasty.

Brianna caught his expression, too, then gazed up at Jeb. "Thank you," she whispered. "I think our job here is done."

Jeb nodded his agreement. "Let's blow this place."

She giggled like a schoolgirl and in that instant, Jeb felt himself falling for her. She tantalized him. He didn't know her. He didn't understand her secrets. He had no idea what made her tick.

Which meant he was going to have to keep seeing her, he concluded. Not that it was a hardship. She fit a little too neatly into his embrace. She smelled of some exotic scent that drove him a little bit crazy. He found himself wanting to kiss that graceful curve of her exposed neck.

None of that was supposed to happen, of course. Getting turned on by the subject of an investigation tended to cloud objectivity. He might not be the professional P.I. his brother was, but he knew that his current state of arousal was big trouble.

Still, he had no choice. Not if he was to save Delacourt Oil. And maybe not even if he was to save himself.

After their triumph on the dance floor, the evening had gone downhill. Jeb couldn't coax more than a one-word response from Brianna all the way home. At her house, she fled from his car. She barely uttered good-bye, much less an invitation to come inside. He had sat in the driveway for fully ten minutes trying to decide whether to follow her. At midnight, he'd finally concluded that he needed to give her the space she so obviously craved. He figured eight to ten hours ought to be enough.

He was up at dawn on Saturday and on the phone to Dylan.

"Some of us actually like to sleep in on the weekends," his big brother protested when Jeb awakened him. "Especially when there's a beautiful woman in bed beside us."

"Stop bragging," Jeb retorted. "Besides, this is important."

"And my plans for the morning weren't?"

"You can get back to them in a minute."

Dylan sighed heavily. "Afraid not. I can hear the patter of little feet running toward the kitchen right now. Soon I'll be blessed with the sound of cartoons at top volume. Then my bride will desert me."

"Okay, okay, you have my pity and my apology. Now will you listen for a minute?"

"Why not? Looks like I don't have anything better to do."

"I went out with Brianna last night."

Dylan whistled. "The lovely spy?"

"We don't know she's a spy," Jeb said defensively.

"Hey, you're the one who pinned the label on her, not me. What's changed?"

Jeb ran his fingers through his hair. "She's… I don't know. She's not what I expected."

"Holy mackerel, you've gone and fallen for her, haven't you?"

"Don't be ridiculous. It was one date. Nobody falls for a woman in one date. Besides, I'm investigating her. How stupid do you think I am?"

His brother laughed. "Not stupid. Just male."

"You are not helping," Jeb accused.

"What do you want from me?"

"Advice."

"About your love life?"

"About the investigation, dammit!"

"Let's take it from the top then. Tell me again why you suspect Brianna of leaking Delacourt secrets."

"Timing, mostly. She arrived and suddenly deals started going sour."

"What does Dad say?"

"That I should stay the heck away from her, that she's totally trustworthy, etcetera."

"Maybe you should listen to him for once."

"I can't ignore my instincts. There's something going on, Dylan. I can feel it."

"Maybe there is, but maybe Brianna has absolutely nothing to do with it. Circumstantial evidence, especially the little bit you have, won't cut it. You need some cold hard facts. There are other geologists. Any one of them could be behind the leaks."

"Out of the blue? They've been here for years."

"But maybe one of them has just been hit with huge medical expenses, or college tuition, or blackmail. The possibilities are endless. I think you'd better back off with Brianna. Start from scratch. Look at everyone who had the information that was leaked. Check into their finances. If you want to fax me a list of names, I'll do some of the financial checks for you. Then you can go from there."

Jeb could see the logic of Dylan's plan, but it grated just the same. If he did as his brother suggested, he'd have to stop seeing Brianna. Right now he had the excuse of the investigation. If he kept seeing her, he would have to admit it was personal, and then what? What if the feelings that had stirred in him last night deepened, and then it did turn out that she was guilty?

He'd be caught smack in the middle of a disaster. "Jeb? Are you listening to me?"

"Yeah, I heard you."

Dylan groaned. "But you don't want to stay away from Brianna, do you? It's already gotten personal. How far has it gone, little brother?"

Jeb saw little point in lying. Dylan was already assuming the worst. "Not far. I kissed her. That's it."

"You think she's a corporate spy and you kissed her. Terrific. That's really using your brain."

"I didn't consult my brain. That's the difference between you and me, Dylan. Sometimes I just react to the moment."

"Then perhaps you ought to severely restrict the moments you spend with Brianna," his brother suggested.

"I'm afraid I can't do that. I've already made plans to see her again this morning." He didn't mention that Brianna knew nothing about those plans. "I want to check a little more closely into her lifestyle."

"Yeah, right."

"You're not helping."

"I'm trying to. You're just not listening. Fax me those names, Jeb. And keep your distance from Brianna. See her today if you have to, but try to think of her as the enemy. Normally I recommend thinking of a suspect as innocent until proved guilty, but maybe that's not such a good idea in this instance. Maybe considering Brianna a bad guy will help you to keep your hormones in check until we know what's really going on."

Jeb accepted his brother's advice without comment. It hadn't worked the night before, but he was willing to give it another try. This time he wouldn't even take coffee, much less pastries, when he paid his surprise visit.

Four

"Tell me about the party, Mama," Emma begged when Brianna stopped by the rehab facility on Saturday morning. "I want to know everything. Was your dress beautiful? Did it have lots of lace and ruffles? What color was it? Pink? That's my favorite, you know."

Brianna held back a chuckle at Emma's idea of high fashion. "I know you love pink, but my gown was bronze and there wasn't a ruffle on it. Sorry, angel. You know I'd look terrible in pink. That's *your* color. You look like a little princess when you get all dressed up in pink."

"I'll bet *you* looked like a princess even if you were wearing some other color," Emma said loyally.

"I don't know about that." Brianna thought of her escort, who had looked very much like a prince in his fancy tux. The formal attire suited his dark good looks, made him look more than ever like the scoundrel she had to keep reminding herself he was.

Not that he'd behaved that way…for the most part. For the major portion of the evening, he'd treated her with the utmost respect. He'd been a perfect gentleman. And she, perverse idiot that she was, had hated it.

Apparently some long-dormant part of her had wanted him to kiss her, had wanted him to make a pass at her when he'd danced her into the shadows of the huge ballroom. Instead, when he'd merely settled her on a bench and gone for champagne, she had been ridiculously disappointed. He was a rogue, wasn't he?

Later, when she got her unspoken wish, when he kissed her on the terrace, the results had been devastating. Her blood had almost literally sizzled. She hadn't realized that was possible. She had also recognized belatedly just how intoxicatingly dangerous that could be.

After the kiss, they had danced some more, putting on a show, in fact. Then they had talked. And talked. Most of the time Jeb had been totally, utterly charming. Attentive. Witty. Compassionate, especially when it came to helping her claim revenge against Max Coleman. In fact, she hadn't met a man she'd been more attracted to in years.

Or a man who was more out of reach. She had absolutely no intention of risking her job by getting involved with someone at the office, a Delacourt no less. She had no time for a relationship, period. Talk about courting disaster. She simply couldn't risk it, not with so much at stake.

Besides, there had been all those probing questions he'd dismissed as nothing more than small talk. She knew better. He was after something, though she honestly had no idea what. Could it really be as simple as a man wanting to get to know a woman? She might be out of practice at dating, but her instincts said no. She could still recognize idle conversation. She did a lot of networking, especially with men. She knew how to play *that* game. Jeb's questions had been too sharp, a little too pointed. They would have made her uncomfortable even if they hadn't come so close to exposing all her secrets.

"Mama?"

Emma's voice cut into her thoughts. "Sorry, baby. My mind wandered."

"Wandered where?"

"Back to the party," she said, forcing herself to inject a note of enthusiasm into her voice as she described all of the elegant clothes and beautiful decorations.

Emma had too few chances to hear about anything that could carry her away from this confined world in which she lived. Their rare outings were seldom more exciting than the drive-through line at a fast-food restaurant, though hopefully that would change now that Emma was getting more adept at dealing with her wheelchair. Up until now she had stubbornly refused to go anywhere unless she could remain in the car.

"I don't want people to stare," she declared, and that was that.

One day Emma's world would open up again, but until then Brianna did her best to let Emma live vicariously through her own activities. Her site explorations were seldom as intriguing for a five-year-old as last night's dance clearly was.

"It sounds like a fairy tale," her daughter concluded with a little sigh when Brianna had finished. "I wish I could go to a ball and dance."

Brianna's heart broke at the wistfulness in her daughter's voice. In Emma's case, it wasn't just childish yearning to be grown-up. Unspoken was the very real fear that she might never be able to walk, much less dance.

"You will, sweetie," Brianna promised in an attempt to reassure her. "One of these days you will make all of the other girls weep with envy when you arrive with your handsome prince."

"What about *your* prince? Is he very handsome? Can I meet Mr. Delacourt?"

The very idea horrified Brianna. "No," she said curtly, then tempered it by adding, "He's a very busy man."

"But you like him, don't you? You haven't gone out with anyone since Daddy left, so you must."

"This was just a business occasion, Emma, not a real date," Brianna said, ignoring the fact that for a few minutes, out on the terrace, it had felt very much like a date. In fact, it had felt like the start of something important.

Then he'd started in with those questions again, and the mood had been lost.

"Oh," Emma said, clearly disappointed.

Brianna decided it was time to change the subject. "Want to try to stand up for me? Gretchen says you're getting better at it every day."

Emma shook her head. "Not now."

"It's important to keep trying."

Emma's expression set stubbornly. "No," she said as emphatically as she had when it had been the primary word in her vocabulary.

"Please," Brianna coaxed.

"I don't feel like it."

Brianna sighed. She'd had to learn not to push, though it went against her nature. But she knew Emma had to be allowed her rebellions. There were so few things she had control over in her life. The therapists were demanding taskmasters. The doctors poked and prodded. Occasionally Emma had to be permitted to make her own decisions about what she was ready to try.

"Maybe next time, then," Brianna said cheerfully, and gave Emma a kiss. "I love you, baby. I'll be back first thing in the morning. If the weather's nice, I'll bring a picnic and we can eat lunch outside. Would you like that?"

Emma shrugged, then turned away to face the TV, even though Brianna doubted she really cared what was on. It was just a way to show her displeasure with her mother.

Once again filled with the sensation that she had let her daughter down, Brianna left. She'd known there would be days like this, days when she would feel utterly and totally defeated. The doctors, the counselors and Gretchen had repeatedly told her it was perfectly normal, but she wanted so badly to be a positive influence in Emma's life. She wanted her little girl to be motivated, to feel loved. She wanted her to fight her injuries, not her mother.

Brianna was dragging by the time she got home, lost in waves of self-pity and regrets. Though her pulse took an unwanted leap at the sight of Jeb waiting on her doorstep, she was in no mood to welcome him.

Even so, for a fleeting moment she found herself regretting that she hadn't dressed in something other than jeans and a faded teal T-shirt when she'd run out of the house to pay a quick visit to Emma. She looked decidedly frumpy, while he managed to make his own jeans and dress shirt with the sleeves rolled up look like something out of a men's fashion spread in *GQ*.

Why was it that she constantly felt at a total disadvantage with this man? She worked in a man's world. She had never been easily intimidated, but there was no denying that Jeb rattled her. He could shake her composure without even opening his mouth. Possibly it had something to do with the fact that he deliberately kept her off balance. She couldn't get a fix on his real intentions.

And so she approached him with wariness.

"Where have you been this early on a beautiful Saturday morning?" he asked as she neared. "Not the office, I know, because I called there."

Even though his tone was curious rather than accusatory, Brianna instinctively bristled. "Checking up on me, Mr. Delacourt?"

"Now that I've held you in my arms, I think you can stick to calling me Jeb," he chided. "No, I wasn't checking up on you, just looking for you. I thought you might want to do something today. It's a little late now, but we could go out for breakfast."

"Sorry. I've already eaten."

"So that's where you were. Having breakfast with a friend?"

Brianna grasped the explanation eagerly. "Yes. If I'd known you were thinking of coming by, I could have told you I had a prior engagement. Some people actually call ahead."

He shook his head. "Too easy to get turned down. It's harder for you to say no to my face."

Despite her dark mood, her lips twitched with amusement at his feigned vulnerability. "Is that so? Well, I'm sorry, but the answer is still no."

"How about lunch then? Or dinner?"

"I thought you had another ball to attend tonight."

"I'll skip it."

"Won't that upset your date?"

"I was planning on going solo. They have my money. No one will miss me."

Brianna doubted that.

He gave her one of those winning, megawatt smiles. "So, how about it?"

"Sorry, no."

"Another date?"

"No."

"Too much to do?"

"Yes."

"You work too hard," he scolded. "It's not good for you. You need to relax, have some fun."

"I thought that's what I did last night. Now I have to catch up."

"On?"

"Housework. Paperwork. I have an important business trip at the end of next week."

Clearly undaunted, he suggested, "Tell me about it."

"You'd be bored to tears."

"It's my family's business. Why would I be bored?"

Put in her place, Brianna searched for an explanation that would ring true. She couldn't very well tell him that he made her uneasy, that she simply wanted him to go, that she didn't want to get too comfortable with having someone—especially him—around.

"Rumor has it that you don't care all that much about oil, that you're working at the company because your father expects it," she said eventually. "Naturally I assumed hearing about dirt samples and rocks would bore you."

He surveyed her with one of those knowing, penetrating looks that he obviously knew rattled her. "I'll bet you could make it interesting."

"I don't have time to try," she said flatly. Then because her first tactic had clearly backfired, she tried another one. "Before I get down to work, I have to do my chores around here. With my schedule, I have to stick to a routine."

"In other words, you're in a rut."

"I prefer to think of it as living a structured life," she said testily.

"Okay, then, I'll help," he volunteered.

Taken aback by the unexpected offer, she stared at him. "You'll help?" she repeated, as if his offer hadn't been entirely clear. When he nodded, she asked, "Why?"

"Why not? I can run a vacuum or dust as well as the next person, though I'm a little curious why a woman with so much on her plate and making your salary wouldn't have a maid."

"Because I have better uses for my money," she said tersely, brushing past him and going inside, hoping to put an end to this absurd discussion. If she could have, she would have slammed the door in his face, but there were a whole lot of reasons for not doing that, starting with his ability to make trouble for her at the office. Naturally, he didn't take the hint. He followed.

The minute he crossed the threshold, she very nearly panicked. Had she left the door to Emma's room closed, as she usually did? Though the town house was a recent acquisition, purchased in the aftermath of the divorce because she no longer had the funds or the time to cope with the upkeep on the house she and her ex had shared, she had decorated a room for her daughter. It was filled with dolls and stuffed animals, the overflow from a collection too big for Emma's room at the rehab center.

The bed was a little girl's dream, a white four-poster with a pink eyelet canopy and matching comforter. Emma had picked it out just before the accident, but she had never slept in it. It had been delivered during those awful days when they hadn't known if she would live or die. When Larry would have sent it back, Brianna had insisted on keeping it, clinging to it as a talisman that her daughter would get well and come home again.

"Excuse me a minute," she said, and dashed upstairs to check the door. If she couldn't talk Jeb into leaving, she had to be sure he wouldn't spot any evidence that she had a daughter.

Upstairs, she found the door to Emma's room closed. She turned the key in the lock as an added precaution, then pocketed it. Thank heavens, the only pictures of Emma were in her bedroom, a place she was all but certain she could manage to keep Jeb from entering.

When she went back downstairs, she found Jeb surveying the living room with open curiosity. She thought she detected surprise at the simplicity of her surroundings. Other than Emma's room, she had done little to turn the town house into a home. She hadn't wanted to spend the time and she hadn't had the money. The truth was, every spare cent she had went into Emma's care. The insurance covered a lot, but far from everything.

"I know it's understated," she said defensively, "but I like it."

He seemed surprised by her defensiveness. "Did I say anything about the decor?" he asked.

"No, but I could see the wheels churning in that mind

of yours. You know what I earn and it's clear I don't spend it on knickknacks."

His gaze clashed with hers. Though there was a teasing glint in his eyes, she couldn't help thinking he was dead serious when he asked, "So, where do you put all that money, Brianna?"

She forced a lighter tone into her voice. "Maybe I gamble," she suggested. "Maybe I have a thing for expensive jewelry and it's all socked away in a safety-deposit box."

He laughed as if he found the responses every bit as absurd as she had intended. "And maybe you just don't see the point in spending a lot on a place where you spend so little time," he suggested mildly, giving her choice a surprisingly innocent spin.

"Exactly," she said, seizing the explanation. "Now, if you don't mind, I really do have work to do, and I'm sure you have better ways to spend your Saturday."

"Actually this suits me just fine. I said I'd help and I will. What needs to be done first? Don't be shy. I've done my share of hard labor. I spent one backbreaking summer in the oil fields at Dad's insistence. I survived that. I can survive whatever chores you'd like to assign me."

Daunted and admittedly a little intrigued by his persistence, she tested him by pointing to the hall closet. "The vacuum's in there. The mop's in the kitchen. All the floors need doing."

"You've got it," he said willingly, then caught her arm when she would have headed for the stairs. "There's just one catch."

She bit back a sigh. "I should have known. What is it?"

"I take you out for a nice, leisurely lunch when we're

finished." Before she could protest, he added, "Topped off by some decadent, gooey dessert."

Brianna laughed at his triumphant expression. Clearly he was convinced he knew exactly how to tempt her. And the sorry truth was, he did.

"How did you know my weakness for decadent desserts, Mr. Delacourt?" she demanded, trying hard to imply that he'd obviously been poking around in highly classified documents to learn that tidbit about her nature.

He winked. "Sweetheart, I know more about you than you think, and what I don't know, I intend to find out."

Threat or promise? Brianna wondered, suddenly nervous all over again. But there was no backing out now, not when he was already turning on the vacuum and attacking the carpet with a vengeance. She'd just have to keep her guard up. Unfortunately, that was rapidly getting to be easier said than done. Jeb Delacourt had a nasty habit of surprising her in ways that made him more and more appealing.

Jeb tried to imagine what his brothers would think if they could see him pushing a vacuum from room to room in a place that wasn't even his own. They'd probably be astonished he even knew how to turn it on, especially since his own place tended to suffer from severe inattention between the maid's visits.

He, however, considered this to be a very clever way of getting to poke through all the rooms in his chief suspect's house. It gave him plenty of time to check out her possessions, to determine if she was living beyond her means.

Unfortunately, he had to admit all of the evidence pointed to the opposite. If anything, Brianna's lifestyle appeared spartan. The furniture was comfortable, but not new or expensive. There were a few pictures on the walls, but most were prints, not originals. The china closet held an assortment of elegant dishes and crystal, but the sets were by no means complete, suggesting that what she did have had been wedding presents.

The dust he found on them when he ran a finger over the surface of a plate suggested they were seldom used.

So what *did* she spend her money on? Was she just a very frugal woman? Was she simply salting it away for retirement? He certainly hadn't believed for a minute her deliberately taunting remarks about throwing her money away on gambling or investing in jewels.

Just when he was concluding that perhaps his suspicions were unfounded, he came to a locked door. He tried the handle twice to be sure the door was locked and not merely stuck. Why would a woman who lived alone need to lock a room? What did she keep hidden behind that door?

As with most interior locks, this one could be picked in a heartbeat, but not with Brianna just down the hall. If she found him inside that room, no explanation he came up with would be good enough. He decided to try an innocent game and see how it played out.

"Hey, Brianna," he called.

She poked her head out of the room he already knew was her home office. When she saw where he was standing, did her complexion turn pale or was that his imagination? She took a step toward him, then seemed to force herself to stop.

"What is it?" she asked.

"Do you want me to vacuum in here? The door seems to be stuck."

"Leave it," she said readily, perhaps even eagerly. "There's nothing but a bunch of junk in there. I use it for storing boxes I haven't unpacked." The explanation made sense on the surface, but it didn't satisfy Jeb.

Why lock a room if the only things in it were junk that hadn't been unpacked? His imagination, already stirred, ran wild. He began to envision boxes stuffed with…what? Hundred-dollar bills? Jewels? Stolen equipment? A spy's home computer hookup?

He needed to get a look inside that room, but it was impossible today.

Resigned to leaving it for another time, he merely waved an acknowledgment to Brianna, switched the vacuum back on and moved down the corridor as if he'd accepted her explanation at face value. He noticed that only when he was well away from the mysterious room did she retreat into her office once more.

A half hour later he was finished with the vacuuming and mopping in the kitchen when a brainstorm struck. He poked his head into Brianna's office.

"Okay, boss," he said with a mock salute. "I'm done. What's next?" She glanced up distractedly as if she'd almost forgotten he was there.

Her blue-green eyes seemed to take a moment to adjust. "What?"

"Anything more for me to do?"

"No, I think you can get time off for good behavior," she said with a smile that almost seemed genuine. "Thanks for the help, though."

"You ready to go to lunch then?"

She shook her head. "Not just yet. I want to go over

these reports one more time. You can go on, if you have other things to do."

She was still trying to get rid of him, he thought with something that bordered on irritation. If his ego were one iota weaker, he'd be insulted. There was no time for that, though, because he had a plan and she had just played right into it.

"I don't mind waiting. In the meantime, why don't I get started on some of those boxes for you?" he suggested.

"Boxes?" she repeated blankly.

Bingo, Jeb thought. There were no boxes in that spare room. He'd guessed as much. How would she handle it if he persisted?

"In the spare room," he reminded her. "I could at least get them unpacked and you could put the stuff where you want it later."

"Absolutely not," she blurted.

For an instant there was unmistakable panic in her eyes. But she covered it quickly. A polite mask slipped back into place. He had to give her credit for putting on a terrific act, when it was obvious that he was too close to some secret she didn't want to share.

"I just meant that you've already done way too much," she said in a rush. "If I haven't needed what's in those boxes by now, then it's probably not important."

She dropped her pen on her desk and stood up, brushing at imaginary lint on her jeans. "Maybe we should go to lunch. I'm sure I'll be able to work better after I've had something to eat. I missed breakfast completely."

Jeb seized on the remark, which directly contradicted what she'd told him earlier about her whereabouts. Had he just caught her in another lie? "I thought you told me you'd been out to breakfast with a friend."

Bright patches of color flared on her cheeks. "True," she said, clearly improvising. "But I didn't feel like having anything more than coffee."

Jeb didn't believe her tortured explanation for a minute. But why lie about something so innocuous? Where had she really been so early in the morning on a Saturday? Had she been getting together with a contact to reveal more Delacourt secrets?

Rather than exonerating her as he'd begun to hope he was going to do, it seemed he was accumulating more and more circumstantial evidence against her. Lies on top of lies. A secret room. And behavior that he could only describe as edgy. She wasn't forthcoming about even the simplest things. There had to be a reason for it, and he doubted he was going to like it.

He met her gaze evenly, watched as her chin lifted a defiant notch. "Do you want to go to lunch or not?" she asked, her gaze unflinching.

"Oh, I definitely want to go to lunch," he responded. There were too many things about Brianna O'Ryan that fascinated him.

Unfortunately, not all of them were suspicious.

Five

Brianna hadn't been this jittery since her wedding day. For once in the past few days it had nothing to do with her physical attraction to Jeb. It was all about the man's clever attempts to dig up information she didn't want to reveal. She hadn't been deluded for a minute back at the house. He had been after information, not her company.

Well, maybe not entirely. From time to time she had caught him watching her with what could only be interpreted as masculine appreciation. But in general, his attention had been focused on tripping her up, especially with all those helpful little offers that would have gotten him into Emma's room. Was his fascination with the locked door curiosity or something more?

From the moment he'd shown up in her office, she had suspected that he was after something. She had worked at Delacourt Oil for months without catching more than a glimpse of him. Now he'd paid a visit to her office, taken her to a very public event and shown up on her doorstep, all in one week. She doubted it was because he'd suddenly found her irresistible.

Since he was impossible to shake, she knew she'd better confront him directly—and soon—or she would make herself crazy wondering. She vowed to make it the first topic of conversation once they reached whatever restaurant he'd chosen for lunch.

But instead of heading for some casual outdoor café suitable for their attire, Jeb stopped his fancy sports utility vehicle in front of a gourmet deli in a No Parking zone.

"I'll be right back," he promised, darting from the car before she could question him or point out the likelihood that he was courting a ticket.

Maybe such mundane things as parking tickets didn't matter to the very rich.

He returned much faster than she'd anticipated, and he was carrying a huge picnic hamper. "Since it's such a beautiful day, I thought we'd go to a little park I know. Okay with you?"

"Sure," Brianna said, more charmed than she cared to admit. She'd figured him—all of the Delacourts, for that matter—as a see-and-be-seen type. Of course, she was hardly dressed for one of Houston's best restaurants or country clubs and, after his efforts with the vacuum and mop, neither was Jeb. Maybe this was all about protecting his image, rather than taking her on some romantic little excursion.

Thoroughly frustrated, she sighed heavily. She was usually good at reading people. Why couldn't she get a fix on this man? Probably because he didn't want her to, she thought wryly.

"What?" Jeb asked, glancing at her as he wove through heavy Saturday traffic.

She forced a smile. "Nothing."

"It didn't sound like nothing."

"Just relaxing. You know what they say—taking a deep breath and releasing it not only cleanses the lungs, it also restores the spirit."

"Is that so? I must have missed that. It sounded to me like the sigh of someone with a whole lot on her mind."

Brianna chafed at his easy reading of her moods. "Isn't that pretty much what I said?" she retorted testily.

"Not really. So, what has you stressed-out?"

She wondered what he would think if she blurted out that he was the problem, he and his motives for seeking her out. Instead, she said, "Too much to do, too little time. Isn't that what keeps most of us all churned up?"

"Not me," he claimed. "I'm a pretty carefree guy. Probably has something to do with running. After you've gone five miles in the morning, it's pretty hard to worry about anything else. It's a great stress reducer. You should try it."

Brianna laughed. "I wouldn't make it around the block."

"Why not? You look as if you're in pretty good shape."

She winced at his less-than-dumbstruck reaction to her body. "Thanks, I think."

He regarded her with amusement. "We're not talking about beautiful," he noted, "which you are. We're talking about fitness. Don't you have to be in good shape to go hiking and climbing around prospective oil sites?"

"I suppose," she conceded. "I never thought much about it. I just do it."

"It's not a job for a desk-bound weakling," Jeb pointed out. "Do you ever get to a gym?"

"Never," she admitted. When would she fit that in?

During one of the six or seven hours she now managed for sleeping? The closest she came to having a real fitness program was climbing up and down the stairs to her office at Delacourt Oil headquarters at least once a day. It was great for the thigh and calf muscles, to say nothing of her cardiovascular system. She was hardly ever breathless when she reached the fourth floor, but she was usually very grateful that her office was no higher.

"Maybe we'll go running together one morning," Jeb suggested. "You could come out to our beach house for the weekend. That's the best place for a morning run."

Brianna ignored the casual invitation to spend a weekend with him, refusing to take it seriously. Instead, she concentrated on the supposed purpose of such a visit. "I'd never keep up and you'd be frustrated."

"Darlin', seeing you in a pair of running shorts might frustrate me, but your pace wouldn't bother me one bit," he teased. "Think about it. I'll bet once you got started, you'd be hooked for life."

Brianna doubted it, and decided to change the topic. "You mentioned a beach house. Has it been in your family for a long time?"

"Years," he said. "My brothers and Trish and I love it, but my mother hated it. She would never have set foot in the place if she hadn't enjoyed mentioning its existence so much. She felt it gave her a certain cachet to be able to say she'd spent the weekend at her beach house. Dylan bought it from my parents a few years ago. Now it's pretty much a weekend bachelor pad." He glanced at her. "I was serious a minute ago. We could go sometime."

A whole weekend with the man, when she could

barely keep it together for a few hours? Not likely. Brianna shook her head. "I don't think so, but thanks, anyway."

"It's a big house, Brianna, a place to relax and get away from everything. I wasn't suggesting anything else."

She didn't believe him for a minute. Jeb was a very virile male. If he invited a woman away for the weekend, it wasn't to take walks on the beach and play cards. She met his gaze, though, and for once his expression was absolutely serious.

"You've obviously spent too much time listening to all the office gossip," he scolded mildly. "If I'd done half of what I've been accused of doing, I'd never be able to drag myself into work."

"What's the old adage? Where there's smoke there's usually fire."

"I date, Brianna. I'm single. Why shouldn't I? But I don't engage in casual affairs. There are plenty of women who like to imply otherwise for reasons of their own."

"Such as?"

"You'd have to ask them that. Maybe it's as simple as hoping that a little talk will make it so." He shrugged. "Those are the ones I never see again, so it pretty much backfires if that was their intention."

She had a feeling he was giving her a rare glimpse into his head, maybe even into his heart. "If they're so willing, why not take what they're offering?" she asked.

"Sex is easy. Too easy. Relationships are hard and, in the end, they're the only things that matter. I guess I'm holding out for something that matters."

Brianna shivered. She'd never met a man who actu-

ally believed that before. Most were all too eager to accept easy sex. If Jeb was actually telling the truth—and
she had no reason to doubt him—it said a lot about his
character. He wasn't the kind of man who would run
when the going got tough. He wouldn't abandon a wife
and an injured child when they needed him the most.

She might not understand his motives, she might
be concerned about all this sudden attention—but one
thing was clear. Jeb wasn't a thing in the world like
Larry. Which was too bad, because as much as she
would like to have a man like that in her life, Jeb Delacourt was still the last man it could be.

Jeb watched the emotions churning in the depths of
Brianna's eyes and concluded that things had gotten entirely too serious in the past half hour. She looked to be
near tears and, for the life of him, he had no idea why.
He just knew it did something to him deep inside to see
her like that. He reached across the seat and squeezed
her hand, which was maintaining a white-knuckled grip
on the strap of her handbag.

"Relax," he coached. "Remember? Deep breath.
Heavy sigh. Whatever works."

An uncensored smile—the first he'd seen—flashed
across her face. It was warm enough to cause a tight-
ening sensation in his chest.

"You're making fun of me," she accused without
rancor.

He grinned. "Now, why would I want to do that?"

"To make me laugh. It's what you do. You're a
charmer. I watched you last night. Every woman you
talked to was chuckling by the time we walked away."

"Is that a bad thing?"

"Absolutely not. It just makes it harder to know when to take you seriously."

He pulled to a stop at the curb beside one of his favorite small parks, then turned and met her gaze. "I've already told you that I don't do serious," he said quietly. Then it was his turn to sigh. Before he could stop himself, he added, "Something tells me you could change that, Brianna, and to be perfectly honest, it scares the hell out of me."

He wasn't sure which of them was more taken aback by his words.

Until they were out of his mouth, he hadn't even realized he'd been thinking that way. He'd recognized his attraction to her, accepted it as a fact of life, but more? He hadn't even begun to contemplate that.

Her startled gaze locked with his. Pink tinted her cheeks. She opened her mouth, probably to protest, then fell silent instead.

He rubbed a finger over her knuckles until they eased their grip. "Don't panic, darlin'. I'm just giving you fair warning."

"But I don't want—" she blurted.

"What? A fair warning."

"No," she said, then seemed to catch herself. "I mean I don't want anything, not from you."

Jeb nodded. "I know. That's what makes me think something's going to happen. You're the first woman I've met in years who clearly wants absolutely nothing from me." His expression turned wry. "Not even my company."

"That's not—"

He cut her off before she could utter a blatant lie. "I make you nervous, Brianna. If I hadn't brought up Max

Coleman's name, you would never have agreed to go out with me last night. You would just as soon I'd disappear. I'm not blind to that. You couldn't wait to get me out of your house."

"That's just because…" She shrugged, then leveled a look straight at him. "You were so persistent. I was convinced you had to be after something."

Jeb forced back an admission of guilt. "Such as?"

"I have no idea," she said, sounding thoroughly frustrated by her inability to assess his motives.

He sensed then that she really didn't know what had brought him poking into her life. Did that mean she was innocent? Or did she simply think that she'd covered her tracks too well ever to be discovered? Or that she merely assumed him to be some form of affable rake, rather than an investigator on a mission? His assigned jobs at Delacourt Oil were innocuous enough. His father tended to keep him where he could do no harm. His investigation of the soured land deals had been instigated at his own initiative, so why would she or anyone else suspect what he was up to?

"An honest woman," he said lightly. "That's all I'm looking for, Brianna."

She flushed at that. From embarrassment or guilt? He couldn't help wondering.

"Then you're looking in the wrong place," she told him. "No one's totally honest all the time, Jeb. Not even me. I tell the same little social lies as anyone else, shade the truth on occasion when it won't harm anyone."

"How about big lies?"

"Not if I can help it."

"What about secrets, Brianna? Do you have any of those?"

"Don't we all?"

Her tone was light, but the color had drained from her complexion, renewing his fear that she did have things to hide. Were they just general things she wanted no one to know, or specific things she didn't want him to discover? Such as the fact that she'd been betraying his family?

"How about this?" she suggested. "If I ask you for a million dollars, will it change your mind? Maybe make you go away?" There was a vaguely wistful note in her voice.

Jeb laughed, even though he found her desire to be rid of him troubling on any number of levels. "It might slow me down, make me think twice, but only if you could convince me you were serious."

"I guess that's out then," she said with what seemed to be feigned regret. "I'm not that good an actress."

"Then let's back-burner all this serious talk for the next hour or so and enjoy our lunch."

She seemed relieved by the suggestion. Though her expression remained guarded as they chose a spot in the shade, by the time they'd spread a blanket on the ground and opened the hamper, she was chuckling at his deliberate attempts to make her laugh. She still didn't sound carefree, but she was definitely not as guarded as she had been.

"I knew you couldn't resist me," he teased.

"Oh, I can resist *you,* but I'm a sucker for a bad joke," she retorted.

"How about expensive champagne? Are you a sucker for that, as well?" he asked, holding up a bottle and two crystal flutes.

"Absolutely." She accepted the glass he poured for

her, then asked, "By the way, how did you get all of this put together in such a hurry? You couldn't have been in that deli more than fifteen minutes. Do you have a standing Saturday order?"

"Nope, but I will admit that I called it in before I left the house this morning."

"What if I'd said no?"

"You did say no. More than once, as I recall."

She lifted her glass in a mock salute. "Okay, then, what if you hadn't been able to persuade me to change my mind? Would all of this have gone to waste or did you have a stand-in in mind?"

"I would have taken it home and dined all alone," he said with exaggerated self-pity. "Such a waste."

Brianna dug into the picnic basket and came up with caviar and toasted triangles of bread to put it on. "Do you often dine at home on caviar?"

"Not if I can help it," Jeb said. "I hate the stuff, but women seem to like it. I was out to impress you."

"Fried chicken would have done the trick, especially if you'd cooked it yourself. I do love to see a man in an apron, especially if he's in front of a stove, instead of a grill."

"Sorry. You're fresh out of luck. I can order up a gourmet dining experience from any restaurant in town, but I can't boil water. I'm afraid there have been too many testy housekeepers in my past, begging me to stay out of their kitchens."

"And here I thought anyone worthy of the Delacourt name would have to be capable of great feats of daring everywhere from the boardroom to the kitchen."

"Wrong family. The men in my family grew up piti-fully pampered." He grinned. "But I'm willing to learn, if you're willing to teach me. I get bored with pheasant under glass and beef Wellington."

"You are joking, aren't you?"

He chuckled at her startled expression. "About the pheasant or the cooking lessons?"

"Both."

He shook his head. "Only about the pheasant."

"There are cooking schools if you're serious," she pointed out.

"I'd rather be tutored, one-on-one."

"I'm sure they'd arrange that, as well."

"I meant by you."

She laughed. "I know you did. Sorry. My days are crowded enough as they are. While you're dining on pheasant, I'm popping something frozen into the microwave. The last time I had time to cook a real meal was..." She hesitated, then shrugged. "I honestly can't remember that far back."

"Let's make a deal," Jeb said impulsively. "One meal a week, I buy the ingredients. You teach me to cook. You can pick the night and the menu."

He told himself the suggestion was only a way to guarantee that she would keep seeing him, keep allowing him into her home so he could keep an eye on her, but he knew better. It had long since gotten personal. He was just looking for excuses to keep seeing her. First it had been the invitation to join him for a run, then the even more impulsive invitation to the sacrosanct bachelor beach house, now this. He was pathetically eager to find some niche for himself in her life.

And she was plainly just as eager to keep him out. She was shaking her head before he finished making the suggestion.

"No time," she insisted.

"That must mean my father is working you entirely too hard. I'll have to speak to him."

"Don't you dare," she said, sounding genuinely alarmed. "I love my job. Yes, it does take a lot of my time, but I'm more than willing to put in the hours. How many people get a chance to do something they love and get paid for it?"

"Probably not as many as there should be," Jeb said, thinking of his own situation. He was trapped in a business he didn't care much about one way or the other. He stayed out of family loyalty and inertia, he supposed, unlike Michael and Tyler, who genuinely loved every aspect of it. They were the true oilmen in the company. They were the ones who deserved to inherit it, though his father seemed dead set on carving it into equal shares for all five of them.

"Does that include you?" Brianna asked, studying him intently.

Since she'd already heard the rumors about his dissatisfaction, he saw no reason to deny it. "Pretty much."

"Surely you have options. Why don't you leave? Do what you love?"

"I'm not sure I have an answer for that. Maybe it's as simple as middle-kid syndrome."

"Meaning?"

"There are five of us. The oldest and the youngest have already staged rebellions that shook the family. I suppose I'm just staying put to please my father, maybe help keep the peace a little longer. Isn't that what us middle kids do? Try to please? Try not to make waves?"

"Since I was an only child, I have no idea. What would you rather be doing?"

Jeb couldn't very well reveal that his dream was to join his brother as an investigator or, at the very least, to turn internal corporate spy for his father. So, he thought wryly, it seemed he was going to have to keep a big-time secret, too. Maybe the total honesty thing wasn't as easy as he'd always assumed.

"I'm still figuring that out," he evaded. "How did you get interested in geology and oil, anyway? It's pretty much a man's world."

A smile crossed her lips, then faded. "My dad was a wildcatter. He had more dreams and ambition than success, so I guess I caught the fever. But I was more practical than he was. I wanted to learn how to find the stuff with scientific data, not just gut instinct."

Jeb wondered if it was her father who'd been the beneficiary of her research for Delacourt Oil. Was that why she was betraying the company, to give her dad a long-overdue break?

"Where is your dad working now?"

"He died several years ago," she said, her expression revealing that the sorrow of that was still very much with her. "A severe thunderstorm came up when he was on a rig in the Gulf of Mexico. He drowned."

"I'm sorry. You must miss him a lot."

"Every day," she said. "My mom died when I was still in grade school, so it had just been my dad and me for a long time. It was a bit of a nomadic existence, so I rarely kept the same friends for long. You're fortunate to have such a large family, to have spent your whole life in one place."

"Most of the time," Jeb agreed with a touch of irony. He couldn't help thinking that her life could have been his. But for the whims of fortune, her father could have succeeded wildly in the oil business and his own father could have failed.

She reached for a strawberry from the container in the basket, then slowly bit into it. The ripe berry spilled juice on her lips. Jeb's gaze locked on the red moisture in fascination as she ran her tongue across her lips to catch the errant drips. His body reacted as if it had been his tongue tasting that sweet juice…tasting her.

This was bad, he thought, reining in his hormones. Very bad. Brianna had gone from suspect to desirable woman in the past twenty-four hours. His suspicions didn't seem to be keeping pace with his libido. Pretty soon his head was going to lose the race. Since his father didn't seem concerned about the leaks, why should they worry him so? Maybe he should just give up his investigation and openly court Brianna, assuming she would allow it.

Unfortunately, he wasn't the kind of man who liked to leave a job unfinished, which meant his hormones needed to be kept in check just a little longer.

"Maybe we should go," he suggested with more regret than he wanted to admit to.

Wide blue-green eyes met his, then darkened to the shade of a storm-tossed sea as the moments ticked by. Desire? Passion? Was that what he saw churning in the depths? Heaven help them both if it was, because he doubted he was strong enough to resist it for long.

And then, if it turned out she was as guilty as he feared, there would be hell to pay.

Six

The picnic Brianna took to the rehab center on Sunday was nothing at all like the one she'd shared with Jeb the day before. Peanut butter and jelly sandwiches, potato chips, cold sodas and chocolate chip cookies might not be on a gourmet menu, but they were all her daughter's favorites. Emma greeted the spread with enthusiasm, the previous day's sulking forgotten.

This was what her life was about, Brianna reminded herself a dozen times as she and Emma shared their meal. She couldn't afford distractions, and Jeb had definitely proved himself to be that. He'd kept her from her work the day before. He'd made her forget all about her resolve not to let any man into her life, at least not until Emma was totally recovered and leading a normal little girl's life again. He'd even made her long for the kind of passion she hadn't experienced since the early days of her marriage. In all, he'd been a worrisome reminder of the effect an attentive man could have on a woman. She had to resist him, and Emma was only one reason why.

"Mama, guess what?"

Brianna brushed a stray curl from Emma's forehead. "What, baby?"

"Gretchen says the picture I drew is the best one in the whole center. She says I gots 'tistic talent. What's that?"

Brianna smiled. "Artistic talent," she corrected. "It means you can draw."

"Oh, yeah. Anyway, she's going to hang my picture on the wall right up front in the reception area. She'll put it in a real frame and everything, so everybody will see it when they come in."

"Really? That's wonderful. Have you shown that one to me?" Most of Emma's drawings were on the walls in her room right here at the center.

Most were of brightly colored flowers and rainbows. She rarely parted with any of them.

Emma hesitated, then shook her head. "No."

"Why not?"

"I was afraid you'd be mad."

"Why on earth would I be mad?"

"Because this one is of my family, just you and me. I left out Daddy," Emma said with a belligerent thrust of her chin. She looked as if she expected to be chastized and didn't care.

"Oh," Brianna said neutrally. "Why did you leave out your dad?"

"He never comes to see me. Why should I put him in a picture?" she asked, then added despondently, "I might as well not even have a daddy."

Personally, Brianna agreed with her daughter, but she had tried hard not to say negative things about her ex. She hadn't wanted to influence Emma's feelings.

After all, Larry was her father even if he happened to be a lousy one.

"You know, it still might hurt his feelings to know that you left him out. He loves you, sweetie. He just feels really, really bad about causing you to be hurt like this."

Emma shook her head stubbornly. "He never comes because he's ashamed to see me like this."

The hurt in Emma's eyes was hard to take. For what had to be the hundredth time Brianna tried her best to explain away Larry's insensitivity. "Only because he caused it," Brianna swore, cupping Emma's chin so she could gaze directly into her eyes. "Not because he's ashamed of you. Never that."

"Well, I don't believe you." Emma's eyes filled with tears. "I hate him. I hate him!"

Not half as much as Brianna did at that moment. She gathered Emma close and rocked her. "You don't really hate him. You miss him. I don't blame you. One of these days he'll come back and the two of you will remember all the wonderful times you shared."

"I don't want him to come," Emma insisted with a sniff. "Not ever. I want a new daddy."

She didn't want to set herself up for disappointment with the old one who'd failed her, Brianna concluded, and who could blame her? There were times like this when she wanted to track her ex-husband down and strangle him for adding to Emma's insecurities.

Maybe she should, too. She hadn't before, because she'd been too glad to have him out of her own life. She knew he had accepted a transfer from his company, that he'd moved out of the area. It would be a simple matter to locate him, as long as he hadn't quit since then. For Emma's sake, maybe she had to make the effort. She would ask the counselors about that the next time she spoke with them.

For now, though, she needed to console her daughter, to reassure her that she was as lovable—as beautiful—as always. She might not be able to do much about the accident's physical scars, but she had to deal with the emotional ones. That meant taking extra time, time she didn't have, to distract Emma. When she thought of the work piled up at home, she almost moaned, but it would get done eventually. This was more important.

"Why don't we go back inside and play a game?" she suggested.

Emma regarded her tentatively. "You can stay?"

"Absolutely."

"Will you play Go Fish with me?"

"Whatever you want." She tweaked her daughter's nose. "I know why you want to play that, though. You always beat me."

Emma grinned. "I know. You don't pay attention, Mama. You have to concentrate."

That impish smile, almost as perfect as it had been before the accident, was what gave Brianna strength. One day it would be back full force. One day she would have her daughter whole and her life on track. Until then, she would just have to do the best she could.

And steer very far away from the one man who could lead her off course and quite likely straight into her own emotional disaster.

Brianna was barely seated behind her desk on Monday morning when she was summoned to Bryce Delacourt's office. By the time she got there, she'd imagined all sorts of dire reasons for the unscheduled meeting.

Since his secretary wasn't at her desk, Brianna tapped on the door, then stepped inside.

"You wanted to see me, sir?"

Bryce was on the phone, but he beckoned to her distractedly. She went in and took a seat across from him. Surreptitiously she tried to see what was on his desk to learn if that would give her any clue about why he had called her in at such an early hour. Unfortunately, the papers were totally innocuous, mostly business correspondence she couldn't really read upside down.

A few moments later, Bryce hung up and beamed at her. The smile caught her off guard. Maybe this wasn't about some calamity, after all. There had been some in recent months, two land deals that had fallen through when competitors had stepped in and topped their bids at the last second. Bryce had taken those in stride, but he might not if there was a third. He was a man who didn't like losing.

"Coffee?" he asked. "It's strong, but I can't vouch for how good it is. I never really got the knack for making it, but my secretary won't be in for another hour and I needed something to jump-start my day."

"No, thanks. I have some back in my office."

"Wise woman."

"What is this about, sir? Is there a problem?"

He seemed startled by her assumption. "A problem? No, indeed. You're doing a fine job, Brianna."

He fiddled with the papers on his desk as if he were uncomfortable. If he was, it was totally out of character. Bryce Delacourt was the most self-confident man she'd ever met, even more so than his son, and Jeb had proved over the weekend that he was no slouch in that department.

"I hear you went out with my son on Friday night," Bryce said finally.

Was he objecting to the two of them being seen together? She tried to gauge his reaction but couldn't. She phrased her response cautiously. "He took me to a charity function he had to attend, yes," she said, curious about where this was heading.

"Did you have a good time?"

"It was a lovely party."

"And Jeb? How did the two of you get along?"

"We enjoyed ourselves."

He gave a little nod of satisfaction. "Good," he said, sounding relieved for some reason. "I was just wondering. That's all, Brianna."

She stared at him, thoroughly confused by the whole encounter. "That's all you wanted to ask me about?"

"That was it," he confirmed.

Still bemused, she got to her feet and started for the door, then decided she shouldn't mince words. If he had a problem with her seeing Jeb, he needed to know it wasn't likely to happen again.

"Sir, do you object to me seeing Jeb? It's nothing to worry about, I assure you. This was a one-time thing," she said, ignoring the fact that it had been repeated on Saturday. Apparently Bryce didn't know about that. She stuck to explaining away Friday night. "He just offered me a chance to get a little revenge."

He chuckled knowingly at that. "Against Max Coleman, I imagine."

Brianna nodded.

"Did it work?"

She grinned. "Like a charm."

"Good. Can't say I'm sorry about the way things

turned out with Coleman, because it brought you here, but he deserved to have his nose rubbed in it."

"I couldn't agree more," she said fervently.

"Then I'm glad my son was able to help you accomplish it. Was the revenge as sweet as you'd hoped?"

She thought about Max's reaction and her own satisfaction at seeing him lose his cool facade. "Yes, sir."

"I'm glad." He hesitated. "Just one thing, Brianna."

"What's that, sir?"

"Maybe I have no business saying this, but I like you. Jeb is my son. He's a good man, but he has something of a reputation with women."

"It doesn't matter. Like I said, this was a one-time thing."

He waved off the explanation. "Actually, what I wanted to say was that you shouldn't believe everything you hear."

"I shouldn't?"

"Jeb's got staying power. He just hasn't met the right woman yet." Then, as if he sensed he'd said too much, he gestured toward the door. "That's all. You can get back to work now."

Brianna nodded and left. As she walked into the outer office, she all but ran straight into Jeb. He stared at her in amazement, then began to chuckle.

"So he got to you first, I see."

"What?"

"Asking about our date, I imagine."

"Yes." She began to get the picture. This hadn't been anything more than fatherly nosiness and, maybe at the end, a subtle pitch. "And now it's your turn?"

"That's my guess." He leaned down and whispered,

"Is there anything I should know? Did you reveal any of our deep, dark secrets?"

"Not a one," she assured him. "I did my best to downplay the whole thing."

"That wouldn't stop Dad. He's an independent thinker. He draws whatever conclusions suit his purposes. Two dates in one weekend would really get his attention."

"He only knows about one, I think, and I never mentioned Saturday."

"I guess all his spies haven't checked in, then." His expression sobered.

"I'm sorry if he made you uncomfortable."

"Actually, I thought it was rather sweet."

"Don't mistake meddling for sweet," Jeb warned.

"Since we have nothing to hide, I'm not worried about it."

"It won't always be that way," he said with an irrepressible wink that made Brianna's pulse ricochet wildly, just when she was about to conclude that she could handle these occasional chance meetings without losing her composure.

Promise or threat? The man had a way of delivering these unexpected little gibes so that she couldn't tell. If he did it just to keep her off balance, he was doing a darn fine job of it.

"Digging into my social life now, Dad?" Jeb said, after he'd poured himself a cup of the awful brew that passed for coffee when his father's secretary wasn't around. He normally avoided it like the plague, but he needed a couple of minutes to figure out how to handle what was likely to be an uncomfortable interrogation.

"Actually, I was checking to make sure you weren't going against my wishes and putting that woman on the spot."

"Even if I were, do you think she'd realize what I was up to? Believe it or not, I have learned a few things on those occasions when I've worked with Dylan. I don't run roughshod over a suspect. In fact, I am capable of great subtlety and discretion when the situation calls for it."

"What the hell does that mean? Did you spend the whole evening pumping her for information that was none of your business?"

"I spent the evening getting to know her. It's not the same thing." He hesitated, then conceded, "Not exactly, anyway."

"Blast it, son, I thought I told you to back off with those ridiculous suspicions of yours. Do I have to fire you to get the message across?"

At any other time, Jeb might have welcomed exactly that. If his father fired him, he'd be free to pursue his own interests. Unfortunately, if his father fired him now, there would be no one to follow up on these insider leaks.

"You're not going to fire me," Jeb said, sprawling in the chair opposite his father as if he didn't have a care in the world.

"Don't test me."

"Dad, you just talked to Brianna. Did she seem the least bit upset?"

"No," his father conceded grudgingly. "She told me not to make too much of the whole evening." His expression turned sly. "That must mean you're losing your touch. Most women are falling all over themselves trying to trap you into marriage."

"Generally speaking, Brianna wants nothing from me. Friday night just gave her a chance to show Max Coleman how well she's doing after he stupidly fired her."

"That makes me curious," his father said. "How did you happen to know that Max was going to be at this event and that the promise of seeing him would guarantee that Brianna would go with you? I know she's not in the habit of dating the men around here."

"Whether it's a woman or my job, I do my homework," Jeb said. He studied his father. Maybe this would be a good time to see just how subtle he could be. "Any idea why Max let her go? He's not generally that dumb when it comes to business."

"As far as I know, it was something that just came up out of the blue." Now there was an evasive answer if ever he'd heard one. Bryce Delacourt would have checked out every little detail before hiring someone who'd been fired from their last job.

"Just a whim?" Jeb asked, not bothering to hide his skepticism even though the response pretty much confirmed Brianna's explanation.

"That's what I said, isn't it?"

"And you didn't dig any deeper?"

"I saw no need. She was right for the job we had here."

Any pretense of subtlety vanished. "Dad, that's not like you. Maybe she was fired for leaking information to Max's competitors."

"Okay, that's it," Bryce said, his complexion turning dangerously red. "You *are* fired."

To Jeb's astonishment, his father sounded not only angry but totally serious. It was time to do some fast fence-mending. "Dad, I'm sorry."

"Not half as sorry as I am."

"You don't really want to fire me," Jeb protested.

"No, I don't, but you're leaving me with no recourse. I won't have you harassing one of our best employees."

It was time to cut his losses. "Okay, I'll stay away from Brianna, at least when it comes to work."

His father eyed him suspiciously. "Meaning what, exactly?"

"If she's willing, I have every intention of continuing to see her socially. You may be able to dictate what I do when it comes to the company, but you have nothing to say about my social life."

"You think she's a spy, but you want to date her, anyway? I'm not buying it."

"Maybe you've convinced me she's not a spy," he hedged.

"Bull."

"Okay, how about this? She's a fascinating woman. Why wouldn't I want to date her?"

His father continued to regard him skeptically. "And that's all it is? Your hormones have kicked in?"

"Exactly."

His father sat silently, evidently weighing Jeb's truthfulness. "Okay," he said at last. "You're not fired. Date Brianna, if she's willing, but if you hurt her, son, you'll answer to me."

Jeb's gaze narrowed. "You're awfully protective of her."

"Because she's one of ours. Everybody in this company is like family to me, not just you boys. Now, I meant what I said. She's not the kind of woman who deserves to have you playing fast and loose with her heart."

"Okay, okay, I get the message."

He headed for the door before his father could change his mind. That meant he missed the satisfied smile that crossed Bryce Delacourt's face.

Brianna wasn't all that surprised when the bouquet of flowers turned up in her office later that afternoon. Nor was she shocked when it was followed by a box of candy. Anyone who knew anything at all about Jeb knew he played the courting game like a pro. What stunned her, though, was the expensive little French porcelain box in the shape of a picnic hamper that came with a note that said, "To our first real date."

Not only was it a romantic gesture, it suggested that he had been extremely observant when he'd been at her house on Saturday. He'd apparently noticed the small collection of such boxes she had displayed on a bookshelf. They were the only remotely frivolous possessions she had.

Maybe he'd just remembered them because he'd been the one who had to dust them. She frequently cursed the delicate collection when she had to clean.

At any rate, she might be able to ignore flowers and candy, but she couldn't let the box's arrival go by without calling to thank him. His secretary put her straight through.

"I thought I might hear from you," he admitted. "What did it? The roses, the chocolate or the little box?"

"The box, of course. You could have sent the other two to just anybody, but that little picnic hamper was special."

"I saw you collected little boxes."

"Not many men would be that observant."

"Not many have the incentive I do."

"Which is?"

"I want to charm you into saying yes to dinner."

Brianna paused. "I can't. Dinners are tough for me. I usually leave the office late, and I have things to do after that."

Her visits to Emma topped the list, but she refused to tell him about those. It wasn't just because of work, either. She suspected he would immediately show an interest in her daughter as he already had in other things that mattered to her. He would ask to go along sooner or later, and she didn't want to set Emma up for more heartbreak when another man came and went in her life. She could take the hurt, but her daughter shouldn't have to. Sunday's visit had proved just how deeply her father's desertion had hurt Emma.

"Sorry," she added to take the sting out of the rejection.

"Are you telling me there isn't one single night in the week when you're free?"

"Not a one."

"You pick the time, then." He hesitated, then added lightly, "Or should I just walk away now and nurse my bruised ego?"

She should tell him yes, she thought, but the idea of telling him to back off held little appeal. Despite all the risks, a part of her—the part that had responded to his kiss—wanted to see him again.

"Saturday," she said at last. "I could make time on Saturday."

"Afternoon?"

She chuckled. "Unless you want to do the vacuuming again."

"I'll be there at ten," he said. "Have the dust mop and that vacuum waiting."

Brianna laughed. "Jeb, you really don't have to do my cleaning."

"If it means a couple more hours around you, I do. I'm bringing my own furniture polish, though."

"Why on earth would you do that?"

"Because yours doesn't have lemon in it. I'm a sucker for lemon-scented polish. Our housekeeper used so much of the stuff, the place always smelled like a citrus grove."

"Do you have any other little idiosyncrasies I should know about?"

"Quite a few, actually, but you'll just have to take my word for it until I know you better. Discovering all of them could take a very long time." This time there was no mistaking the promise in his voice.

"Jeb." It began as a protest, but she fell silent before she could complete the thought. What could she say, anyway? *Don't think too far ahead? Don't expect too much? Don't make promises you don't intend to keep?* The sad truth was that she was the one opening a door she didn't intend to leave open for long. She was the one looking for an interlude, not a commitment. He was the one who ought to be warned to take care.

"Hey, are you okay?" he asked, after the silence had dragged on for fully a minute.

"Just peachy," she assured him. "I'll see you Saturday morning."

"Don't be surprised if I can't wait that long," he warned. "I'll probably pop up in your office with coffee and pastries before that."

"Then you should know that chocolate croissants are a favorite of mine," she teased. "You can win a lot of points with one of those."

He laughed. "I'll remember that, Brianna. In fact, I just may leave for the bakery right now."

"Don't. I'm on my way to a meeting and I'll be tied up for the rest of the day," she said, glad to have a legitimate excuse for postponing their next encounter. She touched a finger to the tiny porcelain picnic hamper on her desk. She was too vulnerable to him right now. No gift she'd received in years had touched her heart like this one.

"If you insist on putting business before pleasure, I suppose there's nothing I can do about it," he grumbled.

"You should be grateful. It's your business."

"Michael and Tyler would be grateful. My father would probably be ecstatic. All I am is disappointed."

"You'll survive."

"Don't be so sure of that."

"Goodbye, Jeb," she said pointedly.

"Bye, Brianna."

She slowly returned the receiver to its cradle, then swiveled her chair to stare out the window at the Houston skyline, which was glittering in the bright sunlight. What was she getting herself into? she wondered. What in heaven's name was she getting herself into?

She just knew that in the past few days she'd remembered what it was like to feel like a desirable woman. She wasn't quite ready to let that feeling go.

Seven

The chocolate croissant turned up on Brianna's desk on Tuesday morning, but Jeb wasn't with it. Nor did he show up on Wednesday or Thursday. He considered it a tactical retreat. Not only did he want to keep her guessing, he needed time to assess his own shifting motives for seeing her.

Although he'd promised his father that he would back off in his investigation, he still had his doubts about her integrity. He didn't want to, but suspicion and cynicism were second nature to him. How could he not be suspicious, with her mysterious after-work disappearances that kept her from accepting dinner dates, that locked room in her home, the contradictions in her lifestyle?

But maybe none of that mattered. Maybe it wasn't up to him to worry so much about the company. If his father wasn't concerned, why should he be? There was a certain amount of irony in the fact that he was fighting so hard to protect a company he claimed to care nothing about.

The truth was, he really felt attracted to Brianna, contradictions and all.

Maybe he should just go with that and the rest be damned. Obviously clearer heads needed to be consulted. Since Saturday was a long way off and he was restless, he called his brothers.

Michael and Tyler were always eager for an evening out. Michael was the button-down type, who had perfected the art of the business lunch. He owned more suits than any man Jeb had ever known. Tyler, by contrast, would have lived in jeans and T-shirts if he could have gotten away with it in the office. He wanted badly to work in the oil fields, but his ploy to learn the business literally from the ground up hadn't persuaded their father to let him out from behind a desk.

Jeb chose a favorite Tex-Mex restaurant for their meeting. He had cold beers waiting when his brothers arrived. Tyler showed up first, grabbed the beer bottle by its long neck and took a deep drink before turning his attention to Jeb.

"What's up with you? Dad on your case again?"

"Not exactly."

"Woman trouble?"

Jeb laughed ruefully. "Am I that predictable?"

Tyler grinned. "It's usually one or the other with you. Face it, big brother, you're a babe magnet. Some of them are bound to be trouble. Who is it this time?"

Normally he didn't talk about the women in his life. Most of them weren't likely to be around long enough to matter. But since he had a feeling that Brianna would be—and this was exactly the reason he'd wanted to see his brothers—he saw no point in hedging.

"Brianna O'Ryan," he confessed.

His brother, who was younger only by ten months,

whistled. "Dad's pet geologist. You *are* asking for trouble."

Jeb jumped all over the description. "Why do you say that? Why do you think she's Dad's pet?"

"Because he brought her in over everyone in the department. He practically glows when he talks about her outstanding credentials. You'd think the woman was going to single-handedly save the company from ruin by finding oil where no man has gone before."

"Must be talking about Brianna," Michael guessed, slipping into the unoccupied seat at the table.

"So you've seen it, too?" Jeb asked.

"Seen what?"

"How enamored Dad is of Brianna," Jeb explained.

Tyler leaned closer to Michael, the youngest male in the family but the one most likely to inherit the kingdom because of his total fascination with and dedication to the oil business. Of all of them, he was the one with the head and the heart for it.

"Careful," Tyler warned in a stage whisper. "Our big brother here seems to have a thing for the beautiful Brianna."

"Forget about her," Michael cautioned without hesitation.

"Why?" Jeb demanded, unhappy about being warned off so emphatically.

"Face it, bro, you don't have a sterling track record when it comes to women. If you do anything to upset Brianna, anything that might cause her to bolt from Delacourt Oil, Dad will have your hide."

Jeb sighed. "Yeah, he said as much."

"You and Dad have discussed this?" Michael asked, clearly amazed. "When? I haven't heard any loud explosions at corporate headquarters recently, and my office is right next door to his."

"You were probably too busy wheeling and dealing," Tyler suggested. "You are the only man I know who conducts contract negotiations while walking on the treadmill so you don't waste time. I believe the category of type A personality was created just for you."

Michael shot him a disparaging look. "You, on the other hand, are so laid-back, it's a wonder you get anything done."

"But I do," Tyler assured him. "And I won't be the one dying at forty of a heart attack."

Jeb chuckled despite himself. He'd heard this particular discussion a hundred times. Neither of them was ever going to change, and despite the sibling barbs, they loved each other.

"Could we stick to the point here?" he pleaded.

"Which is?" Michael asked, feigning confusion.

"Brianna."

"I say go for it," Tyler said. "If you know the score and are interested anyway, maybe she'll be the one who has staying power. Goodness knows, the types you usually choose don't."

"I say go for it at your own peril," Michael added.

"What do you think of her, though? Honestly."

"Beautiful," Tyler said at once.

"Smart," Michael added.

"Sexy," Tyler contributed.

Jeb scowled at him. "Okay, I catch your drift." He glanced at Michael, phrasing his next question very carefully. "Do you trust her?"

Both of his brothers stared at him as if he'd lost it. "What the heck does that have to do with anything?"

Tyler wanted to know. "You're dating her, not handing over classified information."

"That's not entirely true," Michael said slowly. His gaze clashed with Jeb's. "Is it? What are you afraid of?"

Jeb decided to bite the bullet. He might not entirely trust Brianna, but he would trust these two men with his life. He could say what was on his mind and know that it would go no further than the three of them. His father would never learn from them that he was still asking questions.

"Do you think there's any connection between Brianna and the deals that went bad?"

"Are you crazy?" Tyler blurted. "If there were, Dad would have fired her."

"You're the one who said it earlier," Jeb reminded him. "Dad is very protective of her."

"You're not just engaging in idle speculation, are you?" Michael asked, his expression thoughtful. "Is there anything, anything at all, to back up your suspicions?"

"Not much," Jeb admitted. "Certainly not much concrete. Just timing and coincidence."

"Then forget it. If Dad's not worried, there's no reason for you to be," Michael reassured him. "Dad can be blind to a good many things, but not when it comes to business. He would have been all over this like white on rice if there were anything remotely suspicious going on."

"And you don't think those deals that fell through were anything more than coincidence?" Jeb asked, trusting Michael's instincts as much as his father's.

"Absolutely not," Michael insisted. "You've been spending too much time with Dylan. He's made you

suspicious of everything. I was involved in those negotiations myself. It made me mad as hell to lose out at the
last minute, but it happens. There's no point in crying
over it. Competition these days is tough. There's certainly no point in trying to lay the blame on an insider."

"You're absolutely certain?" Jeb asked.

"As certain as I can be."

Jeb sighed. "You have no idea how badly I was hoping you'd say that."

His brother had just cleared the way for him to date
Brianna O'Ryan with a clear conscience.

Friday morning when Jeb walked into Brianna's office with coffee and yet another chocolate croissant,
she greeted him with a groan.

"Not another one," she pleaded, staring at the bag
in his hand.

His smile faltered. "I thought you loved these."

"I do, but I'm going to be as big as a house if you
keep feeding them to me. And Carly has flatly refused
to eat them when I've tried to foist them off on her."

He pointedly surveyed as much of her as was visible.
"Maybe a small toolshed," he countered with a grin.
"Never a house. As I recall, Carly doesn't have anything to worry about either. She could probably work
off the calories just running that smart mouth of hers."

"Don't knock my assistant. She may be chatty, but
she's pure gold when it comes to details. In fact, she's
the one who recited the precise number of calories in
one of those things. I think my arteries clogged just
hearing her."

"Which is why you need to start running with me,"

he said. "Then you could eat all you want and not worry about it."

She shook her head at his logic. "We've been over this. I couldn't run far enough or fast enough to work these off."

"Every run starts with just one step. I'll come over at nine tomorrow instead of ten and show you."

"Sorry. No can do. I have an early meeting."

He perched on the corner of her desk, which put him way too close.

Then he leaned down and whispered conspiratorially, "Tell the truth, Brianna. Are you sure you're not just making excuses to get out of starting a new fitness regimen?"

"Of course not," she insisted, crossing her heart with an exaggerated gesture. Impulsively she touched his cheek. "Thanks for tempting me, anyway."

"We're not talking about the invitation to exercise, are we?"

"No way. This is all about the chocolate croissants. You can pass this one along to Mrs. Hanover when you leave. You will make her a very happy woman. Carly hasn't given her the calorie lecture yet."

"And if your secretary is happy, I will never have a problem getting a call put through, will I?" he mused. "I can see the benefit in that."

"As if anyone in this company would refuse to put your calls through," Brianna said.

"I don't like to use my clout," he said. "Especially when the call is strictly personal."

"But you have no qualms about using a bribe?"

"Nope," he said unrepentantly. "Absolutely none." He headed for the door. "See you in the morning."

Brianna stared at the door for a long time after he'd closed it behind him. It had only been a little over a week since the first time he'd popped into her office, and already she was starting to look forward to the unexpected treats, the surprise visits. She was in over her head, all right. Way over her head.

For the next few weeks, Jeb wormed his way into Brianna's life. Quite simply, he wore her down. He could tell that she quickly tired of saying no, so he gave her dozens of opportunities to say yes. He popped into her office for midmorning coffee breaks, lured her out for lunches. He even managed to get her to go for a long walk, though she stubbornly refused to lace up sneakers and run with him.

He tried his darnedest to get inside her head, to figure out what made her tick, but there was always a part of herself she held aloof. It remained as mysterious as that locked room, and kept him from ever fully trusting that what they had was real in any way that mattered. Being on the receiving end of the same kind of treatment he was known for doling out was darned frustrating. Now he knew why women hated it.

It also made him more determined than ever to break down the barriers between them. Getting her to agree to go to dinner seemed like a good place to start. What kind of relationship could be built on stolen moments? He wanted a whole evening, just for the two of them. It became as much a cause as the investigation that had started all this.

Four weeks after he'd started seeing Brianna, Jeb finally saw his chance. She was going out of town on business, a four-day trip that would take her away from

Houston and whatever demands there were on her time. Jeb decided to tag along, though he didn't mention the fact to her until they were at the airport, where she had assumed he intended only to drop her off. When he headed instead for a parking lot, she stared at him.

"You're going in?"

"Actually, I'm going with you," he said cheerfully, keeping his attention riveted on the road.

"Excuse me?"

"I haven't been to London in ages. I thought we could see a couple of plays while we're there, maybe even take an extra day or two and drive to Cornwall. Have you ever been?"

He could all but feel the heat of her anger radiating in his direction. "Jeb," she began, her voice tight. "This is a business trip, not a vacation. I have a conference to attend, along with some very important meetings."

"You won't be working twenty-four hours a day."

"Close to it," she protested. "This is a very bad idea. What will people think if they discover that the boss's son is tagging around after me?"

"Do you honestly care what people think?"

"When it comes to my professional reputation, I certainly do. I can't imagine why you thought I'd go along with you on this."

Jeb decided to pull rank. He glanced over and met her furious gaze evenly. "Because my father approved it."

Her expression faltered. "He did?"

"He said it would be good for you to take a break. We have his blessing to stay as long as we like."

"Dammit, I can't stay," she protested.

"Can't or won't?"

"It doesn't really matter. The bottom line is, I have to

get back as quickly as my business is wrapped up. That means putting in as much time as it takes to get it done."

Jeb pulled into a parking space, cut the engine, then slowly turned to look at her. "Is it always going to be this way? Are you going to squash any attempt I make to get closer to you?"

She seemed genuinely shocked by the accusation. "That's not what I'm doing. The last few weeks have been lovely."

"But they're not going anywhere. Is that what you're telling me?"

"Yes. No." She stared back at him in frustration. "Jeb, we can't have this conversation in a parking lot when I have a flight to catch."

"Fine," he said, stepping from the car. "Then we can have it on the plane. We'll have lots of time."

She seemed about to argue, but then with a little huff of apparent resignation, she joined him for the walk into the terminal. She didn't say much else until they were in the air, and even then, most of her remarks were addressed to the flight attendant. Jeb began to get the message that she was royally ticked off at him. What he'd hoped would be a pleasant surprise had seriously offended her.

"Brianna?"

She glanced up from the report she'd been studying intently since takeoff.

"I'm sorry."

"For?"

"Overstepping. Assuming that you would want this time as much as I do."

The tension in her face eased just a little. "I do," she said softly. "I think maybe that's what made me so angry. I don't want to want you so much." A smile flickered. "And you were awfully pushy and presumptuous."

Sensing victory, Jeb grinned. "I'm a Delacourt. What can I say? We're a pushy bunch."

"It's not something to be proud of."

"Pushy has its rewards," he pointed out. "I'm here with you, aren't I?"

"On a *business* trip," she reminded him.

"I'll stay out of your way when you're working. I promise."

Her gaze narrowed. "I assume you have your own room."

"I'm pushy, darlin', not crude. Of course I do." His gaze settled on her face. "Unless you'd like me to cancel it."

"I don't think that will be necessary," she retorted with the first real smile she'd given him since they'd arrived at the Houston airport. "Then, again, you have four days to change my mind."

"It will be my pleasure," Jeb assured her, relieved that the mood had shifted.

Watching Brianna in action was an eye-opener for Jeb. She worked the international crowd at the European oil industry conference like a pro, as comfortable in that role as she no doubt was with collecting her rock and soil samples. Jeb lingered in the background, amused and often green-eyed with jealousy as she charmed man after man.

As low-key as he tried to remain, there were those who recognized him and wondered if he was there as backup in case Brianna faltered in some way.

He was as deeply offended by the question as she

would have been. "Absolutely not. The company has complete faith in her. I'm just here as an observer."

"And what is it you are observing," one sly gentleman had the nerve to ask. "Our meetings or Mrs. O'Ryan?"

"If you had a choice, which would you pick?" Jeb retorted lightly, preferring not to slug the man and cause an incident likely to get reported back home.

As if she sensed trouble, Brianna picked that precise moment to slip into place beside him. She beamed at both of them. "Do you mind if I steal Jeb away for a moment? We have business to discuss."

"Of course not," the man responded. He then muttered something that sounded like, "Lucky man."

Brianna's smile remained frozen in place until they were alone in an elevator. "Are you beginning to see why I didn't want you along? People are speculating."

Jeb shrugged. "Let them."

"Even if it leaves my professional reputation in tatters?"

"Brianna, your professional reputation is the last thing on their minds," he grumbled. Only after the words were out did he realize his mistake.

"What are you saying?"

"That every man down there was envying me, not worrying about how brilliant you are."

"Wasn't that my point? I'm supposed to dazzle them with my intelligence."

"Then you'll have to tone down the beauty," he said. "Which I doubt you could do if you wore the dowdiest dress ever made." He stood facing her, putting one hand on the elevator wall on each side of her. "Face it, Mrs. O'Ryan. You're a knockout."

"Me?" she asked incredulously.

"Yes, you," he said, then slowly lowered his head. "And I've been wanting to do this all evening long."

He claimed her mouth with an urgency he hadn't known existed.

Possessiveness, need and desire combined to form a white-hot burst of combustion that would have melted anything else he touched. With Brianna, though, she met that blazing heat with a passion of her own. For once, she held nothing back.

"Sweet mercy, I want you," Jeb murmured against her neck as he fought for some measure of self-control. They were in an elevator, for goodness' sakes. Unless he managed to jam the thing between floors, it was no place for what he desperately wanted to do with Brianna.

She gazed back at him with dazed eyes. Her hips cradled his arousal, welcomed it. "My room," she whispered eventually.

Jeb studied her intently. "You're sure?"

She laughed at that. "I haven't been sure of anything since the day we met. But I need this." Her eyes caught his. "I want this."

Only when the elevators doors slid open did Jeb move away. Then he grabbed her hand and all but dragged her down the hall. She was fumbling in her purse for her key. Impatient, he took the tiny evening bag and barely resisted the urge to upend it on the carpet to find the elusive key.

"How the hell can it be missing when there can't be more than a tube of lipstick in here with it?"

"One of those feminine mysteries," Brianna responded with a nervous chuckle. "Let me."

She took the purse and dumped everything out. The

key fell amidst a flurry of tissues, coins and cosmetics. While she gathered those, Jeb opened the door, then scooped her up and walked inside. His mouth was on hers, even as he kicked the door closed behind them.

He reminded himself that Brianna deserved care and finesse, but the rake of her fingers down his suddenly bare chest pretty much put an end to reason. She had very wicked fingers. Somehow, without him quite knowing how, she had his shirt off and his pants undone before he could blink.

Not that he objected. It just meant his plan for slow and easy gave way to raging demand. She slipped out of her prim tailored suit, but when she reached for the lacy scrap of a bra, he stilled her hands.

"My turn," he insisted, easing open the front hook, then trailing his fingers along bare flesh as the lacy cups fell away. Her nipples peaked into such hard little buds that he simply had to taste them, drawing a gasped response. Head thrown back, she seemed to savor every stroke of his tongue.

Before everything spun wildly out of control, Jeb grabbed a condom from his wallet, then stepped out of his pants and tossed them aside. The rest of his clothes followed, along with her panties. They stood facing each other, he fully aroused, Brianna suddenly looking shy.

"I guess we should have canceled your room after all," she murmured.

He touched her cheek, rubbed his thumb over her kiss-swollen lips. "We can save that for next time," he suggested. "You know what they say? Variety is the spice of life."

She regarded him wryly. "I don't think we need to worry about that just yet."

Jeb moved to the bed, then beckoned to her. "Let me make love to you, Brianna."

She eased onto the bed beside him, allowed him the role of the aggressor that she had claimed for herself earlier. Then they traded off again, tormenting each other until their bodies were straining for release.

When it came, it was explosive, like nothing Jeb had ever experienced before. It wasn't just the passion—which had rocked him to his core—it was something more. For the first time in his life, making love had touched his heart. He felt complete, as if something he hadn't even realized was missing from his life had just returned. How could he possibly have gotten so lucky?

With Brianna cradled in his arms, he was still trying to make sense of his good fortune when her phone rang.

"Ignore it," he pleaded.

"I can't. It could be…it could be important."

"More important than this?"

She didn't respond. Instead, she sat up and lifted the receiver. "Hello?" Bright patches of color tinted her cheeks and then she handed the phone to him. "It's for you."

Jeb grabbed the phone. "This had better be good."

"It is," Michael assured him. "But I think you might want to put your pants on and get back to your own room before you hear it."

"Just tell me."

"We lost another deal today. Aside from Dad and me, the only other person who knew about it was Brianna. Be careful, Jeb. I think your doubts about her may have been well-founded after all."

Eight

Her expression filled with alarm, Brianna studied Jeb as he hung up after speaking to his brother. He could feel her gaze on him, sense the unspoken questions, but he wasn't ready to deal with any of it yet. Avoiding the bed in which he'd just spent so many hours discovering the wonders of her body, he searched the room for his scattered clothing.

"Jeb, what is it?" she asked finally. "What's happened?"

Jeb was already pulling on his pants. "An emergency," he said, praying she would leave it alone. He simply couldn't get into this with her, not now. "I have to get back to Houston."

Of course it wasn't enough of an explanation for her. "Is it your father?" she persisted, regarding him worriedly.

"Dad's fine," he said more curtly than he'd intended, then winced when he saw the hurt in her eyes. "Sorry."

"Do you want me to come back, too?"

"No. I'll handle it. You stay here. Finish your business." He couldn't help the wry note that crept into his voice. Brianna didn't miss it, either, though it was clear she didn't understand what was behind it.

"Jeb, something is obviously wrong. Can't you tell me about it?"

"No. I can't talk about it. It's private family business."

"I see."

Again there was the hint of hurt that made him feel as if he were the one who'd done something wrong, rather than the other way around.

"Does this have something to do with me? If so, don't you think you ought to explain?"

He seized on her quick leap to that particular conclusion. Was it a guilty conscience that caused her to ask? he wondered. "Why would you assume it has something to do with you?" he asked, watching her reaction intently.

She reached for her robe and hurriedly dragged it on, as if to shield herself. That she felt she needed to do that with him was incredibly telling. What else did she feel the need to hide from him? And why? A short time ago, he'd been so sure that he knew everything that was important about her.

"Because of the way you're acting," she said, moving to stand in front of him so he couldn't possibly avoid looking at her.

Irritated at having given himself away, he scoffed, "Oh, really? How am I acting?"

"You haven't looked me in the eye since you hung up the phone. Either it's about me or it's something you don't want to share with me. After what just went on in this room, I thought we were closer than that. You were the one who's been pushing for us to get closer. Now you're backing away. The only reason I can see for that is whatever that phone call was about. I'll ask you again, was it about me?"

He turned away long enough to grab his jacket, then met her wary gaze. "The truth is, I'm hoping like hell it has nothing to do with you."

He walked out before she could question what he meant. All the way back to Houston, he cursed himself up and down for missing something, for allowing his attraction to Brianna to obscure the reason he'd gotten involved with her in the first place. He'd put his suspicions on hold and he couldn't put the blame for that all on his father's shoulders. He'd wanted her to be innocent for his own, totally masculine reasons.

Well, no more. His blinders were off now. Obviously, she'd been playing him for a fool, keeping him occupied while she went right on with her nasty little business of betraying Delacourt Oil.

How could she? And how could he have been so wrong about her? At least this proved that his investigative instincts had been right from the outset. He would find the proof he needed this time, no matter what he had to do to get it. Even if that meant continuing to play out this charade of a relationship they were supposed to have until he won her trust. Maybe then she'd slip up and reveal the answers he'd been seeking.

He thought of the few hours they had spent in her hotel room bed and tried not to regret that for a few minutes he had actually thought he might be falling in love with her.

It was ironic that Brianna of all people had been the first woman in years he'd started to let down his guard with. She had turned right around and betrayed him. It was the second time in his life he'd been fooled by a beautiful face and a sweet smile. It would also be the last, even if he had to spend the rest of his life celibate.

After a sleepless night and a long flight, he was exhausted by the time the plane touched down in Houston. Even so, he went straight to his brother's office.

"You look like hell," Michael greeted him, his expression grim.

"Feel like it, too," he said candidly, pouring himself a cup of coffee before sinking into a chair. It was better than usual, which meant Mrs. Fletcher, not his father, had made it. "Start at the beginning and tell me everything."

"And then what?"

"I'll go after the hard evidence we need to convict her," he said heatedly.

His brother's sympathetic gaze searched his. "You've fallen in love with her, haven't you?"

"Absolutely not."

"Jeb?" Michael chided. "Lie to me if you must, but not to yourself."

"Even if I have, it doesn't matter. Not anymore."

"Can you separate your feelings from what you'll have to do to bring her down?"

"If she's betrayed my family, I can."

"We don't know that for sure," Michael cautioned.

"You were sure enough of it to track me down in her bed last night. Now will you just spit out what we do have and let me get started?"

Michael sighed. "Okay, here it is. Brianna checked a site for us about four months ago. It was a site Tyler had scouted out. You know how he is, all gut instinct. He swore there was the smell of oil in the soil. Brianna went in to see if she could back it up. She did all of that scientific stuff that's beyond me, then brought her report to Dad and me. It was the most promising site we'd seen in the past couple of years. I started negotiating to buy it. Earlier this week, I thought the deal was all but sewn up. The owner and I had reached a verbal agreement on price."

"Which with anyone honorable would have been enough to close the deal," Jeb pointed out.

"True enough, but another bidder emerged. Paid handsomely for the mineral rights alone. The owner, who'd always been uneasy about giving up his family's land, signed without even coming back to me for a counterbid."

"The whole damn thing smells," Jeb said. "Are you absolutely certain you, Dad, Tyler and Brianna were the only ones inside the company who knew about this land?"

"Absolutely. People on her staff run some of the core sample tests, but they never know where the samples come from. That's always been the practice around here. It keeps people from being tempted to start speculating in buying up land before they turn over the results. Dad has always been adamant about absolute secrecy."

"What about the owner? Maybe he figured if he had Delacourt Oil on the hook, then the land might be worth even more to another buyer. We've already seen he doesn't understand the meaning of a verbal agreement."

"Anything's possible," Michael conceded, "but this guy is an old codger. I don't think his mind works that way. I don't think he went looking for another buyer. But when one came along, I think the chance to keep his land in his family and sell only the mineral rights was too good to pass up. And I doubt he even thought about the business implications for us."

"Maybe he has a greedy wife or heirs who caught

wind of his intentions and got into the act at the last minute," Jeb suggested, then realized that he was grasping at any straw that might clear Brianna's name. He didn't want to believe her capable of this.

"That's possible, too. I didn't start digging around for answers. I called you. Maybe that was a mistake." He regarded Jeb uneasily. "If you want me to, I'll call Dylan. Let him handle this. He might be more objective."

Though he knew Michael was only trying to spare his feelings, Jeb was insulted by the offer, by the implication that he couldn't handle a simple investigation just because Brianna was the prime suspect. "No, dammit! I said I'd do this and I will." He forced himself to calm down, then asked, "What has Dad had to say about this?"

"Not much. I expected him to go through the roof, but he shrugged it off yet again. He was absolutely insistent that I not call you in London, ruin your trip, and get you all stirred up, as he put it."

"Doesn't sound much like Dad, does it? What the hell is going on with him? Is he losing his touch?"

Michael hooted at that. "Dad will still be a better businessman than any of us when he has one foot in the grave. At least to hear him tell it."

"What do you think?"

"I think we need to know what's going on, even if Dad blows a gasket when he finds out what we've been up to."

Jeb nodded. "Then I'll go home, shower, and get right on this. Give me the name and address of the guy who sold the land. I'll start with him, then check out the guy who bought it."

"The guy who bought it is Jordan Adams," Michael

said, waiting while the significance of that sank in. "Doesn't make much sense, does it? He's always been known as a straight arrow."

"I suppose anyone can change if the stakes are high enough," Jeb said, though he agreed that it didn't sound like the Jordan Adams he'd heard about his whole life, the one who'd been so kind to Trish when she'd been alone and in trouble.

"What will you do when Brianna gets back?" Michael asked.

"She won't make a move without me knowing about it," Jeb said grimly. For once he took no pleasure in the thought of becoming her shadow.

The rest of the European conference was a blur for Brianna. Without really understanding what had happened during that brief phone call, she recognized that it had changed everything. She also knew that sleeping with Jeb had been a terrible mistake. She had been heartsick when she had seen the way he looked at her while he was on the phone that night—and the way he'd avoided her gaze afterward.

When he had walked out of her hotel room, she had known that whatever they had felt for each other had died. His leaving had had a finality about it, despite the cryptic remark that he hoped the phone call had nothing to do with her. For whatever reason, he no longer trusted her. That much had been plain. Why was beyond her. In the end, though, their feelings were a lot like a young seedling that had been trampled underfoot, too weak to withstand such a devastating injury.

If she hadn't feared something like this from the beginning, maybe she would have been more willing to fight for a future. Maybe she would have kept him from leaving, demanded an explanation. As it was, she simply resigned herself to no longer having him in her life. She'd been fine before he'd pushed his way into her daily routine. She would be again. All along she had told herself she wanted nothing more than an interlude. Well, she'd had that. And at least Emma had been spared the heartache of his going.

Intellectually, she accepted the sudden turnaround in his behavior, but her heart was another matter. She couldn't seem to stop the aching sense of loss that accompanied her on the flight home.

When she got into Houston, it was late. She went back to her town house, caught a few hours of restless sleep, then went into work. She kept glancing at the door, hoping Jeb would appear, maybe offer the explanation that he hadn't given her in London. Each time the phone rang, she waited expectantly for her secretary to announce his call. By noon, she realized he wasn't going to call and she was accomplishing nothing.

"Go home," Carly advised. "You're jet-lagged or something."

"In other words, I'm wasting my time and yours here."

Carly grinned. "Pretty much."

Maybe if she spent the afternoon with Emma, she could push thoughts of Jeb out of her head. Maybe her daughter would help her to get her perspective back.

"Okay, you're right. I'm out of here," she told Carly, then announced her departure to Mrs. Hanover as she passed her secretary's desk.

The older woman stared at her in surprise. "Do you have a lunch meeting? I didn't see one on your calendar."

The question proved just how predictable Brianna

had become. When she didn't have an engagement for lunch, she ate at her desk, usually a bowl of soup that Mrs. Hanover heated in the microwave.

"No meeting. I'm just struggling with jet lag more so than usual. I'll take some work home, catch up on sleep and be back in the morning."

"Shall I forward your calls? Especially if Mr. Delacourt checks in?"

Brianna wasn't anticipating a call from Jeb—or any other Delacourt, for that matter. "No. Just take messages. I'll check in later and return any that are important."

"Very well. You have a nice rest."

"Thanks. I'll see you in the morning."

Outside, she drew in a deep breath of fresh air, but it did little to refresh her. It was hot and humid with storm clouds building in the west.

She used her cell phone to call the center to let Gretchen know she was coming and that she'd be bringing lunch. On the way she stopped at a fast-food restaurant and picked up one of their kid's meals, along with the latest collectible toy. She'd also brought back coloring books and a doll from England. Imagining Emma's delight brought the first real smile since Jeb had left her room so abruptly.

When she reached the rehab center, her mood was lighter. Concentrate on Emma, she told herself as she walked down the corridor toward the sunroom. Nothing else matters. *Nothing.*

Jeb was on his way to lunch when he spotted Brianna getting into her car on the opposite side of the parking garage. For an instant his heart seemed to stop.

He hadn't realized she was back at work, though he had known her flight was due in the night before. He'd thought she would take the morning off at least to catch up on her sleep. He should have known better. She was as much of a workaholic as anyone in his family.

He promptly called and canceled his plans to meet Tyler for lunch, then set out to follow her.

In the heavy midday traffic, it was all he could do to keep her car in sight as she traveled across town. Where the devil was she going in the middle of the day? He knew her routine almost as well as he knew his own. She never left the office unless she had a lunch meeting, and she always scheduled those for a nearby downtown restaurant to save time.

Could she be going to meet her secret contact? Was that why she was heading to some obscure, out-of-the-way location, so she wouldn't be spotted?

He warned himself to stop imagining things, to stick to the facts. The only fact he had was that she was in her car, heading away from Delacourt Oil. His conversations with the seller of those mineral rights hadn't given him any evidence directly pointing to Brianna. Nor had his terse phone call to Jordan Adams, who clearly resented the implication that he had been involved in anything shady. After that conversation, Jeb had been thoroughly chastised by Trish and then Dylan, both of whom had assured him that Jordan Adams would never do anything underhanded.

"He bought those rights out from under us," Jeb countered. "How did he know about it, unless someone leaked the information?"

"You'd have to ask him that," Dylan said. "But I guarantee you he didn't buy the information. His son's the sheriff over here. Where do you think Justin got his sense of right and wrong? Jordan's as much a straight shooter as you'll ever run across. And Harlan Adams, Jordan's daddy, is the most honorable man in the entire state. It's his moral compass that guides the whole family."

Jeb had sighed and let the matter drop. Maybe Jordan Adams had come by the information legitimately, but the whole deal still smelled to high heaven and he intended to get to the bottom of it before Delacourt Oil was ruined.

That brought him back to Brianna. He followed her for nearly forty minutes as she led him eventually into a more residential area with shaded lawns and lush gardens. When she turned into a gated drive, he slowed and waited before turning in after her. He paused long enough to read the discreet sign on the gate: Corcoran Treatment Facility.

What on earth was she doing here? He took note of the neatly tended grounds, the man-made lake that was home to several ducks, the park benches on which several uniformed nurses sat. There were patients in wheelchairs on the lawn as well, most of them adults, though surprisingly few of them senior citizens.

A rehab center, from the looks of it. For what, though? Psychiatric problems? Stroke or heart attack recovery? He'd never heard of the place, though it was evident that it was very exclusive and more than likely very expensive. Was this where Brianna's money was going? Into care for…who? An elderly relative? An errant sister or brother? Maybe even the ex-husband she never mentioned? Maybe she was still tied to him by duty, if not legalities. There was only one way to find out.

After giving her a few minutes of lead time, he parked and followed her inside, then asked at the desk where he could find Brianna O'Ryan. "She just came in. I believe she's visiting a patient."

"Of course. She's down the hall in pediatrics, probably in the sunroom. That's where Emma usually is this time of day."

Pediatrics? Emma? Heart beating as wildly as if he'd been in pursuit of a hardened criminal, Jeb headed in the direction the woman at the desk had indicated.

In a large room, splashed with sunlight, he found Brianna bent over a pint-sized angel in a wheelchair. The child was holding a doll and gazing at it with something akin to awe.

"All the way from England?" she asked. "You brought her to me all the way from England?"

Brianna nodded. "She reminded me of you."

In fact, Jeb noted, she did have the same golden hair, the same big blue-green eyes, though no doll's could shine as brightly as the child's.

Something Brianna said made the child laugh and brought his heart to a halt. Suddenly it all came together—the eyes, the coloring, the laugh. The child's hair was strawberry blond, but he would have bet anything it would darken to Brianna's auburn by the time she was an adult.

Her daughter, he thought in shock. He knew it as certainly as if they'd been introduced. All this time and Brianna had never said a word about having a child. What did that say about their relationship? Why would she hide the fact that she had a little girl? Especially one she obviously loved as much as she loved this one? He had seen the adoration in the way she'd touched her daughter's cheek, in the way her gaze had lingered on the little angel's face, the way her own face had brightened at the child's laughter.

Did his father know? Was that why his father wanted Brianna treated with kid gloves? Because he sympathized with the fact that she had a little girl in an expensive treatment facility? Whatever injuries the child had sustained, whatever the cost of her care, Jeb knew his father. Not only would he sympathize, he would see to it that the treatment was paid for by the company's generous insurance plan. Brianna wouldn't have to betray Delacourt Oil to get money.

So what the devil was going on here? He needed time. He needed to think.

Thoughts churning, he left the building, then almost got into his car and drove away, but something stopped him. He'd been way too busy the past few weeks leaping to conclusions based on faulty information and half-truths. It was time to get everything out in the open once and for all. Past time.

He crossed the parking lot, then leaned back against the side of Brianna's car and waited.

It was an hour before she finally emerged from the building, her shoulders slumped, exhaustion written all over her face. When she spotted him, her footsteps slowed, but her eyes flashed with anger.

"What are you doing here?" she demanded, clearly displeased to see him.

"I could ask you the same thing."

"What I'm doing here is none of your business. You had no right to follow me."

"But I did," he said, dismissing that much as a *fait accompli*. "So, who is she, Brianna? Your daughter?"

She stared at him, anger, confusion and misery mingling on her face. "You came inside? You saw Emma?"

He nodded. "We have to talk about this, Brianna."

"No."

"Yes."

"Why? Because you say so? I don't think so. This is my private life, Jeb. It has nothing to do with you."

This time he was the one who felt a sharp shaft of pain cut straight through him. Now he knew exactly how she had felt in that hotel room.

"Really? I thought what happened in London brought us together," he said, much as she had. The irony wasn't lost on him, but he went on just the same. "I thought we were as close as any two people could be. Now I discover you're keeping a huge part of your life a secret. What does that say about our relationship?"

"We don't have a relationship," she said flatly. "You proved that when you walked out on me without telling me why."

"It's not the same," he insisted, despite the guilty pang that told him it was darned close to being the same. Still, he defended his actions. "That happened in an instant. It was something I couldn't share at the time. I would have gotten into it eventually."

"Would you?" she said skeptically. "Well, maybe I would have gotten into this eventually."

Frustrated, Jeb raked his fingers through his hair. "Brianna, we have to talk about this. There's more at stake here than hurt feelings."

"Such as?"

"I'll explain when we sit down somewhere we can talk. I won't do it in the middle of a parking lot."

"Some other time. I'm beat."

"No, today. Right now." He gestured toward the benches by the lake. "We can do it over there, if you prefer. Or we can go to your house or to a restaurant. I don't care." He leveled a look straight at her. "But we are going to talk about it. Maybe once the air is cleared, I can help you."

"Help me?" she echoed, looking genuinely baffled. "Why would I need help?"

"We'll talk about that, as well."

She stared right back at him, challenging him, then finally nodded as if she were too weary to fight him. "Okay, fine, but not here. A restaurant," she said, as if she hoped that a confrontation in a public place would be easier. Or maybe simply to get him far away from her daughter.

He gestured toward his car. "I'll drive."

"But—"

"I'll drive," he repeated.

"You really don't trust me, do you? Do you honestly think I'll take off?"

"Right this minute, I don't have any idea how I feel about you or what you're likely to do," he told her truthfully. "Bottom line, I don't think I ever knew you at all."

There was another flash of hurt in her eyes, but she dutifully climbed into his car, then pointedly turned her gaze toward the window with the clear intention of ignoring him until they arrived at whatever destination he chose.

Jeb wanted to say something, but nothing came to him. He felt as if he were riding with a stranger. And though the restaurant was only a few blocks away, it was the longest drive Jeb had ever taken.

Nine

Brianna felt as if she were suffocating. She could see the accusations, the hurt in Jeb's eyes, and wished she could feel something besides anger. He had betrayed her by following her today as if she were some sort of common criminal. Worse, he had pushed himself into a part of her life that was supposed to be hers alone. Emma was her burden, her joy. *Hers.* How dare he intrude on something so private without an invitation?

Would she have invited him eventually, as she had claimed? More than likely, especially with their connection deepening as it had in London. But not now, not today. Not with their relationship already in upheaval.

He chose a restaurant where they weren't likely to run into anyone they knew. It was well past lunchtime, so most of the booths were empty. A few people remained at the counter, but most of those were drinking coffee or eating a slice of one of the homemade pies on display in glass cases.

Brianna sat silently while Jeb ordered coffee for himself and iced tea for her.

"What would you like to eat?" he asked politely.

"I'm not hungry."

Ignoring her, he ordered a salad for her and a club sandwich for himself.

She noticed that he knew exactly what dressing she preferred, knew to order her tea unsweetened. How could a man who remembered such details know so little about the kind of woman she was? How could he not know how deeply she would resent his prying?

He reached across the table and touched her hand. The caress was brief, as if he knew he no longer had the right to assume any sort of intimacy but had been unable to resist.

"Tell me about her," he said.

When she would have balked at the request, he added quietly, "Please. She's a beautiful little girl. There's no mistaking that she's yours."

Maternal pride swelled in her chest. "She is pretty, isn't she? You should have seen her before…" she began, but her voice trailed off.

"Before what?"

She hesitated, then gave a mental shrug. What was the harm now? He already knew the most important part, that she had a little girl.

"Her name is Emma," she said at last. "She's five."

"How long has she been at the rehab center?"

"For a year now."

He was clearly shocked. "That long? How terrible for you both."

"Her injuries were severe."

"What happened?"

She drew in a deep breath, then told him about the accident, about Larry's desertion, about being fired and, eventually, about Emma's longterm prognosis. "She will walk again," she said fiercely. "No matter what I have to do, no matter what it costs, she will walk."

"No wonder you don't talk about your marriage," he said. "And no wonder you despise Max Coleman. The two men who should have stood beside you during all of this abandoned you."

"Which just proves how lousy my judgment is," she said pointedly.

He flushed guiltily. "And by tailing you today, I haven't exactly proved myself to be someone you could trust either, have I?"

There was a hint of contrition in his voice, and she responded to that. She still didn't understand what had motivated him to do what he'd done, but maybe it had been nothing more than curiosity. "It's understandable, I suppose. I lied to you. I've been lying to everyone at Delacourt, except your father. He's known from the beginning. In case you didn't know it, he's an incredible man. He didn't have to hire me. Nor did he have to take on his insurance carrier to make sure Emma got the care she needed, but he did all of that. I will never forget that."

"So the accident, all of it, happened before you came to Delacourt Oil?"

She nodded.

"Why did you insist on the secrecy? It doesn't make sense," Jeb said. "Being a single mom isn't something to be ashamed of. And surely you're not embarrassed about your daughter needing rehabilitation?"

"Absolutely not," she said fiercely. That was Larry, not her. And yet, in her own way, hadn't she been guilty of keeping Emma hidden as if she were ashamed of her? Wouldn't that be a plausible interpretation for an outsider to make?

"What was it, then?" Jeb asked. "Why the silence?"

"It's complicated. Your father brought me into a very responsible position. There were others in the department who probably thought they should have gotten the job. I had a lot to prove. I didn't want anyone to think I couldn't give it a hundred and ten percent."

"So, this was all about professional pride?"

"More or less."

"Why not tell me, though? Maybe not on our first date, but later?"

"The timing never seemed right." She met his gaze. "I'm sorry. It wasn't that I didn't think you would understand. I guess I just got used to keeping Emma all to myself. After all, Larry abandoned both of us. I couldn't take a chance that you might do the same thing—not for my sake, but for hers. Her self-esteem is already very fragile."

"I guess I can understand that," he conceded. "But don't confuse me with men like Larry O'Ryan and Max Coleman."

She wanted to believe him, wanted to believe that this was the end of it, but something told her that the trouble between them was far from over.

That phone call hadn't been about Emma. And she hadn't imagined his reaction to her after receiving it.

"Okay," she said, putting down her fork and meeting his gaze evenly. "I've been as honest as I know how to be. Now it's your turn. What was that phone call in

London all about? And why did you say earlier that you would try to help me? Why would I need help?"

He hesitated, then shook his head apologetically. "Sorry. I can't get into it. Not yet."

The warmth that had been in his eyes just moments before vanished. As if someone had flipped a switch, the same cool distance she had felt in the hotel room was back again. She couldn't let it rest until she knew what had put it there between them.

"Why not?" she persisted. "I thought we were getting all of our cards out on the table, clearing the air once and for all. Or is that just a one-way street?"

"You've given me a lot to think about."

"What does one thing have to do with the other?"

"I can't explain."

"Well, isn't that just dandy? You turn my life into an open book, poke and prod into my privacy, but your life is off-limits." She was suddenly struck by a thought. "Why did you follow me today? Was it just a casual whim or something more?"

There was a telltale flush in his complexion, but he tried to shrug off the question. "Impulse, I suppose."

Suddenly she recalled the talk at Delacourt in the past when Jeb had taken off. He'd gone to help his brother, a well-respected private investigator. Carly had been fascinated. In fact, hadn't she predicted that Jeb would one day abandon his father's company to become a full-time investigator?

So, Brianna wondered, had the phone call been about another case? And if so, how in the world was she involved?

She met his gaze evenly. "I don't think so," she said finally. "It had something to do with that phone call, didn't it? Are you watching me, Jeb?" His gaze turned heated as he surveyed her with leisurely enthusiasm.

"Absolutely," he said. "You know I love watching you."

She waved off the glib, all-too-male explanation. "I'm talking about surveillance."

Tellingly, he refused to meet her gaze. His reaction was all but an admission that she had hit on the truth.

"That's it, isn't it? You were actually tailing me as part of some sort of investigation," she said, fury mounting as the implications sank in. She regarded him coldly. "I think you'd better explain."

"I'm not at liberty—"

"Cut the nonsense, Jeb. You're the one who said I needed help. Why? Explain, or I will go straight to your father and tell him you've been harassing me, and if need be I'll file suit. I can make a pretty damned good case, too."

He looked shocked. "Harassment? You're going to charge me with sexual harassment? What happened between the two of us was both private and consensual and you know it."

This time around she was playing hardball. She wouldn't lose another job through no fault of her own. Even though the circumstances were different, with Emma on the mend, she had her fighting spirit back.

"It won't sound that way when I'm through," she warned him. "I might not have fought Max Coleman when he fired me without justification, but I will take you and Delacourt Oil to court, if I have to. I'm not running this time, Jeb, so you'd better spill everything right now or it's going to get very ugly and you are going to be right in the middle of it. If I know your father, he won't be happy about it, either."

"Ugly," he echoed incredulously. "You want to talk about ugly? How about selling out Delacourt Oil? After everything you've just told me about how my father brought you in and helped you with your daughter, let's talk about how you turned right around and betrayed him and his company."

This time it was Brianna who stared in shock. "I beg your pardon."

"I learned for a fact today just how clever you are at concealing things, Brianna. What's the big deal about hiding a little corporate espionage?"

She was stunned into silence. When she could finally gather her thoughts, she whispered, "You think I've been leaking inside information?"

"Why not? Even with the best insurance, that treatment center must be costing you a pretty penny. You can probably use the extra cash. And what mother wouldn't do anything when her child's future is at stake?"

The words hammered at her, but what hurt more was that Jeb was the one uttering them. Brianna quivered with outrage. How could she have slept with a man capable of thinking such awful things about her? What he was accusing her of was reprehensible. For him to insinuate that she had hidden Emma's existence because she hadn't wanted anyone to guess how desperately she might need money was insulting, to say nothing of infuriating. Had he believed it of her from the beginning? Was that why he'd started seeing her in the first place, why he'd turned up at her house so often? It made a horrible kind of sense.

Jeb's harsh accusation hung in the air. She stared at

him in shock. She knew about the failed deals, the suggestion that the competition had had inside information, but to be accused of being a part of it? How could anyone think that, especially a man who knew her as well as Jeb did? Of course, right now, after today's discovery, he must not think he knew her well at all.

Still, she faced him with indignation. "Excuse me? Maybe you'd better spell out just exactly what you think I'm guilty of."

"You already know precisely what I'm talking about. Three deals have soured in recent months. One went bad just this last week."

"And that's what the call was about," she guessed. And it was also why he'd said he hoped that it had nothing to do with her. Obviously he'd already tried and convicted her, though.

"That's right. Somebody has to be leaking inside information. Only you, my father, Michael and Tyler knew about this deal. I know *they* wouldn't sell out the company."

"So obviously that leaves me," she said sourly. She thought over the conversations she'd had with Jeb's father about the two earlier deals. Bryce Delacourt had assured her it was just the nature of the business. He hadn't seemed overly upset by the losses. Now she knew better. He'd had his son investigating her all along. Was that why he'd been so delighted that the two of them were getting close, because it put Jeb right in the middle of the enemy camp?

Then to compound their suspicions, right in the middle of his investigation yet another deal had gone bad. Despite their closeness, Jeb hadn't even hesitated before blaming this one on her, too, because he'd been waiting all along for her to slip up.

"You believe I'm guilty, don't you?" she suggested, her voice like ice, even though she was quivering inside. "After everything we've shared the past few weeks, after everything I've told you today about how much I owe your father, you still think that I could hurt your family like that."

For an instant, he regarded her with obviously conflicting emotions. For one single moment, she thought he might say, "Of course not. I believe in you."

Instead, when he finally spoke, he said, "I don't want to, Brianna, but yes. I think if you were desperate enough, you would do anything to protect your daughter. It's the only logical conclusion."

It took every ounce of self-control she possessed to get to her feet with some measure of dignity and stare him down. "If you think that, then you can just go straight to hell," she said quietly. "And take your stinking job with you."

Outside, she was still shaking as she flagged down a cab. It had felt good to tell him off, even better to throw her job back in his face, but now what? What would she and Emma do?

"Brianna?" he shouted, racing from the restaurant just as she slammed the cab door and gave the driver directions to the rehab center, where she'd left her car. When the driver hesitated at Jeb's shout, she met his gaze in the rearview mirror. "Go."

"Whatever you say, ma'am."

She managed to hold back the tears that threatened until she got into her own car. She fumbled with the keys, but finally managed to get them into the ignition.

She was shaking so badly she knew she had no business driving, but the threat that Jeb would return here and force another confrontation finally steadied her nerves.

Rather than go home, which was obviously the second place he would look for her, she drove around until by instinct or chance she happened on the park where they had shared that first picnic. She pulled into a parking space, then climbed out of the car.

The day was every bit as lovely as it had been on that Saturday afternoon, the sky as blue, the sun as brilliant, but Brianna saw it all through a haze of bitter tears.

Everything she'd worked for, everything she'd struggled to hold together for herself and her daughter, was falling apart, and all because of a lie. Whoever was causing the finger of suspicion to be pointed in her direction deserved to suffer for it. Since Jeb thought he already had his culprit, it was up to her to prove her own innocence.

Leaving Delacourt Oil wasn't the solution. It had been a knee-jerk decision made out of pain and heartache. She had vowed to fight Jeb once today before she had even realized exactly what the stakes were. Now that she knew, the fight was even more critical. She couldn't walk away from it. This wasn't just about a job, it was about her reputation. It was about the one man on earth who should have trusted her selling her out when the chips were down.

But she couldn't think about Jeb now. It hardly mattered that he had been her lover. What counted was the damage he could do to her future in the profession she loved. He had to be stopped from making these absurd accusations public before he destroyed her. Later she would shed whatever tears needed to be shed for losing a man she might have loved.

Jeb was at his wit's end. He'd searched high and low for Brianna, but she was nowhere to be found. She'd taken her car from the rehab center and vanished. He knew without a doubt, though, that if there was one place she would return, it would be the center.

He went back there, spent a half hour in the parking lot debating with himself, then went inside.

"Could I see Emma O'Ryan?" he asked a willowy blond nurse behind the desk.

"And you are?"

"A friend of her mother's, I work with Brianna at Delacourt Oil. I'm Jeb Delacourt."

"Ah, the handsome prince. Emma talks about you all the time. I'm Gretchen Larson."

"Emma talks about me? We've never met."

"No, but her mother told her all about the ball you took her to. Emma was enchanted. She's pretty sure you're at least as handsome as the prince in *Cinderella.* Normally, I'd never let a stranger in to visit, but Emma will be thrilled to see you for herself."

Jeb chuckled. "Think I'll disappoint her?"

"Why Mr. Delacourt, are you fishing for compliments?"

"No, more like reassurance. I don't want to scare the girl."

"Believe me, she'll be delighted to see you. She doesn't get a lot of visitors besides her mother. She left a couple of hours ago, by the way."

"I know," Jeb said succinctly.

Gretchen came out from behind the desk to display

a curvaceous body that once upon a time would have sent his hormones into overdrive. Now it did nothing. Only one woman seemed to have the key to his heart these days, and she was justifiably furious with him. Thinking about how anguished she'd looked when she realized he thought her guilty filled him with regret. He'd blundered badly, yet again, laying out suspicions instead of facts. He wouldn't blame her if she never forgave him.

Was that what he wanted? Forgiveness, rather than the truth? It said a lot about the state of his heart that he thought it might be. In the meantime, there was Emma, and the feeling he had that he needed to know this child who was so important to Brianna.

When they neared the sunroom again, it occurred to Jeb that he should have brought along a present on his first visit. Such a momentous occasion called for one.

"Is there a gift shop?" he asked suddenly.

"I'm afraid not," Gretchen told him. "But it's okay. Your company is what matters. If you suggest a game of Go Fish, you'll have a friend for life."

Jeb couldn't recall ever playing such a game, but he was willing to learn.

They found Emma in the sunroom, staring out the window with a despondent look that no child of five should ever have.

"Emma, you have a visitor," Gretchen called out.

The girl struggled with the controls on her wheelchair, but eventually managed the turn. When she spotted Jeb, her eyes brightened with curiosity.

"Who're you?"

Jeb held out his hand. "I'm Jeb Delacourt."

Emma's smile spread. "Mommy's prince," she said as she placed her fragile little hand in his.

"I don't know about that, but I am her friend." He gestured toward a chair. "Mind if I stay a while so we can visit?"

Gretchen leaned down to whisper in Emma's ear, drawing another grin. Then the nurse winked at Jeb. "Call if she has you on the ropes. I'll rescue you."

"Thanks." He turned his attention to Emma. "I hear you play a mean game of Go Fish."

She nodded, curls bouncing. "It's my favorite."

"Want to play?"

She flipped up a tray on the wheelchair, then reached into a side pocket and whipped out a deck of cards. "I'm really, really good, you know."

"So I hear. I'm afraid you'll have to explain the rules to me. I don't know them."

"It's really, really easy," she said, as she awkwardly dealt the cards.

She launched a detailed explanation of the card game that left Jeb more confused than enlightened, but he was ready to try. When Emma had beaten him six games straight, he studied her intently. "You aren't by any chance the national Go Fish champion, are you?"

"No, silly. They don't have a championship for that."

"Well, they should. You'd be a shoo-in."

She patted his hand. "Don't feel bad. I beat Mommy all the time, too." She leaned close and confided, "I think she lets me win so I'll feel better."

"I doubt it. Your mother is a very competitive woman. I think the real truth is that she's no match for you."

Emma beamed. "Do you really think so?"

"Absolutely." He cupped her tiny hand in his. "Thank you for teaching me, Emma. I had fun."

"Even though you lost?" she asked doubtfully. "It probably wasn't polite for me not to let you win at least once."

"Never let someone win just to be polite," he said. "It's important always to do your best."

She regarded him shyly. "Will you come to see me again?"

"I would like that very much." He hesitated. "There's just one thing."

"What?"

"Could you not tell your mom that I stopped by?"

"You mean like a secret?"

Jeb nodded, swallowing back the guilty feeling that he had no business getting Emma to hide things from her own mother. But he knew Brianna wouldn't approve. In fact, she was likely to blow a gasket if she learned he'd been by to see her daughter.

Something had happened to him in the past hour, though. He'd fallen in love with another of the O'Ryan women. Spending time with Emma had, in some way, reassured him about Brianna. Any mother would fight to save a child this incredible. It was a defense no jury on earth would ignore. He certainly couldn't, and he had more reason than most to want Brianna to pay for her crimes against his family's company.

"Can this be our secret, just for now?" he asked Emma.

She nodded, apparently intrigued with the idea of sharing a secret with mommy's prince. "I won't say a single word. Not to anybody. But you'd better tell Gretchen, too. She and Mommy talk a lot."

Since that hadn't even occurred to Jeb, he was grateful for the advice. "Thanks. I'll talk to her on the way out. By the way, are you allowed ice cream in here?"

Emma grinned. "Uh-huh. Chocolate's my very favorite in the whole world."

"Then the next time I come, I'll bring chocolate ice cream. Shall I bring enough for everyone, so we can have a party? You can be the hostess."

Her eyes widened. "You would do that?"

If it meant seeing her surrounded by other children, instead of all alone staring out the window, he would bring anything she asked. "Absolutely," he assured her.

"When will you come back?"

"As soon as I can," he promised.

"Tomorrow?"

Why not? "Tomorrow, it is. I'll make the arrangements with Gretchen on my way out."

"Mr. Delacourt?" Emma asked, her expression vaguely worried.

"What, angel?"

"You won't forget, will you? Like my daddy did?"

Jeb felt the unfamiliar salty sting of tears at the plaintive question. "No, I will not forget," he vowed, leaning down to press a kiss against her forehead. "You can count on it. I will be here tomorrow."

If he had to move heaven and earth—and one stubborn female—to make it happen.

Ten

Brianna's head was ringing. Actually, it was the phone that was ringing, but it had done it so persistently for the past few hours that it seemed to echo in her head. She sat in her darkened living room and stared in the general direction of the offending instrument and willed it to stop.

Eventually it did, only to start up again ten minutes later. Apparently Jeb wasn't going to give up easily. She knew that's who it was, because he'd left a message the first half-dozen times he'd called. In an act of desperation, Brianna had finally switched off the machine. Then he'd settled for simply letting the phone ring.

Tired of the constant sound, the next time it rang, she snatched it up. "I have nothing to say to you," she snapped before slamming it back down again.

Of course, that was a mistake. In answering it, she had proved to him that she was home. Moments later, he leaned on the doorbell, then pounded on the door.

"Brianna, I know you're in there. We need to talk."

She started across the room, then stopped. No, she thought to herself, talking was a waste of time. Nothing she said could possibly penetrate a skull as thick as his had to be.

"Brianna, dammit. Open the door."

"No," she said just as loudly. At this rate, they were going to disturb any neighbors not already rattled by the constant phone calls.

"Please," he said, lowering his voice to a plea.

She leaned against the door, sighing heavily. As furious as she was, her heart still leaped at the sound of his voice. What sort of idiot did that make her?

"No," she said again, this time in a whisper.

"What?"

"I am not opening the door."

"This is silly. We're two rational adults. We ought to be able to discuss this in a civilized manner."

"One of us may be civilized. I'm not so sure about you," she countered. "You're trying to beat down a door in the middle of the night."

"I am not trying to beat it down. I am simply trying to get your attention. Besides, it's not the middle of the night. It's barely nine o'clock. And I would have been here earlier, but you've apparently been sitting inside in the dark pretending you weren't at home."

"Have you been watching the house?" she asked, appalled by the idea that he'd been staking out the place in plain view of her neighbors.

"Pretty much," he admitted unrepentantly.

"Jeb, this has to stop. Go away. I don't want to talk to you. You made your opinion of me plain earlier today."

"I was angry."

"A lot of hard truths get spoken in anger."

"Brianna, please, if you'll just tell me what really happened, I'll straighten everything out. I swear it."

"How terribly sweet of you," she said sarcastically. "Obviously, you assume there are things to straighten out. I, on the other hand, would prefer some indication that you realize I am innocent. Let me spell it out for you, Mr. Delacourt. I have done absolutely nothing wrong. Period. End of sentence. End of conversation."

To emphasize it, she walked away from the door, went into the kitchen and poured herself a glass of soda with lots of ice. Then she put on the earphones to her stereo and turned it up full volume, so she wouldn't hear anything more than the muffled sound of Jeb's voice and the ongoing pounding on her door.

To her astonishment, he was still at it an hour later, when she forced herself to go off to bed, where she knew she wouldn't get a single minute's sleep all night long. If persistence counted for anything, he would have gotten a lot of points tonight.

As it was, she would have preferred even a hint that he believed in her.

Without that, they had nothing.

"You did what?" Bryce Delacourt's voice climbed to a level that could have shattered glass. "I thought I told you to stay the hell away from Brianna with these crazy suspicions of yours! When you said you intended to go on seeing her, you assured me it was personal. I'll admit I was delighted. She'd be perfect for you. She's nothing like those shallow, insipid women you usually prefer. The fact that she's threatening to take you to court, rather than trying to get you to marry her, proves that."

Jeb felt his father's wrath and indignation almost as deeply as he'd felt Brianna's the night before. "It was personal," he said stiffly.

He had turned up here this morning to admit to the mess he'd made of things, not to hear a lecture. He should have known he couldn't do one without being subjected to the other.

"But you still had to go digging around in her life," his father accused. "I don't blame her for being furious. What kind of man tries to incriminate a woman he supposedly cares about?"

"I didn't try to incriminate her. Believe me, no one wants her to be innocent more than I do. As a matter of fact, I had dropped everything. I hadn't checked out a lead in weeks." He thought of the lengths he'd gone to just to be alone with her in London. "She mattered to me, Dad. She still does."

"Then what the hell happened? Is this the way you treat someone who matters? No wonder you're not married."

Jeb ignored the assessment of his courting skills, or lack thereof. "I got a call from Michael about another deal that went south. The only person who knew about it outside of family was Brianna."

"So that made it okay to go charging off with a bunch of half-baked accusations? Even though you knew this woman? Even though you should have known that she would never betray us? Even though you had very strict instructions from me to leave her be? What sort of judgment was that? And who the hell's in charge around here, anyway?"

"You are, but—"

"But what? Did you get together with your brothers and conclude I'm not capable of making rational decisions anymore?"

Jeb winced. His father had hit all too close to the truth, but he wasn't about to admit to it.

Fortunately, Bryce Delacourt didn't wait for an answer. In fact, he seemed pretty much uninterested in anything Jeb had to say. He was more interested in trying to get his own point across.

"Well, let me assure you that I have all of my wits about me," he said emphatically. "I also have the title that gives me the right to fire the whole blasted lot of you, which right this moment I am sorely tempted to do."

"Dad—"

"Just stop it. I don't want to hear your excuses. All I want to hear is that you intend to find some way out of this mess."

"I tried to talk to her. She won't listen."

"Can you blame her? What did you intend to say? That you're sorry, I hope."

"I was going to repeat what I've already said, that I'd help her."

"Help her?" his father repeated incredulously. "That's what you said? How magnanimous. The only help the woman needs is to be protected from you. You've all but called her a spy. I'm surprised she didn't wring your sorry neck."

"I don't think she wanted to get that close," Jeb admitted ruefully.

"I can't say I blame her. Let's start with her supposedly incriminating decision to hide her daughter from you. Did it never once occur to you that she might have told you about her daughter in her own good time, that after being abandoned by Emma's father she needed to know she could trust you? Well, you've certainly reassured her on that score, haven't you?"

He shook his head. "The woman has been through hell the last year. Now you've gone and made it worse. You've twisted her secrecy into something ugly, when you should have been supportive. You're every bit as bad as that no-account husband of hers."

Being compared to Larry O'Ryan was about as in-sulting as anything his father could have said. Unfor-tunately, Jeb couldn't come up with a ready defense of his behavior. When his father described it, even Jeb thought he was a louse.

"I'm sorry."

"Sorry won't cut it. I just pray I can talk her into coming back to work here," his father said.

Even though he knew he'd handled things very badly, Jeb was stunned that his father was so readily dismiss-ing the bottom line, that Brianna had betrayed Dela-court Oil. Wasn't this a time for caution? Weren't there issues that needed to be resolved first?

"Dad, you're not thinking clearly," he protested. "You can't just bring her back. No matter how sorry you feel for her, it still seems more than likely that she's been betraying the company. Maybe she thought she had to, maybe she was desperate, but you can't ignore what she's done."

"I can and I will, because you don't have squat in the way of proof. You're supposed to be this hotshot in-vestigator. You claim you've learned how to do the job from your brother, so I assume you know the rules. Do you have so much as a single shred of evidence to prove that Brianna has done anything wrong?"

He doubted that her secrecy, that mysterious locked room at her house, or any of the rest would satisfy his father. He thought of his conversations with the old codger who owned the last land they'd lost and with Dylan about Jordan Adams's integrity. "No," he finally admitted, "but—"

"But you went off half-cocked, anyway. You accused Brianna of doing something so malicious, so totally out of character, that we'll be lucky if she doesn't file suit against us. Slander comes to mind, along with wrongful dismissal."

Jeb tried to reclaim some of the high ground he'd obviously lost in the past few minutes. "She quit. She wasn't fired. If she were innocent, wouldn't she have fought back?"

His father scowled at him. "Now there's a brilliant technicality if ever I heard one. In the end, we have the same result. We've lost one of the best geologists in the business and hurt the reputation of a woman who doesn't deserve it." His expression darkened. "You created this mess. Now fix it."

Jeb stared. "Fix it? How?"

"I don't give a rat's behind. Crawl, if you have to. Just do it." Jeb was actually more than willing to try to patch things up with Brianna, at least on a personal level. He didn't even question the incongruity of wanting to be with a woman he thought guilty of a crime. Somehow he'd made excuses for her that she hadn't asked him to make. If he tried hard enough, he could rationalize everything she'd done. He just couldn't figure out how to explain that to her when the woman flatly refused to talk to him.

As for repairing the damage and getting her back to Delacourt Oil, he figured there were miracles that had been pulled off more easily. He doubted a man in his precarious position with the Almighty had any right to call for assistance.

* * *

Brianna was still muttering curses hours after her blowup with Jeb. Most of them now, however, were aimed at herself. She had walked away from a fight. She hadn't even tried to defend herself to Jeb, although how she was supposed to do that when the man was blind as a bat was beyond her.

The situation was complicated by the fact that until he had followed her, found out about Emma and then started hurling accusations, she had almost let herself fall in love with him. She had begun to trust him more than she'd ever anticipated trusting anyone again.

Now, like Larry, Jeb had betrayed her. Rather than supporting her, he had added to the problem, much as her ex had. But that was personal and Jeb's accusations were professional. Her professional integrity had never, ever been called into question before. She owed it to her future to fight back with all she had. She just wasn't sure how much fight she had left in her, which meant getting someone in her corner. The same attorney who'd handled her divorce came to mind.

She called Grace Foster's office and made an appointment to find out what her options were. If Delacourt Oil intended to press charges against her, she needed to be ready with a battle plan of her own.

She was about to leave the house when Mrs. Hanover called.

"Brianna, dear, are you all right? I expected you in by now. You've had several urgent calls. Carly's been able to handle some of them, but others insisted on speaking to you directly."

Obviously the news of her quitting hadn't made its way down the corporate ladder from the executive suite.

Maybe Jeb hadn't had the nerve to pass along the word. She had enough confidence in herself left to be pretty sure that his father wasn't going to be happy about it. She was just as glad that no one knew. It would make it easier to go back and fight.

"I'm sorry, Mrs. Hanover. I should have called first thing. Something's come up that I have to deal with. I won't be in today. Possibly not for several days."

She heard her secretary's sharp intake of breath. "Is it anything I can help with?"

"No, but thanks," Brianna said. "I'll be in touch. I'm sorry, but I have to go now. I have an appointment."

"What should I tell Mr. Delacourt the next time he calls?"

"Which one?"

"Jeb."

"Tell him to go straight to hell," she muttered, then apologized. "Sorry."

"Oh, dear," Mrs. Hanover murmured. "Are you sure about this, dear? If this is about something he's done, shouldn't the two of you be trying to work it out? He seems like such a nice young man."

"Yes, he does give that impression, doesn't he?" Brianna concurred. "Too bad it's a charade. The man is a snake."

"Oh," the older woman said with a shocked gasp that didn't seem entirely due to Brianna's sharp assessment. "Oh, my."

There were rustling sounds, a muffled protest and then Jeb announced, "This is the snake."

"Were you listening on the other line? That would be pretty much in character for you."

"No, I just walked in in time to hear my character impugned."

"Welcome to the club. I have to go." She hung up before he could try once again to persuade her to listen to him. If he kept at it, sooner or later she would weaken. She couldn't allow that to happen, not when her stupid heart kept yelling at her to do just that. What did a heart know, anyway? If ever a situation called for cool, rational thought, this was it.

The attorney she met with agreed. Grace Foster was as indignant on Brianna's behalf now as she had been during the divorce. She was more than ready to take on the entire Delacourt empire if need be. "You say the word and I'll file the papers," she assured Brianna. "We'll win, too. You'll never have another financial worry."

Brianna had always liked the woman, but never more so than she did at that moment. It wasn't just because of her unrestrained faith in Brianna's case, but for her clear assumption that Brianna was innocent.

"Just so you know, I didn't sell any secret information to our competitors," Brianna told her.

"Even if the divorce hadn't told me everything I needed to know about your character, I would have known that the minute you started talking. Otherwise, I would never have taken the case. I like fighting for the underdog, but I'm not an idiot. I don't take cases I don't think I can win, not against people like the Delacourts."

"I don't have a lot of money," Brianna warned her. "You know where every cent is going. And Larry's behind in his child-support payments again."

"Which makes it all the more important that we beat

the stuffing out of them in court, so you'll get enough to pay my exorbitant fees."

"And if we lose?" Brianna asked worriedly.

"We won't. Now you go spend some time with that little girl of yours and forget all about this mess. When the time comes, we'll whip their butts."

Brianna grinned at her confidence. "I like the way you think."

"If you think I'm a tough act now, wait till you see me in court on this one. It'll make what I did to Larry look like child's play."

Brianna was brimming with confidence herself by the time she left the attorney's office. She'd taken the first and most important step in fighting back. She'd found an advocate who believed in her completely. She couldn't help wishing that Jeb had had the same sort of faith.

"But he hadn't," she reminded herself wearily. And therein lay all her troubles.

She managed to push them out of her mind while she visited with Emma, who seemed curiously excited about something she refused to discuss.

"You have to go now, Mama."

"Why? I have some extra time this afternoon. I thought we could spend it together."

Emma shook her head. "Not today."

"How come?"

"I got things to do," Emma said importantly.

"What things?"

"It's a surprise."

Brianna knew better than to argue with a kid planning a surprise. She'd had enough of her own spoiled over the years.

"Okay, pudding, I'll leave, but you owe me a really long visit tomorrow."

Emma lifted her arms for a hug. Brianna knelt down and gave her daughter a tight squeeze. "I love you, baby."

"I love you, too, Mama. Now, go."

"I'm going." Down the hall, she paused to speak to Gretchen, who was subbing for the day supervisor. "I've been banished."

"I'm not surprised."

Brianna's gaze narrowed. "What's going on?"

"Nothing."

"So, you're in on the surprise, too? Okay, I'll back off, but a word of warning. I have recently learned that secrets have a way of backfiring."

Gretchen looked vaguely guilty. "I'll keep that in mind."

After she'd left the rehab center, Brianna found herself at loose ends.

She thought of going to the office, but it was too soon. Let Jeb sweat a little. For the first time in years, she regretted not having made more of an effort to stay in touch with old friends. Unfortunately, many of her friends had been Larry's, as well. Rather than forcing them to take sides, she had simply walked away from most of them, blaming it on the amount of work she had, as well as Emma's demanding care.

She drove to a mall and tried to shop, but now definitely didn't seem like the right time for a shopping binge. She finally ate a quick slice of pizza in a food court, then went to a movie. It was a romantic comedy that only served to remind her of the budding romance she'd had with Jeb that had died before it could really flourish.

By the time she got home, she was feeling well and truly sorry for herself. Finding Jeb on her front stoop didn't improve her mood.

"I've come to eat crow," he told her.

"Sorry. I don't have any."

He held up a bag filled with chocolate croissants. "I brought along my own, just in case."

He looked so thoroughly dejected, so totally ill at ease, that Brianna relented just a little. How could she really blame him for leaping to the defense of his family? Wasn't family loyalty one of the things she loved about him? If only he hadn't turned on her in the process.

She sighed and sat down on the step next to him. He regarded her hopefully.

"Forgive me?"

"No."

"But you're thinking about it, right?"

"Maybe."

"I shouldn't have leaped to conclusions," he admitted.

"No," she agreed. "Not about me." She regarded him curiously. "Why did you?"

"Circumstantial evidence, combined with some crazy idea that I could prove to my father what a fantastic investigator I could be. So far, the whole plan has pretty much backfired. He's ready to fire me."

"I can't say I blame him."

His lips twitched. "So much for sympathy."

"From me? You must be kidding."

His gaze sought hers in the gathering twilight. "Can we start over?"

"That depends."

"On?"

She leveled a look straight into his eyes. "Do you actually believe I would ever betray your family?"

His silence lasted a beat too long. Brianna stood up. "I guess that answers my question."

"I want to believe you," he said fiercely. "Believe me, there is nothing I want more."

"But it's not the same, is it?" she said wearily. "No, I suppose it's not. I'm sorry."

"Yeah, me, too."

"Brianna, come back to work. Dad wants you there."

"And you?"

"It's not up to me," he said candidly.

"But you'd prefer I stay away so I can't give away any more company secrets," she said, re-considering her decision to stay while she fought his accusations. It would be untenable. "Sorry. I'm not coming back knowing that you're going to be looking over my shoulder, waiting for me to slip up."

"What will you do?"

"Believe it or not, I am a damned fine geologist. I'll find another job."

"Even with this cloud hanging over you?"

She sucked in a breath at the implied threat that he would leak his suspicions to the world. "No one except you knows about this so-called cloud," she said evenly. "I suggest you keep it that way, or the lawyer I saw earlier today will take you and Delacourt Oil to the cleaners. By the time we're through, maybe I'll be CEO—and you'll be the one wishing we'd never met instead of me."

Eleven

After he left Brianna's, Jeb decided to get stinking drunk and forget about the mess he'd made of everything. He called his brothers for the moral support he knew he could count on. One thing about the Delacourts—the younger generation anyway—they stuck together.

Dylan was too far away to come, though to Jeb's chagrin, he sounded almost as disgusted as their father about Jeb's rush to judgment. That left Michael and Tyler to offer sympathy. They were better at drinking. Each came to his place with a six-pack of beer and clothes to wear to work the next day, since none of them was likely to be in any condition to drive home.

"Did Dad rake you guys over the coals, too?" Jeb asked, as he sipped his second beer. He'd gotten a head start while they were on their way over.

"He mentioned his displeasure," Michael said, in what was probably a massive understatement. "He reminded me that he had specifically told me to keep you out of it after that last deal fell through."

"What about you, Ty?"

"I lucked out. I was out of the office all day long," Tyler said. "Besides, I'm only a bit player. I'm only guilty by association with the two of you. I wasn't in on the deal, I didn't get Jeb all stirred up, and I didn't tangle with Brianna." He grinned. "Hey, I guess that makes me the good son for a change."

Michael lifted his beer in salute. "Lucky you."

Tyler studied Jeb. "How's Brianna taking all this?"

"She's mad as a hornet. She's also hurt," Jeb said, thinking of the sorrow in her eyes when she'd realized that he still had doubts about her integrity. His continued offers to help her had only inflamed her more.

"Can you blame her?" Michael asked. "It would be bad enough if one of us started hurling accusations her way, but for you to do it must have really crushed her. I should have left you out of it. I wasn't thinking. Dad was right about that. Now I've messed up whatever the two of you might have had going."

Jeb was surprised at his brother's sympathetic tone, even more surprised that it was directed at Brianna. "I thought you were all for nailing her."

"Only if she's guilty," he insisted. "I assumed you'd quietly assemble some evidence before you went to her. In fact, I pretty much thought you'd jump through hoops trying to prove her innocence."

Jeb winced. "Okay, that's what I should have done. I foolishly thought I could get her to open up by trying the direct approach."

"Women hate the direct approach," Tyler said. "Puts 'em on the defensive right off. You might as well kiss the evening goodbye after that. Subtlety and charm, that's the ticket."

Michael chuckled. "Listen to him, Jeb. Nobody knows women like our brother."

"Unfortunately, his advice is a little too late to do me any good." He regarded Tyler intently. "So, tell me, how can I bail myself out of this mess?"

"Which mess are you referring to? The one that's left your personal life in a shambles? Or the one in which you're about to get your butt sued for professional slander?"

"Could be they're one and the same," Michael pointed out, just as his cell phone rang. He scowled at the intrusion but didn't hesitate to answer it. Surprise registered on his face before he said, "Yes, it's me."

Jeb and Tyler watched as their brother's expression went from surprise to displeasure to indignation, all without him having a chance to open his mouth.

"Must be a woman," Jeb decided.

"A woman with a lot on her mind," Tyler said. "Do you suppose he blew off a date to come over here tonight?"

Jeb chuckled. "He's loyal, but not that loyal."

"He could have forgotten."

"Michael, the man who has two calendars in the office, one at home and another in his briefcase?" Jeb scoffed. "I don't think so. It's got to be about business."

"Maybe it's a reporter who's gotten wind of what happened with those land deals," Tyler speculated.

Jeb shook his head. "Reporters ask questions. They don't deliver monologues." He studied his brother. "And I don't think they deliberately put the subject on the defensive if they hope to get information. Look at him. He's turning purple. I give him less than a minute till he explodes."

"Nah. Michael thrives on confrontation," his brother said.

Michael glanced over and scowled at them. "Could you two go elsewhere to do your play-by-play?"

Jeb grinned. "We wouldn't be able to do it from another room. It's illuminating to watch a man of action from a front-row seat."

Michael muttered an obscenity, then turned his attention back to the caller, who apparently hadn't let up for a second during his distraction.

"Okay, okay," he said finally. "You've made your point. I'll get back to you."

When he hung up without saying anything more, Jeb and Tyler exchanged looks.

"That's it?" Jeb questioned. "No witty repartee? No hard-line comeback?"

"Blasted female," Michael said.

"Told you it was a woman," Jeb said triumphantly.

"Not just any woman," Michael retorted. "But a very angry Grace Foster. Have you had the pleasure?"

"Uh-oh," Tyler murmured knowingly.

"Who's Grace Foster?" Jeb asked.

"The thorn in Michael's side, the woman who got away, the one who makes his blood boil and his hormones tap-dance," Tyler said, when Michael's expression only darkened.

"She's also Brianna's attorney," Michael said. "She just shared a very generous piece of her mind with me, along with some legal warnings. We've got trouble, bros. Personal issues aside, Grace may be a pain in the behind, but she knows her law." He stared hard at Jeb. "Can you switch investigative gears and do it in a hurry?"

"Meaning?"

"Go to bat for Brianna," Michael said at once. "Instead of trying to prove she did it, prove she didn't. Find the guilty culprit and save the day. Once Brianna gets past the fact that you doubted her in the first place, she'll love you forever."

Jeb studied Michael. "If that's what you really want."

"It will have the added benefit of bailing Michael here out at the same time," Tyler added. "Not that I think he wouldn't enjoy going a few rounds with the barracuda attorney, but my hunch is he'd rather do it in the bedroom than the courtroom. Right, Michael?"

"Go to hell," Michael retorted succinctly. "How about it, Jeb? Can you save the day? Isn't that what you really want?"

Still sober enough to find the challenge provocative, Jeb considered the idea of forever. A couple of months ago just the mention of the word would have made him shudder and run for the hills. Now he couldn't think of anything he wanted more, and he wanted it with Brianna. He wanted to make things right, not for the company's sake, not for his father's, but for Brianna and for himself. He wanted them to have the future that had seemed so promising just a few days ago, before things turned ugly.

"I want it," he said quietly. "I want to make things right." Neither brother seemed especially shocked by his declaration.

"Do you believe in her?" Michael asked, then pointed toward his head. "Not here, where you're analyzing all the circumstantial evidence, but down here, in your gut? Do you believe Brianna incapable of the kind of corporate espionage we're talking about?"

"Yes," he said at once, surprising himself. Why the hell hadn't he listened to his heart sooner? That was easy. Because he'd been trying too blasted hard to prove what a hotshot investigator he was. He'd wanted a quick solution that would impress his father. Instead, he'd botched things royally, infuriated his father and lost Brianna. That was quite a triple play.

"Okay, then, let's get serious and try to analyze this," Tyler said briskly. "We're obviously missing something."

None of them had had so much to drink that they couldn't think clearly.

They concentrated so hard it was surprising that the clatter of all those mental wheels turning wasn't audible.

"There's something fishy about these deals," Michael said eventually. "Dad never seemed all that broken up when they fell through."

"I agree," Tyler said. "The sites were promising, too. I even took a look at this last one. I'd been hoping to convince Dad to let me go down there and run the operation, but when Jordan Adams stole it away, Dad just shrugged it off. I figured that was because Jordan had been so good to Trish after she had the baby. I thought maybe Dad figured he owed Jordan and decided to let it pass."

Jeb stared hard at his brothers. "So what are you saying? That Dad's losing his competitive edge? Since when does he let sentiment get in the way of good business?"

Michael hooted at that, just as he had the first time Jeb had suggested it. Tyler was equally dismissive. "Never. If he let those sites go without a fight, there had to be a reason for it. Maybe he knew something the geologists and I missed."

Since scientific data was far from Jeb's area of expertise, he asked, "Such as?"

"That the balance of oil to potential investment wouldn't work in our favor," Michael suggested from the perspective of a number cruncher. "Just because there's oil on a site doesn't mean it would be cost-effective to drill."

"Or maybe there were environmental regulations pending that would have made it all but impossible to drill at that location. It could have been tied up in court for years," Tyler suggested.

"Wouldn't any smart competitor have known that, too?" Jeb asked.

"Some are willing to take the risk," Tyler said, as Michael nodded his agreement.

"But a man like Jordan Adams?" Jeb asked. "From everything I've heard about the man, he wouldn't deliberately get into a battle with the environmentalists. He's always tried to balance corporate interests with the public good, according to Dylan."

"That's what I've heard, too," Michael said.

"Let's go back to the leaks for a minute," Jeb suggested. "Is there anyone else who could possibly have known about the pending land deals? Brianna's not the only person in that department. I know you told me that Dad insists that the samples be tested without any identifying data, but there could have been a slip-up."

"Maybe one," Michael agreed. "But three? I doubt it."

"There are people in that department who've been there a lot longer than Brianna," Jeb argued. "Wouldn't they know the safeguards? Maybe they'd know how to get around them. They might also resent the fact that Brianna was brought in as head of the department, bypassing them. Selling out Delacourt Oil and implicating her in this could have been a form of payback."

"Anything's possible," Michael said. "But those safe-guards are pretty secure."

"I'll check them out, anyway," Jeb decided.

"I don't know about you, but I'm beat," Tyler announced as the antique grandfather clock in the foyer struck midnight. "I'm crashing on the sofa. Michael, you can have Jeb's guest room, since I know you need your beauty sleep so you won't look any more wrinkled than those perfectly pressed suits of yours."

"And you could obviously sleep in your jeans and no one would know the difference," Michael retorted.

"It's way too late to get into a discussion of your fashion sense, or lack of it," Jeb said. "Good night, guys. Thanks for coming over."

He walked away to the familiar sound of his brothers bickering. His head was swimming, and not from booze. He had a lot to think about, a lot to resolve before he went back to Brianna one more time with hat in hand and begged for forgiveness.

Brianna spent the morning with Emma without getting a single clue about what her daughter had been up to the previous day that was so important she had wanted her mother to leave. Gretchen had clearly been sworn to secrecy, as well. Maybe it had something to do with Emma's progress.

Maybe she was struggling to take those first critical steps and didn't want Brianna to know until she'd mastered them.

"Dear God," she murmured, "please let that be it."

"What, Mama?" Emma was staring at her with a puzzled expression.

"Nothing, baby."

"Mama, how come you got so much time to be here? Are you on vacation?"

There were times when her daughter was too darned smart. Brianna debated how to handle the question. She didn't want Emma to worry about her loss of a job.

"Something like that," she said finally. "I'm thinking about going to work for another company."

Emma looked surprisingly dismayed. "Why? What's wrong with Mr. Delacourt's company? I thought you liked it there."

"I do, but sometimes change is good."

Emma shook her head. "No. I don't like change. I want you to stay there."

Brianna stared at her. "But why? What difference does it make where I work?"

"Because," Emma said, folding her arms across her chest and regarding Brianna with a stubborn expression. "I just like this place, that's all."

"You've never even been to the office with me."

Emma reached for Brianna's hand and clung to it. "Don't leave, Mama. Please."

Brianna was clearly missing something. Had she somehow communicated that Delacourt Oil was the only reason she was able to afford such expensive care for Emma? Was her daughter frightened that she would have to leave this place before she was ready?

"Sweetie, what is it? Why would it bother you so much if I changed jobs?"

Emma sighed heavily. "Don't you get it, Mama? It's because your prince is there."

"My prince?"

"Mr. Delacourt, remember?"

Some prince, Brianna thought bitterly. "Mr. Delacourt isn't my prince," she said. "He's just someone who took me to a party."

"Not a party, a ball," Emma corrected.

Obviously the story had caught Emma's imagination even more than Brianna had realized.

"That was just one night, baby. It didn't mean a thing."

"Yes, it did," Emma said adamantly. "I want you to have a prince, Mama."

"And someday I'll find one," Brianna assured her. "Just not Mr. Delacourt."

Emma scowled at the response, then deliberately turned her wheelchair away and rolled across the room to join one of her friends in front of the TV.

"Well, what on earth was that all about?" Brianna wondered aloud.

"Talking to yourself?" Gretchen asked. "That's a bad sign."

"Believe me, my life is filled with bad signs these days." She regarded the nurse intently. "What's up with Emma? Does she seem upset to you?"

"No. In fact, she's been more upbeat than usual the past couple of days. Why? Did something happen just now?"

"I mentioned that I might change jobs and the idea really disturbed her. It doesn't make sense. It's not like she's met anyone from work or been in the office. I didn't get this job until after the accident."

"Maybe it's just that she knows you've been happy at this job," Gretchen suggested. "Children sense a lot, sometimes from what we don't say as much as what we do."

"Maybe."

The nurse gave Brianna's hand a squeeze. "Don't worry about it. I'm sure she'll forget all about it by tomorrow. You know how kids are, one minute the world is ending, the next they're floating on air."

"I suppose," Brianna said, though she wasn't reassured.

She stopped to give Emma a kiss on her way out, but got little more than a heavy sigh in response. Only after she reached the parking lot did she realize how completely at loose ends she was. She didn't feel like another lonely lunch in some crowded food court, and seeing a movie in the middle of the day had only depressed her the day before. It had been a reminder that she was unemployed.

Since it was lunchtime, she decided it might be a good time to visit her office and pick up her personal belongings. Most people—Jeb included—were likely to be out of the building. She wouldn't have to spend a lot of time coming up with explanations for why she had left so suddenly.

When she walked in the door, Mrs. Hanover's expression brightened. "You're here. Does this mean you're back for good?"

"Afraid not." Brianna held up the box she'd brought along. "I just thought I'd sneak in and pick up my things."

"You're not going to stick around to see anyone?"

Brianna shook her head.

"Carly will be sick that she missed you. She's been trying to reach you all morning." Her secretary followed her into her office. "I just don't understand this. Why would you quit?"

"It's a long story."

Mrs. Hanover sat down and patted the place next to her on the sofa. "I have time. Tell me."

Brianna was tempted. Not only did she trust the woman completely, but she desperately needed a friendly shoulder to cry on. Only the realization that she would be placing the longtime Delacourt employee in the middle of a battle that wasn't hers to fight kept Brianna from telling her everything.

"Trust me. It's better if you don't get involved," she told her. "Thanks for caring, though."

"She's not the only one who cares."

At the sound of Jeb's voice, Brianna whirled around. "What are you doing here?"

"Hoping to find you."

Mrs. Hanover got to her feet, gave Jeb a beaming smile and hurried from the room. "I'll just give you two some privacy," she said, closing the door behind her.

Brianna wasn't at all sure she didn't hear the sound of a key turning in the lock. It would be just like the woman to guess at the cause of Brianna's decision and conclude on her own that Brianna and Jeb should be coerced into working things out.

"Did you hear that?" she asked, staring at the door.

"What?"

"Did she actually lock us in here?"

Jeb grinned. "Wouldn't put it past her. Shall I check?"

Brianna sighed and shook her head. "I don't think I want to know."

"Does that mean you're willing to stick around and talk to me?" he asked, regarding her hopefully.

"You can talk. I have things to do," she said, slipping past him and settling at her desk. She opened the drawers and started tossing personal belongings into the box she'd brought along.

"What are you doing?"

"Packing up."

"You can't leave," he protested.

"I quit. Leaving is usually the next step."

"But you love it here."

"I did," she agreed. "But you've made it impossible for me to stay."

He walked around her desk until he was standing between her and the drawer she'd been emptying. "Listen to me."

Given no choice, she sat perfectly still, but she refused to meet his gaze. Even so, she was surrounded by the scent of him. He was close enough that she could feel the heat radiating from his body. He drew her like a magnet. Only sheer will kept her from touching him.

"There is no reason for you to leave."

She did meet his gaze then. "You think I'm a spy, but you want me to stay?" she asked incredulously. "Why doesn't that add up?"

"I don't think you're a spy," he said, raking his hand through his hair in evident frustration.

"Hey, you're the one who made the accusation. Are you taking it back?"

"Yes."

"Why? New evidence that cleared me?"

"No. Not yet, anyway."

"Well, do let me know when you've managed to clear my name," she said sarcastically. "I'll let you know where to send the apology."

"In care of Grace Foster, I suppose."

Brianna stilled. "You've talked to Grace?"

"No, but Michael has. She's quite an advocate."

"That's why she earns the big bucks." She studied him. "So, that's what this is about. You're running scared?"

"I am not running scared. Dammit, I know you have every right to be furious with me."

"No kidding."

"Put yourself in my place. There are three deals that fell through, all of them since you arrived. You're the only person outside of family who had access to the information. What was I supposed to think?"

"That I was innocent until proven guilty," she suggested dryly. "Call me crazy, but I thought that's what the Constitution guaranteed. Or is there a different standard here at Delacourt Oil?"

"Dammit, Brianna. You're not being fair."

She stared at him in amazement. "*I'm* not being fair? You pursued me. You made me fall in love with you. And not ten seconds later, it seemed, you turned right around and accused me of committing a crime. Pardon me, if my head is spinning."

Jeb looked thunderstruck. "What did you say?"

"The short version is that you're a jerk."

He regarded her ruefully. "I meant the part about falling in love with me."

"A momentary lapse in judgment, I assure you."

He tucked a finger under her chin and forced her gaze to meet his. "You can't fall out of love that easily."

"I sure as hell fell into it too fast. I can correct that just as easily."

"Don't." His gaze locked with hers. "Please don't."

His hushed tone calmed her own urge to rant and rave some more. "Don't what?" she whispered, not at all proud of the way her heart was skittering crazily.

"Don't fall out of love with me," he pleaded. "Give me some time to get this straightened out."

"And then what?"

"We'll start over."

"You going to wait for me while I serve my jail term?" she inquired, the edge back in her voice.

"Nobody's going to jail," he insisted. "At least not you."

"Why not?"

"Because you haven't done anything."

He said it with more conviction than she'd expected, but she still couldn't bring herself to put her faith in him. After all, the kind of doubts he'd had about her integrity didn't just vanish overnight because clearer heads prevailed. It would be a long time before she risked trusting him again, with either her fate or, even longer, with her heart.

"No," she said softly. "I haven't done anything to harm Delacourt Oil. I just wish you'd realized that from the beginning."

"So do I," he said, then leaned down and touched his lips to hers. "It's going to work out, Brianna. I swear to you, that I will move heaven and earth until your name is cleared."

"I wouldn't have been implicated in the first place if you hadn't been so quick to rush to judgment," she pointed out.

"Believe me, nobody knows that better than I do. I'm sorry."

The apology sounded heartfelt, but Brianna wasn't ready to let go of the hurt and anger. Not just yet.

"You'll pardon me if I don't entirely trust you to get the job done," she said. "I think maybe I'll do a little investigating on my own."

"We could work as a team."

She shook her head. "I don't think so. You and I have somewhat different goals. You want to nail a spy. I want to clear my name."

"It's the same thing."

"You didn't feel that way a couple of days ago."

"Because I was an idiot."

She allowed herself a faint smile. "Yes," she agreed. "And if you expect me to let you off the hook, you're going to have to work really hard at it."

If he really cared about her, if he really did trust her, after all, maybe trying to erase her doubts about him would motivate him to find the real culprit behind the leaks. Just in case, though, she intended to do everything in her power to clear herself.

Sometimes the only way to get a job done right was to do it yourself.

Twelve

There was a huge leap between deciding to do a little investigating of her own and actually cross-examining the people she'd once worked with and respected. Brianna wasn't at all sure she was up to the task. It wasn't in her nature to poke and prod in a subtle way that wouldn't immediately give away what she was doing.

However, she also realized that this was the one time when her direct approach wouldn't work. She'd have the entire oil exploration department at Delacourt Oil in an uproar. Then again, was it even possible to blunder any more than Jeb had when he'd set out to investigate her? Probably not.

She eventually decided to start with the most talkative member of the department. Roy Miller was younger than she was and was one of the few people who hadn't been openly hostile when she'd taken over. A new hire himself, he conceded he hadn't been hoping to get the job for himself. He'd told her bluntly that he'd welcome learning from her, "even if some of these old fossils think you couldn't possibly know more than they do."

When she phoned, he readily agreed to meet her for

lunch. The first thing he asked, after they'd been seated was, "What the devil is going on? Everyone says you quit and that you're under suspicion for leaking corporate secrets to the competition."

Brianna smiled ruefully. "It's nice to know the grapevine is up and running."

Roy looked shocked. "It's true?"

"It's true that I quit. It's true that secrets were apparently leaked. As the person who conducted the fieldwork, I'm definitely at the top of the list of suspects."

"I can't believe it. You're the most honest, straight-shooting person I know."

"Thank you."

"If I had to hazard a guess about anyone, it would be…" His voice trailed off and he squirmed uncomfortably. "Maybe I shouldn't say."

"Please," Brianna pleaded. "You know the people in the department better than I do. You've been in the field with some of them and worked side by side with them analyzing data. I really need to get to the bottom of this or my reputation in this business will be ruined. Getting fired by Max Coleman will be nothing compared to leaving Delacourt Oil under a cloud of suspicion."

Roy continued to look uneasy. "Look, I'd really like to help you out, but what happens if I'm wrong? If I stir things up over what turns out to be nothing, I could be the next one fired. Jill and I have a baby on the way. I can't afford to lose my job."

Unfortunately, Brianna could relate to his concerns. "I swear to you that whatever you say won't go any further. I'll find some other way to substantiate whatever you tell me so you won't be involved at all."

"I don't know, Brianna."

"Please," she pleaded. "What if I mention names and you just give me a gut reaction? Yes, no, maybe. At least I'll have a starting point."

"Okay," he finally agreed, though with obvious reluctance.

"Homer Collins," she said, mentioning the senior geologist and the man who had thought he was a shoo-in for the job she'd gotten.

"No," Roy said with conviction, then elaborated. "He might have been unhappy at first, but he's too much a company man to betray the Delacourts. He's also getting close to retirement. He wouldn't risk it."

Brianna was heartened by the sharp-eyed analysis. Whatever reservations Roy had had seemed to have given way to the desire to be as helpful as possible. Since his assessment was the same one she would have made, she was reassured that her instincts hadn't totally deserted her.

"Gil Frye," she suggested next.

There was a slight hesitation, a darkening of his expression before he finally said, "He just bought a huge boat and a beach house in Galveston. Does that answer your question?"

A sudden influx of money from a grateful competitor? At the very least, the timing of his acquisitions was worth checking out, Brianna decided. She refrained from comment and moved on.

"Karen Cole?"

"Jealous as sin of your success, but no. She doesn't have the stomach for that kind of intrigue."

It had to be Gil, then, Brianna concluded.

"You've missed a couple of people," Roy pointed out.

"Aside from you, those are the only geologists."

"But a couple of them have extremely loyal assistants. Hart Riker, for example. He would jump off a cliff if Karen mentioned seeing something she wanted at the bottom. And Susan Williams has been with Homer for years. She might want one more crack at being the right hand to the top dog. And no one knows their way around Delacourt like Susan. If there's a locked room, I guarantee she knows where to find the key. It's how she made herself so indispensable to Homer."

"But after all these years of being totally trustworthy, would she suddenly go out on this kind of a limb?" Brianna asked, unable to imagine the quiet, well-mannered woman taking such desperate measures.

"I can't answer that. You asked for a gut reaction and that's what I'm giving you."

Brianna nodded. "Okay, let's talk about the safeguards for a minute."

Roy scoffed. "Safeguards? You've got to be kidding me. Most of us may be stuck in the lab, but the locations of the sites under consideration are common knowledge. Maybe no one has every last survey marker pinned down, but the general location is easy enough to figure out. Nobody walks to these places. Travel records are easy enough to get. If you go back to the same place a couple of times, don't you think we can guess the rest? It's for darn sure you're not going there to relax. These are not garden spots."

"Then you know where we've been testing most recently?"

Roy ticked them off readily. "Hidden Gulch, Nevada. Harrison Ranch, Texas. Winding Gorge, Texas." He met her gaze. "Should I keep going?"

Brianna was appalled. "No. You've made your point.

After all these years, wouldn't someone have mentioned that to the Delacourts?"

"Why? No one intended to use the information against them."

"Until now," Brianna pointed out.

Roy's expression faltered. "Yes. Until now. I'm sorry, Brianna." He glanced at his watch. "I'd better go. I've got testing to do this afternoon, and Homer wants the results on his desk before I leave for the day."

"Homer's acting head of the department?"

"He'd stepped in before the end of the day yesterday. I don't know if anyone appointed him or if he just saw an opportunity and grabbed it. I'm not going to argue with him, though. And Susan is in her glory setting up meetings. She was always appalled at how few you held. 'Meetings establish common goals and build morale,'" he quoted.

His precise mimicry brought a smile. "Thanks, Roy. You've given me a lot to think about."

He shook his head. "No, I haven't," he reminded her with a half-smile. "We haven't even talked."

"Of course not," Brianna agreed.

After he'd gone, she sipped another glass of iced tea and pondered the information he'd passed along.

"Learn anything interesting?" Jeb inquired, appearing out of nowhere and slipping into the seat opposite her.

Brianna almost choked at the sound of his voice. "You!"

He offered one of those irrepressible grins. "Glad to see me?"

"Dismayed would be more accurate," she muttered, despite the contradictory leap of her pulse. "What are you doing here? I don't suppose this is pure coincidence."

"Nope. I followed you."

She saw little point in protesting that. It had gotten to be a habit, albeit an extremely annoying one. "Can't you do your own investigating?"

"I am."

"No, you're just tagging along on mine."

"Somebody's got to keep an eye on you. Hasn't it occurred to you that whoever did leak those secrets might not be happy about you poking around trying to find answers?"

"So, this is all about protecting me?"

"Of course."

"In a pig's eye. This time a few days ago, you were intent on nailing me yourself."

"A momentary blip in judgment, for which I have apologized."

"You could crawl over hot coals on your hands and knees and it wouldn't get you off the hook," she told him.

He winced at the image. "I know you're mad—"

"Try furious."

"Have a glass of wine. It'll relax you."

"That's a bad habit to get into, though spending too much time around you could drive me to it."

"If we were someplace other than the middle of this restaurant, I could make you take that back," he said.

"I doubt it."

"Don't dare me, Brianna. You know I'm a man who thrives on challenge. Besides, I discovered very recently that I'm addicted to a certain smart-mouthed geologist, and I'm suffering from withdrawal. I might do just about anything to get another fix, even if I have to steal it."

"Suggesting that you're not above thievery might not be wise under the circumstances," she pointed out, though she had to work to keep her lips from curving into a smile. He did know how to make a woman feel desire…right before he turned around and stabbed her in the back, unfortunately.

He held up his hands in a gesture of surrender. "Peace? Let's talk about your pal Roy. Did he have anything interesting to say?"

She thought of her promise to the other man. "Not a word. We were just having a bite to eat and a casual conversation about the weather."

"Fascinating stuff, weather."

"Absolutely."

"I heard Homer's name mentioned, along with Gil's, Karen's, and a few others."

"What were you doing, hiding under the table?"

He leaned down and peeked pointedly under the edge of the tablecloth. "I'll admit the view from there might have been intriguing, but alas, no. I was behind the potted palm."

Brianna glanced at the offending plant and sighed. "If you were that close, then I'm sure you caught most of the conversation. You don't need a play-by-play from me. Draw your own conclusions."

She stood up and started for the door, deliberately leaving the check on the table for him to pay. He tossed some money down without a whimper of protest, then followed. He caught up with her at the cashier's booth at the parking lot next door.

"Where are we going?"

She frowned at him. "I am going to run some errands. I don't know about you."

"I could tag along. It would save on gas."

"You own an oil company. The cost of gas shouldn't be a consideration."

"We all have a responsibility to conserve our natural resources."

Brianna rolled her eyes. "No," she said emphatically. She was going to see Emma, and she did not want him accompanying her.

"Is going to see your daughter one of those errands?" he inquired, accurately pinpointing the cause of her reluctance with one guess.

"Okay, yes," she admitted.

To her surprise, he merely nodded. "Fine, then. I'll catch up with you later."

"Please don't."

He shook his head. "Darlin', until this is settled you're not going to be able to shake me. Just relax and enjoy it."

Relax around the man who'd gotten her into this fix in the first place with his absurd suspicions? The man who now claimed to be totally in her corner? Not a chance, Brianna thought. If he was any more on her side, she'd probably end up in jail.

Jeb had, in fact, heard enough of Brianna's conversation with Roy to give him new avenues of investigation to explore. He'd still hoped she would trust him enough to share them with him. Discovering that she did not cut straight through him. Of course, there were some who might say—Brianna among them, no doubt—that he deserved to know what it felt like to have someone he loved not trust him worth spit.

Since he didn't have access to some of the same computerized financial checks that his brother did, he called Dylan and asked him to check out Gil Frye's finances. In the meantime, he decided to have a chat with both Homer and Karen to see how deeply their animosity toward Brianna ran. He intended to tell them he was just paying a little morale-boosting visit to the department. They could make of that whatever they liked.

Homer Collins was the epitome of a dedicated scientist from his flyaway white hair to his rumpled, careless attire. Jeb could recall the first time as a child that he had seen Homer in the lab and wondered if he was experimenting with something as exciting as Frankenstein. Both Homer and his father had chuckled at his vivid imagination.

He found Homer in the lab again, surrounded by test tubes and piles of computer printouts analyzing the data he'd assembled.

"Hey, Homer."

The older man glanced up, looking a bit dazed behind his thick glasses. "Oh, Jeb, it's you. Can I help you with something?"

"I just stopped by to see how things are going with Brianna out of the picture."

"A sorry situation," Homer said, sounding genuinely distraught. "I would never have thought her capable of selling out this company, not after your dad put such faith in her."

"Are you so sure she did?"

Homer seemed startled by the question. "If she didn't, who would have?"

"I was hoping you might have some ideas," Jeb said.

"Haven't given it much thought. I've been too busy trying to take up the slack since she left."

"She's only been gone a day," Jeb pointed out mildly.

"It doesn't take long for work to pile up, if everyone's not pulling their weight," he responded defensively.

Jeb patted his shoulder. "Yes, I'm sure you're right. Thanks for pitching in. I just wanted you to know we're all counting on you to stay on top of things until we can get this worked out and get Brianna back here."

Homer regarded him with surprise. "She'll be back?"

"If I have my way, she will be."

"Yes, I had heard that the two of you…" His voice trailed off and he shrugged. "Well, never mind. You know what's best, I'm sure."

"Any idea where Karen Cole is?" Jeb asked, letting Homer's unspoken innuendo about Jeb's personal relationship with Brianna pass.

"Where she usually is, I imagine, in the field. She left this morning to do a follow-up report on one of the sites Brianna checked out."

"Why? Was there some question about the results?"

"With what's happened, everyone's going to be second-guessing every move Brianna made," Homer said. "We need to be ready for the questions."

Jeb supposed he had a point, but it still grated on his nerves to hear someone so eager to accept the fact that Brianna really had been a spy. Of course, he'd been just as bad. Worse, in fact, since he'd known her well enough to know better.

As he wandered back to his own office, his cell phone rang. He flipped it open. "Yes?"

"Jeb, it's Dylan. I got that information on Frye, but I don't think it's going to help you."

"Oh?"

"He's a financial paragon. The man's been depositing

his checks like clockwork. No extra money going into his accounts. He doesn't have credit cards. His mortgage payments are modest. His two big splurges were the beach house and boat you already know about. He made the down payments with money he had in savings."

"What are you saying?"

"He looks clean."

"Damn. I thought he was going to be our best shot."

"Anything's possible, but from where I sit, he's not your man. Want me to run checks on the others in the department?"

"Not yet. I'll get back to you."

"Jeb?"

"What?"

"Could this be a game of smoke and mirrors that Dad's been playing?"

Shocked by the suggestion, Jeb halted where he was. "Dad? Why the hell would he do something like that?"

"You've got me there, but I don't like the way this is going. Be careful. You may be stirring up a hornet's nest over nothing."

"Dylan, those sites were stolen out from under Delacourt Oil. That's not nothing."

"You only have Dad's word for that, right?"

"Yes," he said, then corrected himself. "No, not exactly. Michael confirmed it. He was in on the negotiations for one site himself. And Brianna has never denied that we lost sites she'd been checking out."

"Think about it, though. Dad hasn't gone ballistic. Not even once. That is totally out of character."

"True," Jeb agreed.

"All he's done is try to warn you away from getting involved, correct?"

"Yes."

"Ask yourself why," Dylan suggested.

"I've asked myself that a million times, but I don't have an answer."

"One comes to mind, but it's so far-fetched even I have a hard time believing it."

"Try me."

"No," Dylan said slowly. "I think I'll let you work it out for yourself."

"Dylan," Jeb protested, but he was wasting his breath. His big brother had just hung up on him, and if he wasn't very much mistaken, Dylan had been chuckling. Jeb couldn't see a blasted thing to laugh about.

Brianna's visit with Emma wasn't nearly the distraction she'd hoped for. Once again, her daughter kept watching the door as if she were expecting someone else to drop by. Since there were no other visitors that Brianna knew about, her behavior was strange. Questioning her about it only drew shrugs and denials.

"I gots to go to therapy, Mama," Emma said eventually, dismissing her.

"Okay, baby. I'll see you tomorrow," Brianna said even as Emma whooshed past in her wheelchair. Brianna sighed. She ought to be grateful that her daughter was so eager to keep up with her treatment, but she couldn't help feeling just a little hurt by the abrupt departure.

"Put the time to good use," she muttered as she left the building, waving at the daytime nursing supervisor who'd just returned from a week-long vacation. Gretchen wouldn't be on until evening. Brianna missed chatting with her. Maybe Gretchen would have some insights into Emma's odd behavior, though the last time they'd talked, she had been as tight-lipped as the child. There were definitely secrets being kept around the rehab center, and Emma was at the center of them. Unfortunately, Brianna had bigger mysteries to unravel.

Dismissing it as a problem she couldn't solve, she tried to focus on her so-called investigation. If she knew Jeb, he had headed straight back to Delacourt Oil to question all the people Roy had mentioned at lunch.

Sitting behind the wheel of her car, she considered her options. "Why am I pussyfooting around with this?" she demanded aloud.

The person who could tell her precisely what had happened with this last deal was Jordan Adams. He'd bought the land. Why not ask him how he'd found out about it? The worst he could do would be to lie or evade her questions. In the best-case scenario, he could put the whole thing to rest with an honest reply.

Because she dealt with charter companies all the time to book flights to some of the out-of-the-way sites she needed to explore, she called a pilot she knew and made arrangements with him to fly her to Los Piños immediately. Whatever the cost, if she could prove her innocence on this trip, it would be worth the battering to her savings.

By the time they arrived across the state, Jordan Adams had left his office and headed home. She found him there in the middle of his dinner.

"I'm so sorry," she said, when he came to the door with a napkin in his hand and a puzzled frown on his face. "I would have called, but I was afraid you wouldn't see me."

"Why on earth wouldn't I see you?" Jordan said, his manner surprisingly friendly. "Come on in and join us. Dinner's just getting started. It's a little crazy because the grandkids are here, but if you don't mind chaos, there's plenty of food."

The thought of intruding, along with her own dark mood, kept her from accepting. She shook her head. "No, really, I don't want to interrupt. I'll just wait out here, if you don't mind. Join me whenever you've finished."

Jordan studied her face intently, then nodded. "Give me a minute. I'll be right back."

He returned almost at once, carrying two glasses of lemonade. "It's a warm night. I thought you might want something to drink," he said, offering one glass to her.

"Thank you."

He settled into the rocker next to hers, rocked for a moment, giving the evening's peacefulness a chance to soak in. "Okay, Brianna," he said eventually. "What can I do for you?"

"It's about the deal you made for the Harrison Ranch mineral rights."

He nodded slowly. "I thought that might be it. What can I tell you?"

"Did that deal just fall into your lap?"

He chuckled. "Is that your polite way of asking if someone leaked the information about Delacourt Oil's findings to me?"

"Pretty much," she said candidly.

"No, at least not in the sense you mean. I'd really rather not get into this with you, though."

"I'm sure I can understand why," she said bitterly.

"I doubt that," he said in a wry tone she couldn't quite

interpret. She decided to play on his well-known sense of decency and honor.

"Look, my professional reputation is on the line over this. I know that I'm not the one who told you. And I'm not out to have somebody prosecuted. I just want to be able to go to Bryce Delacourt and offer him something to prove that I had nothing to do with leaking inside information. I need to clear my name."

Jordan, the epitome of a gentleman, swore. "It's come to that, has it?"

Brianna nodded miserably. "I've already quit my job. Jeb's investigating me. I need answers."

"I could use a few myself," he said fervently. "Don't worry, Brianna. If you need work, you have a job with me. I know your reputation and your credentials. I would have offered when you left Max Coleman, but Bryce beat me to it. So that's one worry off your shoulders. In the meantime, I'll give you an affidavit that swears you had nothing to do with the information I was given."

She was astounded by the job offer and the offer of an affidavit. "Thank you. A sworn statement ought to help."

"It's yours, but you're not going to need it," he assured her. "Not with Bryce."

Something in his voice set off alarms. "Because?"

"I knew I should have stayed the heck out of this," he murmured to himself, then met her gaze evenly. "Because Bryce gave me that information himself."

As his words sank in, Brianna began to shake, the reaction part fury, part relief. "Do you know why he would do that?"

"Actually, I think I do, but you'll have to ask him."

"Oh, believe me, I intend to."

Thirteen

Brianna couldn't begin to imagine what would lead Bryce Delacourt to sabotage his own company, but she intended to find out. In fact, she was mad enough at being caught in the middle of some intrigue he'd obviously masterminded that she would have blistered his ears with her opinion if his secretary hadn't informed her that he'd suddenly been called away on business.

"When will he be back?" she asked, during the call she made from the plane on her way back from seeing Jordan Adams.

"I'm not sure," Mrs. Fletcher said with a touch of apparent indignation at his failure to be more forthcoming. "He shouldn't be gone more than a day or two. If he checks in, shall I have him call you?"

"No," Brianna said. This meeting needed to be face-to-face. She owed him that much in return for all he'd done for her. "But I would appreciate it if you would contact me the minute he returns."

"Absolutely. I'll add your name to the list of people waiting to speak to him."

"Put it at the top," Brianna said insistently. "This is urgent."

"Funny," Mrs. Fletcher said, sounding anything but amused. "Jeb said the same thing. Is there something going on I should know about?"

Brianna almost smiled at the increased level of exasperation in the woman's voice. She prided herself on knowing absolutely everything going on at Delacourt Oil. She had been with Bryce since he started the company more than thirty years earlier and she clearly didn't like being left in the dark.

"I'm not sure yet," Brianna told her candidly.

"Does this have something to do with the reason you just up and quit out of the blue? I can tell you that Mr. Delacourt was furious about that. He told Jeb exactly how he felt. Not that I was eavesdropping," she said hurriedly. "But when Mr. Delacourt gets angry, you can hear him in the next county."

"I'm sure you can," Brianna said wryly. "And yes, this is related. I'm just not sure how yet."

"Well, for whatever it's worth, I hope you'll change your mind and come back. Mr. Delacourt has a lot of faith in you. Ever since Trish refused to become involved in the company and went off to marry that rancher, he's been down in the dumps. I think he actually thought of you as a substitute for his daughter."

Funny way to treat a daughter, Brianna thought, but then Mrs. Fletcher didn't know the whole story about how Bryce had apparently set Brianna up to take the fall for something he'd done.

"That's nice of you to say. I've always been fond of him, too," Brianna said. But that could change, she thought. Right now she was seriously considering murdering the man, if he was guilty of what Jordan Adams had suggested.

When she got to her place, she found Jeb once again waiting on the doorstep. She wasn't entirely sure how she felt about the man's persistence. However, there was no earthly reason for him to see her ambivalence.

"This is getting to be a habit," she said. "A bad one."

Jeb ignored the gibe. "Where have you been? Those errands must have really piled up."

She frowned at his sarcasm. "Where I go and what I do are none of your concern."

"Now, darlin', you know that's not entirely true. Even if I weren't crazy about you, there's the little matter of corporate espionage to be considered."

"Oh, get off it. I'm not guilty and you know it. That's just an excuse to hang around here and drive me crazy."

He regarded her with evident curiosity. "Do I?"

"Do you what?"

"Drive you crazy?"

"Isn't it obvious?"

"I was thinking of crazy in a good way," he said, regarding her with a crooked grin.

She bit back a chuckle. "And I wasn't," she retorted.

"I guess I'll have to work on my technique."

"You might want to start by not making unsubstantiated accusations."

"I've apologized for that." He held up a bag. "And I've brought dinner. Chinese. All your favorites."

"You don't know my favorites."

"Sure, I do. Mrs. Hanover told me what she orders for you when you're staying late at the office. Carly advised me that crow would be better, but I couldn't find it on the menu."

"Mrs. Hanover has a big mouth. She probably ought to be fired."

"In order to fire her, you'd have to come back to work." He regarded her hopefully. "Are you considering that?"

"Nope. Not until this mess is cleared up, anyway." Suddenly overwhelmed by how complicated her life had become, she blinked back tears, turned away and focused her attention on finding her key.

"Brianna?"

"What?"

"I really am sorry for my part in all of this."

Once again, he sounded genuinely contrite, but that didn't make the mess go away. It didn't clear her name. She gazed down at him. "Speaking of which, what did you do today to stir things up?"

He held up the bag. "Can I come in and share this with you? We can talk about it."

Chinese and Jeb's company? How could she turn either of them down, when her refrigerator was empty and her spirits were low? Otherwise she was likely to spend the long evening indulging in a heavy bout of self-pity that would serve no useful purpose whatsoever. If he spent the evening doing little more than aggravating her, having him around would be worthwhile.

"You might as well," she said grudgingly.

He grinned and followed her inside. "I would have preferred a little more enthusiasm, but I'm grateful for whatever I can get."

Brianna dished up the lukewarm sweet-and-sour chicken and the spicier Kung Pao chicken, then popped them into the microwave. "What would you like to drink?"

"Soda, beer, iced tea—whatever you have is fine," Jeb told her, moving efficiently to set the table.

Brianna couldn't help noticing that after only a few visits, he was as familiar with her cupboards as she was. For some reason, she found it annoying that he was so blasted comfortable in her home. She had allowed that. She had invited him into her home, into her life—into her bed, dammit —and he had turned right around and betrayed her.

She moved directly into his path, blocking his movements. With knives and forks in one hand and napkins in the other, he stared down at her. "What?"

"How could you do it?" she asked plaintively. "How could you turn on me?"

"I never turned on you," he protested.

"It sure as hell felt that way."

"I hardly knew you when this began. I was protecting my family."

"Not then," she said. "Later. After…"

"After we'd slept together?" he asked, his gaze locked with hers. Heat shimmered in the air as the memories of that night in London came flooding back. "After we'd started to fall in love?"

"Yes," she whispered. "After that."

"It was still about family." He shrugged ruefully. "At least, I thought it was. I told myself I had a duty."

Something in his tone alerted her that something had changed. "And now? Has something happened to change that?"

His gaze locked with hers. "You know it has."

"Has it really, Jeb? When it comes right down to making a choice, who will you choose?"

"Not who," he told her. "What. I'll choose the truth, whatever it is."

"No matter who gets hurt?" she asked, thinking of his father and his apparent involvement.

"Brianna—"

She cut him off. "Someone is going to get hurt, Jeb. It's too late to stop it now. This whole ridiculous thing has spun out of control, and all because you wanted to prove something to your father." Or because his father had some crazy scheme up his sleeve, she amended to herself.

Jeb winced at the accusation. He dropped the silverware and napkins onto the table, started to say something and then stopped. Instead, he reached out and touched her cheek with a tenderness that made her heart ache.

"Not you," he said softly. "You're not going to get hurt, Brianna. I'll see to it."

"I've already been hurt," she reminded him. "And there's more to come. You, your family. It really is spiraling out of our control."

He regarded her with obvious confusion. "I don't understand. Do you know something?"

She thought of what Jordan Adams had revealed earlier about Bryce's involvement. Should she share that with Jeb now? Warn him? No. She wouldn't do to him what he had done to her. She wouldn't act on unsubstantiated rumors or pass along half-truths. Not that she believed for a second that Jordan Adams had lied to her. She just didn't know *all* of the facts. She wouldn't until she had talked to Bryce. It was a courtesy she wished someone had extended to her at the outset.

"Not yet," she said finally. "But I'm getting close, Jeb."

To her surprise, he said, "So am I."

"Will you tell me?"

He hesitated, then shook his head. Brianna sighed. Once again, they were at a stalemate. The lack of trust hovered in the air, an unwanted guest standing squarely between two people who'd had such high hopes for the future only a few short days ago. Given time, love could be the most powerful emotion on earth. In its earliest moments, however, it was as fragile as a spring blossom in a late blizzard.

In the end, she thought that was what she might never forgive Jeb for.

He had restored her faith in men, only to snatch it away within days. He had proved once and for all that the only person she could really count on was herself. It was a desperately lonely way to live. She already knew that. But it was safe, and sometimes safe was the best a woman could do.

Jeb hated what was happening to him and Brianna. For every step closer they took, there were a dozen more to separate them. The distance was growing by the minute.

He had seen the hurt and anguish shimmering in her eyes the night before, along with the tears she had determinedly blinked back. It might have been easier if she had raged at him and let the tears flow. But that quiet resignation, that unshakable acceptance that the future was over for the two of them, was impossible to battle.

Wherever the chips fell, he had to bring an end to

this. He wasn't looking forward to confronting his father with his suspicions, but it had to be done. If he was wrong, he had no doubt that his relationship with his father would suffer irreparably just as his with Brianna had.

"What the hell am I supposed to do?" he asked Michael, who had the reputation of being the calm, rational one in the family.

"Do you really think Dad was involved in all of this in some way, that he set it up?"

"Dylan suspects it and, frankly, I think the whole thing stinks to high heaven. There is not one shred of evidence that Brianna—or anyone else, for that matter—was involved in leaking this information. I just wish I'd done the legwork before I started casting blame on Brianna, instead of after. I should have listened to Dad when he warned me to leave it all alone. Obviously he knew more than he was saying."

"At least you've learned a valuable lesson, even if it was the hard way."

"I don't suppose you'd like to come along when I talk to Dad?" he asked halfheartedly, already knowing the likely response.

Michael held up his hands. "No way. I've got enough problems keeping Grace Foster in check. I'll just wait nearby to pick up the pieces after the explosion."

"Coward."

"Sensible," Michael corrected. "Somebody has to be in one piece to run this place when the dust settles."

"Thanks for your support," Jeb said, though without real rancor. Michael was just being sensible, as always. "Where's Tyler?"

"If he's smart, nowhere near Houston. Forget it, Jeb. You're on your own."

Jeb glanced toward his father's office next door, then sighed. "Wish me luck."

"Always, bro. Something tells me you're going to need it. I can't wait for a full report."

Jeb drew in a deep breath, then marched out of Michael's office, through the reception area, past an indignant, protesting Mrs. Fletcher and straight into his father's office.

Stunned by the sight that greeted him, he halted halfway in. Brianna was facing his father, her hands braced on his desk, the color high in her cheeks. At the sight of Jeb, the flush deepened. His father heaved a sigh of apparent resignation.

"Okay, sit down, son. You might as well hear this, too. Brianna, take a seat." For the first time in Jeb's memory, his father looked less than totally sure of himself. His gaze met Jeb's, then Brianna's, then fell.

"Much as it pains me to admit it, I've made a damned mess of things," he muttered.

Jeb wasn't about to argue with that, even without knowing the whole story. "Maybe you should start at the beginning, Dad."

"I'm not sure I know precisely when that was. I suppose it goes back to losing Trish and Dylan."

"Dad, you didn't 'lose' them," Jeb protested. "They made different choices for their lives, but they still love you. And what does that have to do with this?"

"Maybe they do still love me, but it seemed as if nothing was working out the way I'd planned. I built this company from nothing, and I did it for the five of you. I dreamed of all of us working together. I wanted an oil dynasty."

Jeb glanced at Brianna and saw that she was listening intently, if somewhat skeptically. He couldn't blame her. All of this Delacourt family history must seem like the weakest of excuses for what had apparently happened. Not that he fully understood what that was just yet. His father's cryptic remarks were hardly illuminating.

"Go on," Jeb encouraged.

His father's gaze met his. "This all started as a way to keep you interested in the company," he murmured so low that Jeb had difficulty hearing him.

When he grasped what his father was trying to say, he stared incredulously. "Me? This was about me?"

"Yes."

"I think you'd better explain that one."

"I didn't want you defecting, too. I knew you wanted to join up with your brother as an investigator. I thought maybe if you had that kind of work to do around here, you wouldn't be so anxious to leave. I began planting the idea that we had problems." He smiled. "I certainly didn't have to say much. You leaped right on it, but I knew as soon as you started looking very deep, you'd see that there was nothing, so I..." His voice trailed off.

Jeb got the picture just the same. Even though it was what he'd begun to suspect, he was still incredulous. "So you sabotaged your own deals?"

"More or less," his father admitted. He regarded Brianna apologetically. "I never meant to get you involved, but I have to admit I was grateful when my son began showing an interest in you. That was the icing on the cake. I'd hope you would be one more reason for him to stick around. I thought maybe you could do what I couldn't, spark his interest in staying right here at Delacourt Oil."

"So Jordan Adams was right," Brianna said, clearly every bit as stunned as Jeb. "You manipulated this, from beginning to end."

"Guilty," his father admitted.

"You wanted to turn it into some sort of bizarre matchmaking scheme?" she asked, clearly dumbstruck by the absurdity of the lengths to which he'd gone.

"At first, it was just a way to hold on to Jeb. In the end, yes, I was matchmaking. I saw the two of you getting closer and I wanted something to happen. I knew if you spent enough time together, it would. I know my son, Brianna, better than he thinks I do. I knew he would leap to defend the company and, given time, he would leap to defend you." He surveyed the two of them. "In a way, that's exactly what's happened, isn't it?"

Jeb didn't even try to deny that part. "Dad, why the hell would you cook up a crazy scheme like that?" he asked. "It's not your style. You've done a lot of things to keep us tied to the company, but you've always left our personal lives alone."

His father shrugged, his expression sheepish. "I kept hearing from Trish and Dylan and from Jordan Adams before them about what a wonder Harlan Adams was, how he meddled in everyone's lives and they loved him for it. I suppose I figured I could pull it off, too. That I could keep what was left of my family together and watch it grow."

Jeb would have laughed if the situation weren't so pathetic. "You were jealous of Harlan Adams?"

"Not of his money or his power," his father said. "Of his family. His keeps growing, and mine is getting smaller and smaller. I'm sorry. I can't say it enough. I just pray I haven't messed up everything for the two of you. That would be my biggest regret."

He walked out from behind his desk and gave Brianna's shoulder a squeeze. "I truly am sorry. I sincerely regret any pain I've caused you. I hope you'll forgive me and I hope you'll stay on here."

Jeb waited for her reply almost as eagerly as his father, but she seemed dazed. "I need some time. I have to think about all of this," she said eventually.

"That's all I'm asking," his father said. "Think about what you'd be giving up if you left, too. Whatever you decide, though, I will see to it that Emma continues to get the care she needs. She's a remarkable little girl and you're a remarkable woman. I would have been blessed to have you become a part of this family. And if this stubborn son of mine has a grain of sense left, he'll make it happen, despite what I've done."

"Dad," Jeb warned. He didn't want his father making his proposal for him. Jeb had a hunch Bryce wouldn't have any better luck than Jeb himself was likely to have. They were both lucky that Brianna wasn't the type to go for the jugular, even if she had hired an attorney who would. They had both made terrible mistakes and deserved whatever she felt like dishing out in the way of punishment.

His father moved to stand in front of him. "I owe you an apology, too, son. I wouldn't blame you if you never spoke to me again."

Jeb heard the genuine regret and real fear in his father's voice and let some of his anger slip away. "Oh,

I think you can count on hearing quite a lot from me once Brianna and I have settled a few things."

His father nodded, accepting that things between the two of them were far from over. "Then I'll leave you to it."

Brianna watched Bryce Delacourt walk out of his office with a sense of dismay. She thought she understood what had driven him to make such a mistaken attempt to control his family. She could almost forgive the depth of desperation that must have been driving him. She knew that she, too, would do anything to keep Emma in her life and, when the time came, to assure her happiness with the right man at her side. Hopefully, though, she wouldn't resort to such a risky brand of matchmaking.

But if Bryce's motives were clear, Jeb's were anything but. She didn't understand how a man who purported to love her could have so thoroughly misread her. She wasn't even sure anymore that it mattered. Bottom line: when the chips were down, he'd distrusted her. She simply couldn't get past that. She doubted that she ever would.

When she met his gaze, she saw that he was waiting, watching her warily.

"I can't believe my father did something like that," he said finally.

"It was all about family," she said. "The same way it was with you. Perhaps the two of you are more alike than you realize."

Jeb didn't seem at all comfortable with the comparison. "I imagine you're not crazy about any of us at the moment."

"Not especially," she agreed candidly.

"This may not be the right time to get into this, but I'd like another chance with you," he said. "I want you to know that up front. I'd like to prove that I'm not quite the jerk I must seem right now, that none of the Delacourts are. Give us a chance, Brianna. Let me make things right."

"I don't think that's possible," she said coolly, even though her heart ached.

"Just say you'll try."

She shook her head, ignoring the pangs of regret. "No, Jeb. I need someone in my life I can count on, not someone who'll think the worst of me so easily." She might not have a lot of answers right now, but she knew that much. She stood and turned to go.

To her surprise, he didn't argue. "Will you accept my father's offer and stay at Delacourt Oil?" he asked instead.

She turned back, met his gaze. "I honestly don't know."

He reached out as if to touch her cheek, then let his hand fall away. "I hope you do, Brianna. Not just for my sake or my dad's, but for Emma's. This job has given the two of you stability, and I'd hate to see you lose all that because the Delacourt men are fools."

"Not fools, Jeb, just misguided."

"If you can see that, then maybe someday you will forgive us."

Brianna wished she could believe that, wished that this whole nightmare had never even begun, but wishing couldn't change anything. She felt every bit as betrayed as she had when Larry had walked away from her and Emma without a backward glance.

"I have to go," she said.

Jeb nodded, though there was no mistaking the regret in his eyes. "Do what you have to do."

What she wanted to do was hurl herself into his arms and pretend that everything was going to be okay, but that was out of the question. Instead, even though her heart was breaking, she made herself walk away.

Fourteen

Brianna debated long and hard about whether to return to Delacourt Oil. The decision had nothing to do with the job itself. She loved it. She always had. It wasn't even about the potential harm that had been done to her reputation, because the people who really mattered, the industry big shots like Jordan Adams and Bryce Delacourt, had known all along that she was guilty of nothing.

Rather, it had everything to do with the knowledge that she was bound to bump into Jeb from time to time. She knew from Mrs. Hanover and Carly that he was still very much in evidence. Apparently he and his father had made their peace. No one believed in the importance of family more than she did. Because of that, she was glad for them, even if it did complicate her own decision.

She couldn't go on indefinitely in this professional limbo. Jordan Adams had put his money where his mouth was. He had made her a firm offer to join his staff, which would mean moving to Los Piños.

A few days ago she had gone for a visit and she genuinely liked the small town, liked the people in Jordan's company, loved all of the Adamses, whom Jordan had insisted she meet. But the thought of uprooting Emma or, worse yet, leaving her over in Houston, even temporarily, was out of the question.

"I'm sorry, Jordan," she said when they met again after she'd weighed the decision for days. "I can't do it, as much as I would like to. The timing just isn't good for my daughter."

"I understand," he said, though with obvious disappointment. "Once she's back on her feet again, if you change your mind, the offer holds. You'll always be welcome here, Brianna. I feel as if I owe you at least as much as Bryce does for my part in that whole farce."

When she would have spoken, he held up a hand. "No argument. And this isn't just about that, either, in case you thought it was. You're a fine geologist. We'd be lucky to get you."

He studied her, his expression serious. "Mind if I butt in on something that is none of my business?"

She laughed. "Everyone else has. Why not you?"

"I don't think Emma is the only reason you're turning me down."

She had a hunch she knew where he was heading and decided to nip the speculation in the bud. "Of course it's about Emma. Everything I do has to be about my daughter's welfare."

"She could get the care she needs over here, even if we had to fly in therapists," he pointed out. "Which I would be more than happy to do. She could have a full-time nanny or a nurse and be at home with you. In some ways she would be even better off than she is now. I think she might thrive in this environment. Kids do." His gaze locked with hers. "But you'd still turn me down, wouldn't you?"

Brianna winced at the accuracy of his assessment. Obviously he had sensed something in her that she hadn't wanted to see.

"If you love Jeb, work it out. Give him a chance to make up for hurting you. One thing Bryce had right about this family is that each and every one of us understands the power of love. We respect it. And we know it's the one thing in life you should never back away from, especially not out of fear of being hurt."

"I appreciate what you're saying, but you're wrong. I don't love Jeb and he doesn't love me," she insisted. "If he had, he would never have done what he did."

"What did he do that was so terrible?" Jordan asked quietly. "Think about it, Brianna. He tried to defend his family, even when it cost him the love of a woman he cared about. Isn't that the kind of man you'd like in your corner when the chips are down?"

Brianna sighed. "Maybe so," she conceded. But it wasn't going to happen. There was simply too much water under that particular bridge. She didn't waste time pointing out that the chips had been down and Jeb hadn't been there for her.

"Think about what I've said. I don't mind losing you, if it's for the right reasons. Be honest with yourself, at least."

Brianna thought she was being honest with herself. She couldn't love a man who'd betrayed her. She wouldn't.

Even if her heart said otherwise.

When Brianna walked out of his father's office two weeks earlier, Jeb had feared that she was just as literally walking out of his life. Letting her go without a fight was one of the hardest things he'd ever done, but he knew she needed time to heal before she would even listen to anything he said.

When he heard she was interviewing with Jordan Adams, it gave him a few bad moments. A few days later, when his father told him that she'd made the decision to come back to Delacourt Oil, relief washed through him.

"Give her some space," his father advised. "Let her get her feet back under her."

"As if I'd take courting advice from you," Jeb said dryly. "You must have a short memory. It was your meddling that brought us to this point."

"That doesn't mean I don't understand a thing or two about the way a woman's mind works," his father said defensively. "Your mother and I have been together for close to forty years now. That didn't happen without a few rough patches. We worked them out."

Jeb couldn't argue with that. The longevity of his parents' marriage was due to more than inertia. Obviously there was a deep-rooted sense of commitment and understanding between them.

"Okay, what would you do?" Jeb asked. "I can't just sit idly by and wait for something to happen."

His father looked relieved and a little pleased by Jeb's question. "There's another O'Ryan female, you know."

"Emma?"

"Exactly. I imagine she gets lonely from time to time. Goodness knows, her own daddy doesn't pay her any visits. It seems to me that a smart man who's very sure that he wants her mother would be wise to get to know the daughter."

"Emma and I already spend time together," Jeb admitted.

His father regarded him with surprise. "You do? Does Brianna know that?"

"Not unless Emma's told her, and I don't think she has. I'm sure I would have heard about it."

His father chuckled. "Yes, I imagine you would have. She's a cute kid, isn't she?"

Now it was Jeb's turn to be surprised. "You've seen her?"

"From time to time. Whenever I get a hankering to see my own grandbabies, I go and spend time with Emma. She takes the edge off the need."

"When did this start? She hasn't mentioned it."

"Hasn't mentioned you to me, either. I guess she has her mother's ability to keep a secret."

Jeb sighed. "Dad, why not go and see your own grandchildren? Dylan and Trish would welcome you."

"Once you've taken a stand, it's hard backing down," his father said. "Pride tends to get in the way."

"To hell with pride."

"That's easy for you to say. You haven't been there."

"Haven't I? It seems like I've been apologizing to Brianna since the day we met. That stubborn woman hasn't weakened yet, but I'll keep going back until she does. You just told me to fight for her. Can't you do the same when it comes to Trish and Dylan and their kids? You fought hard enough to keep me here. Why not do at least as much to keep them in your life?"

His father's glance strayed to the framed pictures on the corner of his desk, snapshots that Jeb had brought him from Los Piños not all that long ago. He sighed heavily. "You're right, son. You're absolutely right. I've let your mother influence me on this for far too long. If she refuses to come, I'll go alone."

"You won't regret it, Dad."

"Thanks for giving me the push I needed."

Jeb left his father's office with a sense that he'd finally accomplished one mission. It appeared that at least one family reunion was destined to take place. Now if only he could force his own reunion with Brianna, he thought his world might be just about perfect. Considering what a disaster he had almost made of everything, it was probably more than he deserved.

Brianna buried herself in work. She wanted to prove to anyone with lingering doubts that she was absolutely and totally devoted to Delacourt Oil.

Not that anyone in the department had dared to voice their doubts aloud.

Bryce had apparently had a talk with all of them, reassuring them that the suspicions and rumors had been completely without merit. He had accepted full responsibility for the situation, though he hadn't gone into detail.

According to Roy, almost everyone had taken him at his word. He hadn't really given them any choice.

"Susan will never believe that you weren't guilty of something, even though she's not precisely sure what," Roy said. "She's just miffed that Homer's term at the helm was so short-lived. I've heard rumblings that both of them may retire before the end of the year."

That was not an outcome Brianna really wanted. Homer was an excellent scientist. He stayed on top of the latest technology and was as savvy as they came in the lab. She made it a point to have a talk with him on her first day back on the job. This time she confided in him about her own situation with Emma.

"I deliberately kept that quiet before so that no one would feel I wasn't capable of giving my all to this job. That was a mistake. Secrets are never healthy."

Homer seemed taken aback, not by the revelation, but by her willingness to share it with him. "Why are you telling me this now?"

"Because I need you here and I want you to know why. Your experience is valuable to this department. I can't do everything. I want someone I can rely on as backup when my daughter's needs take precedence over my job."

He nodded slowly. "We would have done that for you before," he pointed out. "If only you'd asked."

"I know that now. But I've learned from my mistakes. Can I count on you, Homer?"

"Of course. The others will pitch in, too. Delacourt Oil is a family. Despite whatever faults he might have, Bryce Delacourt has seen to that."

If only Homer knew just how much it was about family, Brianna thought wryly. "Yes," she agreed. "He has."

Amazingly enough, her talk with Homer did make her life simpler. Suddenly things that had taken so much of her time were quickly and expertly handled by other members of the team without her even having to delegate them. She found that she could leave the office by four-thirty or five, rather than six-thirty or seven. That meant more time with Emma.

Unfortunately, Emma increasingly had plans of her own. For a five-year-old, she seemed to have an incredibly active social life all of a sudden. She was rarely in the sunroom when Brianna arrived. Where she was seemed to be a deep, dark secret. Gretchen always made

Brianna wait at the nurse's station while she went to fetch Emma.

But whatever was going on, Brianna couldn't deny that her daughter appeared happier than ever. She was smiling all the time now. In fact, if it weren't for the fact that she was still tied to that wheelchair to get around, she would have been almost her old self again.

Her old self. The phrase lingered in Brianna's mind. She couldn't help wondering what it would be like to be her old self again. What had she been like a million years ago—before Larry, before the accident, before Jeb? Had she been merely innocent and naive? Too trusting? Or had her expectations simply been too high, more than any mortal could possibly live up to? Was she partly at fault for what had happened in her marriage, for what had happened between her and Jeb? She spent long, restless nights second-guessing herself.

During the day, she spent far too much time glancing up at the sound of voices in the outer office, staring at the door, hoping that Jeb would break the silence she had imposed on him. She was growing more listless, more unsure of herself, day by day. She weighed her professional expertise against her competence as a woman and wondered if she hadn't spent too much time favoring one over the other.

Maybe that was why she was so terribly lonely. How was it possible for a woman who crammed so much into a single day to be so gut-wrenchingly lonely? How could she possibly miss a man who'd been in her life such a short time, a man who'd let her down?

She supposed it didn't really matter how. The point was, she missed Jeb.

Enough to risk giving him a second chance? That

was the debate she had with herself morning, noon and night. She still hadn't reached any conclusion when she ran into him at a crowded restaurant near the office one day. Taken by surprise, they stared at each other. Her heart skittered as wildly as it had on their very first date. Something that might have been longing darkened his eyes.

"Brianna," he said.

That was all, but it was more than enough. The low rumble of his voice caressing her name set off goose bumps. "Hello, Jeb." Her polite tone masked her nervousness, or at least she hoped it did.

"Are you eating alone?"

She nodded.

"Join me."

When she would have refused, he gestured toward the waiting crowd. "I'm next in line. You'll have a long wait if you don't accept."

She couldn't think of a single valid reason to turn him down except stubborn pride. "Yes, I suppose you're right. Fine. Thank you," she said, just as the hostess gestured for Jeb to follow her. Brianna fell into step with him.

After they'd been seated, she devoted her full attention to the menu, even though the words blurred and her concentration was no better than a two-year-old's. She managed to keep up the facade, though, until the waitress came to take their order. Fortunately Brianna knew the menu by heart. She ordered a chicken Caesar Salad and iced tea, then wondered what on earth she would do until it came.

"How have you been?" Jeb asked.

"Busy."

"Busy must agree with you. You look wonderful." His avid survey suggested that the comment was more than polite chitchat. He couldn't seem to get enough of looking at her.

Finally she drew in a deep breath. "This is silly. I feel as if I'm with a stranger."

"I don't," he said quietly. "Anything but."

"Jeb…" The rest of the protest died on her lips, when he placed his hand on top of hers and rubbed a thumb across her knuckles. The effect was shattering. Coherent thought fled, just because of that tender caress. It shouldn't be that way, not after all this time, not after everything that had happened.

"I've missed you, Brianna. It's only been a couple of weeks, but it seems like longer."

He said it so solemnly, so sincerely, that she couldn't possibly doubt him. A part of her wanted to admit that she had missed him, too, but pride kicked in. She would never let him see that this separation had cost her anything at all.

"Have dinner with me tonight?" he suggested.

She almost choked at the suggestion. "Jeb, we can't even get through lunch. How could we possibly manage dinner?"

"This was a chance meeting. It caught you off guard. Dinner would be easier."

"I don't see how." It would just be more time to suffer pangs of regret over what would never be.

His gaze turned challenging. "You're not afraid, are you?"

The schoolyard taunt brought a brief flicker of amusement. "Jeb, we're not ten years old. You can't dare me to go out with you."

"Sure I can," he said unrepentantly. "I just did, in fact."

"What would be the purpose?"

"To spend an evening with a woman I like, share a little conversation, some good food." His gaze locked with hers. "Start over."

"I thought we'd decided that starting over isn't possible."

"No, that was your call. I believe anything's possible when two people care enough."

Brianna sighed. "Maybe that's the problem. Maybe I just don't care enough," she lied.

"I don't believe you," he said at once. "Quite the opposite in fact. I think you care too much. That's why you're scared. I've already hurt you once. You're not willing to risk it again."

He met her gaze evenly. "I'm not Larry. I'm not simply walking away because the going's a little rough. I'm in this for the long haul, Brianna. Get used to it."

Stunned by his fierce declaration, Brianna regarded him worriedly. "What does that mean?"

"That the days of my sitting on the sidelines to give you the space you need are over. I'm back in the game, jumping into the fray, hot on your trail."

She shuddered at the firm conviction she heard in his voice. He meant every word. It had been simple pretending that she would get over him when he wasn't around to pester her. If he intended to change that, how long would her resolve last?

Until the first kiss? Longer? Until the first time he managed to seduce her? She didn't doubt for a second that he could. She'd gone all weak-kneed when she'd spotted him waiting in line just a few minutes ago. She'd caved in to his request that she join him with hardly a whimper of protest. When he put his mind to it, he'd be able to persuade her to do anything he wanted, no question about it.

"I won't have dinner with you, Jeb," she said every bit as firmly as he'd spoken.

"Coward."

"Maybe so," she conceded.

"It doesn't bother you that you could be throwing away your best chance at happiness?"

"Considering how miserable you managed to make me after just a few short weeks, that's a fairly brazen assumption on your part," she noted.

"I'm a brazen kind of guy," he said, clearly not the least bit put off by her assessment of their shaky past.

Trying to gather her wits for another argument he might actually listen to, Brianna sipped her tea, then forced herself to meet his gaze. "Why me, Jeb? There are probably hundreds of women in Houston who would swoon if you paid any attention to them. Why pick me?"

"I didn't pick you," he said, though he looked vaguely uneasy at the question. "Fate did."

She chuckled at that. "Fate? Or your father?"

"Same difference. Not one of those hundreds of women you're talking about ever caught my attention, not the way you did. For years, too many years, I drifted along. I worked at Delacourt because it was easier than figuring out what I really wanted to do. I dated any woman who struck my fancy, because it was easier than sticking with one and having to work things out. In the past few weeks I've taken a hard look at myself, and I don't like what I see. I was deluding myself that I could be a real investigator. I'm too impatient. I jump to conclusions. I think there's a niche for me at Delacourt, but that's not it. I've been talking to Dad about getting into marketing, about putting the company on the map. If there's one thing I know how to do, it's to sell something I believe in."

His gaze locked on her. "I believe in us," he said solemnly. "I'm not a romantic, Brianna, that's why you ought to believe what I'm about to say, because it doesn't come easily. You're a part of me. I know that as surely as I know that the sun will rise."

This time the shiver that washed over her wasn't panic. It was anticipation. He sounded so certain, so absolutely, unequivocally certain. If only she could be half as sure.

Maybe, for now, his certainty was enough to justify giving them another chance. Time would prove whether he was the salesman he claimed to be, whether he could convince her that love really could conquer the past.

Fifteen

Jeb's confidence grew after that lunch with Brianna. Even though she had continued to flatly refuse his invitation to dinner, he knew she had been tempted. He had seen it in the flush in her cheeks, the yearning in her eyes. She was struggling with herself. He just had to hang in there. More than ever, he suspected that Emma was the key.

They had already formed an unshakable bond. He had fallen just as deeply in love with the little girl as he had with her mother.

Most of his visits were made in the morning, when he knew Brianna would be at work at Delacourt Oil. After a couple of weeks, he learned to time the visits to coincide with Emma's therapy. According to the therapists, she seemed to respond to his encouragement in a way that she did with no one else.

"I think she's come to see you as a surrogate for her father. She wants desperately to prove herself to you," the psychologist told him. "Be careful that you don't shatter the trust she's placed in you."

As he had with her mother, Jeb couldn't help thinking. But he wouldn't let Emma down. Not ever. He reminded himself of what he owed to both of them as he walked into the therapy room in search of Emma. When he spotted her on her feet between two railings, his heart leaped into his throat. She'd been standing for longer and longer periods lately, her muscles getting stronger each day, but she hadn't tried to take a step that he knew of.

"Hi, Jeb," she said, turning a beaming smile on him.

"Hey, princess. Going someplace?"

She nodded. "Watch."

A frown of concentration knit her brow as she struggled to put one tiny foot in front of the other. Jeb mentally cheered her on, his fingers curled tightly into his palm to hide his nervousness. If there had been something nearby he could grip, he would have done it.

Emma's right foot inched forward. She wobbled unsteadily for a heartbeat, then moved the left until they were even. Her eyes widened and a huge grin split her face.

"I did it, Jeb. I really did it. I walked."

Jeb would have given anything at that moment for Brianna to have been there beside him to celebrate the triumph. Patience, he reminded himself.

One day they would share things like this. He just had to have patience and remain steadfast in his determination to win her back.

Looking into Emma's upturned face, Jeb was overwhelmed with gratitude. She was showing him the way, proving that one tiny step was every bit as important as a giant leap. He started to go to her, then glanced toward the therapist, who nodded. He moved in then and swept Emma up in a bear hug.

"You were magnificent, angel. Pretty soon you'll be running so fast that none of us will be able to keep up with you. Wait until your mother sees. She is going to be so proud."

Emma immediately shook her head. "You can't tell her. Not yet."

"But why, darlin'?"

"Because I want to be really, really good."

"Good's not important. Trying is what counts. You're getting it, Emma. It's all coming back."

"Not yet," she repeated. "You said I had to keep it secret that you're coming to see me. This is my secret. You have to keep it."

Jeb couldn't argue with her fair-is-fair logic, but he knew how hurt Brianna would be by being left out of this triumph. "A few days, then," he compromised. "But you have to show her, Emma. It will mean the world to her."

"I know, but it's a surprise for her birthday, and that's not for weeks and weeks yet."

Weeks and weeks? He was supposed to keep something this monumental to himself for that long? Brianna would never forgive him. "Days," he repeated firmly. "I think Saturday would be a really good day for you to put on a show for your mama."

He had an idea. "Maybe we could throw a surprise birthday party for her then."

"But it won't be her birthday yet," Emma protested.

He grinned. "I know, so imagine how surprised she'll be. We'll have presents, cake, ice cream, the whole nine yards."

Emma began to get into the spirit of it. "Decorations, too?"

"If you like."

She planted a kiss on his cheek. "Thank you."

"What kind of theme do you think your mom would like? How about Mickey Mouse?"

"No," Emma said firmly and without any hesitation. "It has to be Cinderella."

Jeb was startled by the choice. "Why Cinderella?"

"Because you're a prince and you made her a princess."

"Oh, baby," he murmured, giving her a squeeze. If only she knew how little he'd done to make her mother feel like a princess. If anything, Brianna thought of him as the wicked wizard in her life.

"Is it okay? Can I have a princess dress, too?"

"Absolutely," he agreed, willing to give this precious child anything her heart desired. "I'll find you the best princess dress in all of Houston."

And while he was at it, he might find a ring suitable for a princess for her mother. Maybe a spell would be cast over this party and Brianna would finally see just how right they were for each other.

Unfortunately, on Friday morning, the day before the planned surprise party, he got caught paying a visit to Emma. Brianna came in while they were playing a challenging game of checkers. The little girl was beating the daylights out of him and wasn't one bit shy about savoring the victory.

"I beat you three times," she said triumphantly. "Where's my prize?" Jeb brought a rare beanbag toy out of his pocket.

"So that's where those have been coming from," Brianna said. "I'd wondered. Emma wouldn't tell."

Jeb's head snapped around. He studied her face, trying to gauge her mood. She looked more startled than furious at finding him there.

"Emma's got her mother's ability to keep a secret," he said mildly.

"So I gather." Her gaze narrowed. "What are you doing here, Jeb?"

"Spending time with the daughter of the woman I love," he said emphatically, and watched the color climb in her cheeks.

"Don't say that." Her worried gaze shifted toward Emma as if to remind him that the child was likely to hang on anything he said.

"It's true."

She looked as if she might argue, then turned on her heel. "We need to talk," she said, and strode from the room, evidently sure that he would follow.

Jeb gave Emma a wink. "See you later, sweetie." She regarded him worriedly. "Is Mama mad?"

"Maybe a little, but don't worry your pretty little head about it. I'm going to fix it."

Emma tugged on his hand. "You'll be here tomorrow, right? You won't forget?"

"Not a chance."

Outside in the parking lot, where another monumental fight had begun only a few weeks earlier, the anger Brianna had contained in Emma's room spilled over. She was practically quivering with rage. She faced him squarely, then poked a finger into his chest.

"You…are…not…going…to…fix…it."

"Sure I am." He silenced her planned protest with a kiss that left them both gasping. "I love you. I love your daughter. I want us to be a family."

"Families don't go sneaking around behind each other's backs," she retorted.

Jeb regarded her with amusement. "Couldn't prove that by me."

She faltered a bit at that. "No. I suppose not. That doesn't make it right, not what I did, not your father's meddling, not what you've been doing."

"We all did it for the right reasons," he pointed out mildly. "Maybe we should make a pact right here and now that we won't do it ever again."

"And just like that, you think everything will be okay?"

"Not just like that, no. But love's a powerful motivator, don't you think? It made you do everything you could to protect Emma. It made me do everything I could to protect my family."

"Words, Jeb. Just words."

"No, darlin'. When I say them, you can take them straight to the bank. If you ask me, the last couple of weeks have been more dishonest than anything that came before."

"How can you possibly say that? You nearly destroyed me."

He looked directly into her eyes. "But I never stopped loving you. Not for a second. And if you would be honest with yourself, you'd admit that you might be furious with me, you might be hurt, but you haven't stopped loving me, either." He touched a finger to her lips to silence her. "Think about it, Brianna. We'll talk later."

"Stay away from Emma," she yelled after him as he walked away.

"Not a chance. No more than I intend to stay away from you. In my heart you're my family now, and I won't leave you willingly." He came back, bent down and kissed her until the heat generated could have melted the asphalt beneath their feet. He gave her a wink when the kiss ended. "If you're honest with yourself, you'll admit that you don't want me to give up on either one of you. I let you down once, Brianna. Never again."

Brianna had to confess she was shaken by Jeb's declaration. She was even more shaken by the discovery that he had been spending time with Emma behind her back. When she finally went back into the rehab center, she found her daughter worriedly watching for her.

"You didn't yell at Jeb, did you?"

"It was nothing for you to worry about. We just had to get a few things straight."

"He's my friend, Mama. He's been here lots and lots, not like Daddy. Jeb thinks I'm pretty and smart. He says I can do anything I want to do. Mr. Delacourt does, too."

She had known about Bryce's visits because he'd told her. Now she realized how much she owed him. Owed both of them.

How many times had Brianna said the same thing? At least once a day.

Obviously that hadn't registered. Emma had needed to hear it from someone she equated with her father. Maybe Brianna did owe Jeb and his father for helping to restore Emma's self-confidence. That didn't excuse what Jeb had done by sneaking around behind her back to pay these visits.

Would she have okayed them, though? Of course not. She would have been too fearful that Emma would get hurt when Jeb left. She had accepted the inevitability of his leaving from the outset, but apparently he was determined to prove that her fears were groundless. If her daughter trusted him so completely, maybe she could too. Sometimes kids were better judges of character than adults. They were also quicker to forgive.

Whom had she really been hurting all these weeks by denying her feelings for Jeb? Not him. He was staying the course, waiting for her to wake up. Not Emma. Apparently her daughter had been having the time of her life with her newfound friend. No, the only person hurt had been herself. Brianna had been the one who'd been left out and lonely. What was it they said about pride making a lonely bedfellow? It was true.

She sighed heavily. "Mama? Are you okay?"

"Not yet, baby, but I'm getting there," she said with a smile. "Would you mind if I run along now? There's someone I need to see."

"Jeb?" Emma inquired hopefully.

Brianna couldn't help wondering if her daughter was turning into a budding matchmaker. If so, she'd fit right in with the Delacourts.

"Yes, Jeb," she confirmed.

"He likes you, Mama. He's told me so."

Brianna felt a smile slowly spread across her face. "Yes, baby, I think I'm just beginning to realize that."

Unfortunately, she had a terrible time finding the man now that she'd finally gotten everything worked out in her mind. His secretary said something about him having gone shopping for party supplies. "I think he had some other stops, as well. Then I imagine he's going home. You might try there later."

"Thanks," Brianna said, though she was suddenly far too impatient to wait. There were only a few major party stores in the immediate vicinity. Maybe she could track him down.

She found him on the second try, pushing a shopping cart loaded with paper plates, napkins, streamers and balloons. For some reason, all were decorated with images of what appeared to be Cinderella. He was studying an elaborate centerpiece of Cinderella's coach.

"Having trouble deciding?" she asked, startling him.

He glanced toward his shopping cart with a look of dismay, then scowled at her. "What are you doing here?"

"Looking for you. Is somebody in your family having a birthday?"

"Something like that." His gaze narrowed. "What's so important that you had to track me down? It's not Emma, is it? Has something happened since I left?"

His concern was genuine, and she realized with absolute certainty then that she hadn't been mistaken about the depth of his feelings for her daughter. "Emma's fine. I needed to talk to you."

He seemed perplexed, and a little anxious. He seemed especially concerned about that supply of paper goods. "Now?"

"If you have the time."

He actually seemed a little torn. "Let me finish up here and I'll meet you at your place."

Brianna concluded that he wanted to get her as far away from these decorations as possible. What she couldn't figure out was why. "Here will do," she said, just to see what his reaction would be.

Clearly startled by her willingness to say whatever was on her mind so publicly, he finally gave a reluctant nod of acceptance. "Okay, what is it?"

She had thought of a thousand different ways to get

into this while she was searching for him. Now, face-to-face, she was tongue-tied. "I forgive you," she said at last, hoping he would know how to interpret that.

"Okay," he said slowly, clearly not as bowled over by the declaration as she'd hoped.

She ran her tongue over lips that were suddenly as dry as the Sahara. "I love you."

His mouth curved into the faint beginnings of a smile. "I know that."

She scowled. "Jeb, you're not making this any easier."

"I'm listening, aren't I?"

"Yes, but you could jump in anytime."

"And say what?"

"Dammit, Jeb, do you still want to marry me or not?"

Apparently she had finally found the right words. He let out a whoop in the middle of the aisle. His mouth slanted over hers and suddenly the stir of voices dimmed. All Brianna knew was the taste of Jeb as his kiss devoured her. All she heard was the sound of her blood rushing through her veins. All she smelled was the faint scent of his aftershave and something that could have been bubble gum.

Bubble gum? She drew back and stared at him. "Why do you smell like bubble gum?"

He grinned. "Check the bottom of the basket."

She found at least a hundred packages of the stuff in every flavor imaginable. "Do you have a secret fetish I need to know about?"

"My only addiction is you," he assured her. "This was a special request from a friend of mine."

"Emma," Brianna said with sudden understanding. "And the decorations?"

"Are none of your concern," he insisted. "And if you're smart, you'll stop asking questions, so I'm not forced to lie to you."

"More secrets?" she asked, but with less concern than she might have just a day ago.

"Only one," he promised, then amended, "well, two, actually, but you'll know soon enough. And that is absolutely all I intend to say on that subject." He studied her intently. "Did you really mean it, about marrying me?"

She nodded.

"Then I propose a celebration. How about tomorrow morning at ten? Meet me at the rehab center. We can share the news with Emma."

It was not exactly the celebration Brianna had envisioned, but Jeb's suggestion had its merits. Emma needed to know, though Brianna had no doubts at all that she would approve. Seeing how close the two of them had become had melted her heart and brought her to this point.

"Tomorrow at ten," she agreed at last.

When she arrived at the rehab center promptly at ten, she found Jeb waiting for her just inside the entrance. "Come with me," he said, drawing her in the opposite direction of the sunroom.

"Where are we going?"

"You'll see. Trust me."

A few days ago those two words would have given her pause, but Brianna had finally realized that she could trust Jeb, that he was a man who would always fight to the death for his family. She and Emma would be lucky to become Delacourts, to have such a passionate advocate for the rest of their lives.

Now he paused outside a door leading into the treatment area. Emma had always been adamant about Brianna not accompanying her here. She stared at Jeb. "I don't understand."

"You will," he promised, opening the door.

"Surprise!" Emma's voice led the chorus.

Brianna stared around her at the Cinderella decorations, the assembly of guests, including Bryce Delacourt, Carly and Gretchen. "Jeb?" she asked in confusion.

He squeezed her hand. "It's Emma's surprise. An early birthday party."

"But—"

"Don't ask. Take it on faith," he said.

To be sure, there was a table stacked with gifts, and Emma's eyes were shining with excitement. There was also a cake, and a stack of ice cream cups ready for serving.

"We have to eat first," Emma declared. "So the ice cream doesn't melt."

Tears in her eyes, Brianna went over and kissed her. "I don't know what to say, baby."

"Don't cry, Mama. It's a party."

The small crowd made quick work of the ice cream and cake, then settled back to watch Brianna open her gifts. There were small tokens of affection from the staff, a lovely silk scarf from Bryce, and then one small box remained.

"From me," Jeb declared, handing it to her. "And just so you know, I already had it before yesterday."

Brianna's fingers shook as she ripped away the fancy ribbon and elegant paper to find a jeweler's box inside.

"Hurry, Mama," Emma begged. "I want to see."

Brianna glanced down into her face. "You know what's inside?"

Emma's head bobbed. "Jeb told me, but he wouldn't let me see."

"Because it's your mama's present," Jeb reminded her. "She should see it first."

Brianna flipped the lid on the box, then gasped at the beautiful ring inside. It was a diamond solitaire, exquisite in its simplicity and perfection.

"Nature's finest," Jeb whispered in her ear. "For someone who knows what mysteries the earth is capable of hiding."

She was dumbstruck, not just by the beauty of the ring, but by Jeb's announcement that he'd bought it even before she had proposed to him the day before. He'd intended to risk his heart in this very public way. He was that confident in the love they shared.

She reached up and touched his cheek. "I love you," she told him quietly.

"Are you going to marry him, Mama? Is he going to be my new daddy?"

Brianna gazed down at her baby and nodded. "Yes, but something tells me you knew that even before I did."

"I didn't *know,* Mama, but I was hoping."

Jeb slipped the ring on Brianna's finger, then gave her hand a squeeze. "Now for Emma's present. We saved the best for last."

Brianna couldn't imagine anything that could top this, but she turned toward her daughter.

"Wait, Mama. I have to get it."

Before Brianna realized what her daughter intended, Emma stood up.

She beamed at Jeb, then turned toward Brianna and

walked straight into her arms. Tears were streaming down Brianna's face, even as she folded Emma into a fierce hug.

"Happy birthday, Mama. Jeb said I couldn't wait till your real birthday to show you. That's why we had the party today."

Brianna glanced up and mouthed a silent thank-you to the man in question, then met her daughter's excited gaze. "There is no present in the world I would have loved more," she told her. "To see you walking again is a miracle."

"Not a miracle, Mama. I told you I would."

Then it seemed as if everyone was laughing and crying. "Yes, baby, you certainly did."

She felt Jeb's hand on her shoulder. "That's one thing your daughter and I have in common," he said quietly. "When it comes to you, we will always keep our promises."

From that moment on, there wasn't a single doubt in Brianna's heart that they would.

* * * * *

MARRYING A DELACOURT

One

If Michael Delacourt had had any idea that this latest harangue about his health was going to bring the bane of his existence, Grace Foster, back into his life, he would have tuned Tyler out. Instead, he let his brother drone on and on, then fell right straight into the trap.

"You're a heart attack waiting to happen," Tyler Delacourt began as he had at least once a week like clockwork. He made the claim with brotherly concern, usually from the comfortable vantage point of the sofa in Michael's office on the executive floor at Delacourt Oil. He was slugging down black coffee and doughnuts as he spoke, unaware of the irony in his comments. "You have to learn how to slow down—before it's too late."

Too late? Hogwash! Michael was getting sick of hearing it, especially from a man who shunned exercise unless it was related to bringing in a new gusher. Worse, Tyler's consumption of cholesterol showed a total disregard for its potential effects on *his* heart.

Besides, Michael thought irritably, he wasn't even in his thirties yet.

Okay, he was close, weeks away, in fact. Still, by all accounts this was the prime of his life. Just as he was doing this morning, he did thirty grueling minutes every day on the treadmill he kept in his office. Hell, he was in better shape now than he'd been in when he'd played college sports. Could Tyler say the same?

"I'd like to see you set the pace I do on this treadmill," he countered as sweat poured down his chest and his muscles burned from the exertion.

But even as he dismissed his brother's concern, Michael was forced to admit that he exercised the way he did everything else—as if driven. His bewildered mother used to say he'd come out of the womb three weeks early, and he'd been in a hurry ever since. It was a trait that definitely set him apart from his laid-back brothers—Dylan, Jeb and, especially, Tyler.

Michael was not prone to a lot of introspection, but he could hardly deny that his type-A personality affected all aspects of his life, personal as well as professional.

To top it off, he had no social life to speak of, unless his command attendance at various benefits and dinner parties counted. He was as wary of females as a man could get. The minute a woman started making possessive little remarks, he beat a hasty retreat. Maybe someday, when he had some spare time, he'd sit down and try to figure out why. In the meantime, he simply accepted the fact that there was no room in his life for a woman who'd have to take second place to his career at Delacourt Oil.

Of the four Delacourt brothers, he was the only one who really gave a damn about the family business. He had his father's instincts for it. He had the drive and ambition to take the company to new heights, but Bryce Delacourt was fiercely determined that the company he'd launched would be divided equally among his off-spring. He grumbled unrelentingly about how ungrate-ful they were for not seeing that, never noticing that Michael was grateful enough for all of them.

Still, Delacourt Oil was his father's baby, which he could split up any way he wanted to. It wasn't that Michael was unwilling to share with his siblings. It was just that he wanted to be the one on top, the one in charge, and he would run himself into the ground if necessary trying to prove that he was worthy of the po-sition. None of the others understood that kind of single-minded determination. Even now, Tyler was shaking his head, disapproval written all over his face.

"That's just it. You exercise all out, as if you're try-ing to conquer Mount Everest, the same way you do ev-erything," Tyler chided, refusing to let the subject drop. "You keep that blasted phone in your hand the whole time, too, so you're not wasting time."

"It's efficient," Michael said, defending himself for perhaps the thousandth time. He tossed his portable phone on the sofa next to Tyler to prove he could give it up anytime he wanted to.

"It's crazy," Tyler contradicted. "Face it, you're a compulsive overachiever. Always have been. When was the last time you took a day off? When was the last time you took an actual vacation?"

"To do what?" Michael asked, perplexed.

"Go to the beach house with the rest of us, for in-stance. We haven't had a decent bachelor weekend in a couple of years now."

"Dylan and Jeb are married. I doubt their wives

would approve of the sort of weekends we used to have over there," Michael said wryly.

Tyler grinned. "Probably not. Okay, so the wild bachelor days are over for poor Dylan and poor Jeb. That doesn't mean you and I can't spend a few days catching rays and chasing women. How about it? A week of sun and fun."

Michael was tempted. Then he thought of his jam-packed schedule. "I don't think so. Not anytime soon, anyway. My calendar's booked solid."

"You *are* turning into a pitiful stick in the mud," his brother declared sorrowfully. "If you won't do that, how about going over to Los Piños for a few days to visit Trish and Dylan and their families? Spend a little quality time with our niece and nephew. Trish was saying just the other day that a visit is long overdue."

Guilt nagged at Michael for about ten seconds. "Yeah, well, I've been meaning to get over there, but you know how it is," he hedged.

"I know exactly how it is. Your niece is going on three years old and you haven't seen her since she was baptized when she was a month old. When Dylan and Kelsey got married, you barely stuck your head in the church over there long enough to hear their *I do's* before you took off for some can't-miss conference."

"I was speaking at an OPEC meeting. Are you saying I should have turned down that chance?"

Tyler waved off the defense. "I'll give you that one. But if it hadn't been OPEC, it would have been something else. What exactly are you afraid will happen if you take some time off? Do you think the rest of us are going to steal the company out from under you?"

He peered at Michael intently. "You do realize what

a joke that is, don't you? Trish wants no part of the business. She's happy as a clam running her bookstore and devoting her spare time to her husband and daughter. Dylan is perfectly content playing Dick Tracy across the state. Jeb is doing in-house security and wallowing in family life."

"That still leaves you," Michael pointed out, aware that he was grasping at straws.

Tyler laughed. "You know perfectly well that I'm trying my best to convince Dad to let me stay out in the field, exploring for oil. I'm heading back out onto one of our rigs in the Gulf of Mexico in another couple of weeks. I miss it. I miss Baton Rouge."

Michael studied him. "Who's in Baton Rouge, little brother?"

"I didn't say anything about a person. I mentioned an oil rig and a city."

"But I know you. There has to be a woman involved."

Tyler scowled. "We were talking about me competing for your job. It's not going to happen, Michael. Not only do I love what I do, it keeps me out from under Dad's thumb. Face it, none of your siblings wants a desk job here, thank you very much. It's all yours, big brother. There is no competition. This office in the executive suite is yours for life—if you want it."

Michael inwardly admitted that everything Tyler had just said was true.

But that knowledge didn't keep him from working compulsively. "I love what I do, so shoot me," he muttered.

"You need a life," Tyler retorted. "You might think it's enough to be at the top of the list of Houston's most eligible bachelors, but you're going to look mighty funny if you're still there when you hit ninety."

"Why worry about my social life? A minute ago you claimed I'm destined to die of a heart attack before I turn forty. If that's the case, there's no point in leaving behind a wealthy widow."

Tyler waved off the attempt to divert him. "You're missing my point."

"Which is?"

"You need some balance in your life, Michael. Believe it or not, I actually recall a time when you were fun to be around, when you talked about something besides mergers and the price of crude oil."

Michael uttered a resigned sigh. Clearly, his brother was on a mission.

Tyler was usually a live-and-let-live kind of a guy, but periodically he turned into a nag. This kind of persistence could only mean that he'd been put up to it by the rest of the family. The one way to shut him up was to make a few well-intentioned promises.

"Okay, okay, I'll try to get a break in my schedule," Michael promised.

Tyler looked skeptical. "Not good enough. When?"

"Soon."

He shook his head, obviously not pacified by such a vague response. "Trish says her guest room is ready now," he said. "You can see your niece. You can see Dylan and his family. I'll even ride over with you on the company jet. We'll have ourselves an old-fashioned reunion."

Michael wasn't fooled for a minute. Tyler wasn't going on this proposed jaunt out of any great desire to hold a family barbecue. He'd been assigned to deliver his big brother into the protective arms of their baby sister.

Michael shuddered at the memory of the last time they'd all ganged up on him like this. He'd wound up in a deserted cabin in the woods for a solid week with no car and no phone. Instead of relaxing him, the forced solitude had almost driven him up a wall. He hadn't been able to convince his siblings that they hadn't done him any favors. A two-day visit with Trish's family would be heaven by comparison. He was smart enough to accept it while he still had a choice in the matter. His family wasn't above kidnapping him, and he doubted a court in the land would convict them for it once they made a convincing case that they'd done it for his own good.

"Set it up," he said, resigned to the inevitable. "Just let me know the details."

"We're leaving in fifteen minutes," Tyler announced, his expression instantly triumphant.

"But I can't—"

"Of course, you can," Tyler said, cutting off the protest. "Hop in the shower, get into your clothes and let's go. I have your suitcase at the airport and the pilot's on standby. Your secretary's canceled all your appointments for the next week."

"A week?" Michael protested. "I agreed to a couple of days."

"Your secretary must have misunderstood me," Tyler said with no evidence of remorse. "You know how she is."

"She's incredibly efficient, and I *thought* she was loyal to me."

"She is. That's why she wiped the slate clean for

the next week. So you'll be able to take a long overdue break. You're free and clear, bro."

Michael frowned at Tyler. "Awfully damned sure of yourself, weren't you?"

"What can I say? I'm a born negotiator. It runs in the family. Now, hop to it."

Not until twenty-four hours later did Michael realize the full extent of his brother's treachery, when he found himself shut away on Trish's ranch, abandoned by his sister, her husband and the very niece he'd supposedly come to see.

Tyler had long since departed, claiming urgent business elsewhere. Probably a woman. That one he'd denied existed over in Baton Rouge. With Ty, it was always about a woman.

At any rate, one minute Michael had been sitting at Trish's kitchen table surrounded by family, the next he'd been all alone and cursing the fact that he hadn't been an only child.

"It's Hardy's family," Trish had explained apologetically as she sashayed past him with little more than a perfunctory kiss on his cheek. "An emergency. We absolutely have to go. We shouldn't be gone more than a day or two."

Since the phone hadn't rung, he had to assume this crisis had occurred before his arrival. Naturally no one had thought for a second to simply call him and tell him to stay home.

"I hate doing this to you," his sister claimed, though she looked suspiciously cheerful. "The cattle shouldn't be any problem. Hardy's got that covered. You don't mind staying here and keeping an eye on the horses, though, do you? Somebody will be by to see that they're fed and let out into the corral, but you might want to exercise them."

Already reeling, at that point Michael had stared at his baby sister as if she'd lost her mind. "Trish, unless it has four wheels, I don't ride it."

"Of course you do."

"I was on a pony once when I was six. I fell off. All advice to the contrary, I did not get back on."

"Well, you're a Texan, aren't you? You'll get the knack of it while you're here," she'd said blithely. "We'll get back as soon as we can. Whatever you do, don't leave. I won't have your vacation ruined because of us. This is a great place to relax. Lots of peace and quiet. Make yourself right at home, okay? Love you."

And then she was gone. Michael felt as if he'd been caught up in a tornado and dropped down again, dazed and totally lost. He knew he should have protested, told his sister that he'd be on his way first thing in the morning, but she already had one foot out the door when she asked him to stick around. She made this sudden trip sound like a blasted emergency. She made it seem as if his staying here was bailing her out of a terrible jam, so what was he supposed to say?

Not until Trish, Hardy and little Laura had vanished did he recall that Hardy didn't have any family to speak of, none that he was in touch with anyway. With an able assist from Tyler, the whole lot of them had plotted against him again.

Okay, he thought, Tyler might be gone, Trish and her family had abandoned him, but there was still Dylan. Michael comforted himself with that. This time at least he wouldn't be out in the middle of nowhere without a familiar face in sight. And they'd left him with a working phone. He picked it up, listened suspiciously just in case they'd had the darn thing disconnected, then breathed a sigh of relief at the sound of the dial tone. He punched in his older brother's number.

But Dylan—surprise, surprise—was nowhere to be found.

"Off on a case," his wife said cheerfully. "Stop by while you're here, though. Bobby and I would love to see you. And if you need any help at the ranch, give me a call. My medical skills may be pretty much limited to kids, but I can rally a few of the Adamses who actually know a thing or two about horses and cattle. They'll be happy to come over to help out."

Wasn't that just gosh-darn neighborly, Michael thought sourly as he sat on the porch in the gathering dusk and stared out at the field of wildflowers that Trish gushed about all the time. Frankly, he didn't get the fascination. They didn't *do* anything. Maybe after a couple of glasses of wine, he'd be more appreciative.

He was on his way inside in search of a decent cabernet and livelier entertainment, when he heard the distant cry. It sounded like someone in pain and it was coming from the barn, which should have been occupied by nothing more than a few of those horses Trish was so blasted worried about. Not that he was an expert, but no horse he'd ever heard sounded quite so human.

Adrenaline pumping, Michael eased around the house and slid through the shadows toward the small, neat barn. He could hear what sounded like muffled crying and a frantic exchange of whispers.

Thankful for his brother-in-law's skill in constructing the barn, he slid the door open in one smooth, silent glide and hit the lights, exposing two small, towheaded boys huddled in a corner, one of them holding a gashed hand to his chest, his face streaked with tears. Michael stared at them with astonishment and the unsettling sense that the day's bad luck was just about to take a spin for the worse.

"We ain't done anything, mister," the older boy said, facing him defiantly. Wearing a ragged T-shirt, frayed jeans and filthy sneakers, he stood protectively in front of the smaller, injured boy. The littler one gave Michael a hesitant smile, which faded when confronted by Michael's unrelenting scowl.

Michael's gaze narrowed. "What are you doing here?"

"We just wanted someplace to sleep for the night," the little one said, moving up to stand side by side with his companion whose belligerent expression now matched Michael's. His fierce loyalty reminded Michael of the four Delacourt brothers, whose one-for-all-and-all-for-one attitudes had gotten them into and out of a lot of sticky situations when they'd been about the same ages as these two.

"Come over here closer to the light and let me see your hand," he said to the smaller child, preferring to deal with the immediacy of an injury to the rest of the situation.

"It ain't nothing," the bigger boy said, holding him back.

"If it's bleeding, it's something," Michael replied. "Do you want it getting infected so bad, the doctors will have to cut off his arm?"

He figured the image of such an exaggeratedly gory fate would cut straight through their reluctance, but he'd figured wrong.

"We can fix it ourselves," the boy insisted stubbornly. "We found the first aid kit. I've already dumped lots and lots of peroxide over it."

"It hurt real bad, too," the little one said.

The comment earned him a frown, rather than praise for his bravery. "If he'd just hold still, I'd have it bandaged by now," the older boy grumbled.

"You two used to taking care of yourselves?" Michael asked, getting the uneasy sense that they'd frequently been through this routine of standing solidly together in defiance of adult authority.

The smaller boy nodded, even as the older one said a very firm, "No."

Michael bit back a smile at the contradictory responses. "Which is it?"

"Look, mister, if you don't want us here, we'll go," the taller boy said, edging toward the door while keeping a safe distance between himself and Michael.

"What's your name?"

"I ain't supposed to tell that to strangers."

"Well, seeing how you're on my property," he began, stretching the truth ever-so-slightly in the interest of saving time on unnecessary explanations about his own presence here. "I think I have a right to know who you are."

The boys exchanged a look before the older one finally gave a subtle nod.

"I'm Josh," the little one said. "He's Jamie."

"You two brothers?" Michael asked.

"Uh-huh."

"Do you have a last name, Josh and Jamie?"

"Of course, we do," Jamie said impatiently. "But

we ain't telling." Michael let that pass for the moment. "Live around here?"

Again, he got two contradictory answers. He sighed. "Which is it?"

"We're visiting," the little one said, as Jamie nodded. "Yeah, that's it. We're visiting."

Michael was an expert in sizing up people, reading their expressions. He wasn't buying that line of bull for a second. These two were runaways.

There wasn't a doubt in his mind about that. Hadn't they just said they'd been looking for a place to spend the night? He decided to see how far they were willing to carry the fib.

"Won't the folks you're visiting be worried about you?" he asked. "Maybe we should call them."

"We're not sure of the number," Jamie said hurriedly, his expression worried.

"Tell me the name, then. I'll look it up."

"We can't," Jamie said. "They'll be real mad, when they find out we're gone. We weren't supposed to leave their place. They told us and told us not to go exploring, didn't they, Josh?"

"Uh-huh." Josh peered at Michael hopefully. "You don't want us to get in trouble, do you?"

Michael faced them with a stern, forbidding expression that worked nicely on the employees at Delacourt Oil. "No, what I want is the truth."

"That is the truth," Jamie vowed, sketching a cross over his heart and clearly not one bit intimidated.

"Honest," Josh said.

Michael feared he hadn't heard an honest, truthful word since these two had first opened their mouths. But if they wouldn't give him a straight answer, what

was he supposed to do about it? He couldn't very well
leave them in the barn. He couldn't send them packing,
as desperately as he wanted to. They were just boys, no
more than thirteen and nine, most likely. Somebody,
somewhere, had to be worried sick about them. Maybe
he could loosen their tongues with a bribe of food.

"You hungry?" he asked.

Josh's eyes lit up. His head bobbed up and down
eagerly.

"I suppose we could eat," Jamie said, clearly trying
hard not to show too much enthusiasm.

"Come on inside, then. Once you've eaten, we'll figure out where to go from there."

In Trish's state-of-the-art, spotless kitchen, they
turned around in circles, wide-eyed with amazement.

"This is so cool," Jamie pronounced, his sullen defiance slipping away. "Like in a magazine or something."

"There's even a cookie jar," Josh announced excitedly.
"A really big one. You suppose there are any cookies?"

"We'll check it out after you've eaten a sandwich,"
Michael said. He poured them both huge glasses of
milk and made them thick ham and cheese sandwiches,
which they fell on eagerly, either in anticipation of
home-baked cookies or because they were half-starved.

Watching the boys while they devoured the food, Michael realized he needed advice and he needed it now.
He needed an expert, somebody who understood kids,
somebody who knew the law. Even as that realization
struck him, he had a sudden inspiration. He knew the
perfect person to get them all out of this jam. He walked
into the living room, grabbed his portable phone and
punched in a once-familiar number.

Grace Foster answered on the first ring, just as she

always did. Grace was brisk and efficient. Best of all, she didn't play games. If she was home, why act as if she had better things to do than talk? He'd liked that about her once. Heck, he'd liked a whole lot more than that about her, but that was another time, another place, eons ago.

Now about all he could say was that he respected her as a lawyer, even if she did make his life a living hell from time to time.

"What do you want?" she asked the instant she recognized his voice.

"Nice to speak to you, too," he countered.

"Michael, you never call unless there's a problem. Since we don't have any court dates coming up, just spit it out. It's Friday night. I'm busy."

"Whatever it is can wait," he retorted, troubled more than he liked by the image of Grace being in the midst of a hot date, one that might last all weekend long. He preferred to think that she led a nice, quiet, solitary—*maidenly*—existence.

Although he'd intended only to ask for advice, instead he said, "I need you to get on a plane and get over to Los Piños tonight."

He said it with absolute confidence that she wouldn't refuse, not in the long run. She might grumble a little, but once she understood the stakes, she wouldn't turn him down. He wondered just how little he could get away with revealing. Maybe just the lure of sparring with him would be enough.

His ego certainly wanted to believe that.

"Excuse me? Why would I want to do that?" she asked. "It's not like your every wish has been my command, not for a long time now."

She employed that huffy little tone that always turned him on although she intended the exact opposite. He could envision her sitting up a little straighter, squaring her shoulders. She had no idea that her efforts to look rigid and unyielding only thrust out her breasts and made her more desirable than ever. He bit back a desire to chuckle at the mental image.

Grace was a real piece of work, all right. She might be pint-sized and fragile-looking, but she had the soul and spirit of a warrior. It was a trait he suspected was going to come in handy.

"You'll come because you know I wouldn't ask unless it was important," he told her patiently. Then he dangled an impossible-to-resist temptation. "And you can hold it over my head for the rest of our lives, okay?"

"Now that is an intriguing idea," she said with considerably more enthusiasm. "Care to fill me in?"

What a breeze, he thought triumphantly. Even easier than he'd anticipated. He hadn't even had to pull out the big guns and tell her about the kids.

"I'll fill you in when you get here. Can you be at the airport in an hour? I'll have the Delacourt jet fueled up and ready. The pilot can see to it that you find me once you land over here."

"Michael, really, there has to be someone else you could call, someone closer."

"There isn't," he assured her.

"But I have plans. I've had them for ages. I hate to cancel."

Damn, she was still trying to wriggle off the hook. "No," he said firmly. "It has to be you. This is right up your alley." He sighed heavily, then added as if it were costing him a great deal to say, "I need you, Grace."

"Hah! As if I believe that for a minute. You're over-selling, Michael."

"Trust me. You're the only one for this job."

This time she was the one who sighed heavily. "Okay, okay. When you start laying it on this thick, my curiosity kicks in. But I have to finish up what I'm doing here. Make it ninety minutes," she said. "And, Michael, this is going to cost you. Big time."

"I never doubted it for a second," he said.

Only after he'd hung up did he stop to wonder why he'd instinctively turned to Grace, rather than his sister-in-law or one of the Adamses right here in town. He told himself it was because this situation all but cried out for a woman to deal with the two runaways, but he hadn't gotten where he was in life by deluding himself. His sister-in-law was not only obviously female, but a doctor as well.

No, he had called Grace Foster, because as much of a pain in the butt as she was to him personally, she was the smartest lawyer he knew. If these boys were in some kind of trouble, he couldn't think of a better ally than Grace.

But it was even more than that, he admitted candidly. A part of him liked wrangling with Ms. Grace Foster more than just about anything except watching a new million-dollar gusher spewing crude into the Texas sky.

Two

Grace could hardly wait to hear what had caused Michael Delacourt to condescend to beg her for help. As annoyed as she was at being imperiously summoned across the state on a Friday night, her curiosity had gotten the better of her.

And contrary to what she had deliberately led him to believe, he had not caught her in the middle of a pressing engagement. A long, boring weekend had stretched out ahead of her, so Michael's call had been a welcome diversion, a chance to break out of the rut she'd fallen into in recent months. She slaved like crazy in court all week long, then did more of the same on weekends so she wouldn't notice how truly barren her social life had become.

But even better than a break in routine, the promised chance to hold this over the man's arrogant, egotistical head for the rest of their lives had been an irresistible lure. Given the number of court cases on which they found themselves on opposing sides, it was an edge she couldn't ignore.

There was more to it, of course. There had been a

time in the distant past when she had almost allowed herself to think about a future with Michael. But then she'd realized she would always play second fiddle to the family business. It was a role she flatly refused to accept.

Grace had already spent an entire childhood trying to figure out why she hadn't been smart enough or pretty enough for her father to love her.

Norman Foster had left her and her mom when Grace was barely five. The unexplained departure of her adored father had all but destroyed her self-esteem. It had taken years to restore it, to accept that his going had had nothing at all to do with her. She wasn't going to waste the rest of her life wondering why she didn't have another man's full attention.

She had broken off with Michael the same day she'd graduated from law school. She'd had clues from the beginning of their relationship that work came first with him, but his failure to appear at the important graduation ceremony had made it all too evident where she fit into his priorities. Even his profuse apologies and a barrage of expensive gifts—all of which she'd returned—hadn't convinced her he would ever be able to change.

After pursuing her with flattering determination for a few weeks, he had accepted that the breakup was final. When he'd actually stopped calling, she'd suffered a few serious twinges of regret, but on balance she knew she'd done what she had to. She knew better than to think a man would change.

That didn't mean that she couldn't thoroughly enjoy the occasional sparring match with Michael. He was, after all, exceptionally smart, exceptionally sexy and, when he allowed himself to forget about work, highly entertaining. It gave her a great deal of pleasure, however, to remind him from time to time that he wasn't God's gift to women. She figured she had at least a little credibility since she was one of the few who'd ever walked away from him.

Over the years she had observed his pattern from a nice, safe distance. Most of the women he dated were eventually abandoned by him through benign neglect, never in an explosion of passionate fireworks. She suspected that most of those relationships contained less passion than some of the occasional conversations she and Michael had over legal matters. In the deep, dark middle of the night, she took a certain comfort in that.

Tonight as she settled into the fancy Delacourt corporate jet, she glanced around at the posh interior and smiled. Of course Michael expected her to be impressed by the bottle of chilled champagne, the little plate of hot hors d'oeuvres. No doubt he still thought of her as the small-town girl who'd been wide-eyed the first time he'd taken her on a trip in this very same plane.

They had gone from Austin, where she'd been in school, to Houston for a visit to the family mansion. Michael had wanted to introduce her to his family, especially his charismatic, much-idolized father. She had been stunned, if not impressed, by the evidence of their wealth. Even with Michael at her side, she had wondered if she would ever truly fit in there.

These days it took a lot more than champagne and canapés to impress her. Apparently Michael had forgotten that in recent years she'd worked for a lot of people every bit as rich as the Delacourts. In fact, she'd prided herself on taking quite a bit of money away from them.

Oh, yes, she thought with anticipation, this little trip

to Los-wherever-Texas held a lot of promise. For Michael to be anywhere other than in his office or at some gala where he could network was so rare that the explanation was bound to be a doozy. She could hardly wait to hear it.

The flight didn't take long. When they landed, a car was waiting for her at the airport and the pilot gave her very thorough written and verbal directions, then regarded her anxiously.

"Are you sure you wouldn't like me to drive you, Ms. Foster? I don't mind, and Mr. Delacourt suggested that would be best."

Grace understood the insulting implications of that. She drew herself up to her full five-foot-two-inch height.

"Thanks, Paul, but I am perfectly capable of driving a few miles," she said coolly. Beyond his low regard for her driving skills, she knew what Michael was up to. He wanted her wherever he was at his beck and call, with no car available for a speedy exit. "Thank you, though. You can let Mr. Delacourt know that I am on my way."

The pilot, who'd been around during the days of their stormy relationship, grinned at her display of defiance. "Whatever you say, Ms. Foster. Nice seeing you again."

"You, too, Paul."

Satisfied that she had won that round, Grace got behind the wheel of the rental car, studied the directions one last time and tried not to panic. The truth was, she had a very unfortunate sense of direction. To top it off, the sky was pitch-black, the moon little more than a distant, shimmering sliver of silver. And it wasn't as if there were a lot of street signs out here in the middle of nowhere.

"I can do this," she told herself staunchly.

Twenty minutes later she was forced to concede that she was hopelessly lost. She drove around for another ten minutes trying to extricate herself from the tangle of rural roads that apparently led nowhere close to where she wanted to go. By the time she finally abandoned her pride, she was highly irritated. With great reluctance, she called Michael at the number the pilot had discreetly written at the bottom of the page.

"The plane landed forty-five minutes ago. Where the devil are you?" Michael demanded.

"If I knew that, I wouldn't be calling."

He moaned. "Don't tell me you've gotten yourself lost."

"It wasn't me," she protested. "It was these stupid directions. Whoever heard of telling somebody to turn at a blasted pine forest? I saw a pine tree, I turned. Now I seem to be staring at a pasture. There are cattle in the pasture, and I am not amused."

He chuckled.

"It's not funny. Laugh again and I'll be back at the airport and out of here."

"Not likely," he muttered.

"Michael," she said, her tone a warning.

"Sorry. It's just that this is one of your many charms," he said. "For a woman who has a law degree and a thriving practice in a major metropolitan area, you are absolutely pitiful when it comes to getting from one place to the next. I am amazed you ever make it to court on time."

"Will you just tell me how to get from here to there?" she snapped. She was not about to tell him that only years of practice and sticking to the same, precise route assured her of getting to the courthouse. Unanticipated detours gave her hives.

"Sweetheart, you're in a ranching area," he said, pointing out the obvious with what sounded like a little too much glee. "There are a lot of cows. Can't you just back up, turn around and get right back on the highway where you made the wrong turn?"

"You stay on the phone," she instructed. "I'll be back to you for further instructions when I am facing the highway."

It took another frustrating twenty minutes to backtrack and finally make her way to the turnoff Michael assured her would lead to where he was.

When she found him waiting for her on the front porch of a spectacular house with two boys sound asleep in the rocking chairs flanking him, her annoyance promptly gave way to amazement. This was obviously going to be a whole lot more fascinating than the weekend she'd anticipated spending with her case files and her law books.

"Whose house is this and why are you here?" Grace asked as she and Michael settled in the living room with the cup of tea she'd insisted she preferred over wine. She wanted all her wits about her for this conversation.

"My brother-in-law built it for Trish," Michael explained. "And I'm here because I've got a whole family of conspirators."

"Another forced vacation?" She'd heard all about the last one. The tale had circled the Houston grapevine before landing in the society column of the daily paper. Imagining Michael's indignation, she had laughed out loud at the story, but she was wise enough to stifle a similar urge now.

"You don't have to look so amused," he said, his own expression thoroughly disgruntled.

"I guess even the high-and-mighty Michael Delacourt has someone he has to answer to on occasion."

"If you're going to start taking potshots, I'm going to regret calling you."

"It's all part of the package," she informed him. "But let's get down to business."

She gestured toward the stairs. The boys had been awakened and sent off to bed in a guest room. Since they'd barely been alert enough to acknowledge her existence, she imagined they were sleeping soundly again by now.

"Who are they?" she asked.

Michael appeared not to have heard her. They were alone in a cozy room that had been designed for the comfort of big men. He was sprawled in an oversized chair, looking frazzled. Even here he was dressed in slacks and a dress shirt with the sleeves rolled up and the collar open. No jeans and T-shirts for this man. No wonder he made the society pages so often. He always looked like a million bucks.

Grace liked her power suits as well as the next person, but on the weekends, she settled into shorts or comfortable, well-worn jeans, faded, shapeless T-shirts, and sandals. She'd deliberately worn her weekend wardrobe to demonstrate how unimpressed she'd been by this out-of-the-blue invitation.

Now, with her shoes kicked off, she was curled up in a matching chair opposite Michael regretting the fact that she'd left all those power suits at home. She could feel the tensions of the week easing away, right along with her defenses.

This was just a little too cozy. She'd barely resisted the urge to flip on every light in the room, so it was bathed only in the glow of a single lamp in the corner. The atmosphere was disturbingly romantic and Michael was enchantingly rumpled for a man who usually looked like he'd just stepped out of an ad for Armani suits. She had to force herself to concentrate on the topic at hand.

"Michael, who are they?" she asked again, when she realized his attention was focused intently on her. He looked as if he were trying to memorize every little detail about her. Under other circumstances it might have been flattering. Under these circumstances, it rattled her in a way she didn't want to be rattled.

His gaze finally snapped up. "Jamie and Josh," he replied. "Beyond that, your guess is as good as mine. They refused to disclose a last name."

"Smart kids. It'll slow you down tracing where they belong. Any idea where that might be?"

"Not a one. I found them in the barn."

She was relieved to be able to finally slip into lawyer mode. "Like a couple of stray cats?" she asked. "Or burgling the place?"

"Looking for a place to sleep, they said."

"Did you believe them?"

"I believe they weren't there to steal anything. I also believe they're in some sort of trouble. They wouldn't give me a clue about where they came from, wouldn't let me call anyone to let them know they were okay. They claimed to be visiting in the area, but they wouldn't give me a name."

"Runaways," Grace deduced, her heart aching. She'd seen the sorry state of their clothes. More than that, she'd detected the worry in their eyes that not even being half-asleep could disguise. They had to be exhausted if they were risking sleep. Otherwise they'd probably be at the top of the stairs eavesdropping or slipping out an upstairs window as she and Michael discussed their fate.

"Looks that way to me," Michael agreed.

"Have you checked the local paper, turned on TV to see if they've been reported missing?"

"No, I just called you."

"Why?" she asked, bewildered by him turning to her. She would have expected him to go straight to his family. With the Delacourt resources, including a private eye for a brother, wouldn't that have made more sense? Even if he was ticked at most of them at the moment, they were the closest, most obvious people to call.

"What about Dylan?" she asked. "Isn't he living over here now?"

"He's away."

"And Trish? Maybe she knew about the boys hiding out in the barn but didn't say anything."

"I can't imagine Trish going off and leaving two runaways behind. She'd have brought them in and mothered them to death," he said wryly.

"Maybe you should call her and ask."

He looked vaguely uncomfortable. "Not a good idea."

"Why not?"

A scowl settled on his face again. "Because, if you must know, I have no idea where she is. She deliberately kept me in the dark about her destination. Made up a bunch of hogwash that turned out not to be true."

"So that makes me what? Third choice after Dylan and Trish?"

"Nope, first," he insisted. "Like I told you on the phone, this is right up your alley. You know about all this family law stuff. You're compassionate. You're a woman."

"And your sister-in-law, Dylan's wife, is *what?*" she asked wryly.

Because the Delacourts were big news in Houston, she'd been able to keep up. She knew all about their marriages.

Michael shrugged off the question, as if it wasn't worthy of a response. "Unreachable by phone?" she suggested. "Out in the hinterlands delivering a baby, perhaps?"

"I don't know. I didn't try. Look, Grace, I know this is an imposition, but you're the best. Face it, I'm out of my element. When that happens, I know enough to call in an expert."

If she'd been on her feet, she'd probably have fainted at the admission. "That has to be a first," she commented.

"What?"

"You admitting you're at a loss."

He regarded her evenly. "I'm not blind to my faults, Grace."

"Just not interested in correcting them?" she surmised.

His gaze narrowed. "Do you really want to take that particular walk down memory lane?"

Her cheeks burned. She swallowed hard and shook her head, reminding herself that his calling her wasn't personal. He hadn't dragged her over here because he'd been pining away for her for the past few years. It was about those two scared boys upstairs. Nothing else. Period. She had to keep that in mind. It would be way too easy to get caught up in all of this, to imagine that they were partners, a team…a family.

No sooner had that thought slammed into her head, than she jerked herself sternly back to reality. They were nothing to each other. *Nothing.* Old friends, at best. And this weekend was nothing more than a tiny, last-gasp blip on their flat-lined relationship. It was not evidence that there was life in it.

"No, of course not," she said briskly.

"I thought not." He studied her intently. "So, what do I do with them?"

He sounded genuinely perplexed, as if the decision-making king of the business world had finally butted up against a problem he couldn't solve with a snap of his fingers or a flurry of memos. Grace found the uncertainty more appealing than she cared to admit. For Michael Delacourt to show his vulnerability, especially to her, was something worth noting.

"What options have you considered?" she asked, curious to know exactly where he was coming from. "And speaking of experts, why didn't you just call the police and let them deal with the situation?"

To her relief, he looked genuinely appalled by the suggestion. "They're a couple of scared kids. How could I call the police? They haven't done anything wrong."

"They've run away for starters, and you don't know that they haven't done more," she pointed out realistically. "They could have been roaming around for weeks breaking into places, stealing food, jewelry and who knows what else."

"If they were stealing food, they weren't much good at it. They were starved," he said, ignoring the rest.

"Think back, Michael. All boys that age are starved at least a half-dozen times a day," she reminded him.

"Yeah, I suppose you're right."

She was still mystified by what he expected. "Look, Michael, what exactly do you want me to do?"

"Talk to them. Handle it. Figure out what's going on. Get them back home." He raked his hand through his thick, dark brown hair in a gesture of frustration that pretty much destroyed the usual neat style. "I don't know."

She found that appealing, too. Because her reaction irritated her, she snapped, "Just get them off your plate and onto mine, I suppose."

His expression brightened. "Exactly."

"Sorry, pal," she said, getting to her feet. She needed to get out of here before she succumbed to Michael's charm and the very real distress of those two boys. This was heartache she didn't need. There were plenty of other people around who could step in here and solve this, professionals with nothing at stake except doing their jobs.

"I think handling a couple of kids ought to be a piece of cake for a man who controls a multinational corporation," she said. "You'll be good for each other. Consider it your good deed for the century. Just think, you'll have it out of the way right at the start."

With the pointed barb delivered, she skirted past him and aimed for the door. Conveniently, her overnight bag was still there. She'd barely made a grab for it, though, when he stepped into her path. Even though Michael went through life with an economy of movements, he had always been able to move as swiftly as a panther when he chose to. Apparently right now he was highly motivated.

"You can't leave," he protested.

"Oh, but I can."

"Grace, don't do this to me. You're a lawyer. You know how to cut through red tape, get things done."

She regarded him with amusement. "And you don't? Please. Compared to convincing a foreign government to let you steal mineral rights, this is just a little inconvenience. Deal with it."

"Do you want me to beg?"

She grinned at the prospect, then regarded him curiously. "An interesting possibility. Are you any good at it?"

"Let me give it a shot."

He reached for her hand, pressed a kiss against her knuckles that sent shockwaves cavorting right through her. It wasn't exactly begging, but she had to admit it was an excellent start. Something inside her was melting right along with her resolve.

"Please, Grace. Stick around through the weekend at least. Help me get a straight story out of those kids. Once we've figured out what to do, you can race straight back to Houston and I won't bother you again for another half-dozen years or so."

She withdrew her hand, because she didn't like the sensations his touch was kicking off. "Nice try, but I'm not convinced yet that you really need me. Any old lawyer would do. Doesn't Delacourt Oil have a slew of them on retainer?"

He frowned at that. "None like you."

She regarded him with surprise. "I almost believe you mean that."

"Believe me, Grace, I have never meant anything more, never needed you more," he said with convincing solemnity. "Never."

There was a time when those words would have made her pulse ricochet wildly. Unfortunately, they still had a disconcerting effect. Ignoring it, she shook her head and took another step back, a step toward putting a safe emotional distance between them.

"Maybe this will be good for you, Michael. Put you in touch with real human beings for a change."

He appeared genuinely offended by the implication. "I deal with real human beings all the time."

"You just don't find them nearly as interesting as the bottom line, is that it?"

"You're not being fair."

"Probably not," she agreed. "But we both know life isn't always fair."

His gaze locked on hers. "But you are, Grace. Fairness is what you're all about. You fight for the underdog. Nobody knows that better than I do. I've seen you take some of my friends to the cleaners to make sure their ex-wives get what they deserve. Hell, you've taken me apart on the witness stand to pry out some ugly truths about friends of mine. We both know how tough you are when it matters. You handled that situation for Jeb's wife when you thought the company was misjudging her. If it hadn't been straightened out to your satisfaction, you would have fought like a tiger for her."

"You lucked out. Brianna was in love with Jeb and he was smart enough to go to bat for her in the end. Otherwise we would have sued your pants off and won."

He grinned. "That's what I mean. You don't care *who* you go up against, if you think the cause is just."

"There's a difference this time," she said.

"What's different?"

"You and I would be on the same side. I think I like it better when we're battling on opposite sides," she admitted candidly.

"Safer that way?" he inquired, an all-too-knowing glint in his eyes.

She was surprised that he could read her so well. "Smarter," she corrected.

He regarded her with amusement. "You don't still have a thing for me, do you, Grace? Being here with me isn't dredging up old memories, is it?"

She bristled at the suggestion. "Of course not."

"Then it shouldn't be a problem, right?" he said, clearly laying down a challenge. "We'll leave the past off-limits, stick strictly to the situation at hand."

It rankled that he thought it would be so easy to avoid rekindling their old passion. But if he could spend this weekend with her and keep it impersonal, then she certainly could...or she would die trying.

"Fine," she said, picking up her bag again, this time turning toward the stairs. "Okay, where's my room? Since I'm staying, I'm obviously too beat to think straight. We'll tackle this in the morning."

And in the morning, maybe she'd be able to figure out why Michael Delacourt was the only male on earth who could still twist her right around his finger without even trying.

Three

Michael had never been so relieved to see anyone in his life as he had been to see Grace pull into the driveway the night before. The fact that his heart had done a little hop, skip and jump had been gratitude, nothing more, he assured himself. The woman was far too prickly for him to consider another run at anything more, especially when there were plenty of willing women who'd be grateful for his attention and who wouldn't grumble if he had to cancel a date every now and again.

Not that he didn't understand why Grace had been furious when he'd missed her law school graduation years ago. He'd known exactly how important that day was to her. She had struggled and sacrificed to go to college, worked herself to a frazzle to succeed. She had earned that moment of triumph, and he should have been there to witness it.

Even understanding all that, he'd gotten caught up in a tough negotiation and hadn't even glanced at a clock until it was too late to make the ceremony. He'd apologized in every way he could think of, but she'd been unforgiving. Still was, as far as he could tell.

At the time, he'd told himself it was for the best. After all, how could a man in his position be expected to work nine to five? If he followed the workaholic example set by his father, his career was destined to be time-consuming. If Grace was going to be unreasonably demanding, it would never work out. Better to find that out before they were married.

He winced when he thought of how he'd tried to deftly shift all of the blame to her, tried to make her feel guilty for his neglect, as if it were her expectations that were at fault, not his insensitivity. No wonder she'd taken every opportunity since to make him squirm in court. He was amazed that she'd shown up here at all, much less stayed. But, then, Grace had too much grit, too much honor, to let her distaste for him stand in the way of helping someone truly in need.

One glance at those two boys and Michael had seen her heart begin to melt. Despite her tough exterior, she was a soft touch. Always had been. Even when she'd been struggling to pay tuition, refusing to accept so much as a dime from him, she'd never been able to turn away a lost kitten or a stray dog. She'd craved family the way some people needed sex. He'd counted on that to work in his favor when he'd called her.

And speaking of sex, being in such close proximity to her was going to be sheer torture. Just because he'd recognized that they weren't suited for marriage didn't mean that recognition shut off his hormones. The minute she'd stepped out of that rental car, looking annoyed and disheveled, he'd promptly envisioned her in bed with him, and in this scenario he was doing some very clever and inventive things to put a smile back on her face. He doubted she would have been pleased to know the direction of his thoughts.

He was none too pleased about them himself, since he'd been in an uncomfortable state of arousal ever since his first glimpse of her the night before. He figured an icy shower was going to be his only salvation and, if Grace was sticking around, he might as well get used to taking them.

Uncontrollable lust or not, he had no intention of strolling down that particular dead-end road again. He had trouble enough on his hands with Jamie and Josh under his roof—or Trish's roof, to be more precise about it.

He considered hanging around upstairs for a while longer, giving her plenty of time to solve the problem of the runaway kids, but guilt had him showered and dressed and on his way downstairs just after dawn. To his surprise, he was the last one up.

When he wandered into the kitchen, he found Grace blithely flipping pancakes for two wide-eyed and eager boys, whose blond hair had been slicked back and whose faces had been scrubbed clean. Grace's influence, no doubt.

They were currently falling all over themselves to get the table set for her. Given the fact that she was barefoot and had chosen to dress in shorts and a T-shirt, he could understand their reaction. He was pretty darned anxious to do whatever he could to please her, too. Unfortunately, his ideas would have to wait for another time, another place...probably another lifetime.

"Grace says as soon as we eat, we're going to talk about what to do with us," Josh announced, sounding surprisingly upbeat about the prospect.

Obviously he was crediting Grace with the good judgment not to do anything against his will.

"We're not going back," Jamie inserted direly, his gaze pointedly resting first on Michael, then on Grace. "So, if that's what you're thinking, you can forget it."

Obviously he was not as willing to assume Michael's good will or Grace's powers of persuasion as his little brother was.

"Back to where?" Michael asked, hoping to get a quick, uncensored response.

Grace shot a warning look at him. "That's enough for now. We'll talk about it after breakfast," she soothed, a hand resting gently on the boy's shoulder. "We'll all be able to think more clearly after we've eaten. How many pancakes, Jamie?"

"Four," he said, his distrust clearly not extending to the matter of food.

"I want five," Josh said.

"You can't eat five," Jamie countered. "You're littler than me."

"Can so."

"How about you both start with four and see if you want more?" Grace suggested, deftly averting a full-scale war between the two boys. She turned her attention to Michael for the first time since he'd entered the kitchen. "And you?"

"Just coffee. Lots and lots of coffee."

"The pancake offer only goes around once," she advised him. "I'll give you four, too. You look like you could use a decent breakfast for a change. You probably have the executive special back home."

"What's that?" Josh asked.

"Half a grapefruit and dry toast," Grace said with obvious distaste. "Keeps them lean and mean."

"Oh, yuck," both boys agreed in unison.

It was too close to the truth for Michael to contradict Grace's guesswork or the boys' disgust. "Whatever," he mumbled, pouring himself a cup of coffee and taking his first sip gratefully. It was strong, just the way he liked it.

When they were all seated at the round kitchen table, plates piled high with pancakes that had been drowned in maple syrup, Grace regarded Michael with interest. "In all the confusion last night, I forgot to ask. Where exactly are we? You said Los Piños on the phone. The pilot neglected to give me any details about our flight plan."

"And we all know your sense of direction is seriously flawed," Michael teased. "Los Piños is in west Texas. That's the opposite side of the state from Houston, in case you were wondering."

"How exactly did Trish manage to lure you over here before deserting you?"

"She didn't. Tyler came into my office and nagged until he got me on the company jet under the pretense of bringing me over here for a big family reunion."

"And you bought that, after what they did to you last time?" she asked, looking incredulous.

"What happened last time?" Josh asked, his face alight with curiosity, his overloaded fork hovering in midair.

"They took him off to a cabin in the woods and left him," Grace said with a certain amount of obvious delight. "One whole week."

"Cool," Jamie declared.

"No cell phone. No TV. No newspapers. No financial news," Grace added cheerily, as if she knew exactly what had driven him up a wall during those seven endless days. "Did they stock the refrigerator, or were you expected to catch your dinner in the lake?"

Michael scowled at her but didn't bother to reply. He was not about to discuss his lack of expertise with a fishing rod or the fact that Trish had left him with a freezer filled with meals prepared and labeled, complete with microwave instructions.

"No TV?" Josh asked with evident shock. "What did you do?"

"Cursed my family for the most part," Michael said. He'd also read half the books on the shelves, even the classics that he'd avoided back in school. "Could we drop the sorry saga of my sneaky relatives, please? Just thinking about it is giving me indigestion."

"What amazes me is not their sneakiness, but your gullibility," Grace said, ignoring his plea to end the topic. "Once, maybe, but twice? That radar of yours must be slipping, Michael. You've obviously lost your edge. I hope none of your competitors get wind of that."

He frowned at her taunt. "My edge is just fine, thank you. I got you over here, didn't I?"

She laughed. "Touché."

"What does that mean?" Josh asked.

"It means he got the last laugh, at least for now," Grace told him. "Now eat. Your pancakes are getting cold."

Jamie regarded Michael worriedly. "If you're here on some kind of vacation, does that mean this place ain't yours?"

"No, it *isn't* mine," Michael said, in a probably wasted attempt to correct the boy's pitiful grammar. "It belongs to my sister."

"Oh," Jamie said flatly. He looked as disappointed as if Michael had revealed that there was no Santa Claus.

Of course, these two probably hadn't believed in Santa for quite some time, if ever.

"Does that bother you for some reason?" Grace asked Jamie.

"It's just that it's real nice, the nicest place we've been in a while. Even the barn was real clean."

"Were you hoping to stick around?" Grace inquired casually.

"Maybe," Jamie admitted, clearly struggling to keep any hint of real hope out of his voice. "For a little bit. Just till we figure out what to do next. I gotta get a job if I'm gonna take care of me and Josh."

Michael was about to question what sort of a job he expected to get at his age, but Grace gave him a subtle signal, as if she knew what he'd been about to say and wanted him to keep silent.

"Where's home for you guys?" she asked instead, sneaking in the very same question she'd wanted Michael to back away from earlier.

"Ain't got one," Jamie said, returning her gaze belligerently.

"Okay, then, where did you run away from?" When they didn't answer, she said, "You might as well tell us. Otherwise, we'll just have to call the police so they can check all the missing persons reports."

Josh regarded them worriedly. "If we say, can we stay here? I can do laundry and make my bed. We won't be any trouble. Honest."

It was already too late for that, Michael thought. He was harboring two runaways and a woman he had a desperate desire to kiss senseless. Talk about a weekend fraught with danger.

"No," he said a little too sharply. He saw the look of

betrayal in their eyes and felt like a heel. Before he could stop himself, he moderated the sharp refusal. "Tell us the truth and then we'll talk about what happens next."

"You'll really listen to what we got to say?" Jamie asked skeptically.

"We'll listen," Grace promised.

"We gotta tell," Josh said, regarding his big brother stubbornly. "Maybe they'll let us stay."

"I say we don't," Jamie insisted. "They're grown-ups. They'll just make us go back. They'll say they gotta, because it's the law or something. You want to be separated again, like last time?"

He seemed unaware of just how revealing his question was. Michael was uncomfortably aware of an ache somewhere in the region of his heart. These two were getting to him, no doubt about it. As for Grace, they'd clearly already stolen her heart. She was regarding them sympathetically.

"You were in foster care, weren't you?" she guessed. "And not together?"

"Uh-huh," Josh said, shooting a defiant look at his brother. "Nobody would take both of us last time or the time before that. They said we were too much trouble when we were together."

"I'm old enough to look out for my own kid brother," Jamie said, regarding them both with his usual belligerence. "We'll be okay. You don't have to do nothin'. Soon as we eat, we'll go."

"Go where?" Michael asked, feeling as if the kids had sucker punched him. He tried to imagine being separated from Dylan, Jeb and Tyler when they'd been the ages of these boys. He couldn't. They were bound together by a shared history, by family and by the kind of fierce love and loyalty that only siblings felt despite whatever rivalries existed.

He focused his attention on Jamie, since he was clearly the leader. Josh would trustingly go along with whatever his big brother wanted. "How old are you?"

"Sixteen," Jamie said, drawing a shocked look from his brother.

"I'd guess thirteen, tops," Michael said, turning to gauge Josh's reaction, rather than Jamie's. The boy gave him a subtle but unmistakable nod. "How about you, Josh? Eight? Nine?"

"Eight," Josh admitted readily. He was apparently eager to provide any information that might persuade Michael and Grace to keep the two of them at the ranch. "Last week. That's when Jamie came for me, on my birthday. We've always been together on our birthdays, no matter what. We promised."

"And that's a very good promise to try to keep," Grace said. "Families should stick together whenever they can."

As she said it, she kept her gaze locked on Michael. He got the message. There were now evidently three against one in the room should he decide to fight for an immediate call to the proper authorities. Grace wasn't going to turn these two over to anybody who would sep-arate them again, though how she hoped to avoid it was beyond him. There were probably a zillion rules about how to handle this, and he'd brought her here precisely because she knew them. Now she was showing every indication that she might just ignore all zillion of them. For the moment, however, it had to be her call.

She was the expert.

"How long have you been in foster care?" she asked,

apparently inferring from Michael's silence that he was willing to withhold judgment until all the facts were in.

"Since Josh was four," Jamie finally confessed. "We were together in the first place, but then they got mad at me, 'cause I wouldn't follow all their stupid rules, so I got sent away to another family. They kept Josh till he ran away to find me. When they dragged him back, he cried and cried, till he made himself sick. Then they said they couldn't cope with him either."

Michael swallowed hard at the image of a little boy sobbing his heart out for his big brother. Instead of being treated with compassion, he'd been sent away. What kind of monsters did that to a child? He glanced at Grace and thought he detected tears in her eyes.

"How many places have you been since then?" she asked gently.

"Four," Jamie said without emotion. "Josh has been in three."

"Because you keep running away to be together?" Grace concluded.

"Uh-huh."

"What happened to your parents?"

"We don't got any," Jamie said flatly. His sharp gaze dared his brother to contradict him.

Even so, Josh couldn't hide his shock at the reply. "That's not true," he protested, fighting tears. "We got a mom. You know we do."

"For all the good it does. She's been in rehab or jail as far back as I can remember," Jamie said angrily. "What good is a mom like that?"

"I'm sure she loves you both very much, despite whatever problems she has," Grace said. "Sometimes things just get to be overwhelming and people make mistakes."

"Yeah, like turning her back on her own kids," Jamie said with resentment. "Some mistake."

Michael was inclined to agree with him, but he kept silent. This was Grace's show. She no doubt knew what to say under very complicated circumstances like this. He didn't have a clue. He just knew he wanted to crack some adult heads together. The vehemence of his response surprised him. Grace was the champion of the underdog, not him. He'd wanted to distance himself from this situation, not get drawn more deeply into it. But with every word Jamie and Josh spoke, he could feel his defenses crumbling.

"Where are you from—I mean originally, back when you lived with your mom?" Grace asked the boys.

The question surprised him. He'd just assumed the boys had to be from someplace nearby. How else would they have wound up in Trish and Hardy's barn? Realistically, though, how many foster homes were there likely to be around Los Piños? How much need for them would there be in a town this size, anyway?

"We were born in San Antonio," Jamie said. "But we moved around a lot, even before Mom ditched us. I can't even remember all the places. She liked big cities best because it was easier to get…" He shrugged. "You know…stuff."

Michael was very much afraid he did know. He held back a sigh.

"And your last foster home?" Grace asked. "Was it near here?"

The boy shook his head. "Not really. When I got Josh, I figured this time we'd better get far away so they could never find us. I figured they'd just give up after a couple of days. It's not as if anybody really cares where we are. We've been hitching rides for a while now. Like a week, maybe."

"Yeah," Josh said. "We must have gone about a thousand miles."

"It's only a couple of hundred, doofus," Jamie said.

"Well, it seems like a lot. We didn't get a lot of rides, so we had to walk and walk. Jamie wouldn't get in a car with just anybody. He said we could only get in pickups where we could ride in the back."

Michael listened, horrified. He saw the same sense of dismay on Grace's face. Clearly, they both knew all too well what might have happened to two small boys on the road alone. Obviously Jamie, at his age and with his street smarts, understood the dangers as well, but it was also clear that he thought those were preferable to another bad foster care experience or another separation.

"We told the truth," Jamie said, looking from Grace to Michael and back again. "You gonna let us stay?" He didn't sound especially hopeful. His expression suggested he was ready to run at the first hint that Michael and Grace might not agree to let them stick around.

"Why don't you boys go and check on the feed for the horses?" Michael suggested. "Grace and I need to talk things over and decide what's best." He scowled at Jamie. "And don't get any ideas about taking off while we do, okay? We'll work this out. I promise."

He meant that promise more than he'd ever meant anything in his life.

Unfortunately, he had a feeling that the solution to this particular problem wasn't going to come to them over a second cup of coffee. And judging from Grace's troubled expression, she knew it, too.

Four

Grace wanted to cry. As the boys straggled dejectedly out of the kitchen as if the weight of the world were on their narrow shoulders, she couldn't bear to meet Michael's gaze. She was afraid if she did, the tears would come and she wouldn't be able to stop them.

She identified with Josh and Jamie a little too much. She could remember exactly what it felt like to have no one around she could count on. After her father's departure, her mother had sunk more and more deeply into a depression from which she never recovered. Grace had been eighteen when her mother died, a sad, lost woman.

Because for so many years Grace had been as much caregiver as child, she had felt the loss even more deeply, felt even more abandoned and alone. She blinked back tears at the memory of that time. She had been so frightened and so determined not to show it.

That was when she had met Michael and, for a time, she had felt connected. She had leaned on him, drawing strength from the attention he had showered on her, envisioning herself a part of his large family even though at that time she'd never met them.

But, in the end, he hadn't been able to give her what she desperately needed—a storybook family in which she would come first with him, just as he did with her. Graduation day had been a brutal awakening for her. She had realized then that the only person she could truly count on was herself. She'd clung to her independence ever since, not wanting to risk more disillusionment with another man.

But while her lifestyle suited her now, she didn't want that for Jamie and Josh, who were already far too used to fending for themselves. She wanted them to be surrounded by people who cared, people they knew would be there for them always.

"Grace?"

Michael's concerned voice drew her back to the present. "What?" she said without glancing up.

"You okay?"

"Of course," she said, forcing a brisk, confident note into her voice. It was her courtroom tone, the one she drew on so no judge or jury would ever sense a hint of vulnerability. Even so, she wasn't quite ready to look him in the eye.

"This is a hell of a mess, isn't it?" he said.

"Now there's an understatement, if ever I heard one."

"What are we going to do?"

Her gaze came up at that. *"We?"* she echoed, not bothering to hide her surprise. "I thought you intended to dump this into my lap."

"Look, if you don't want my help, that's fine by me. Believe me, nothing would please me more than to turn this over to you and get on with my nice, peaceful vacation."

She regarded him skeptically. "'Peaceful' and 'vacation' are not two words I normally associate with you," she said. "You're here under duress, remember?"

"The prospect has become considerably more appealing overnight."

"How unfortunate, since we have a crisis on our hands," she declared, emphatically echoing him.

"I knew it was a mistake the minute I said that," he muttered.

He didn't sound half as disgruntled as she was sure he meant to. In fact, he sounded like a man who'd unwillingly been deeply touched by what those boys had already been through in their young lives. For the first time ever, she thought maybe she knew Michael Delacourt better than he knew himself. She had always known that he possessed a heart. He just wasn't in touch with it very often. He wouldn't allow himself to be, because he wanted nothing to compete with the time he devoted to Delacourt Oil.

Those boys had reached him in a way she suspected he rarely allowed to happen. She wasn't about to let him back away from the experience. Just as he was about to rise from his seat—probably intent on beating a hasty retreat—she put her hand on his.

"Oh, no, you don't. You're not getting out of this that easily."

He sank back down with a sigh of resignation, then reached for a piece of paper. "Okay, what's the game plan?" he asked.

He sounded as if he were strategizing a corporate takeover and wanted every detail nailed down in advance. He almost seemed eager to get started. Or maybe, she thought more realistically, he was simply anxious to get finished.

Despite Michael's sense of urgency, Grace considered their options thoughtfully. "I'm going to make a few discreet inquiries," she began slowly.

He regarded her worriedly, as if he already sensed that he wasn't going to like the role she had in mind for him. "What about me?"

She regarded him with a certain amount of delight. "You're going to go out there and see how much more information you can pry out of Josh and Jamie."

"Such as?"

"A last name would be helpful. So would their mother's name."

"Grace, those two fell in love with you at first sight. They were all but falling all over themselves earlier to please you. If they wouldn't talk to you, how do you expect me to get them to open up? They don't trust me. The only reason they didn't sneak away from here last night was because they were too exhausted to try."

"It's not too late to change that. You can become their new best buddy." She looked him over carefully. He was in another pair of slacks with creases so sharp they could have cut butter and a shirt that probably cost more than everything in her suitcase. "One little suggestion, though, before you go outside."

"I could use more than one suggestion, sweetheart. I need a damned manual."

"You were a boy once, Michael. You had brothers. Surely you recall what that was like."

"Of course, but Jamie and Josh are nothing like we were."

"For good reasons."

"I know that. What I don't know is how to get

through to them, especially Jamie. He's got solid concrete walls built around himself."

"Are you surprised?"

"Of course not, but—"

"Michael, give it up. You're a bright man. You can do this. For starters, how about changing into a pair of jeans and some boots? Dressed like that, you'd intimidate a CEO. That outfit might be fine for an afternoon at the country club, but out here you are seriously overdressed."

To her surprise he chuckled.

"What's so funny?"

"I was wondering how long it was going to take before you tried to get me out of my clothes." He winked at her on his way out of the room. "Turned out to take a whole lot less time than I'd imagined."

Michael's taunting good humor was short-lived. He exited the house in the jeans and scuffed boots he normally wore to the oil fields feeling about as confident as a man facing a firing squad.

He stood silently for a moment, drawing in a deep breath of the scented morning air. He had a feeling it was the first time in years he'd actually been aware of the air he was breathing. The last time had probably been at the beach house where he'd always enjoyed sitting on the porch with a cup of coffee and the scent of salty sea breezes surrounding him.

"Whatcha doing?" Josh asked, slipping up beside him and regarding him curiously.

"Trying to decide what that scent in the air is," he admitted. "Take a deep breath and see if you can tell."

Josh gave an exaggerated sniff. "Must be those roses

over there," he said, indicating a garden Michael hadn't noticed before. "They smell real sweet, just like that."

Michael laughed.

Josh stared at him. "What's so funny?"

"Some would say it's about time I stopped to smell the roses," Michael told him.

"What's that mean?"

"It means I'm usually too busy to pay attention to what's going on around me."

The boy nodded. "One of my foster dads was like that. He was never home. Sometimes he stayed out all night. When he did, my foster mom would cry."

Michael doubted Josh had any idea what the man had probably been up to on those nights away from home. Obviously, though, seeing his foster mom cry had troubled him. He gave the boy's shoulder a sympathetic squeeze. "That must have been tough on you."

"Yeah, well, when you're a foster kid, you get used to stuff," he said with a shrug.

Michael resolved then and there that there would be no more *stuff* for Josh and Jamie to learn to take in stride. He would do whatever it took to see that they landed in a good home this time, maybe even try to make them eligible for adoption if their mother wasn't ever going to get her life straightened out. The courts were looking more favorably on making that happen these days, rather than leaving children in limbo forever. Whatever he and Grace decided to do, though, they had to move quickly, before logic got all tangled up with emotion.

He glanced down and saw that Josh was mimicking his wide stance, his hands locked behind his back just as Michael's were. He bit back a sudden desire to smile.

"Where's Jamie?" he asked Josh.

"In the barn. He's not touching anything," he assured Michael hurriedly. "Just looking."

"Looking is fine," Michael assured him. "Does he like horses?"

Josh's head bobbed up and down. "He loves horses more than anything. He really, really wants to learn to ride," he confided. "Even more than me. Do you think we could? Could you teach us?"

What was it with everyone trying to get him on a blasted horse?

Michael wondered.

"We'll see," he hedged, then felt terrible when he saw the disappointment rising in Josh's eyes. Maybe he could get someone from White Pines over here to give the boys lessons. He couldn't do that, though, until he and Grace had made some progress in finding out their legal status. That had to be cleared up before everyone landed in a heap of trouble.

"I'll make you a deal," he said, hunkering down until he was at eye level with Josh. He'd pulled off multimillion dollar negotiations with less finesse than this conversation was likely to require.

"What kind of a deal?" Josh asked, regarding him with innate distrust.

"You tell me your last name so Grace and I can get your situation straightened out, and I'll get someone over here to give you riding lessons."

"I don't know," Josh replied, clearly torn. "Jamie would be real mad if he found out."

"Jamie wants to ride. Maybe he'd consider it a fair trade-off."

Obviously tempted, Josh brightened. "Let's go ask him," he said, tugging on Michael's hand.

Michael had a feeling Jamie's hide was tougher than Josh's. No matter how badly he wanted the riding lessons, Jamie might not be willing to tell Michael what he needed to know.

"No," Michael said, halting their forward motion. "This deal is between the two of us. I won't tell your brother you told me."

"But he'll know," Josh reasoned. "How else could you find out?"

"If he asks, I'll tell him I had my brother do some research. He's a private investigator."

"But that's a lie."

Michael winced at his shock. "I know, but once in a very long while, when it's to protect someone's feelings, a very small lie is okay."

Josh was still hesitant. "But I promised I wouldn't tell. Not ever."

"Some promises can be broken if it's for a really, really good reason," Michael reassured him. He couldn't help wondering if he wasn't teaching Josh to bend way too many of the values he'd been taught. Maybe these were lessons that should have waited until he was old enough to make the right distinctions about the circumstances. Too late now, though.

Josh regarded him worriedly. "You swear we'll get to ride the horses?"

"Cross my heart," Michael said, sketching a cross across his chest.

Josh beckoned him closer. Michael bent down. "Miller," he whispered. "That's our last name. Our mom is Naomi Miller."

"Josh!"

The shout of betrayal echoed across the corral. Neither of them had seen Jamie emerge from the barn. Whether he had heard all of the words from that distance or not, he clearly suspected that Josh was confiding something he shouldn't.

Before Michael could react, Jamie raced across the ground and tackled his brother, throwing him to the ground, then landing on top of him, fists flying.

For a moment, Josh gave as good as he got, but Jamie was bigger and stronger. When Michael figured the odds were way too uneven, he reached down and snagged Jamie by the back of his shirt. The boy came to his feet flailing at Michael. One punch caught him squarely in the jaw, jarring his teeth. He figured it was no more than he deserved for his role in this.

"Enough!" Grace commanded, appearing out of nowhere, her voice calm but unyielding.

Jamie stilled, but the anger in his eyes continued to cast sparks in Michael's direction.

"What is this all about?" she demanded, her gaze on Michael. Jamie and Josh stared at him, clearly wary of what he might say.

"Just a little disagreement," he said mildly. "Nothing to get excited about."

"It is not a little disagreement when Josh has the beginnings of a black eye and cuts all over him and you're rubbing a swollen jaw." Her gaze landed on Jamie. "Well?"

"I'm not telling," he said sullenly. He stared pointedly at his brother. "I don't tell secrets."

Josh flushed, tears welling up in his eyes.

Michael sighed. The last thing he'd meant to do was

cause a rift between the brothers. He knew it wouldn't last, but for now they were both hurting in ways well beyond whatever physical injuries they'd suffered.

"This is my fault," he confessed.

Grace stared at him in surprise. "It is? Why?"

"I asked Josh for some information. We made a deal. It was a fair deal, but I should never have put him in that position," he said candidly. He regarded both boys intently. "I'm sorry."

"What good's sorry now that you got what you wanted?" Jamie demanded, not the least bit pacified by the apology.

"He's gonna get us riding lessons," Josh said so softly it was barely audible.

Jamie gaped. "That was the deal? You traded our secret for riding lessons?"

"I know how bad you wanted them," Josh said defensively. "I did it for you."

"He did," Michael said. "And I'll get somebody over here this afternoon."

"Yeah," Jamie said bitterly. "And right after that, you'll turn us in."

"Nobody's turning anybody in," Grace assured him. "This just makes it easier for me to get information." She regarded Jamie evenly. "I'm a lawyer and I am on your side."

Jamie continued to regard her with suspicion. "We can't afford to pay a lawyer."

Grace returned his look with a solemn expression. "Do you have any money at all?"

"A couple of dollars," Jamie said.

Josh looked surprised. "You said we was broke."

"This was for emergencies," Jamie said defensively.

"Give me one of the dollars," Grace said.

Jamie balked. "What about the emergencies?"

"Once you give me that dollar, I'll be working for you. I'll take care of any emergencies," she explained.

Jamie still looked dubious. "Honest?"

"Honest."

He took a crumpled bill from his pocket and handed it to her. Grace smoothed it out, folded it and put it in her pocket.

"Now you have yourself a lawyer," she said. "With me on your side, nothing will happen to the two of you unless we all agree it's for the best."

"All of us?" Jamie repeated skeptically. "That means me and Josh have to say yes, too?"

"Absolutely," she assured him.

Michael regarded her with surprise. Surely she knew that making such a promise was risky. What if the court overruled their judgment? Just as Jamie had said earlier, grown-ups in general and judges in particular could be notoriously capricious, even in interpreting the letter of the law.

Jamie seemed to be wavering, his distrust of the system weighing heavily against his longing to ride one of the horses.

"Do I get to pick which horse?" he asked.

"As long as whoever comes to give the lesson approves it," Michael said. When Jamie looked ready to protest, he added, "Just to make sure you won't get hurt. Once you've had your lessons, you can ride any horse around here."

"Satisfied?" Grace asked.

Josh stared up at his big brother hopefully. "Is it okay?"

Jamie shuffled his sneakers in the dirt, trying very hard to bank his obvious excitement. "I suppose."

"All right!" Josh shouted, slapping Michael's hand in a high five.

Michael had to admit, he felt a little of the child's glee himself. A glance at Grace suggested she was just as happy. A smile had spread across her face and lit her eyes. Only Jamie refused to give any outward hint of his exuberance. All alone, he headed back into the barn. After a slight hesitation, Josh trailed after him.

"I guess you're pretty proud that your divide-and-conquer technique paid off," Grace said, a surprising hint of condemnation in her voice.

"I'm glad we have the information we need," he agreed. He met her gaze evenly. "But I wish there had been another way to get it. I don't want those boys to lose their trust in one another."

She regarded him with obvious relief. "Good. Then you won't try that again."

"Since you obviously disapprove of my methods, does that mean you don't want the ill-gotten information?"

"No," she said quickly. "Of course, I want it."

"The last name is Miller. The mother is Naomi. Any luck with your other calls?"

"Nothing so far, but it's hard to get a line on something like this without giving away more than I'm getting. It'll be easier now that I'm not just trying to track down two needles in a very large haystack."

Michael regarded her worriedly. "Grace, how much trouble will you be in if someone wants to make a big deal out of the two of us letting those kids stay here instead of turning them in right away? I imagine there are pretty strict regulations governing this sort of thing.

We can't just decide to keep the kids here without some-body's approval, right? Not even for a few days?"

"I can handle it. What about you? If some newspa-per gets wind of your involvement, this could land on the front pages of the papers all over Texas."

"I've weathered worse," he assured her. It came with the territory. There were a lot of people eager to dig up dirt on a family as powerful as the Delacourts. There wasn't much to be found, but a lot could be made of a little indiscretion if a reporter cared to put a negative slant on it.

"All that matters is getting those boys settled some-place where they'll be together and happy," he told her.

She smiled up at him then, one of those bright, sunny smiles that held nothing back. Drawn to her, he slipped closer, and before she could realize his intention, he leaned down and touched his lips lightly to hers. Silken heat, whisper-soft against his, her mouth was every bit as wickedly tempting as he'd recalled. He had to force himself to stop at just one kiss.

"Thank you for coming to their defense," he whis-pered against her cheek.

She gazed up at him, her lips parted in astonishment.

His resolve fled. The first kiss had felt so good and her mouth was so thoroughly tempting that Michael couldn't resist one more taste. This time when his mouth slanted across hers, a deep sigh shuddered through her and was echoed in his body.

How was it possible after all these years apart, after all of their legal skirmishes, that something as simple as a kiss felt like coming home? Now that he knew that, he could hardly wait to get Jamie and Josh's situation settled, so that he and Grace could start over.

If she'd agree.

Five

Dazed by the unexpected kiss and even more stunned by her response to it, Grace stared at Michael. "What was that all about?"

"Just a little thank-you kiss," he assured her, but his lips were curved into a satisfied smile.

"The first one, maybe," she said, resisting the desire to touch her fingers to her still-tingling mouth. "That second one was something else altogether."

"Was it really?" he asked innocently. "It got to you, did it?" The man was infuriating. Smug.

Accurate, she thought with a barely concealed sigh. It would not do to let him see it, though. "It did not *get to me,* as you put it," she said staunchly. "I am immune to you, Michael Delacourt. I have been for years."

"Then the kiss meant nothing, did it? It's hardly worth all this analysis."

"That's exactly right. It meant absolutely nothing!" She whirled around and headed for the house, fully aware of his faint chuckle trailing after her.

Oh, yes, the man was impossible. He was trying to start something, either to satisfy his ego that he could still make it happen or because he was bored and she was conveniently available as a distraction. As if two runaway kids weren't enough trouble, he was looking for more.

Coming here was a mistake, she told herself as she went into the kitchen and splashed cold water on her flushed cheeks, then stood still and fought to quiet the racing of her pulse.

No, she corrected, staying was the mistake. She should have turned right around the night before and gone back to Houston. She could have driven the rental car all the way, if need be, taking Jamie and Josh with her. Of course, they might well have ended up in New Mexico if she'd tried, but that would have been better than this off-kilter way she was feeling right this second.

Even before she heard Michael's booted footsteps on the porch, she sensed that he was near. She could feel a vague and once all-too-familiar prickling sensation on the back of her neck, the same sensation that warned of danger closing in. She quickly dried her cheeks and turned to face him with what she hoped was a totally calm, disinterested expression. She'd had plenty of time to perfect it over the years. Every time they met, in fact.

"Feeling in control again?" he inquired with amusement flashing in his eyes.

"You really do have an overinflated ego," she pointed out.

"I find confidence to be necessary in business."

"Confidence and ego are not exactly the same," she remarked tartly.

He wasn't put off in the least. In fact, he seemed to

be enjoying the debate, deliberately prolonging it. "I suppose that depends on how you define them."

"Confidence has to do with knowing your own strengths. Ego has to do with overinflating them, giving yourself a little too much credit." She leveled a haughty look straight at him. "It is not an attractive quality."

"Then just think of the fun you can have over the next few days trying to cut my overinflated ego back down to size," he suggested.

"I am not here for your personal amusement or my own," she pointed out huffily. "The only reason I agreed to stay was because of Jamie and Josh."

Michael nodded. "Of course," he intoned solemnly. "I'll try to remember that."

She drew herself up and leveled a stern look straight at him. It usually worked quite well on a reluctant witness. "See that you do."

She had no earthly idea why her words seemed to make him smile, but she caught him doing just that, even though he quickly hid it. She decided it was wisest to let the matter drop. It was evident she wasn't winning the debate, couldn't against a man who didn't play by any rules and didn't seem the least bit wary of the outcome.

"I'd better make those calls," she said. "Is there another phone around here that's more private? I don't want Jamie or Josh to come in and overhear me."

"There's one in the den," he said, leading her toward a small but airy room that faced the sun-splashed fields of wildflowers at the back of the house. French doors opened onto a deck and let in the rapidly warming morning breeze.

While there was a masculine feel to much of the

house, this room had been designed for a woman. The view had been brought indoors with splashes of brightly colored chintz on the sofa and a collection of chintz-patterned teacups on an old oak sideboard. The furniture was scaled-down in size, too, comfortable, but far more feminine than the oversized, darkly upholstered chairs in the living room. Books, some of them lying open as if abandoned in midsentence, were scattered everywhere and ranged in topic from the latest fiction to a colorful book on quilts as art.

Grace instantly fell in love with all of it. It was thoroughly charming and such a stark contrast to the tidy, practical, modern decor in her Houston condo, where a weekly maid chased away dust and disorder.

"What a wonderful room," she said, circling it to admire the lush combination of fabrics, the eclectic touches that hinted of Trish's various interests. This had to be her special domain, a home office, perhaps.

"Trish's haven, as I understand it," Michael said, confirming her guess. "Hardy custom-built all the bookshelves and cabinets."

"They're beautiful," Grace said, thinking that they, like the rest of the house he'd built, had been imbued with such care and love. "Your sister is a very lucky woman."

"I think she'd agree with you." He stood there uncertainly for a moment, his gaze skimming hers. "Well, I guess I'll leave you to make those calls. I'd better make a few of my own. I have to track down a riding instructor."

"Do you need to use the phone first?"

"I'll use my cell phone." He grinned. "I hid it in my

briefcase in case my family got any crazy ideas about cutting off the phone service on me."

She regarded him with a sudden burst of insight. "You know something, Michael? I think you're almost disappointed that they didn't."

"Why on earth would you say that? I hated that last vacation."

"But you liked the fact that they cared enough to make you go, didn't you?"

He seemed startled by the observation, but then he nodded slowly. "You know, you may be right. I suppose we all want someone who'll look out for our best interests when we forget to." He studied her with quiet intensity. "Do you have someone who does that for you, Grace?"

"Sure," she said blithely, hoping he would let it go at that. But of course, being Michael, he didn't.

"Who?"

"That's my private business," she told him stiffly, because there was no way on earth that she would admit that *she* was the only person who looked out for Grace Foster. She watched herself intently for signs of burnout, scheduled vacations that took her far from Houston where no one could reach her, vacations during which she went almost as nuts as she supposed Michael did.

"Well, I just hope whoever it is does the job right," he said softly. Then he turned and left her alone.

Grace sighed. Why was it that holed up here in Los Piños with Michael and two young boys—more people than she ever had crowded around—she suddenly felt more lonely than ever?

Before she could ponder that for too long, the phone

rang. Hoping that it was a reply to one of her earlier inquiries, she snatched it up on the first ring.

"Well, well, well," a teasing masculine voice said. "Who is this?"

Grace stiffened. "Who is *this?*" she shot right back, not prepared to give anything away.

"Tyler Delacourt," he said at once.

Her shoulders relaxed. She had always liked the most charming of the Delacourt brothers. He had a twinkle in his eyes, a flirtatious nature and a heart as big as Texas. While others in the family had never warmed to her, Tyler had. He'd always treated her as if they were co-conspirators in the battle to hold on to Michael's heart.

"Tyler, I didn't recognize your voice," she said, aware of just how much she'd missed him, right along with his brother. Breaking up with Michael had meant losing his whole family, a family she had come to think of as her own, even if they hadn't seen it quite that way. It would have been awkward, though, and far too painful, to stay in touch even with Tyler, so she hadn't. "This is Grace."

"Grace Foster?" Tyler asked.

He sounded a little shocked, but just as delighted as she was. She had to wonder, though, if it was for the same reason. Tyler had done his best to help Michael mend fences with her all those years ago. He'd considered it a personal failure that he hadn't succeeded.

"Oh, my, how did my brother manage to lure you over to his vacation hideaway?" he said.

His amused tone confirmed her fear that he'd leaped to the wrong conclusion. "Don't make too much of it," she warned.

"How can I not? I thought you two weren't on speaking terms."

"We speak," Grace said, then grinned as she thought of the last conversation she and Michael had had during the debacle between Delacourt Oil and Brianna O'Ryan, who was now Mrs. Jeb Delacourt. "To be more precise, we usually shout."

"Is there a lot of shouting going on now?" Tyler inquired with unabashed curiosity. "Did I interrupt?"

"Nope. All's quiet on the western front. Since you obviously called to speak to your brother, why don't I get him for you?"

"Wait," he commanded.

"Yes?"

"Whatever the reason for it, I'm glad you're there," he said quietly.

Grace was startled by his unexpectedly serious tone. "Why would my being here matter to you?"

He hesitated, then said, "It just does, okay? Give him a chance, Grace. Michael's missed you, more than he'll probably ever admit, even to himself. He needs you in his life."

It was a familiar refrain, but she didn't believe it for a second, couldn't allow herself to believe it. "Tyler, don't get the wrong idea. My reason for being here isn't personal. This isn't about Michael and me. Let me get him. I'm sure he'll explain."

Taking the portable phone with her, she went in search of Michael and found him on the outside deck, legs stretched out in front of him, face turned up to the sun, eyes closed. For a man who professed not to know how to relax, he seemed to have found a way.

"Michael?" she said softly, not sure if he'd drifted off to sleep.

He snagged her hand, proving that he'd been aware

of her presence all along. "Come sit with me," he said without opening his eyes.

"Not just now," she said, easing out of his grip. "Your brother's on the phone."

His eyes snapped open then. "Which one?" he mouthed silently.

"Tyler."

"Oh, boy," he muttered, taking the phone. "Hey, Ty, what's up?" Grace turned to leave, but paused when she heard his low chuckle. "Stay out of it, bro. You dumped me over here without a second thought. Now it's up to me how I occupy my time."

Obviously she hadn't been convincing enough during her own conversation with Tyler. He clearly wasn't buying the fact that her presence here wasn't personal. She had to wonder why. Was she a frequent topic of conversation between the brothers? What sort of speculation had Tyler engaged in over the years? He seemed to think she really mattered to Michael, when she knew the opposite was true. But which of them knew Michael best? Once she would have said she did, but after all this time, maybe Tyler did have more insight.

Oh, what did it matter? she asked herself impatiently. Whatever regrets she or Michael had, it was impossible to recapture the past.

Even so, she found herself moving deliberately right back into Michael's line of vision to wait for the return of the phone. Maybe that way she could inhibit whatever he might otherwise be inclined to say about her easy agreement to his request that she fly over. After that earlier taunt about her eagerness to get him out of his clothes—after that kiss—it was clear that Michael wasn't solely focused on her ability to help Josh and

Jamie. That didn't mean the whole family had to start leaping to conclusions.

After a surprisingly brief exchange, Michael hung up and handed her the phone.

"Tyler said to tell you goodbye."

"It was nice to speak to him," she said honestly.

"He always thought you hung the moon," Michael told her. "Said I was a damned fool for letting you get away."

This was not a conversation she intended to have. "You were," she said simply, then turned and went back inside, fully aware with every step she took that Michael's startled, intense gaze was following her.

Grace managed to stay out of Michael's path for the next few hours. She fixed sandwiches, then left them in the refrigerator for Jamie, Josh and Michael, before taking her own lunch and retreating to the den, where she firmly closed the door to prevent intrusions. She barely resisted the urge to lock it.

It was nearly three o'clock before she finally put the phone back on the hook, then uttered a heartfelt sigh. She shrugged her shoulders trying to work out the knots of tension.

The calls had gone about as she'd expected. She'd received a flurry of faxes indicating just how trouble-some Jamie and Josh Miller had been to their various foster families and just how far Naomi Miller was from being fully recovered from her addiction. There was a lot of frustration from social services, who had about given up on finding anyplace where the boys would stay put, much less thrive.

"Why the interest?" a friend in the Houston department had asked her. Shirley Lee Green—mother of four and foster mom to a dozen more over the years—had agreed to make a few inquiries on Grace's behalf. "Those two are on the other side of the state, out of our jurisdiction. At the moment, they're missing." She paused, then asked suspiciously, "You haven't had any contact with them, have you?"

"I can't answer that," Grace said.

"Oh, baby, don't go getting involved in something like this," Shirley Lee had declared, correctly reading her avoidance of the question as assent. "I know you. You'll get your heart broken."

"Thanks for making the calls," Grace said, ignoring the well-intentioned advice from a very good friend, who also happened to be the best advocate she knew for troubled kids. "You're an angel."

"What I am is one worried mama," Shirley Lee retorted. "You know I look on you as one of my own flock. I don't want you getting yourself hurt. You're one of the last good guys."

That assessment was still ringing in her ears when she heard the squeals of delight from outside, then Michael's shouted warning and the softer, more patient voice of another man. Apparently the riding lesson had commenced. Because the last few hours had been so thoroughly frustrating, she couldn't resist the chance to peek outside and see Josh and Jamie engaged in something that obviously made them happy.

What she didn't expect to find was Michael sitting uncomfortably in a saddle, while two upturned faces regarded him with apparent glee. Josh caught sight of her first.

"Hey, Grace, Michael almost fell off the horse," he

shouted. "Me and Jamie didn't. Slade says we're real naturals, didn't you, Slade?"

A lanky cowboy turned toward her and tipped his hat. "Ma'am."

"Hi, I'm Grace Foster," she said.

"Slade Sutton. I work over at White Pines. Harlan Adams sent me over to see if I could turn these three into cowboys." He winked at the boys. "I'm doing right well with these two." He gave a nod in Michael's direction. "He's another story. Doesn't trust the horse."

"He's a business tycoon," Grace confided. "He doesn't trust anything."

Slade grinned. "Ah, that explains it. Think he'd do better with a pretty little filly?"

Grace stole a quick look at Michael and discovered he was taking the teasing in stride. "Oh, he'd like a filly, all right, but he still wouldn't trust her."

"Okay, you guys, that's enough." Michael swung his leg over the horse and dismounted, fairly smoothly in Grace's opinion. She had to wonder if some of his awkwardness hadn't been for Josh and Jamie's benefit, to give them a much needed sense of being better than an adult at something.

He stalked straight to Grace, put his hands on her waist and hoisted her into the saddle before she could catch her breath to protest. "How does it feel up there?" he inquired, regarding her with amusement.

Because she wasn't about to give him the satisfaction of begging to be rescued, she settled herself more securely in the saddle and gave the question some real thought. "Interesting," she said at last. "I like the vantage point. It's not often I get to look down on a couple of tall men."

"Teach her, too," the boys begged Slade.

The cowboy looked up at her. "You care for a little spin around the corral?"

"Why not?" she said gamely.

He led the horse around in a big circle until she got the feel of being in the saddle.

"Ready to try it on your own?"

"Sure." She listened carefully to his instructions, then followed them precisely. She was pleased—and more than a little relieved—when the horse obeyed her commands.

"Another natural," Slade commended her, helping her down at the end of the lesson.

"Can we ride again?" Jamie asked, regarding the horse with longing.

"Not today," Michael said. "We have to let Slade get back to his job."

"I'll be back around this time tomorrow," Slade promised.

The boys turned fearfully toward Grace, all of the animation drained out of their faces.

"Will we still be here?" Josh asked, a telltale quiver in his voice.

"You'll be here," Grace assured him. She and Michael had some serious decisions to make tonight, but in the meantime, the one thing she knew with absolute certainty was that Jamie and Josh weren't going anywhere. Not yet.

Unaware of the undercurrents, Slade merely nodded. "Then I'll see you tomorrow."

Michael walked with him toward his pickup, leaving Grace alone with the boys. Eyes shining again, Josh immediately started in with a blow-by-blow account of their riding lesson.

"It was so cool," he concluded. "It was the very best thing we ever got to do."

Grace smiled at his exuberance, but she couldn't help noticing that Jamie hadn't said a word. "Jamie, was it everything you expected it to be, too?"

He lifted his too-serious gaze to meet hers. "Nobody has ever done anything like this for us before. No matter what you guys do with us, we won't ever forget that you were real nice to us."

She thought she saw him blink back tears before he turned and ran off to the barn, Josh hard on his heels.

"Jamie, what's wrong?" Josh called out worriedly. "Jamie?"

Grace couldn't hear the boy's mumbled response, couldn't swear that she heard him fighting to choke back a sob, but she took a step after him just the same, then stopped herself. Jamie wouldn't welcome her sympathy. The only thing that would really matter to him was her ability to find some way to guarantee them a better future. How in heaven's name was she supposed to do that when an overburdened social services system was just waiting to swallow them up again?

Six

After a full day of sun and exercise, both Jamie and Josh were exhausted. To Michael's astonishment, right after an early dinner, they agreed without protest to go upstairs to take baths and go to bed.

They were almost out the kitchen door when Josh turned and ran back to enfold Grace in a hug. Clearly startled by the gesture, she stood totally still for an instant before allowing her hand to come to rest on the boy's head.

Michael watched the play of emotions on her face—surprise, sorrow, yearning—and wondered for the first time if he had dragged her into the middle of something that she wasn't emotionally equipped to handle. As usual, he'd selfishly thought only of his own desperation when he'd called her. He hadn't stopped for a second to consider what becoming involved with the boys might do to Grace.

Despite her tough demeanor as a lawyer, he knew better than anyone how tenderhearted Grace really was, how easily bruised her feelings could be. He also knew just how badly she had once wanted a family of her

own, how much she had envied him his large collection of relatives. When she had willingly sacrificed all
of that to cut him out of her life, he had finally realized
just how deeply he had hurt her.

Worried by the strain he thought he detected, he
watched her intently.

Finally, after some sort of internal struggle, she
forced a smile for Josh and said in her usual bright manner, "Off with you. Lights out in half an hour, okay?"

"Could you maybe come up and tuck us in?" Josh
asked hopefully.

"Aw, come on, Josh, we're not babies," Jamie protested. He had remained hovering in the doorway. From
his expression it was evident he longed to be where Josh
was, but it was just as clear he thought himself too old
for such an overt demonstration of affection.

Grace seemed to sense his longing, too. "You may
be too big for me to tuck you in, but I'll come up anyway," Grace promised, then grinned. "So be sure to
wash behind your ears, guys. I'll check."

Jamie's expression brightened at the teasing. He was
clearly relieved to have found a way to be included without giving up his adolescent dignity.

"You'll have to catch me first," he retorted.

"You'd be surprised how quick I am when I'm motivated," Grace warned him.

After the boys had gone, she leaned against the
counter and sighed. "Grace?" Michael asked. "You
okay?"

She frowned at the question. "Would you stop asking me that? I'm fine."

"Are you sure you're not in over your head? If you

are, it's my fault and we need to move ahead with this, get it over with."

"We're not going to rush it. My involvement is not your fault," she said, avoiding the thrust of his question. "I'm here of my own free will."

"You're here because I called."

"Michael, don't make a big deal out of it," she said with a trace of impatience. "I'm a lawyer. This is what I do."

"No. This is above and beyond what you normally do," he corrected. "You're living under the same roof with Jamie and Josh. You're seeing on a minute-by-minute basis how deeply they've been hurt in the past. You're seeing how badly they crave attention and love. It's tearing you apart, isn't it?"

"I'll survive," she insisted, her gaze daring him to contradict her or to prolong the discussion.

"I think we need to put a stop to it. Let someone else take over."

"Absolutely not," she said fiercely. Her gaze clashed with his. "If you do that, Michael, I will never forgive you."

Michael knew enough to let it go. It wouldn't help if he became any more a part of the problem than he already was.

"Okay, then. We'll leave things as they are for the time being. Are you ready to talk about what you found out today?" he asked instead.

"Not just yet," she said, her attention seemingly riveted on the dishes in the sink. "Why don't you go on out to the deck? I'll join you after I've finished here and said good-night to Jamie and Josh."

He nodded, sensing that she needed the time alone

to gather her composure. Because he couldn't think of any other way to help her, he gave her shoulder a light squeeze, took his glass of wine and went outside.

That didn't mean he could shake the vision of the strongest woman he knew looking as if she wanted desperately to cry. Worse, no matter what she said, he knew he was the one responsible for turning her heart inside out yet another time. What he didn't know was how to make any of it right...or precisely why he wanted to so badly.

Grace didn't know how to cope with being needed. Oh, sure, her clients needed her. They came to her during an emotional crisis in their lives, but what they needed was legal advice, an advocate in the courtroom, someone impartial who would stand up for them against injustice. They needed Grace Foster, Attorney-at-Law, not Grace Foster the woman.

Jamie and Josh were different. While Michael might have turned to her for her legal expertise, the boys needed something else. They needed someone to care about them, someone they could love and trust.

Josh, still an innocent at eight, was already turning to her for that. Jamie —older, wiser, less trusting—was more cautious. It was as if he recognized that she might like them, but that she was also in a position to turn their lives upside down again. She didn't know how to risk giving them what they needed without setting them up for another possible disappointment.

All she could do was play it by ear, one second at a time. She would not allow Michael to interfere in that. He'd brought her over here. He would just have to accept her decisions.

The boys had already fallen asleep by the time she finished the dishes and climbed the stairs. She leaned down and pressed a light kiss to Josh's cheek, then stood staring down at Jamie. His blond cowlick was standing up, but his face was more at peace than usual. Long lashes were smudges against his pale cheeks. She smiled at those dark lashes. He was going to be a heartbreaker one day soon. He would grow up, flesh out his lanky frame with muscle, and bestow that rare, dimpled smile of his on some girl who'd fall in love just at the sight of it. Grace had the feeling that whatever happened in the next few days would make all the difference in whether Jamie accepted that love or turned away.

"Sweet dreams," she whispered to him, brushing a gentle hand over his mussed hair.

As if he heard her, he mumbled something in his sleep, then shifted restlessly away from her touch. Grace sighed.

After casting one last look at the Miller brothers, she switched off the overhead light and left the room. Now she just had to go back downstairs and face Michael.

What was she going to say to him? After their earlier conversation how could she tell him that she had no intention of calling anyone, not tonight certainly and maybe not even tomorrow, although she knew the time had come to advise the authorities that Jamie and Josh Miller had been found? Michael would be appalled, not only by her lapse of ethics, but by what it said about her emotional involvement. He already suspected she was in too deep.

Desperate to avoid a conflict with him, she sorted through every alternative she could think of. Maybe she could legitimately buy the boys another day or two here with them through some fancy legal footwork, but after that there would be no choice, she finally concluded with a sigh.

Unless she and Michael could come up with another alternative, the boys would have to go back into the foster care system.

Realistically, they would probably be separated again, too. The thought of it broke her heart. She couldn't let that happen. She just couldn't.

In order to forestall the inevitable, she would just have to stretch the truth to suit her purposes. If Michael so much as suspected that it was only a matter of time before social services traced the boys' whereabouts, thanks to her inquiries, he would insist on meeting the issue head-on. It wasn't that he was heartless, just pragmatic. He would insist that a clean, quick break was the right thing for everyone.

Everyone except Josh and Jamie, she thought heatedly. They needed more time together. They deserved it. No matter what happened afterward, she could give them that.

Outside on the deck, there was a gentle spring breeze, scented with roses. Michael looked up when she walked outside.

"The boys asleep?"

"They were sound asleep before I even got upstairs," she said with a smile. "All the fresh air and riding obviously exhausted them. Thank you for arranging the lesson for them."

"It was nothing," he said.

"Not to them. It meant the world to them. They told me no one had ever done anything like that for them before. It's very sad, really. It would take so little to make them really happy."

"I've been thinking," Michael said. "For kids who've been bounced around the way they have, they haven't turned out too badly. Other than running away, I don't see any sign that they're bad kids. Jamie defies authority, but what kid his age doesn't, and he has more reason than most. Why can't the foster parents see that?"

"He may not be giving them a chance," Grace suggested. "He may be so focused on getting back to Josh that he does whatever he can to avoid getting attached. I've known foster kids who always kept their suitcases packed because they just assumed they would eventually get sent away again."

"It's no way for a kid to live," Michael said with surprising passion.

"No, it isn't."

He glanced over at her. "What did you find out today?"

She decided to stick as closely as she could to the truth, as long as she could do it without raising any red flags. "Nothing we didn't already know. They're regarded as problem kids."

"Is anyone looking for them?"

"The appropriate authorities were notified when they disappeared. The police are supposed to be looking out for them."

Michael shook his head. "I meant does anyone actually give a damn that they're missing?"

The vehemence of his question startled her. He sounded angry on Josh and Jamie's behalf. Because he did, she answered candidly. "No. Not the way you mean. The foster parents are more frustrated than worried. I'm sure there are social services people who are good-hearted and who might be worried, but their case-loads are piled high. Jamie and Josh are just two more kids vying for attention on their radar. Runaways are a tragic fact of life."

"Damn," Michael muttered. "So, what do we do next? Call up and relieve their minds, tell them that the boys are safe?"

"If we do, they'll insist on picking them up," Grace warned.

"And if we don't?"

"The boys will have a little more time together." She regarded Michael anxiously. "Would that be so terrible?"

He sighed heavily. "Grace, I can see a thousand and one pitfalls to what you're suggesting."

"So can I," she conceded. "I'm not blind, Michael, or stupid. I'm aware of the risks."

"But you want to take them anyway," he said.

"A few days," she said again. "It seems like the least we can do. You're here. I'm here. We're both respon-sible. If anyone goes crazy, we have the clout to make them see that this was just a gift we were giving Jamie and Josh. What possible harm can come of it?"

Michael shook his head, regarding her worriedly. "It's a gift that could seriously backfire on all of us. You could lose your license to practice law, couldn't you? You're interfering in a court-ordered process. Even with the best motives in the world, keeping them here is wrong."

"I'm willing to chance it," she said defiantly. "If you're worried about your reputation, I'll take the boys and we'll leave here."

He scowled at her. "Don't be ridiculous. I'm not wor-ried about myself. I'm concerned about you and I'm concerned about Josh and Jamie. They're already attached to you. What will happen after a few more days?"

She felt his gaze searching hers.

"And how will you feel when you have to stand by and watch them go?" he asked quietly.

Grace swallowed hard. "It will tear me apart," she said honestly. "But it would tear me apart now. A few more days won't make that much difference. Besides, in the meantime maybe we'll come up with a better solution."

Michael's brow was still knit with concern. "I don't know."

"I'm not asking, Michael," she said finally. "I'm telling you that this is how it's going to be. The only question is whether we stay here with you or I take them back to Houston."

He seemed taken aback by her defiant tone, but then a grin spread slowly across his face. "Stay here, by all means. When the trouble hits the fan, you're going to need somebody to stand up and fight for you."

"And you'll do that?" she asked skeptically.

"Of course."

"Why, Michael? You could be rid of all of us, wash your hands of this little inconvenience. That's what you intended when you first called me."

"Maybe so," he agreed. "But those kids have grown on me, too. Besides, you're here now, back to being a thorn in my side again. I guess a part of me missed that more than I'd realized."

The admission, even phrased as it was, sent a shiver through her. She'd missed it, too. No one had ever challenged her mentally the way Michael did. No one made her feel as much like a woman as he did. She drew in a deep breath and reminded herself that feeling that way was a luxury she couldn't afford right now, not with the fate of Jamie and Josh at stake.

"It isn't personal," she reminded him, wanting to make that very clear.

"Of course not."

"I mean it, Michael."

"If you'd come over here, I'll bet I could prove otherwise," he taunted.

Because she knew he was right, she stayed right where she was. "Not in a million years," she declared.

"Chicken."

"Prudent," she countered.

He laughed. "That's okay. I've just bought myself a little more time to see if I can persuade you to change your mind. I've always loved a challenge, Grace. Surely you remember that."

She did. That, and so much more that it scared the living daylights out of her. For reasons she didn't care to explore too closely, she still couldn't help being glad that he wasn't sending them on their way.

By morning Grace still felt as if she and the boys had been granted a reprieve, even if it had come from Michael and not the proper authorities. As she listened to Josh and Jamie's excited chatter about their next riding lesson and their plans to explore the rest of the ranch— and to Michael chiming in with an offer to accompany them—she felt an amazing sense of peace steal over her. There was something so right about this, something that felt good deep inside.

"Well, while you all are out having your male adventure, I have a few plans of my own," she announced.

Three pairs of eyes turned to her. Michael's and Josh's were alight with curiosity. Jamie's were wary.

"Like what?" he asked.

She winked at him, hoping to wipe that worried look off of his face. "It's a surprise."

"No way," he protested, sounding almost panicky. "You gotta tell."

"Then it wouldn't be a surprise," she said. "It's a good surprise, Jamie. I promise. Now, go on. Get ready to go exploring. I'll even pack you all a picnic lunch."

Jamie cast one last worried look in her direction before eventually following Josh upstairs. That left Michael watching her intently.

"What do you have up your sleeve?"

"You'll see."

"You don't intend to tell me, either?"

"You might blab."

"I am the very soul of discretion, I'll have you know. Nothing gets past my lips, unless I want it to."

"Once two people know a secret, it's not a secret anymore," she insisted.

"I take it you think I'll approve."

"I know you will." She hesitated, then admitted, "There is one thing that concerns me, though."

"What's that?"

"I'll have to go into town to pull this off."

"Not a problem. You have the rental car."

"Easy for you to say," she muttered, then reminded him, "I have no idea where town is."

He chuckled then. "And even if you did, there's no guarantee you'd know how to find it."

"Very amusing. Can you just draw me a map? I'm very good if I have a precise map."

"I thought my pilot gave you a map the other night."

She waved off the reminder. "He gave me directions. That's not the same at all."

"Maybe we should all go into town."

"Oh, no, you don't. That would ruin everything. Just draw me a map."

Michael uttered a resigned sigh, grabbed a piece of paper and drew her a very detailed map, then went over it with her as carefully as if a wrong turn might lead her into a minefield.

"Got it?" he asked.

"That should get me there," she agreed.

"Maybe you should scatter breadcrumbs behind you, so you can find your way back."

"Not a problem," she assured him, waving the piece of paper. "I just reverse these."

"How long should I wait before I send out a search party?" he teased.

"If I'm not back by dinnertime, forget the search party. Just give me a call in Houston. I could decide that you're more trouble than you're worth and high-tail it out of here."

"Not a chance. You might abandon me, but you wouldn't desert Josh and Jamie."

Unfortunately, he had that pegged exactly right. Rather than admit it, she grabbed her purse and car keys off the counter and headed for the door.

"I'll see you later."

"You sound so sure of that," he noted with amusement. "Must be my outstanding directions. They've given you confidence."

She waved them at him. "They'd better be foolproof," she warned him.

"Oh, they are, darlin'. I want you back here too much to take any chances."

There was a heartfelt note in his voice that she was pretty sure didn't have anything to do with wanting her here for Josh and Jamie's sakes. It left her feeling warm all over in a way that was definitely dangerous. Michael was right about the pitfalls of these stolen days extending to the two of them.

She pushed that troublesome worry out of her head to concentrate on Michael's very precise directions. She was determined not to get herself lost.

When she finally pulled into a parking place in front of Dolan's, she uttered a fervent sigh of relief. Noticing that the drugstore had a lunch counter, she decided to treat herself to a soda while she asked advice about stores and planned out her shopping.

At midmorning, the counter was deserted. The woman behind it was trying to soothe a cranky toddler, who was clearly unhappy about being restricted to a playpen. When she turned to greet Grace, the child let out a wail.

"It's not a good day," the woman said, plucking the toddler up and settling her in her arms. "I don't understand it. This is my third. The first two loved being here all day long, getting showered with attention. This one isn't happy unless she's running up and down the aisles pulling all the stock off the shelves."

"I guess all kids are different," Grace said. "You just have to adapt."

"Or go crazy," the woman agreed. "I'm Sharon Lynn, by the way. Are you new in town?"

"Actually, I'm visiting." She considered how to explain the exact circumstances. "I'm staying with someone who came here to visit his sister."

Sharon Lynn's expression brightened. "Ah, Trish's brother, I'll bet. I'd heard they were trying to get him away from his office."

"You know Trish?"

"Sure. Her bookstore's right next door. Of course, it's closed this week because she and Hardy went out of town to give Michael the peace and quiet they thought he needed." She chuckled as if she were in on the joke. "How's he taking it?"

"Probably a lot better than they imagined when they took off on him, but I don't think it's quite as peaceful or quiet as anyone expected."

Sharon Lynn chuckled. "No, I imagine you being here definitely changed the game plan. They didn't mention he'd be bringing a friend."

"Oh, I'm not a friend," Grace protested hurriedly. "Not the way you mean. I came on a mission of mercy." Though she had warmed to Sharon Lynn immediately, she hesitated to say more. The fewer people who knew the whole story about the boys, the better.

"Sounds fascinating. Tell me what I can get for you and you can tell me all about it."

"Just a soda," Grace said. "And I've probably already said too much. You can help me with something, though. I need to do a little shopping for groceries and for a few birthday presents. Can you steer me in the right direction?"

"You're on Main Street. This is our shopping district, so you can't very well get lost."

"That's a relief," Grace murmured.

"What?"

"I'm not so hot with directions. Some consider it a character flaw."

"I say you're either born with a sense of direction or you're not. Blame it on genetics," Sharon Lynn advised. "What sort of gifts are you looking for?"

"For a boy who just turned eight. I'm not even sure what a kid that age is interested in. This one loves horses, but beyond that, I don't know."

"Then he's not yours," Sharon Lynn concluded. "A nephew?"

"No."

Sharon Lynn's penetrating gaze studied her. "And that's all you intend to say, isn't it?"

"Pretty much. Sorry."

"Don't worry about it. If you're around here long, you'll discover that the Adamses are notoriously nosy. You'll also learn when to tell us to take a hike."

"Ah, the Adamses," she repeated slowly. "And you're Sharon Lynn. I should have put two and two together. I've heard of you."

"Through Trish's brother?"

"Actually no, I read about your custody case when I was researching family law."

The case had fascinated her even then, an intriguing story of a baby left on the doorstep of this very store and Sharon Lynn's fight to keep her. How much of that case might prove to be relevant to the situation in which she and Michael had found themselves? And wasn't it her step-grandmother, the legendary Janet Runningbear Adams, who had fought the case and won?

"You're a lawyer?" Sharon Lynn asked, regarding her with surprise.

Grace nodded. "In Houston."

"And that's how you know Michael?"

Grace laughed. "You're good, you know that? Another few minutes, you'd have my entire life history. It's a darn good thing I have to get this shopping done."

"It won't take long. It's not a big town. Stop back for lunch."

"I'll think about it. If I don't get back by, it was very nice meeting you, Sharon Lynn."

"You, too. I hope I'll see you again while you're here."

Grace slipped out of the drugstore before Sharon Lynn could do any more of her innocent prying. She paused outside Trish's bookstore and peered in the window. She could see the same cozy atmosphere in there that Trish had created in her home.

Across the street she found the baking supplies she needed at the general store, then moved on to the other shops looking for inspiration. When she found the cowboy boots, she knew she'd hit pay dirt. She had to guess at Josh's size, but the proprietor assured her she could bring them back if they didn't fit. She added some more western attire, including a pint-sized Stetson, had it all boxed up and put it in the back of her car.

By then it was lunchtime, so she decided to take Sharon Lynn up on her invitation, but she couldn't help being relieved that it was too busy for another interrogation. She bought wrapping paper and balloons before leaving the drugstore, then headed back to the ranch.

She actually made the trip without mishap, not even a single wrong turn. She was back at the house before the guys returned from their adventure, though she beat them by only a few minutes. They came in bursting with excitement, Josh's words tumbling over each other as he told her about their morning. Jamie's exuberance was more restrained, but his expression was equally happy. And both of them kept turning to Michael for approval. Obviously he was rapidly becoming the male role model they both desperately needed.

Michael met her gaze over the boys' heads. "Home safe and sound, I see."

"I told you I would be."

He glanced around the kitchen. "Where's the surprise?"

He sounded almost as disappointed as a kid at not seeing any evidence of it.

"Be patient. It's not ready yet. When's Slade coming by?"

"Any minute now."

As if on cue, Josh shouted, "I think I hear the truck." He darted out the door, followed by Jamie at a more sedate, determinedly unconcerned pace. Michael stepped closer to Grace and before she guessed his intentions, he bent down to give her a quick kiss. "Just so you know I'm glad to see you," he explained.

"You're just relieved those directions of yours panned out," she said.

"That, too," he said with a wink as he went outside to join the boys.

Grace laughed, suddenly feeling lighthearted. Then she turned to the serious task of baking a birthday cake for Josh. When she did it, baking ranked right up there with driving in its potential for disaster. But she'd put so much T.L.C. into this cake, it was bound to be a winner.

Seven

Michael couldn't imagine what Grace had been up to, but the light shining in her eyes was long overdue. She looked happy, though he couldn't help wondering how much longer that would last.

He stood at the rail of the corral, one booted foot propped on the bottom rung and watched as Slade gave Josh and Jamie their lesson. Slade wasn't exactly talkative, but he knew horses. Both boys hung on every word the man said. They eagerly followed every instruction, right down to cleaning the tack and rubbing down the horses after their lesson. It seemed they were learning about responsibility right along with riding, soaking up not only the information, but the masculine attention. It reminded Michael just how badly they needed a male role model in their lives.

"Same time tomorrow?" Slade asked, joining him as the boys walked the horses.

"If you have the time," Michael said. "You can't begin to know what this means to those two."

"I think maybe I do," Slade said. "I get the sense they haven't had a lot."

"No."

"How'd they wind up here, if you don't mind me asking?"

"Long story," Michael said.

"Runaways," Slade guessed. He slanted a look at Michael. "I'm surprised you haven't turned 'em in. A lot of folks wouldn't have considered them their responsibility."

"Here in Los Piños?" Michael said skeptically. "I was under the impression that Harlan Adams set a tough example when it comes to being your brother's keeper around these parts."

"He does, now that you mention it. If he knew about Jamie and Josh, he'd see to it that something was done to help them, no doubt about it. You didn't tell him the whole story when you called over there looking for a riding instructor, did you?"

"No. I thought it best to be circumspect till we had more facts."

"Do you have them now?"

"Not really. Grace is still looking into some things."

"You need any help, White Pines is crawling with good-hearted people who love to meddle. Wouldn't hurt to have Justin Adams on your side. He's the sheriff. And, like I said, Harlan is a man you can always count on to sort out something that's gotten complicated. His wife knows the ins and outs of the law as well as anyone I've ever seen."

"Thanks. I'll keep that in mind."

Slade slanted a look his way. "I could bring my daughter Annie along tomorrow, if you like. She's a little older than Josh. I think they'd get along okay. And she knows all the other kids around here. She'd be happy to take these two under her wing and introduce them around. She knows what it's like to be an outsider. She had a rough patch when she first came to live with me, but she's adapted real well now."

Michael shook his head at that. "Until Grace and I come up with a plan, the fewer people who know about Josh and Jamie the better. Bring Annie, by all means, but let's keep it at that for the time being."

Slade nodded. "See you tomorrow, then." He touched a finger to his Stetson, then left for one last word with Jamie and Josh before taking off.

"What were you and Mr. Sutton talking about?" Jamie asked when they finally returned from the barn after putting out feed for the horses.

"How well you're doing," Michael told him.

"He really said we were doing good?" Josh asked excitedly. "Did you know he was a rodeo champion before his leg got busted up? If he says we're good, that's, like, the best."

"Well, that's what he said. And I've noticed how responsible you're being about taking care of the horses. I'm proud of you both."

"A cowboy's supposed to treat his horse right," Jamie retorted.

He said it as if it were a simple matter of doing what was expected, as if their behavior were nothing special. But despite his words, it seemed to Michael that he stood a little taller because of the praise. He had to wonder how often anyone had bothered to tell the boy what he was doing right, rather than all the things he was doing wrong.

"Can we go inside and tell Grace about the lesson?" Josh pleaded.

Michael nodded, amazed to discover that he was almost as anxious as the boys to share the excitement with Grace. Once he had wanted to share everything with her, but long conversations about anything and everything had soon fallen by the wayside, lost to the demands of his position at Delacourt Oil and her studies in law school across the state.

"Let's go," he said. "But you'd better let me peek in the door first so we make sure we're not spoiling the big surprise."

"Yeah, that's right," Josh said. "She promised us something real special."

"Don't go getting all worked up," Jamie cautioned him. "It's probably just pot roast or something."

"But I love pot roast," Josh said.

"Yeah, but it's not a real surprise," Jamie countered. "It's just dinner."

Michael stayed out of the squabble, but he had a hunch the surprise was more than a good meal. Grace had been too excited.

"Stay right here on the back deck," Michael instructed the two of them. "I'll let you know if it's okay to come inside."

As soon as he was certain they would stay put, he slipped into the house. He was struck at once by the aromas drifting from the direction of the kitchen, most of them enticing, though he thought he also detected something that might have been burnt sugar. Given that and the muttered cursing, he approached cautiously.

"Everything okay in here?" he inquired, drawing a startled look from the woman bent over in front of the oven. Her cheeks were streaked with flour and flushed from the heat, wisps of hair had curled against her forehead and her eyes flashed with indignation at whatever it was she'd been staring at in the oven. He thought she had never looked more beautiful.

"Everything except this blasted cake," she retorted. "It's lopsided." She withdrew the pan to show him. "Would you tell me why a woman who has mastered any number of skills cannot bake a simple chocolate cake?"

To be sure one side of the cake sank to no more than a half-inch, while the other side rose to a full, plump two inches.

"Is this cake going to be one layer or two?" he asked.

"Two, why?"

"Because you can fill in that crater with icing and no one will be the wiser. In fact, knowing how kids like icing, it'll probably be a huge hit."

Her expression immediately brightened. "You're a genius," she declared, giving him a smacking kiss on her way past. "Where are the boys?"

Michael barely resisted the desire to snag her by the apron strings and draw her back for a more leisurely exploration of her mouth. Instead, he said, "They're on the deck, chomping at the bit to get in here to see the surprise."

"Oh, dear, not yet," she protested at once. "I want everything to be perfect." She frowned at the cake. "Well, close to perfect, anyway. Send them upstairs for showers, but don't let them near the dining room."

"Yes, ma'am," Michael agreed. "On one condition?"

"What's that?" she asked, eyeing him warily.

"That I get to steal a kiss from the cook."

"I just kissed you," she pointed out.

He grinned. "Which makes it my turn. Do we have a deal?"

"Michael…"

The protest died as his mouth covered hers. She tasted of sugar and chocolate and smelled of roses. After a fleeting instant of resistance she melted against him, her body fitting itself to his as instinctively as it once had. Breasts, thighs, heat—they were all as familiar to him as the sigh of her breath against his cheek. He held her loosely, but she didn't even try to get away.

"I never said yes," she whispered.

"That's why they call it stealing," he reminded her. "Something tells me I could get into the habit of doing this again."

"Stealing?" she teased. "I suppose in this instance, I'd have to come to your defense. You're very good at it, Michael."

"I'll get better with practice." She murmured something at that. "What?"

"I said if you get any better, we'll have more trouble around here than having two runaways on our hands."

He regarded her with delight. "Sounds promising."

"Just go get the boys," she said. "I have work to do. I need an hour, okay?"

"Do you also need help?"

She regarded him with surprise. "From you?"

"Who else?"

"Since when do you help in the kitchen doing women's work?" she inquired tartly.

He winced at the too-accurate description of the way he'd been a few years ago, leaving everything connected to running their household to her. Fending for himself in recent years had changed all that. If he didn't cook these days, he didn't eat. Not at home, anyway.

"You'd be surprised at the things I've learned to do since you dumped me."

The claim seemed to fascinate her. "Then by all means join me back here and demonstrate," she said.

"Some of them will have to wait till we're alone in the house," he taunted, thoroughly enjoying the quick rise of color in her cheeks.

"I'll…" Her voice trailed off before she could complete the thought.

"You'll what?" he asked. "Look forward to it? Is that what you were about to say, Grace?"

"No, absolutely not," she denied unconvincingly. "I was about to say I'll be frosting this cake. The first batch of caramel sort of burned in the pan, but I think the second batch looks pretty good."

He peered at the gooey, golden concoction. "If you say so."

"I do."

He gave her one last, skeptical look, then went off to shoo Jamie and Josh upstairs.

"Why can't we see what's going on?" Josh asked.

"Because Grace said so," Jamie told him. "It's a surprise, remember?"

"You're the one who said it probably wasn't a real surprise," Josh countered.

"Doesn't matter if it is or it isn't, we gotta do what Grace says. Now hurry up, and don't use all the hot water, either."

"It's not me," Josh protested. "You're the one who uses it all up."

Michael stood at the foot of the stairs listening to the bickering until it finally faded away. Once he'd expected to have sons of his own, expected to fill a house with laughter and sibling controversy, just like this. How had he lost sight of that part of his dream? Had it gone with the departure of Grace from his life, or even before, when he'd buried himself in work at Delacourt Oil just to prove himself?

Did it really matter when or how it had slipped away? he asked himself.

Maybe what really mattered was whether it was too late to get it back…

Eight

Grace took one last look around the dining room and gave a satisfied sigh. Balloons floated everywhere. The table had been set with Trish's best china and the gaily wrapped presents had been piled high at Josh's place.

"It looks terrific, darlin'," Michael said, coming up behind her to rest his hands on her shoulders. "Every little boy's dream birthday party."

"Do you think he'll mind that it's late?"

"No, something tells me that Josh will be over the moon that you thought to do it for him."

"I wonder how many birthday parties he's ever really had," Grace said, feeling sad for him. Her mom had always struggled to make birthdays special, especiallly when they hadn't had much money to spend or when she hadn't had energy for anything else.

"My guess is not a lot," Michael replied. "Not if that was when Jamie always came for him."

"Will all this fuss over Josh bother Jamie?" she asked worriedly. "We don't even know when his birthday is."

"We'll find out and do something special for him, too," Michael reassured her.

"What if it's months from now?"

"We'll do it whenever it is," Michael insisted. "Wherever he is."

Grace sighed. "I hate to think of him being anywhere but here."

"I know. So do I. But let's be realistic. This isn't even our home. No matter what happens, he won't be here. Neither will we."

"But he's been so happy here the last couple of days. They both have."

"Then we'll look into finding them a home close by," Michael said.

He spoke so confidently as if it were as simple as choosing a place and having the kids move in. Maybe the matter-of-fact tone came from controlling a business empire. He was probably too used to people falling in with his plans. This time it might not be that simple, Grace thought.

"How?" Grace asked. "It's not like placing a puppy."

When he realized she wasn't going to be pacified by glib answers, he paused, his expression thoughtful. "Maybe Dylan's wife can help," he said eventually. "She's a pediatrician. She may know people who would be willing to take in a couple of boys. Let's not talk about this tonight, though. Let's just have a party. I'll go call the boys, okay?"

Grace took one last survey, then nodded. "Go get them."

She waited with her heart in her throat until the two boys thundered down the stairs, then skidded to a stop in the entrance to the dining room.

"Oh, wow," Josh whispered, his gaze locked on the stack of presents. "Is this for me?"

Grace nodded. "I know it's a few days late, but I wanted you to have a celebration," she said.

"This is so cool." Josh raced across the room and threw his arms around her, all but knocking the breath out of her.

"I wish you were my mom," he whispered tearfully.

Grace felt her heart crack in two. "I wish I were, too," she whispered, her gaze seeking Michael's. "I wish I were, too."

She blinked back tears, then glanced toward Jamie, who was standing perfectly still, his expression shuttered.

"Jamie?"

He met her gaze. "What?"

"When is your birthday? Michael and I have already been talking about what we'll do then."

The disbelief in Jamie's eyes shifted slowly to hope. "You guys really talked about that?"

"Yes."

He shrugged. "We probably won't be around then. It's not till fall. September fifth. Sometimes I end up having to go back to school on my birthday. That really sucks."

Grace gave him a commiserating look. "I know. My birthday is September seventh."

"Looks like we'll be having a joint celebration this fall," Michael said, meeting Jamie's gaze evenly. "Sound okay to you?"

"Sure. I guess," Jamie said, clearly struggling still not to get his hopes up.

Michael nodded. "That's good then. Now how about sitting down before all this food gets cold?"

"When do I get to open my presents?" Josh asked.

"After we eat," Michael said firmly.

Grace shook her head. "No way. You can open them whenever you want to. It's your party."

Josh looked from her to Michael and back again, clearly wanting to please both of them. "I say I open one now and the rest after we eat."

"Good compromise," Michael praised. "You'll be a terrific businessman someday."

"Like you?" Josh asked.

"Probably better than him," Grace teased. "Michael's lousy at compromise."

"But I'm learning," he declared, winking at her. "I just need the proper incentive."

Clearly impatient, Josh interrupted them. "Can I open one now? Any one I want?"

"Yep," Grace said, then leaned closer. "But if I were you I'd pick that one." She pointed to the biggest box.

Josh grabbed it eagerly and began stripping away the paper. He tugged open the top without even glancing at the markings on the box, then stared, openmouthed, when he saw what was inside.

"What is it?" Jamie demanded. "You look like it's a snake or something."

"It's boots," Josh said, sounding awestruck. "Real cowboy boots."

"No way." Jamie stood up to peer over his shoulder. "I'll bet they're going to be too big."

"Are not," Josh said, taking one out of the box and holding it up next to his sneaker-clad foot.

Grace saw then that she had guessed wrong. The boot was definitely too big, but Josh was clearly undaunted. He kicked off his shoes and pulled the boots on.

"They're perfect," he declared. "See?" He clomped around the room.

"I think Jamie might be right," Michael said. "A cowboy doesn't want a boot that's not a perfect fit."

"But I love these," Josh said, near tears.

"We'll exchange them first thing tomorrow," Grace said, then glanced at Jamie who was eyeing the boots with longing. "I don't suppose these would fit you, would they, Jamie?"

Josh looked horrified. "He can't have my boots."

"If we're taking them back anyway, what difference does it make?" Grace asked reasonably. "You'll get new ones that are the perfect size for you tomorrow."

"Promise?" Josh asked.

"Of course, but you have to let him try them on so we know whether to trade these back in or just get you your own pair," Grace said.

"Can't I wear them for a little while?" Josh pleaded.

"No," Grace said firmly. "If we have to take them back, they can't be worn out."

Looking crestfallen, Josh sat back down and tugged off the boots, tossing them angrily at his big brother. Jamie threw them right back. "I don't want your old boots."

Grace saw the entire celebration falling apart. "That's enough," she said sternly. "No more presents till after we've eaten and if you two don't apologize to each other right now, there won't be any then either."

"It's just that I never had something that wasn't a hand-me-down before," Josh said to her.

Grace fought the sting of tears to remain firm. "That still doesn't mean you get to take out your disappointment on your brother. It's not his fault the boots might fit him instead of you. I'm the one who picked them out and bought the wrong size. Are you going to yell at me?"

Josh looked shocked by the suggestion. "Never."

"Okay, then, how about telling Jamie you're sorry?"

"I'm sorry," he said at once. "I hope they fit you."

Jamie shrugged. "I'm sorry, too."

Grace beamed at them. "That's better."

"Now can we eat?" Michael pleaded, breaking the tension. "I don't know about you guys, but I'm starving."

Grace sat back and watched as all three of them fell on the meal as if it were the best one they'd ever tasted. Heartfelt praise was uttered between mouthfuls.

"You guys are making me blush," she said eventually, but she couldn't help being pleased that the dinner was a bigger hit than the ill-fitting boots.

As soon as they'd eaten every last bite of pot roast, warm rolls and savory vegetables, she stood up and cleared the table. Jamie and Josh jumped up without being asked to help her take the dishes into the kitchen. Even Michael pitched in to get everything rinsed and into the dishwasher.

"Okay, everybody back to their places," she instructed. "I'll bring in the dessert."

Once they were gone, she stood for a moment alone, eyes closed as she savored the sensations that had washed through her over the last hour. She had felt as if she were finally, at long last, part of a real family. It didn't seem to matter that it was an illusion that could be shattered at any time.

For now, all that counted was the fact that she was with a man she had once loved more than life itself and with two little boys who desperately needed a mother and father to love them. She would do anything necessary to spin out this perfect time for as long as possible…for all their sakes.

The cake, with its eight flickering candles and thick caramel frosting, was a huge hit. So were the rest of the presents Grace had brought back from town.

While Grace watched Josh's reaction, Michael kept his gaze focused on her. There was so much love shining in her eyes that it worried him. As if he could read her mind, he knew that she was starting to make plans for these two boys, thinking ahead to a future that was more than likely built on quicksand. She needed a harsh reality check, but he didn't want to be the one to give it to her. How could he, when he was the one who'd dragged her into this? And yet he knew he had no choice.

Later, when she had tucked the boys into bed—not even Jamie had protested that tonight—Michael was waiting for her in the living room with every light blazing. He'd resisted the temptation to spend the rest of the evening on the deck, under the stars. There were too many possible distractions in such a romantic setting. His body was sending too many demanding messages every time he and Grace were alone.

Here, with bright lights to chase away the shadows, they could engage in some straight talk, make realistic, practical plans. In this lighting, maybe he wouldn't get lost in the fantasy himself.

He spent the time while she was gone ticking off all of the rational reasons for putting an end to this situation here and now, not the least of which was the legal tightrope they were walking.

But when Grace walked into the room, looking sad and vulnerable—desirable—every rational thought in his head fled. He realized with stunned amazement that he wanted her, not just for tonight, but for all time. He knew with absolute certainty that he couldn't let her get away again, that if he did he would regret it for the rest of his days.

Unfortunately, he also knew she wasn't ready to hear such a declaration. She wouldn't trust it any more now than she had six years ago. Actions, not words, were the only way to convince her that he was ready to bring some balance in his life. Wouldn't Tyler find it a hoot that in sending his big brother here to get away from it all, to gain a little perspective in his life, he had actually accomplished his goal in a thoroughly unexpected way?

Of course, there was one little problem. He could hardly start out proving his love to Grace by telling her that she had to turn her back on those two boys. Once those words were out of his mouth, she was going to hate him.

He felt her gaze settle on him, saw worry pucker her brow. "Michael, is something wrong?"

"Of course not," he lied. "Why?"

"You look so sad. I don't think I've ever seen you look like that before."

"Not sad, just concerned," he said, broaching the unavoidable topic of Jamie and Josh cautiously, hoping to minimize the damage to their future.

"About?"

"Your attachment to Jamie and Josh."

"I just threw a little party," she insisted staunchly. "What's the big deal?"

"We both know the answer to that," he chided.

"Grace, my bringing you here was a mistake. You're a professional. It never occurred to me that you would get this emotionally involved. It should have, but it didn't."

She regarded him with obvious impatience. "We've been all through that. I'm here now. I'm right in the thick of this."

"But at what cost?"

"Dammit, Michael, I'm a big girl. You worry about your heart and I'll worry about mine."

He regarded her with regret. "If only it were that easy."

"It's as easy as you let it be."

"No, Grace, it's not. I've already been responsible for one heartbreak in your life. I won't be responsible for another." He drew in a deep breath. "We can't put it off any longer. We have to deal with this tomorrow."

She stared at him with what could only be interpreted as panic in her eyes. "Deal with it how?"

"Call the authorities. Let them know Jamie and Josh are safe."

She was on her feet at once. "No. They'll take them away," she said, voicing what was clearly her greatest fear.

"They might," he agreed.

"I won't let you do it, Michael." Tears streaked down her cheeks. "I can't. It's wrong. You know it's wrong."

"I don't know that. Neither do you. If anything, you know the law better than I do. You have to see that we can't postpone this. We're heading for disaster as it is."

For a moment she looked as if she might argue some more, but then a shudder shook her body, even as the tears continued to track silently down her cheeks. He'd seen her like this only one other time, the day she had told him that she didn't want to see him ever again.

Since then, she had never let him see any sign of weakness. If anything, she was tough as nails whenever she had to confront him.

He swore under his breath, cursing himself for calling her in the first place, for not finding some other way to deal with the two runaways now sleeping upstairs.

"Dammit, Grace, don't do this," he pleaded.

"Do what?" she asked without meeting his gaze.

"Make me feel like a jerk."

"As if I could," she shot back, showing a little more spirit.

But even then the tears didn't let up. Michael went to her then and pulled her into his arms, let her tears soak his shirt. She didn't resist. In fact, she probably took perverse pleasure in ruining the pristine condition of his silk-blend shirt. She could ruin a hundred of them, as far as he was concerned, if only she would forgive him for what he was insisting they do.

Oh, he knew that in the end she would come around, do what had to be done, because she was too wise not to see that it was the only way. In the meantime, though, he could hold her close, maybe let her see by his actions that even after Jamie and Josh were gone, he would still be here for her.

Sadly, though, he suspected that after this, she might not consider him a fit substitute, might not want him at all.

Grace was too numb after Michael's announcement to even try to break away from his attempt to console her. Eventually, though, she retreated upstairs, angrily tugged on her nightgown, tried to settle in bed, then gave up in frustration as she thought of all the arguments she should have flung at him.

What was wrong with her? She didn't fall apart in a crisis. She got tougher, especially if Michael Delacourt was involved. She had vowed six years ago that he would never see her cry again. Now here she was blubbering, instead of doing what she did best, instead of fighting tooth and nail for what she believed.

And what she believed with all her heart was that Jamie and Josh deserved a better shot than they'd been given. Instead of coming unglued, she should have been making calls, rallying allies who could make that happen for them.

She paced her room for a while, debating alternatives to Michael's plan to call in the authorities, but nothing she came up with made a lick of sense. In the end, bottom line, the authorities would have to be notified. Did it really matter if it was tomorrow or the next day? Once they were on the scene, the real work of fighting for Josh and Jamie would begin. Maybe it was better if it began sooner, rather than later. She always focused better once the fight had begun.

That acceptance of the inevitable didn't mean she wasn't sorely tempted to steal down the hall, wake the boys and spirit them away from the house while Michael was sleeping. Only the knowledge that he would probably catch them in the act kept her from trying it.

She was determined about one thing, though. No call would be made until after she and Michael had made good on their promise to take Josh into town for new boots. There were no guarantees for the future, but she refused to renege on that particular promise. Something told her there would be enough broken promises to come after that.

Bracing herself to fight Michael over her decision, if need be, she was in the kitchen at dawn making waffles. When the boys came downstairs, they were subdued, as if they sensed that something had happened.

"You okay?" Jamie asked, studying her. "You look kinda funny, like you been crying or something."

"I'm fine," Grace reassured him.

Jamie didn't look convinced. "If Michael's made you cry, Josh and me will beat him up for you," he said gamely.

Grace bit back a smile. "I don't think that will be necessary."

"Are you guys, like, dating or something?" Josh asked.

"We did a long time ago," Grace said. "Now we're just friends." Even as she said it, she realized it was true. Despite all the pain, Michael was her friend. His decision had been made the night before not to be cruel to Jamie and Josh, but, as he saw it, to protect her.

"Oh," Josh said, clearly disappointed.

He and Jamie exchanged a look she couldn't interpret.

"Me and Josh have been talking. We were kinda hoping it was more than that," Jamie explained.

"Oh? Why?" Grace asked, though she thought she knew.

"'Cause if you were gonna get married, then maybe you could be our new foster parents," Jamie said, then sighed. "I guess that won't work, though, will it?"

Now there was a solution she hadn't considered. She could just imagine Michael's reaction to such a suggestion. Once he stopped laughing, the answer would be a resounding no. He didn't have time to fit a wife into his life, much less two boys.

"No," Grace said. "I'm sorry."

"Couldn't you be our foster mom, though?" Josh asked hopefully.

The very same idea had occurred to her more than once in the past forty-eight hours, but Grace had dismissed it as illogical and impractical. A pipe dream.

But was it? She was as qualified as anyone. She had the financial resources. She already cared deeply for the two of them.

She sighed. She also had a one-bedroom apartment and a demanding law career. How could she possibly bring two young boys into her life and give them the time and attention they needed? And it wasn't as if she could walk into the courthouse, make the offer and walk out with them. There were background checks and mounds of paperwork involved.

As her mental debate raged on, the boys watched her intently, clearly sensing that she was actually struggling with their suggestion.

"So, what do you think?" Jamie finally dared to ask.

"I don't know," she said honestly. "This is a very complicated situation." Probably more so, precisely because she had kept them here, rather than turning them in immediately. The court would probably view that as blatant evidence that she had no regard at all for the regulations governing foster care.

"We'd be really good," Josh promised.

"Yeah, we wouldn't give you any problems. No more running away or nothing," Jamie vowed. "And we can help around the house and stuff, do a lot of chores like taking out the trash."

"I'm sure you'd be a wonderful help, but I just don't know. There are a lot of things to consider before making a commitment like that."

"It's because there are two of us, isn't it?" Jamie said, sounding defeated. "If that's it, take Josh. I'll go someplace else."

"Absolutely not," Grace said at once. "You're not going to be separated again. I'm going to see to that, no matter what." She gave Jamie's shoulder a squeeze. "Let me give this some more thought, okay? I'm not ruling it out, but I'm not saying yes either."

"Think really, really hard," Josh pleaded. "We need you, Grace."

Jamie's gaze locked on hers, regarding her with an understanding that was wise beyond his years. Then he turned to Josh. "Stop bugging her, okay? Let her think."

"Think about what?" Michael asked, walking into the kitchen in jeans and a dress shirt with the sleeves rolled up and the collar open. His hair was still damp from a shower.

Grace's heart skipped a beat as the vivid memory of several steamy, shared showers rushed back. It had been six years and she hadn't been able to shake the way the man made her feel with just a glance. She could all but feel his hands on her body, feel him deep inside her. The memory alone was enough to make her cheeks burn.

Right now, though, he was a threat to this make-believe family of hers.

He wanted to tear the four of them apart with what he viewed as a necessary phone call. And even though she knew in her head that he was right, in her heart she suspected she might wind up hating him for it.

"Okay, everybody, eat up," she said as she placed

plates of waffles and bacon on the table. "As soon as we've finished breakfast, we're going into town."

She regarded Michael with a touch of defiance as she said it, daring him to contradict her announcement.

"We'll get Josh's new boots, maybe do a little shopping, then have lunch," she added for good measure. "I vote for pizza. How about the rest of you?"

"All right!" Josh enthused.

"Pizza's okay by me, too," Jamie responded.

Grace met Michael's gaze. "And you? Any objections?"

"Not a one," he said, regarding her with a look that spoke volumes.

It was evident he intended to keep silent about any real objections until they were alone. Grace just had to make sure that didn't happen. She didn't need another well-intentioned lecture. She had a few more hours at most with Jamie and Josh. She wasn't going to have them spoiled by nagging reminders that time was running out.

She actually managed to avoid being alone with Michael until after they got into Los Piños. As Jamie and Josh raced ahead to the shop where she had bought the cowboy boots, Michael clasped her arm in a firm grip and held her back.

"This is a temporary reprieve, because you made him a promise, understood?"

She frowned at his commanding tone. "This is not your decision to make," she retorted.

"Maybe not entirely," he agreed. "But I've made it, because I don't think you can."

"And the rest of us just have to live with it, is that it? This isn't Delacourt Oil, Michael. You're not the boss.

We're equal partners," she declared, then added point-edly, "All four of us."

He regarded her with evident frustration. "You can't expect Jamie and Josh to know what's in their best interests."

"And you do?" she retorted. "Mr. No-time-for-anything-that-isn't-business? Who made you an expert in child-rearing? My hunch is you don't even spend any time with your niece and nephews, except maybe holidays."

His pained expression told her she'd gotten it exactly right. "Okay, Grace, maybe I'm not a dad, maybe I'm not even the most involved uncle in the world, but I can spot a disaster when it's just waiting to happen. We've got to settle this today. Those boys are getting too attached to you and you to them. It's not good."

She knew he was right and, as she'd anticipated, she despised him for it. "Fine. You make that call whenever you decide it's right. I'm going to get those boots for Josh."

She jerked out of his grasp and stalked down the block. Of course, he caught up with her before she reached the store.

"Sweetheart, I'm not the bad guy here."

"Couldn't prove it by me," she said.

"Do you think I want those boys to go back to the kind of lives they were living? Do you think I can't see how awful it was for them to be separated? Hell, I think about something like that happening to me, Tyler, Dylan and Jeb and I can't even imagine it."

"Then help me to do something," she pleaded, gazing up at him. "Don't make that call until we have a real plan, one that nobody with any sense of decency can challenge."

Michael raked a hand through his hair, his expression torn. "Grace—"

Sensing that he was weakening, she made one more plea. "Please. I've never begged for anything from you before, Michael, but I'm begging now. Not for myself, for Jamie and Josh. They deserve a real chance, a real family."

He visibly struggled with her request. "We'll make that plan this afternoon, though, right? No more putting it off?"

"I swear it," she said. "The four of us will sit down and think of something as soon as we get back to the ranch."

"No," he corrected. "You and I will make the decision. Then we'll sell it to the boys together. Deal?"

She had a feeling it was the best she was going to get. "Deal," she agreed.

She started to move away, but Michael snagged her hand again. "Grace?"

She lifted her gaze to his.

"I love it that you care so much."

She sighed. She couldn't help wondering what he'd say if he knew that over the last two days she'd realized that she cared just as much about him.

Nine

At the Italian restaurant, Josh could barely sit still. He kept poking his feet out to stare at his new boots. Then he'd get up and clomp around the table, trying to imitate the rolling gait of a cowboy. Apparently he'd watched a lot of westerns, since as far as Michael knew he'd never met any real cowboy besides Slade and Slade walked with a limp thanks to a tragic accident that had cost him his rodeo career and almost his life.

"I think he likes the boots," Grace noted.

"What was your first clue?" Michael responded, chuckling.

"He's acting like a jerk," Jamie declared with adolescent disdain. "They're just shoes."

Michael exchanged an amused look with Grace, then regarded Jamie intently. "Guess that means you'd rather we'd gotten you something else, instead of letting you keep the boots that were too big for Josh."

Jamie squirmed uncomfortably. "Nah, they're cool."

"Then let's not make fun of your brother," Michael chided.

"Yeah, whatever."

Grace grinned at Jamie. "There's one advantage to Josh being away from the table," she leaned over to confide.

"What?"

"More pizza for you."

Jamie's expression brightened. "Hey, yeah. Gimme that last piece." He was already reaching for it, when he thought better of it. He glanced at Michael. "You want it?"

"No, but you might check with Grace."

"It was her idea for me to take it."

"Ask anyway. It's only polite."

Jamie rolled his eyes, but he dutifully turned to Grace. "You want another piece of pizza?"

"No, it's all yours."

Jamie shot a triumphant look at Michael. "Told you so," he said, grabbing the piece and taking a huge bite out of it to stake his claim.

As soon as he'd wolfed down the pizza, he went off to join Josh, who was watching some kids play the video games at the back of the restaurant. In minutes, he was back again.

"Could we have some quarters to play?" he asked. "We'll do extra work at the ranch to earn them."

Michael was impressed with Jamie's willingness to work for the money.

The kid had learned a lot of lessons, either from the foster parents he claimed to disdain or from his struggles to make it on his own whenever he came for Josh. He took nothing for granted. He expected to work for whatever he got.

Michael handed him a couple of dollars. "Ask them to change them for you at the register," he said. "Consider it payment for the work you've already done feeding the horses."

"Thanks," Jamie said.

"Those kids are so eager to please," Michael said. "How could they have given their foster parents so much trouble?"

"Maybe we're seeing another side of them just because they're so grateful to be together," Grace suggested.

"You ever see a kid who could pull off a charade like this for more than a few minutes at a time? These are good kids, Grace."

"I'm not about to argue with you. I think they're terrific. But maybe we're seeing them at their best, because they see us as their last chance," Grace said quietly.

Michael didn't know what to say to that. But he did know a lot about last chances. If this was the last one he was going to have with Grace, then he was going to have to make the most of it. He glanced at her, saw the wistful way she was staring at Jamie and Josh.

What was she hoping for, really? Did she merely want to find them a home where they could be together? Would she be satisfied with that? Or was she imagining providing a home for them herself?

He thought about the latter and had the oddest feeling that his own expression was probably every bit as wistful as hers. Was he beginning to want the same thing? Not just Grace, Jamie and Josh as a family, but with himself in the picture, too? He wanted Grace back in his life, but did he want the rest? Marriage? A family? Was he truly ready to make the necessary changes in his lifestyle?

The pitiful truth was that his work habits were as

ingrained as breathing. His days were crowded from morning to night. Was that because he liked it that way, because it had to be that way? Or because he didn't have anything else he cared about as deeply?

And how the hell was he supposed to figure out the answer in the next couple of hours? Suddenly he regretted setting a deadline, but he knew he couldn't back off now. That deadline was as right now as it had been when he'd insisted on it.

That didn't mean he couldn't nudge it back just a little.

"Hey, Josh, Jamie," he called, drawing a worried look from Grace. "How about going down to Dolan's for ice cream?"

"Hot fudge sundaes?" Josh asked eagerly.

"You bet," Michael agreed. "Grace? Is that okay with you?"

As if she understood that he was offering more than scoops of ice cream, her frown faded and a smile spread slowly across her face. "Have you ever known me to turn down a hot fudge sundae?"

"Now that you mention it, no. It was the one way I always knew I could lure you away from your law books."

"Not the only way," she teased with a surprising glint in her eyes.

Michael recalled the other way all too clearly. "Maybe we'd better stick to the G-rated method for now, though I am definitely up for the alternative anytime you give the word."

"Is that so?" she asked with amusement.

"Oh, yes," he said fervently. "Try me."

"Maybe I will," she said thoughtfully.

Jamie and Josh scowled at them. "Are you two coming or not?"

"We're coming," Grace said, sashaying past Michael with a provocative sway to her hips.

He shook his head as he enjoyed the view. The woman was definitely dangerous. In the last few minutes he had not only tossed aside his common sense where those kids were concerned, he was about to invite Grace Foster back into his bed, back into his life. He wasn't sure which of them would be in more trouble if she said yes.

Grace wondered how smart it had been to come to Dolan's when she saw Sharon Lynn's eyes light up with fascination the instant they walked in the door. She had a hunch they were about to be treated to a display of the famed Adams meddling.

"Well, well, well, who do we have here?" she asked, her gaze traveling from Grace to Michael to the boys and back. She eventually settled on Michael. "You must be Trish's brother. I can see the family resemblance, even though I barely caught a glimpse of you at Dylan's wedding."

"Guilty," he agreed. "Michael Delacourt."

"And I'm Sharon Lynn Branson."

"She's an Adams," Grace inserted pointedly, just so Michael would know what they were dealing with. It was apparent from his expression that he got the message.

"I've heard about you," he told Sharon Lynn.

"Oh, I'll just bet you have," she said, laughing. "Stories about this family tend to get around."

"I was thinking of the way you helped Trish with

her grand opening. She said it was wildly successful because of you and your family."

"We were just being neighborly," Sharon Lynn insisted, her gaze shifting to the boys. "Now, then, I know Michael and I've met Grace, but who are you two handsome boys?"

Again, Grace was quick to step in. "This is Josh and this is Jamie. They're visiting us."

"Oh, really?" she said. "Nice to meet you, Josh and Jamie."

Grace had the feeling from Sharon Lynn's vaguely curious expression that she wanted to say a lot more, but about that time a toddler crept into view from behind the counter. As if she were satisfied that her mother's attention was elsewhere, she took off toward a shelf full of first aid supplies. Before anyone could react, she had tumbled boxes of bandages on the floor and was trying to get into one of them.

Sharon Lynn sighed as she scooped her up, ignoring the wails of protest. "Got a boo-boo," the baby insisted tearfully. She turned to Grace, apparently sensing a softhearted ally. "See?"

"Yes, indeed," Grace said, though she saw nothing of the kind. "A very bad boo-boo. Maybe a kiss from mommy would be better than a bandage, though."

Deep blue eyes, swimming in tears, brightened. "Kiss?" she repeated, peering at Sharon Lynn.

"You are such a little manipulator," Sharon Lynn declared, but she dutifully kissed the outstretched finger. "Is that better?"

The child nodded happily. "Boo-boo all gone."

"I'll pick up the boxes," Jamie said, already lining them up neatly on the shelves.

Sharon Lynn gaped. "Who raised him? There's not a kid in our entire clan who would volunteer that fast for any kind of cleanup."

"He's one of a kind, all right," Michael agreed.

Sharon Lynn thrust her daughter into his arms. "Take her for a sec, okay? I'll help Jamie get everything back, then I'll be right over to take your order."

"I'll help, too," Josh offered, already tagging along behind her.

"That's okay. I think Jamie and I can handle it." She flashed a grin at Josh. "Looks to me like Michael might need you more than I do."

Michael stood there, a shocked expression on his face, the toddler held away from his body like a painting he was inspecting closely before deciding whether to buy. She beamed at him.

"I think she likes you," Grace said.

"She's pretty cool," Josh decided after a thorough survey. "I ain't never been around anybody littler than me."

It was pretty clear that Michael hadn't been around many people that size either. Grace finally took pity on him and took the toddler. He shot her a relieved look and headed for a stool at the counter. She had a feeling if it had been a bar, he might have ordered a double.

Enjoying the feel of the little girl snuggled in her arms, Grace took a seat next to him. "Don't tell me you were scared by a little bitty thing like this," she teased.

"I was not scared," he protested.

But when the child started to scramble toward him, reaching out her arms, he looked as panicked as Grace had ever seen him. "You sure about that?" she asked.

He frowned. "Of course, I'm sure. It's not like I get

a lot of opportunities to be around babies. I don't want to slip up, that's all."

"So, before you have kids of your own, you'll buy some books, study up?"

"Exactly."

Grace suddenly had a vision of Michael poring over baby books with the same intensity he devoted to geological surveys. Maybe that was how he would approach having a family of his own, all out. Maybe the trick was to convince him that it was something he wanted as badly as he had always wanted the presidency of Delacourt Oil.

And who was she to make fun of his inexperience? It wasn't as if she'd spent a lot of time around children. Once her relationship with Michael had ended, she had put any thoughts of family on a back burner herself. Her friends tended to be other fast-track lawyers who, even if married, had put off having children. Those who had them spent pitifully little time at home with them.

So why was she suddenly being swamped by all these maternal sentiments? Was it the situation with Josh and Jamie? Was it holding this squirming little angel in her arms? Or was it being back with Michael again, thinking about having a family specifically with him the way she'd once dreamed of?

She feared it was the latter, more than anything. After all those childhood insecurities about abandonment, he was the only man who'd ever made her yearn for happily ever after. He was the only one she'd been able to see herself sitting with on a front porch in fifty years, her mind every bit as engaged as her heart. She'd put all those longings on hold for six long years and now, thanks to a few days of close proximity, they were coming back in a flood.

Before she could wonder where all that was likely to lead, Sharon Lynn stepped back behind the counter.

"I understand we're looking at hot fudge sundaes all around."

"That's the plan," Michael agreed.

"With lots of whipped cream," Josh added.

"And nuts," Grace chimed in.

"My favorite kind of customers," Sharon Lynn said. "No cholesterol worries in this crowd."

"Not today, anyway," Grace agreed.

"Is this a celebration?" Sharon Lynn asked as she began scooping vanilla ice cream into old-fashioned glass dishes.

Grace glanced at Michael, saw the glimmer of uneasiness in his eyes. "Not exactly," she said. "Just a treat."

"Yeah," Josh enthused. "We've been getting lots of treats. I even got new cowboy boots. Jamie, too." He stuck out his feet so Sharon Lynn could see over the counter.

"Very handsome," she approved. "How are the riding lessons going?"

At Grace's startled look, she said, "The White Pines grapevine is an extraordinary thing. Not much goes on out there that I don't hear about. Slade's daughter Annie and his wife are two of my best customers. I love 'em. They talk a mile a minute. Even if they didn't, Grandpa Harlan would have filled me in."

Michael's gaze narrowed. "Harlan Adams? He knows about the boys and the lessons? I only told him about needing riding lessons. I thought he'd assume they were for me."

She nodded. "Grandpa Harlan has sources from one end of the state to the next. It's a waste of time trying to keep anything from him."

Michael's expression sobered. "I see."

Sharon Lynn regarded him worriedly. "Is that a problem?"

"I honestly don't know," Michael said.

Grace picked up on his anxiety and studied him warily. "Michael, what are you thinking?"

"That we shouldn't have gotten sidetracked from my original plan. Too many people already know."

"Know what?" Jamie asked with his usual unabashed curiosity.

"That you're staying out at Trish's with Grace and me," Michael said.

Jamie's expression fell, his mood suddenly as dark as Michael's. "That's a bad thing, isn't it?"

"Let's just say I wish the word hadn't spread quite so far."

Sharon Lynn caught what he said as she put the sundaes on the counter in front of them. "Look, I'm not sure what the deal is, but you don't have to worry about anybody in the family blabbing your business to outsiders. If it's possible for a grapevine to be discreet, ours is."

"I hope so," Michael said fervently. "Otherwise we could be looking at a whole heap of trouble."

The instant the uncensored remark was out of Michael's mouth, alarm spread across Jamie's face. He stuck his spoon back in his ice cream and pushed it away. Grace reached over and moved it back.

"There is no need for you to worry," she told him quietly. "Michael and I will handle anything that comes up." She gazed at Michael. "Right?"

"Absolutely," he said with more conviction than he probably felt.

"Promise?" Jamie asked.

"You have my word on it."

"But—"

"Jamie, I promise," she said solemnly.

Finally reassured, Jamie dug into his sundae, polishing it off in no time.

Josh, who'd been too busy scraping every last bit of hot fudge out of the bottom of the dish to pay attention to the tension swirling around him, finished up and climbed off of the stool.

"Can Jamie and me go for a walk around town?" he asked.

"If you don't leave Main Street," Michael said.

Grace regarded him with surprise. "Are you sure—?"

"It'll be fine."

After they'd gone, she sighed. "Jamie's scared. Are you sure they won't just take off?"

"I'm as sure of that as I am of anything," Michael said. "Which isn't saying a lot right now."

Sharon Lynn came around and sat on the stool next to Grace, the baby settled in her lap with a dog-eared picture book. "Obviously I set off a panic earlier. Why don't you fill me in? Maybe I can help."

"Maybe we do need an objective opinion. You and I are a little too close to the situation," Grace said, trying to gauge Michael's reaction. He finally nodded.

With that go-ahead, Grace gave Sharon Lynn a brief summary of the situation.

"Those poor boys," Sharon Lynn murmured more than once.

"Any ideas about how we can keep them together?"

Michael asked. "Grace and I are both committed to making that happen."

"How would you feel if I held a family powwow?" Sharon Lynn asked. "All of us have big homes. And nobody's more devoted to the concept of family than an Adams. Surely among us we could come up with a place for them to stay so they'd be together. Then we could go to social services, present them with a solution they couldn't possibly refuse. I'm living proof that the tactic can work. What do you think?"

"Are you sure there are people in your family who would consider taking in two boys they haven't even met yet?" Grace worried.

"I know it," Sharon Lynn said. "I'd have to talk to Cord, of course, but I'd do it in a heartbeat. I always wanted a ton of kids around. We don't have as much room as some of the others, but we could make it work."

Grace thought of those dry legal pages that had summarized Sharon Lynn's battle for custody of the little girl who had been left on her doorstep. She saw that same kind of commitment and love shining in her eyes now.

Jamie and Josh would definitely be in good hands with Sharon Lynn.

So, why did she feel so empty inside thinking of the boys staying right here with a woman like Sharon Lynn as their mother? Why was saying no her immediate reaction?

Because she wanted them for herself, she realized with a sinking sense of loss. She couldn't delude herself that her response was anything other than pure jealousy over the fact that Sharon Lynn had a family to offer them. It was a selfish, knee-jerk reaction.

"Well?" Sharon Lynn asked. "What do you think?"

Michael's gaze settled on hers. "Grace?"

"It's an option," she said slowly, trying to hide her dismay. "You're very generous to even consider the idea."

"Shall I talk to Cord and the others? See if we come up with any other brilliant solutions?"

"I think we should let her," Michael said. "Right, Grace?"

Grace forced herself to nod agreement, because she wasn't sure she could speak around the sudden lump in her throat.

"And in the meantime, I think maybe you should talk to my cousin Justin," Sharon Lynn went on. "If you've filled the local sheriff in, you might avoid any problems about letting the boys stay here, rather than turning them in the second you discovered them in the barn. Justin can take his own sweet time about filing paperwork when it suits him. Not that he approves of such things, but one look at those boys and how happy they are and I think in this instance it will suit him just fine."

"Thanks, Sharon Lynn," Michael said. "I think we'll do exactly that. Now we'd better go round up those two and get them back out to Trish's, before anybody else starts asking questions about who they are and where they came from."

Trying to make up for her earlier lack of enthusiasm, Grace gave Sharon Lynn a hug. "You really are wonderful. Your kids are very lucky."

"No," Sharon Lynn said fervently. "I'm the lucky one. I've got the sexiest, most loving husband on the planet and three great kids. Why not share that if I can?

I'll call you all later and let you know how things turn out when I talk to the family."

Outside, Grace spotted Jamie and Josh peering in the window of the feed and grain store. They seemed perfectly content for the moment, so she turned to Michael.

"Do you think we should call Justin?"

"I think it might be the smart thing to do," he said. "If he's anything like Sharon Lynn, he'll be on our side. That can't hurt."

"What if he's not?" Grace asked worriedly. "What if he's a by-the-book kind of guy?"

"Dylan says he is," Michael admitted. "But he also says there's no one he'd rather have on his side in a fight."

"How well does Dylan really know him?"

"They worked together when Kelsey's son was missing. Dylan said the only thing that mattered to Justin was getting the boy back, not which rules might have been bent in the process. He even considered going to work for Justin as a deputy. For Dylan to even think about doing that, the man has to be a good guy."

He studied Grace. "You're not convinced, are you? Not about any of it, including Sharon Lynn's willingness to take the boys in if her husband agrees."

"How can I not be glad about that?" she said, but she couldn't manage to force any enthusiasm into her voice.

Michael touched a hand to her cheek. "Grace?"

She forced herself to meet his gaze, saw the concern in his expression. "What?"

"What's really going on here? No evasions this time. I want the truth."

"I don't know," she said honestly.

"You want those boys to stay with you, don't you?" he said, putting into words what she'd been afraid to say.

Her breath caught at the accuracy of his assessment. It had been a long time since anyone had been able to see into her heart like that, since anyone had even tried. She owed him an honest answer.

"I know it's not realistic, that it doesn't make any kind of sense, but yes, I want to keep them in my life," she admitted.

"In your life?" he asked skeptically. "You could do that no matter where they wind up. You really want them with you permanently. I can see it when you look at them. It's exactly what I was afraid of."

"I know it's wrong, even selfish," she finally conceded, then regarded him fiercely. "But, yes, that is exactly what I want. Those boys need a loving home and I want to be the one to give it to them."

"What about your career?"

"I can make it work," she insisted. "I wouldn't be the first woman to have to juggle work and parenting."

"But two kids, out of the blue?" he asked skeptically. "Jamie and Josh are trying really hard right now to do everything they can to please you, but it won't always be that way. Jamie's a teenager. Teenaged boys can be a handful. Are you prepared for that?"

"Yes," she said without hesitation. She might be good for Josh and Jamie, but they would bring even more into her life, something that had been missing for as long as she could remember.

Michael cupped her chin in his palm, his gaze locked with hers, as if he were searching for assurance that she had no doubts about her claim.

Apparently satisfied with what he saw, he nodded. "Then we'll do what we can to make it happen."

Her heart leaped at the conviction she heard in his voice, the certainty that everything would be settled just the way she wanted it. Given Michael's reputation as a determined man and a tough negotiator, she didn't doubt for an instant that he could make it happen.

But then what? Despite her brave words, how would she manage if she won?

What had he gone and done, Michael worried as he sat up late that night while Grace and the boys slept upstairs. How was he supposed to keep his promise to her? And, for that matter, how did he feel about her determination to bring Jamie and Josh into her life on a full-time basis?

Would there be room for him in that equation? Did he want there to be?

When he could no longer stand the way his thoughts kept shifting back and forth with no resolution in sight, he picked up the phone and called Tyler, waking him out of a sound sleep.

"Michael?" his brother asked sleepily. "What's going on? It's the middle of the night. Don't you have something better to do, or did Grace go home?"

"Grace is asleep," he said, then drew in a deep breath. "So are the two boys I discovered hiding out in the barn."

Tyler's sharp intake of breath suggested he'd finally come awake in a hurry.

"Michael, what the devil is going on over there?"

"You have no idea," Michael said wryly. "But I think I could use a friendly face."

"And you'd prefer mine to Grace's? You obviously need another lecture on your priorities."

"It's gotten complicated," Michael said. "Since you got me over here, I figure you owe me."

"I'll be there first thing in the morning," Tyler agreed at once. "It might be a real good time for me to be out of town anyway."

Something in his little brother's voice alerted Michael that he wasn't the only one with a lot on his mind. "Ty, is everything okay?"

"Nothing I can't handle with a little fancy footwork," Tyler assured him. "See you in the morning."

"Thanks, bro."

"Anytime. You know that. Want me to bring Jeb, too?"

"No, I think you and I can handle it. Dylan should be back any day now, too. And Trish. If we need backup, they can step in."

"What kind of backup are we talking about?" Tyler asked.

"Not the six-shooter variety," Michael said with the first genuine laugh he'd uttered in days.

"I'm relieved. Just remember one thing till I get there."

"What's that?"

"There's nothing a Delacourt can't do, once he puts his mind to it. Get more than one of us in a room and we're indomitable."

"I hope so," Michael said fervently. "For once in my life I'm counting on it."

He wasn't sure when he said it if he was thinking of Josh and Jamie, or if he was thinking about Grace.

Ten

Grace tossed and turned for what seemed like hours before finally giving up, tugging on her robe and padding down the hall to the bathroom to get herself a glass of water. On her way she spotted a light on downstairs and opted to head to the kitchen instead.

Was Michael still up? Was one of the boys sick? She peeked into Josh and Jamie's room, saw that they were both sound asleep, then headed for the stairs. It had to be Michael.

She crept down silently, then peered into the living room. He was stretched out in an oversized chair in front of a fire that was little more than burning embers. He was holding a half-empty glass of wine in one hand, but his eyes were closed. She inched closer, intending only to throw an afghan over him and take away the precariously balanced glass, but he opened his eyes as she neared.

"What are you doing up?" he asked, his gaze settling on the deep *V* of her robe.

Grace barely resisted the urge to tug the robe closed. She was not going to let him see that he could make her nervous with nothing more than a glance. "I couldn't sleep," she told him. "What about you? Have you even been to bed?"

He shook his head. "Come over here and sit with me," he suggested.

When she didn't move, he added quietly, "Please."

She wanted to. Oh, how she wanted to throw caution to the wind and slide into his embrace, but were want and need enough? "Why?" she asked, her gaze locked with his.

A smile tugged at his lips. "Just because," he said lightly.

She shook her head. "Not good enough."

"Because I need you, Grace," he said, his voice raw. "There, you got me to say it. Is that enough?"

Was it? Whether it was or not, she was drawn across the room until she was standing beside him. Still, she didn't join him in the chair. Watching her intently, he held out his hand.

The instant she put her hand in his, she knew that the choice had been made. This was the man she had loved for as long as she could remember. This was the man whose slightest touch was magical. Even now, with hands clasped and nothing more, she felt the heat and tension building inside, felt her pulse ricochet wildly. Six years and nothing had changed. He still had the power to make her weak-kneed with longing.

His thumb rested on her wrist. There was a glint of satisfaction in his eyes as he detected her racing pulse. "Come on, Gracie," he urged, using the nickname only he had ever dared. "One more step."

One step, she thought. It sounded so insignificant, and yet it would change everything. It would put her back in Michael's arms, leave her vulnerable and aching and needy. And even if she satisfied that need tonight or tomorrow or the next day, in the end she would be alone again. How could she do that to herself, open herself to that kind of pain?

As she debated with herself, he waited, exhibiting more patience than usual. In the end, that was what convinced her. She had the sense that he would wait forever, if need be. She found that somehow reassuring.

With a sigh, she settled in his lap, snuggled against his chest in a way that had once been as familiar to her as the rasp of his five o'clock shadow against her skin. His cheeks were shadowed now by the beginnings of a beard. With hesitant fingertips, she caressed the very masculine, sandpaper texture, then drifted lower to rest her hand against the heat of his neck.

All the while his eyes glittered, darkened with some emotion she couldn't quite read.

"It's not going to be enough," he said at last. "I thought it might be, but it's not. I want you, Gracie. All of you."

She had accepted that before taking that first step, so the words came as no shock, but the shudder of anticipation did. "I know," she replied softly. "I don't think a day has gone by that I haven't wanted you. Not in six years."

He regarded her with apparent amazement. "Seriously?"

"Have you ever known me to kid around about something like that?"

A smug grin tugged at the corners of his mouth. "So that's why you've been so tough on me whenever you had the opportunity? Sexual frustration?"

She scowled at his assessment, started to pull away, but he held her in place with little effort.

"Don't go," he said.

"Why should I stay?"

"Because you want to," he suggested lightly. "And because I need you to."

She sighed. "Oh, Michael, I wish you wouldn't say things like that."

"Why?"

"Because they confuse me."

"I thought I was being straightforward and honest." He took her hand and moved it to the hard shaft pressing against her. "Here's the evidence, counselor."

"But that's just it," she said. "You and I have different definitions of need, different expectations."

His gaze settled on her breasts. The nipples were pushing against the silky fabric of her robe. "Are you so sure of that?"

"It's not all about sex," she said impatiently. "If it were, I would have stayed with you years ago. You and I never had any problems in bed. All it took was a glance for us to be ready, a touch. I found it maddening that I could be so furious with you, so sure that I had to get you out of my life, and yet my body would betray me, just as it's doing now."

"Are you so sure it's a betrayal?" he asked. "Maybe it's just reminding you of something that's right, something that never should have ended."

"It had to end, Michael. You know it did. You weren't ready to make the kind of commitment I needed, the kind I still need. I have to know I can count on a man, that he's going to be there for me when it's important, not tied up in some endless, insignificant meeting. I need to know that *I'm* not insignificant."

"The future doesn't come with guarantees. Isn't it enough that *I'm* here now?"

"You're only here because you were tricked into coming, because you found two scared boys in the barn and you're too honorable to desert them. Tell me you're not chomping at the bit to be back in Houston, back in your office with a schedule of back-to-back meetings and nonstop phone calls." He hesitated, which was answer enough.

Then, to her surprise, he said, "I'm not. I was before you got here, but I'm not now. I've never been less bored in my life."

"It's been a couple of days," she scoffed. "How long do you really think that will last? You're a compulsive overachiever."

"You're not the first person to say that to me recently."

She couldn't help smiling at his irritated expression. "Tyler, I presume?"

"Exactly. He's never let me forget that I've done a lot of stupid things in my life because of work—or that the worst one was missing your graduation."

"Since the message obviously hasn't sunk in, apparently he hasn't said it often enough."

"Who says it hasn't sunk in?" he protested. "I learn from my mistakes."

"Then why haven't you had a serious relationship in all these years?" she asked bluntly. "And don't try telling me it's because you couldn't get me out of your head. I know better. I read the society pages. There's been a steady stream of beautiful women in your life, but none of them lasted more than a few weeks."

He regarded her with smug amusement. "Interesting."

"What?"

"That you followed my love life so closely."

"The Houston media followed it closely. It was hard for anyone who reads the newspaper to miss. Based on what I read, I'd be willing to bet that sooner or later you got tied up in this or that and just forgot all about the lady of the moment. The next time you surfaced, you just moved on to someone new, probably because the last lover wouldn't take you back. Or maybe because by then you'd forgotten her name."

He winced at the harsh assessment, but he didn't deny it. At last, sounding wounded, he asked, "Is that what you really think? Do you honestly think I'm that cavalier about women?"

"Aren't you?"

"No. I wasn't cavalier about you, either. I made a mistake. A bad one. But I never stopped loving you. You threw me out, remember? You weighed everything we had against that one mistake and dumped me."

Grace thought she detected hurt in his eyes to match the wounded tone in his voice, even after all this time, but surely that couldn't be, surely she'd never had that much power over him. It was true that it had been one mistake—one huge mistake in her eyes—but there had been signs it would happen again and again.

"You know why I did it," she said.

"I know what you said. I even know what you believe, but I think it was something else entirely, Gracie."

She stared at him in astonishment. "Such as?"

"I think you were scared, maybe even more terrified than I was. I think I gave you the perfect excuse to run and hide behind old fears." His gaze locked on hers. "Well? Am I right?"

"I…" Her voice faltered. Not once had she ever considered that she had seized on a mistake to bail out of a relationship that she feared would end down the road anyway. Had being abandoned by her father made her instinctively distrust Michael—any man—right from the start? Although she didn't like what it said about her level of insecurity, she couldn't deny the possibility. If she'd given him a chance to prove himself back then, would Michael have changed or would he have let her down? She hadn't wanted to find out.

"Maybe," she finally conceded.

He gave a nod of satisfaction. "Now we're getting somewhere."

He seemed so pleased, but she was more confused than ever. "Where?"

"Out of the past and into the present," he said. "How about it? Can we start here and now and see where it leads us?"

She stood up to move away from him, because when she was in his arms, she obviously couldn't think straight.

"This isn't the time for this," she said, gesturing vaguely toward the stairs. "The boys—"

"Are a separate issue," he said firmly. "This is about you and me. Are you willing to give us another chance? Or are you still too scared to try?"

Panic welled up inside her. She wanted to seize the opportunity he was dangling in front of her, but how could she when Josh and Jamie's fate needed to be decided? Or was that just another convenient excuse to avoid risking her heart?

"I don't know," she whispered. Then, because the temptation was so powerful, she added, "Maybe."

As if he sensed her struggle and that the concession she was making might be the best she could do, he smiled. "'Maybe' is good enough for now. Go on upstairs and get some sleep, Grace. Tomorrow's going to be a difficult day."

Surprised that he'd let her off the hook so easily, she nodded. "Are you coming?"

"Are you inviting me to share your bed?"

"No."

"I thought not. You go on. I'll be up soon."

She started away, but his voice stopped her.

"Gracie, you don't have to lock your door. I can take no for an answer. I won't sneak in and ravish you."

She chuckled despite herself. "Too bad. It's been a long time since I've been ravished."

His heated gaze sent desire flaming through her. "Just say the word and I can change that," he said.

"I'll keep that in mind." In fact, she thought it was likely that she would think about very little else.

Michael's blood was pumping fast and furiously as he watched Grace go upstairs. A part of him cursed the fact that he'd let her get away. He knew if he'd kissed her, if he'd caressed her, even innocently, he could have persuaded her to make love with him. Then he wouldn't be sitting here in this aching, aroused state, regretting the fact that he had a sense of decency and honor.

She'd been right, though, this was not the time to start something, not with her emotions running high because of Josh and Jamie. He would have been taking advantage of that, using her vulnerability to get her to turn to him for more than emotional support.

He waited for an hour after she'd left him before he too climbed the stairs and made his way to bed. He very nearly paused outside her door and reached for the knob—just to check on her, he told himself—but then he remembered his promise. He moved on to his own room and slid between the icy sheets, once more cursing the fact that he could have had her there to warm them.

He fell into a restless sleep, tormented by dreams in which Grace turned her back on him over and over. By the time he awoke, he was miserable and out of sorts.

A cold shower revived him somewhat. Years of forcing himself to stay focused on the task at hand got him down the stairs in a reasonable mood, ready to tackle their predicament with Josh and Jamie.

Grace barely looked at him, but he noticed she'd abandoned her more provocative shorts and tank tops for slacks and a sedate blouse. Was that for his benefit, a way to warn him off, perhaps? Or preparation for the meeting with Justin?

Jamie looked up from his plate of scrambled eggs and bacon, glanced from Michael to Grace and back again. His fork hit the plate with a clatter. "Okay, what's up? You guys have been acting all weird since we went to town yesterday."

"Everything is fine," Michael began, only to have Grace interrupt.

"We need to tell them," she said, putting a plate in front of him with a thump, then taking her own place at the table.

Michael noticed she didn't touch her food. It was evident that she, too, had lost her appetite, just as Jamie had. Even Josh was merely stirring his food around on his plate, not eating it.

"Tell us what?" Jamie asked.

"Michael and I have made a decision," she began, looking to him for help.

"Right." He searched for a way to put it into words without scaring them half to death.

Jamie shoved his chair back from the table so fast, it tilted over and crashed to the floor. "You promised," he said, his voice quivering with outrage and betrayal as he stared at Grace. "You told me you wouldn't decide anything unless me and Josh said so, too."

"Hold it," Michael said. "Don't go yelling at Grace. She's on your side. We both are."

"Yeah, but you're just like all grown-ups. You make the decisions, then we're supposed to go along with them, right? Well, not this time. Me and Josh are out of here. Come on, Josh."

Josh's eyes had filled with tears during the exchange. "But I don't want to go."

"Didn't you hear them?" Jamie said, exasperated. "They're deciding what to do with us. They just want us to go along with it."

"But they haven't said what it is yet," Josh said reasonably. "I want to hear."

"Please, Jamie," Grace said gently. "Let us explain at least."

He regarded her with obvious misery and distrust. "Why should I?"

"Because I love you," she said simply.

The response clearly took him by surprise. "You do?"

The mix of distrust and hope in his voice almost broke Michael's heart. "We both do," she said firmly.

"That's why this is so important. I would never, ever do anything that I thought would hurt you or go against your best interests. Please believe that."

Jamie seemed to be struggling with himself, but eventually he righted his chair and sat in it. "Okay, I'll listen, but if I don't like it, Josh and me are out of here."

"Fair enough," Grace said.

Before she could say anything, Michael heard a key turning in the front door, then Tyler's shouted greeting from the foyer.

"Who's that?" Jamie asked suspiciously. He was halfway out of his chair again, ready to bolt.

"Settle down," Michael said. "It's my brother."

Grace regarded him with surprise. "Tyler's here?"

Michael nodded. "I called him last night before you came downstairs."

"And of course I came running to the rescue," Tyler said, strolling into the kitchen and pausing to drop a kiss on Grace's cheek. "Good to see you again, Grace."

"You, too," she said, standing. "Are you hungry? I can fix you something."

"Have you ever known Tyler not to be hungry?" Michael asked, but he regarded his brother with gratitude. "Thanks for getting here so fast."

Jamie had settled back in his seat, but his gaze remained wary. "You guys don't look like brothers," Josh said.

Tyler grinned. "That's 'cause he's so ugly, right? I'm the handsome one."

"You got hair like ours, blond," Josh said, ignoring Tyler's claim. "Michael's is real dark. And you got lots of muscles. You must work out a lot."

"Tyler works in the oil fields every chance he gets," Michael corrected.

"Cool," Jamie said, his reserved facade slipping for a minute. "Is it fun?"

"You bet," Tyler told him, dragging a fifth chair up to the table and sliding it in next to Jamie. "Some people," he said with a pointed glance at Michael, "don't like to get dirty. They just want to sit in a fancy office and reap the rewards of all my hard work."

"Somebody has to sell that crude or it's a waste of time bringing it in," Michael reminded him in what was an old argument. Of course, usually the debate took place between Tyler and their father and it usually was conducted with a whole lot more rancor.

"Old turf," Tyler said, winking at Grace when she put a plate in front of him. "Isn't it?"

"I've been hearing it as far back as I can recall," she agreed. "What amazes me is that you haven't bolted for a rival oil company, where you won't have to fight to do the job you love."

Tyler gave an exaggerated shudder. "Not even I am that brave. I'm not sure Dad's heart is strong enough to take it and I don't want to be the one who puts him in his grave."

He put down his fork and turned to Jamie. "Okay, enough about my career choices. Tell me about you."

"I'm Jamie."

"And I'm Josh."

"I heard you were hiding out in the barn when my brother found you. What's the deal?"

As if they instinctively trusted Tyler, both boys began spilling the events of the last few days before finally winding down.

"So today *we're* gonna decide what happens to us," Jamie concluded with a pointed look at Michael.

"We were just about to discuss it when you came in," Michael said. "What's the plan?"

"Michael wants to call Justin Adams. It's been suggested he would be a very good ally," Grace said, pointedly not mentioning that Justin was the sheriff.

Tyler shot a look at Michael. "Do you think that's wise?"

"Dylan trusts him."

Satisfied by their brother's approval, Tyler nodded. "Okay. Then what?"

"We see what he has to say."

His brother looked as if he wanted to ask more, but instead he fell silent. "Tyler, do you disagree?" Grace asked.

"Not exactly," he said slowly. "Have you come up with a best-case scenario, something to give Justin to work with?"

Michael exchanged a look with Grace, then nodded. "Grace wants to take the boys to live with her."

Jamie and Josh whirled on her and stared, wide-eyed. "You mean it?" Jamie asked incredulously.

"I mean it," she said firmly, then cautioned, "Don't get your hopes up, though. There's no guarantee we can pull it off."

"You will," Josh said, scrambling from his chair to give her a fierce hug. "I know you will."

Grace looked at Jamie, who hadn't budged. "Is this okay with you, Jamie?"

Blinking back tears, the boy nodded. Grace held out her hand, and after a slight hesitation, Jamie put his into it.

"Deal," he said in a voice choked with emotion.

Michael felt the salty sting of tears in his own eyes as he watched the three of them, already united, already a family in their own eyes.

But where the hell did that leave him?

Tyler caught his gaze, gave him a sympathetic look before saying, "Hey, Grace, why don't you and the boys take off for a while? Leave the cleanup for Michael and me."

She stared at him, clearly flabbergasted by the offer. "You don't have to ask me twice," she said, then glanced in Michael's direction. "Of course, it might almost be worth it to stick around and see how you look in an apron."

"If you can find one with frills, I'll take a picture," Tyler offered, grinning.

Michael scowled with mock ferocity. "Thanks, bro."

"Get out of here, Grace," Tyler encouraged. "You don't want to stick around for the bloodshed."

She grinned at him. "Come on, kids. Let's take advantage of this magnanimous offer and go out to see the horses."

"Can we ride?" Josh begged.

"Not without Slade here," she said.

Surprisingly, her decision didn't draw a whiff of protest. Apparently the boys had no intention of risking her wrath when she was willing to be their new mom.

After they'd gone, Tyler turned to Michael. "When you want something as badly as you obviously want those three, you fight for it," he advised mildly.

"Don't even go there," Michael retorted.

"You're talking to me," Tyler said. "Don't waste your breath trying to deny it. You've never gotten over Grace.

And I've never seen you take to a couple of kids the way you've obviously taken to those two. What are you going to do about it?"

"Besides begging Grace for another chance?" Michael said wryly. "I've already done that."

"Did she turn you down?"

"She said maybe."

"Then I guess you're just going to have to be more persuasive," Tyler said. "Because I don't want to think that my brother is an idiot. Besides, Delacourts never fail. Isn't that the lesson Dad started drilling into us when we were still in our cradles?"

"Grace refuses to so much as discuss our future until we've protected Jamie and Josh from being separated again."

"Then get Justin over here and get the ball rolling," Tyler said.

"Good advice," Michael agreed. "Mind telling me what we do if it starts careening downhill?"

"We pull out the big guns," Tyler said readily.

"Oh?"

"Dad and Harlan Adams. I can't imagine a bureaucrat anywhere who wouldn't quake in his boots at the sight of those two formidable men."

Michael took heart at the suggestion. It was true. Nobody he knew would dare to say no to his father or to Harlan Adams, and no two men were more fiercely committed to the concept of family. With them on her side, Josh and Jamie were as good as Grace's.

Once again, though, he had to ask himself: Where did that leave him?

Eleven

Grace stood at the fence to the corral and watched as Jamie and Josh groomed the two horses that were their favorites. Slade had taught them well. They were thorough, murmuring to the horses the whole time and drawing gentle nudges at their pockets where both had stored pieces of apple.

"Stop it," Jamie said, laughing when one curious nudge almost landed him on his backside in the dirt. "You'll get your treat when I'm done."

The horse whinnied in response, clearly unhappy about being put off. Jamie finally gave a resigned shrug and pulled out a chunk of apple, then held it out in his open palm. The horse took it daintily, but seconds later the filly was back for more.

"If I keep feeding you, you're going to be too fat to gallop," Jamie chided her.

The horse's only response was to try to burrow her nose into his pocket.

Grace laughed at their war of wills. She prayed that life could go on being like this for Jamie, simple and uncomplicated after years of having too many worries on his young shoulders. He'd been barely older than Josh was now when he'd concluded it was up to him to see that he and his brother were reunited for their birthdays, no matter what the system did to separate them.

She thought about her plan to take them back to Houston with her. It was evident that both boys were eager to go, but was it right to take them away from this ranching world they so obviously adored, where in just a few days they had begun to flourish?

She was still troubled by that when Michael eased up behind her and put his hands on either side of the corral fence, effectively trapping her body against the hard planes of his. A shiver of anticipation skittered over her at the intimate contact.

"They look as if they're in their element," Michael observed. "Don't they?"

She turned to look up at him. "What if I'm doing the wrong thing?"

He regarded her with surprise. "Meaning?"

"Maybe I shouldn't take them away from here. Maybe I should let Sharon Lynn or one of the others around here make a home for them. They'd have friends, fresh air, horses."

"Sweetheart, you'll bring even more to their lives. Besides, we don't even know if Sharon Lynn was able to convince Cord to take them in."

"She will," Grace said with confidence. "Or she'll get one of the other Adamses to agree. Look at them. They're so happy, probably happier than they've ever been."

"Don't you think that's as much because they're together as it is because they're on a ranch?"

"I don't know that for sure," she said candidly. "Shouldn't I give them the option?"

"We don't even know if that option exists," Michael reminded her again. "Let's leave things as they are. You love those boys. You can give them a good life. More important, you *want* to give them a good life. If they need horses to be happy, you'll find a way to see that they have them. My guess is all they really need is a home and you."

Her gaze met his. His reassurance meant the world to her, ironically because she knew he wouldn't let emotion overrule his clear-eyed objectivity. "Thank you for saying that."

"I meant it." He caressed her cheek. "It's all I would need." She didn't know what to say to that. He grinned at her silence. "Left you speechless? That has to be a first."

"I can't think about that now," she told him honestly. "I just can't."

"I know. I'm not pressing you for an answer, just reminding you that the issue is on the table."

She smiled. "I'm not likely to forget that." Her smile faltered then. "What about Justin? Did you call him?"

Michael nodded. "He's on his way."

"Maybe we should warn the boys that he's a sheriff. If he comes in here in a cop car and wearing a uniform, they might panic."

"Which is why Tyler's coming out any second to take them into town," Michael said. "There's no need to get them worked up unnecessarily."

As if on cue, Tyler came out of the house and called to the boys, "Hey, guys, how about riding into town with me? I could use some help."

Both boys hesitated. "What kind of help?"

"Getting there, for starters. You probably know the way better than I do," he said in what was clearly a blatant lie. "And my brother has given me this endless list of things to pick up. I'll never be able to carry them all myself."

"I guess we could go," Jamie said. He glanced at Grace. "Is it okay? If that guy's coming over to talk about us, shouldn't we get to stay?"

"We've agreed on our plan. We won't change it without talking it over with you. In the meantime, a trip into town sounds great to me."

"How come you're not going?" Josh asked.

"Because they've got to wait for this Justin person," Jamie said. "And they want us out of the way."

"You're too smart for your own good," Michael told him, ruffling his hair. "Now scoot." He bent down to whisper, "And make sure he buys you pizza and ice cream. Play your cards right and he might take you to the toy store, too."

"All right," Josh enthused, easily won over.

Five minutes after the three of them had driven off, Grace heard what had to be the sheriff's cruiser coming through the thick stand of pines between the house and the road.

"I'm not sure I'm ready for this," she admitted to Michael.

"Sure you are. Just remember that I'm right here beside you and I'm not going anywhere. Work your charm and your legal magic on him."

Justin exited the car and strolled toward them wearing his crisply ironed uniform and sunglasses that shaded his eyes and left his expression enigmatic. Grace hated not being able to see behind those lenses to gauge his reaction. She thought she knew one way to assure they'd come off.

"Hello," she said briskly, holding out her hand. "I'm Grace Foster, an attorney from Houston. Why don't we go inside and have a glass of iced tea? It's getting warm out here."

"Fine by me," Justin agreed, then turned to shake Michael's hand. "Good to see you again. It's been a long time."

"I know. I don't get over to see my sister and brother nearly enough."

"So they say," Justin said, then chuckled. "Hear they tricked you into coming this time, then ran off and left you to fend for yourself."

Michael gave him a rueful grin. "Don't remind me."

Inside, as expected, Justin removed his sunglasses, but he didn't sit down. He leaned against the counter and waited for her to begin. Grace had dealt with plenty of law enforcement officers in her time. She never let them get the better of her, but now, with so much at stake, she had to struggle against panic.

"How much do you know?" she asked him, gazing into penetrating blue eyes that she imagined could intimidate a suspect in nothing flat. She almost regretted getting him to remove the sunglasses.

"Sharon Lynn filled us in last night. To tell you the truth I expected a call before now."

"We… I…had some thinking to do," Grace said.

"About?"

"My own role in all of this."

Justin waited patiently.

"I want Jamie and Josh to come live with me. I don't want them separated again."

Justin's gaze registered surprise. "I was under the impression you were hoping someone around here might take them in. Sharon Lynn and Cord are considering it."

"I know, but since I talked with her, I've given it a lot of thought. They're great kids. I can give them a good home. Jamie and Josh have agreed. I want to get the ball rolling to see that that's what happens."

Justin regarded her with concern. "You've talked this over with them? What if you can't make it happen? They'll be devastated."

"I made them a promise that they would have a say," she said defensively. "I kept that promise."

"And if the court turns down your request?" Justin asked. "What then?"

"That won't happen," Michael said at once. His gaze met Justin's evenly. "Will it?"

Justin didn't flinch under the intensity of that look. "You know that that's beyond my control."

"Maybe so, but it'll go a long way toward putting the court on Grace's side if you can report that the boys are happy with her and forget about the fact that she kept their presence here a secret for a few days while we sorted things out."

"In other words, you want me to fudge the truth," Justin said.

"For the good of those two boys," Michael stressed.

Justin didn't look one bit happy about the request, but eventually he gave a curt nod. "Let me start making some calls. Try to salvage this situation as best I can." His piercing gaze landed on Grace. "You and I could both land in a heap of trouble for this. If everybody just grabbed up any stray kid they saw and took them home, we'd have chaos. There's a reason for all the rules and regulations, you know."

"I do know, which is why I'm so grateful to you," she said. "Believe me, when you meet Josh and Jamie, you'll see that they're worth the risk."

"If Sharon Lynn hadn't already told me that, I wouldn't be doing this," he said succinctly. He grinned ruefully. "That, combined with the fact that I'm under orders from Grandpa Harlan to take care of this in a way that protects those brothers from being separated. My grandfather gets his dander up at the slightest hint that some adult isn't doing everything possible to give a child the best possible family. He's chomping at the bit to get over here and meet these two, but Janet's trying her best to keep him at White Pines and out of the middle of things."

He shook his head. "I could tell her she's fighting a losing battle, but why waste my breath. She knows it anyway. And just so you know, she also pulled me aside to tell me if you need another legal mind on this to give her a call. Given your intention to ask for custody of those boys, you might consider it. You won't find a better advocate than Janet."

"I appreciate the offer," Grace said sincerely. "And I may do that before we're done. It probably isn't all that smart for me to represent myself."

She held up the pitcher. "More tea before you make those calls?"

"No, thanks. I'm fine."

"Then I'll show you to Trish's office," Michael offered. "You can make your calls from there."

After the two men had left the room, Grace finally felt the knot of tension in her stomach ease. Justin Adams might be a law-and-order, by-the-book sheriff, but he was a good man. Dylan had been right about that and she could see the kindness in his eyes. It was a good thing, since not only her future, but Jamie's and Josh's, were all in his hands.

"I hate standing on the sidelines while someone else gets things done. What do you think is happening in there?" Grace asked Michael when Justin hadn't come back to the kitchen after an hour.

"I think he's doing everything he can to make sure this turns out the way we want it to."

He stood behind her chair and massaged her shoulders, finally feeling them begin to relax beneath his touch. Unfortunately, the contact was having the opposite effect on him. He felt as if he were grasping a live wire. There were sparks detonating inside him. Memories exaggerated them into full-fledged passion and left him aching with need.

He cursed this inability he had to control himself around her. Desire wasn't what Grace needed now. She needed moral support, compassion, maybe even financial backing should her resources be more limited than he imagined them to be. She didn't need lust.

She glanced up at him, surprising him with a grin. "Nice distraction," she teased.

"Is it?" he asked.

And then, because he could no longer resist, he bent down and covered her lips with his. White-hot urgency slammed through him, making his blood roar. Damned, if he didn't think it made his teeth tingle, too. He was sure if Grace looked into his eyes, she would be terrified by the hunger she saw there.

With a shudder, with a last probe of tongue against tongue, he pulled back, sucked in a deep, calming breath, but he didn't take his hands from her shoulders. He wasn't feeling that generous. He craved the contact, any contact that would remind her, remind both of them of all that was at stake.

"Even better than the last distraction," she murmured. "But risky. I want to be here, not upstairs in bed when Justin's through making his calls."

Michael took heart from the implication that he could lure her to bed with a few more potent kisses. "Hold that thought," he suggested. "In the meantime, how about playing cards or working on a puzzle? Knowing Trish, there must be some around here somewhere."

In the past, when things had been good between him and Grace, there had always been a thousand-piece jigsaw puzzle set up for rainy afternoons. He'd been surprised by how much he enjoyed the quiet activity, but he suspected that had more to do with his companion and the sneaky distraction of her foot against his calf under the table than the challenge of the puzzle. She also played a cutthroat game of rummy.

Although her anxious gaze remained firmly fixed on the door, she nodded. "That would be nice."

Michael checked a few cupboards and finally found some playing cards. "Rummy okay?"

"Sure."

He dealt the cards, but she was slow to pick up her hand. "What could be taking so long?" she asked.

"He's just being thorough. It doesn't mean there's anything wrong."

"I hope you're right."

"Watching for him won't bring him back here any faster. Pick up your cards. Otherwise, I'm going to win by default, and I have some fascinating ideas about what my prize should be."

That caught her attention. "Oh, really?" she said, snatching up her hand and studying it with fierce concentration. "You haven't got a chance, buster."

He grinned. "Is that so?"

As he'd anticipated, within minutes, she was thoroughly caught up in the game and happily taking him to the cleaners. When she'd slapped down another winning hand, she regarded him with a triumphant expression.

"Any questions about who's the grand champion?" she asked.

"Maybe I'm just letting you win to keep your mind off of Justin," he suggested.

"Letting me win?" she retorted indignantly. "I don't think so."

"You'll never know for sure, will you?"

She picked up the cards and shuffled. "Okay, that's it. This is war." She placed the cards down on the table with a snap. "Winner take all."

"An interesting bet," he agreed. "Since we're not playing for money, what does it mean exactly?"

Her expression turned thoughtful. "Okay, here it is. It means that if I win this hand, you will agree to one whole month of working nine to five, Monday to Friday, and no more. And just so you know, the month doesn't begin until you are actually back in Houston and back at work."

He started to protest that he didn't have a nine-to-five job, but that was her point, of course. She wanted to see if he could do it, if he'd learned anything at all about putting his priorities in order. He vowed to prove he could, even if he won the hand.

"Agreed," he said, clearly startling her with his ready acceptance of the terms. "And if I win—"

"You won't."

He scowled at her with mock ferocity. "*When* I win, you and Josh and Jamie will let me court you."

Color flared in her cheeks at the suggestion. "Excuse me? You plan to court all three of us?"

"After this is settled, you'll be a package deal, correct?"

"Yes."

"Then me courting you will also affect them."

"I suppose," she said as if she suspected there were a trick in there she hadn't quite discerned.

"Agreed?"

She nodded finally. "Agreed."

Michael looked at his cards then and had to bite back the urge to utter a whoop of triumph. She had dealt him a near-perfect hand. One card was all he needed for victory. He drew his first card, stared at it, then snuggled it into place in his hand.

He glanced across the table, caught the wary expression in her eyes and was about to place the winning hand down on the table, when Justin stepped into the room.

"Okay," he said, his expression grim. "Here's the deal."

Grace was immediately on her feet, all thoughts of the card game clearly abandoned. "Tell me."

"Sit, sweetheart," Michael urged, drawing her back to the table. "Give the man a chance."

Justin pulled up a chair and sat opposite her. "After some grumbling about people taking the law into their own hands, obstructing justice, etcetera, the authorities are willing to overlook all of that and leave Jamie and Josh in your care until a hearing can be set."

Grace uttered a sigh of relief.

"Hang on. That's only the beginning," Justin warned. "In the meantime, if you want to become their foster parent, you have to take the appropriate steps, file all the paperwork, go through the clearances. I'm sure you know the drill."

"Not a problem," Grace said. "I'll get started this afternoon."

He slid a piece of paper toward her. "Here's the fax number. I left the papers they've already faxed here for your signature on the desk in Trish's office. Fill everything out and get it back to them before they close for the day. Otherwise, they're likely to be camping on the doorstep over here first thing in the morning."

"Is there any chance she won't be approved?" Michael asked.

She frowned at the question. "Why would you even suggest that they might turn me down?"

"Because I'm trying to be realistic here. I think we need to know if our failure to turn those kids in right away could affect the outcome of this."

"He's right," Justin said. "The social services worker on the case is just relieved that the boys are okay. So are the previous foster parents. Neither of those families has any intention of fighting to get Jamie or Josh back. But there's a supervisor in the office over there who's mad as hell. He likes to have all the *i's* dotted and all the *t's* crossed before the fact, not after. He won't cut you any slack, Grace."

"Name?" Michael asked.

Justin glanced at his notes. "Franklin Oakley. He's been around a long time. Runs a tight ship. The caseworker says he's the kind to hold a grudge. Worse, he really hates lawyers. Thinks they're the scourge of the system. 'Bunch of damn bleeding hearts' is the exact quote."

Grace looked shaken. "Terrific."

"Don't panic. We'll take care of Mr. Oakley," Michael said quietly.

"How?"

"There are ways."

"Delacourt or Adams influence won't cut it," Justin warned. "If anything, it'll just infuriate him. You know the type. They hate anything that smacks of undue influence, and they especially hate the wealthy and powerful."

"That won't matter if he's no longer in a position to do any harm," Michael retorted.

Grace regarded him with a shocked expression. "Michael, you can't get the man fired."

"I can, if that's what it takes," he said coldly.

"Let's not resort to that just yet," she pleaded. "Let's just play by the rules."

He wanted to warn her that playing by the rules might cost her Jamie and Josh, but this was her call. He had to do it her way. "Okay," he said at last. "We'll try it your way. If things start turning sour, though, we do it mine. If Mr. Oakley had been doing his job right from the beginning, those boys would still be together somewhere. They wouldn't have had to run away in the first place."

Grace still looked troubled, but she nodded. She faced Justin. "Thank you. I know if I had made these calls myself, we wouldn't be where we are. I would probably have told Mr. Oakley some of the same things Michael just said. I owe you."

"You don't owe me," Justin said. "Just try not to break any more laws while you're in my jurisdiction."

"Not a one," Grace vowed. "We'll be model citizens."

"Scout's honor," Michael said.

Grace stared at him. "When were you a Scout?"

"Never. It just seemed like the thing to say."

She rolled her eyes. "I'll keep him in line," she promised Justin.

He chuckled. "That ought to be interesting to see. Sorry I can't stick around."

After he'd gone, Michael caught Grace's gaze. "So, you're going to keep me in line, are you? Just how do you intend to do that?"

"I have my ways," she said airily.

"Sounds promising. I'll be fascinated to see them in action."

She kept her gaze level for a moment, but then her glance fell. She caught sight of the cards lying on the table.

"Want to finish our game before I fill out this paperwork?" she asked.

"No need," he told her, spreading out his winning hand. "It's already over."

She stared at the cards in shock. "How can that be?"

"Just lucky, I guess."

"You cheated. You must have."

"No need, darlin'. You dealt the cards. I won. It's as simple as that. I think you wanted me to win."

"I most certainly did not."

"Well, the cards don't lie. I won, and now I aim to collect on my bet."

"How?" she asked warily.

"Don't look so terrified. If I do it right, courting's practically painless. You just have to get used to bouquets of flowers, the occasional box of candy, a little fine dining, maybe a kiss now and then."

"The boys will love that," she noted wryly.

"They can share in some of it, but the kisses are all yours," he clarified. "In fact, now might be a good time to collect on the first one. We're all alone. You're already looking a little flushed."

She waved the faxes at him. "I have forms to fill out."

"It's just one kiss, a sample of things to come."

"Oh, all right," she said with an exaggerated sigh of resignation. She puckered her lips and waited, eyes closed.

Michael regarded her with amusement, then gave her a gentle peck on the cheek that had her eyes snapping open.

"That's it?" she demanded.

"You wanted something more?"

"Of course not."

He chuckled. "Liar."

As she opened her mouth to tell yet another fib, he angled his head, swooped in and stole another kiss, this one packing the kind of wallop that left them both breathless.

"Now there's an incentive," he murmured.

"An incentive for what?"

"Who knows?" he teased. "A few more of those and I might get home from work every day for lunch."

Twelve

The reality of what she was doing slammed into Grace as she was filling out the stack of papers Justin had received by fax. She had closeted herself in Trish's office, partly to get the necessary paperwork done, but just as much to get out of the path of Michael's devastating kisses. They left her confused and shaken and right now she definitely needed all her wits about her.

A tiny voice in her head shouted that she was making a totally impulsive decision, a decision driven by emotion. Grace Foster, tough, single-focus attorney, didn't do things like that. In fact, her clearheadedness was one of her most prized assets. So why this decision?

Because Jamie and Josh needed to be together. They needed stability and love and she could give them both. Simple as that.

And twice as complicated, she thought ruefully. She was charging into this because she didn't see an alternative. And—she realized with sudden insight—because she needed them almost as much as they needed her. They filled a void in her life, an empty place in her heart. They promised something she hadn't had since she'd split up with Michael: love.

"It's the right thing to do," she murmured, trying to reassure herself. "Definitely the right thing."

She bent over the papers once more. A few minutes later she was just finishing the last form when she heard the thunder of feet hitting the porch. Shouts echoed through the house as Josh and Jamie came bolting inside, obviously exuberant after their trip into town. Their happiness reassured her. Hearing it, she was able to push aside the last, lingering doubts. She put the papers into the fax and sent them. Now all they had to do was wait.

And pray, she thought as she went to find the boys.

She found them in the kitchen raiding the refrigerator as if they were starved. Michael was observing the scene with apparent astonishment.

"Ty, I thought you were going to feed them in town," Michael said, watching them snatch up cheese and lunch meats for sandwiches.

"They're as voracious as a horde of locusts," Tyler declared. "I swear to you I bought them pizza—a large one with everything on it—and sundaes with the works, including double hot fudge. I don't understand where they put it."

Grace chuckled at his incredulous expression. "You don't remember being that age?"

"Of course I do, but we had our limits." He glanced at Michael. "Didn't we?"

"I certainly did," Michael retorted with a pious expression. "You, however, ate everything in sight, now that I think about it. No freshly baked cookie was safe with you in the house. We lost three housekeepers because they couldn't keep up with you."

Tyler shot him an exasperated look. "We did not. The only housekeeper who ever quit did so because you put a frog in her bed."

Josh and Jamie looked up at that, clearly fascinated. "Cool," Jamie declared.

"Did you get punished?" Josh asked.

"Michael never got punished," Tyler said. "He was mother's favorite." He grinned. "Till Trish came along, anyway."

Michael groaned. "You are such a liar."

"Am not. You got away with murder, while the rest of us had to pay a heavy price for every little misdeed."

"What kind of price?" Josh asked, clearly fascinated.

"We were grounded, lost our TV privileges, had to clean our rooms. I'm telling you, our folks were tough."

"Get out the violins," Michael muttered.

Grace laughed. "Something tells me you are making every word of this up, Tyler Delacourt."

"He is," Michael assured her. "Except for his inability to get our father to leave him out in the oil fields, Tyler has gotten his way his entire life. The man was spoiled rotten. He was a skinny little thing, so the housekeepers always gave him the choicest food, the biggest servings of pie and cake. Every time I turned around Mother was bringing him another toy. He was the first one in the family to get his own computer."

"Which you stole so you could run profit and loss statements on Delacourt Oil before you turned ten," Tyler countered.

"It must have been really cool living at your house," Jamie said quietly.

The observation brought a sudden halt to the teasing as the men clearly realized what a contrast their upbringing had been to Josh and Jamie's experiences. Not only had they been together, they had been surrounded by love and material things that Josh and Jamie could only dream about.

"It was cool," Michael told them. "And once you're with Grace, it's going to be just as cool for you."

Grace was startled that he would dangle that possibility out to them before it was a done deal. The less said about it until then, the better. "Michael—"

"No, Grace, don't start doubting it. This is going to happen."

"Things went okay with Justin, then?" Tyler asked.

"Well enough," Grace conceded carefully.

Jamie's eyes registered concern. "There's something you're not saying, isn't there?"

Grace shot an *I-told-you-so* look at Michael. "They've agreed to let you stay with me for now."

"All right!" Josh shouted.

"She said *for now,* dope. That's not forever," Jamie said.

"No, it's not forever," Grace admitted. "But it's a good start. We've got the ball rolling. We'll just have to wait and see what happens."

"How long do we have to wait?" Jamie asked.

"It's hard to tell. They'll set a hearing date, probably in a few days."

"But you're not giving up, right? Will we get to tell somebody what *we* want?"

"Maybe, down the road," she told him. "In the meantime, let's try not to worry about it."

"In fact, let's focus on something else," Michael told

them. "I think I hear Slade. Are you guys ready for another riding lesson? I talked to him earlier, and I think he's going to take you on a real ride today."

"You mean, like, out of the corral?" Josh asked, eyes wide.

"Yep," Michael said. "He says you're ready and the horses are definitely eager for the exercise."

"Are you coming?" Jamie asked Michael. He was already heading for the door, sandwich in hand.

"Nope. I'll be out later to watch you guys. I want to talk to Grace for a bit."

"About us?"

Michael grinned at him. "Not everything is about you. In fact, if I could get my brother out of here, I might snatch a little time alone with Grace."

"So you can kiss her?" Josh wanted to know.

Grace felt the color rise in her cheeks. "There will be no kissing," she said in her haughtiest tone, but Michael only winked.

"Bet I can change her mind," he said.

Tyler dutifully stood up and followed Josh and Jamie to the door. He paused before leaving, though, and directed his own wink at Grace before facing his brother.

"Bet you can't."

"You're on," Michael responded at once.

As soon as they were alone, Grace scowled at Michael. "Hell will freeze over before you get another kiss from me, Michael Delacourt."

He merely grinned. "I love it when you get all huffy."

Exasperated, she started to leave the kitchen, but he snagged her hand.

Despite herself, she felt a wave of anticipation wash over her. "Michael—"

"Yes, Grace."

"I…will…not…kiss…you," she said emphatically. "Especially not so you can win some bet with your brother."

His gaze locked with hers. "How about because it's been a couple of hours since the last one and I don't think I can last another minute?"

Unfortunately, that echoed her own longing. "Maybe," she said. "Keep talking."

"How about because you drive me wild?"

"Better."

"How about because kissing you is the best thing that's happened to me in six years?"

She sighed and stepped closer, tilting her face up. "Me, too," she whispered, slowly opening her mouth to the tantalizing invasion of his tongue.

"Oh, yes," she murmured sometime later. "Definitely, me, too."

When Michael eventually went outside in search of the boys, Grace headed straight for the sink and a splash of cold water to cool off her suddenly over-active hormones. She was still standing there wondering how her life had taken this unexpected twist in such a short time when the doorbell rang.

Wondering who on earth it could be, she opened it to find a distinguished-looking white-haired gentleman on the porch. Even though he was dressed in the worn jeans and chambray shirt of a rancher, there was no mistaking that this was no ordinary rancher. She guessed at once that this was the indomitable Harlan Adams. Who else would have the audacity to drop in on strangers out of the blue?

"You must be Grace Foster," he said, extending his hand. He enfolded her hand in a powerful grip. Gaze steady and filled with curiosity, he surveyed her from head to toe. "Even prettier than I'd been told."

She grinned. "Thank you. You're as charming as *I've* been told."

"So the grandkids have been blabbing about me again," he said with a resigned expression. "Told all sorts of tales, no doubt. Don't believe 'em. I'm not half as bad as they say."

"I suppose that depends on your point of view, Mr. Adams."

"Call me Harlan. Or Grandpa Harlan, if it suits you better. Mind if I come in and sit a spell?" He gave an impatient wave of his cane. "Blasted knee's not what it once was, so they make me use this thing. It's a damned nuisance, but what can I do? It puts Janet's mind at ease."

"I'm sure your wife appreciates your thoughtfulness," she said, leading the way into the kitchen.

"Sometimes she does," he agreed as he sat down heavily. "Sometimes she doesn't quite see it the same way I do."

Grace chuckled. "You mean even after all these years, you two haven't worked out all the kinks in your marriage?"

"Gracious, no. If we had, we'd just have to dream up new ones. Have to keep things lively."

Grace offered him some iced tea, but he opted for coffee instead. "If it's not too much trouble."

"Of course not."

He regarded her with a satisfied smile that had her worrying. "Are you supposed to drink coffee?" she asked as a scoop hovered over the coffeemaker. "I noticed there's decaf here, too."

"Decaf's a waste of time. I like the real thing."

She regarded him evenly. "Which isn't an answer at all."

"Oh, for goodness sakes. It's one little cup of coffee. No need to make a big deal about it."

Rather than argue, she made it weak. "Something tells me you're a sneaky man, Mr. Adams."

"I am, and proud of it," he declared, snatching the cup of coffee before she could change her mind. He took a sip, then made a face. "No *oompf.*"

"Precisely what I intended," she retorted, thoroughly enjoying him. "Now why don't you tell me why you're here? I don't imagine you came all this way just to sneak a cup of coffee."

"Came to meet those boys, of course. And you. I like to know what's going on around these parts, especially with family."

"Family?" she questioned, surprised by the claimed connection.

"Hardy works for me. I rent that bookstore space to Trish. Had a hand in getting the two of them together. That's close enough to being family for me."

"I see. So you've claimed Michael as well."

"He's Trish's brother, isn't he? Of course I do." He winked at her. "We'll have to see about you." He tapped his coffee cup. "You've got promise, though."

"Thank you, I think."

"Justin help you out with this situation?"

"He did."

"Anything I can do?"

"Not at the moment. He was able to get the authorities to agree to let me keep Josh and Jamie for the time being, while the rest is worked out."

"They'd have a good home with Sharon Lynn and Cord," he said. "She seems inclined to offer."

"I know and I appreciate it. I really do, but I'm thinking that they ought to stay with me."

"They'd have two parents here," he countered. "You and that young man gonna offer them that?"

She stared at him. "Michael? And me?"

"You know any other young men around here?"

"We're not... I mean, there's been no talk of anything permanent happening between Michael and me. We're just friends."

"Too bad. From what I've heard, those two boys could use a stable home."

She drew herself up, taking exception to the notion that only a two-parent home could give a child what he needed. She'd seen plenty of examples of a single parent being far better than a man and woman who didn't get along. "I can give them that," she said stiffly.

"Well, of course, you can. But boys especially need a man's influence. Where will they get that?"

Grace had no answer for that. He was right, too. Even though she didn't like admitting it, Jamie and Josh needed a male role model. Once again she was forced to consider whether she was being selfish in trying to keep them. Could she fight their feelings of abandonment alone any better than her mother had been able to fight hers?

"Just something to think about," Harlan Adams said mildly, then pushed himself up and reached for his cane. "Think I'll go outside and meet them now."

"I'll come with you," Grace offered.

"No need. Seems to me like you'd do better to spend a little time thinking about what I said."

"I will," she assured him. "I promise."

"A man can't ask for more than that." He stepped outside, then smiled at her. "It's been a pleasure, Grace. I look forward to seeing you again."

"The pleasure was all mine, Mr. Adams."

But after he had gone, she was left with the disquieting sense that despite his warm remarks, he didn't entirely approve of what she was planning. What she didn't understand was why that bothered her so. Could it be because she feared he might be right?

Michael looked up with surprise when he spotted Harlan Adams exiting the house and heading for the corral. Michael knew Harlan only from scattered casual meetings at Trish's wedding and later Dylan's. But he knew his reputation for taking charge and making things turn out the way he thought they ought to. No doubt it had been only a matter of time before he turned up here to check out what was going on, just as Justin had predicted he would.

"Mr. Adams, good to see you again," he said, crossing the yard to meet him.

"Thought I told you to call me Grandpa Harlan, like the rest of them. Said the same thing to that little gal inside, but she didn't pay a bit of attention to me either."

"Maybe we think it seems a bit disrespectful," Michael suggested.

"It's not if I say it isn't," Harlan said, then gazed around, his expression alight with curiosity. "Okay, then, where are they?"

"Jamie and Josh have gone off on their first real ride with Slade. They should be back any second. Would you care to have a seat over here by the corral? I can bring a chair from the barn."

"If you wouldn't mind, that would suit me fine. Bring two and sit a spell with me. It'll give us a chance to talk."

Uh-oh, Michael thought. "About?" he asked aloud.

The old man grinned. "This and that. It's not an inquisition, boy, so don't go getting your dander up already."

Michael let the comment pass, retrieved two chairs from the barn and took a seat next to Harlan.

"So, tell me," he said, casting a sly look at Michael. "What do you think of Grace's plan to take in those boys? Think she's taking on too much?"

"*She* doesn't think she is," Michael said.

"Now, that's not exactly what I asked you, is it?"

"No, I suppose not."

"Well, then?"

"I think Grace will give them a good home and the love they deserve."

"You gonna be around to be a role model for them?" he inquired pointedly. "Boys need the influence of a strong man."

"I suppose I'll see them from time to time," Michael replied cautiously, not especially crazy about the direction of the conversation. He knew all about Harlan Adams's penchant for matchmaking and his very large role in getting Trish and Hardy together. This was not the kind of pressure Michael needed, not right now when he and Grace were still finding their way.

"Seems to me like you need to do a little more than that, son," Harlan declared.

"It's not up to me," Michael insisted, not liking the glint in the old man's eyes one bit.

"Who's it up to, then? The court?" Harlan scoffed.

"You think the court gives a hoot about the boys the way a father could? The judge isn't going to be there day in and day out. The judge isn't going to hug them or discipline them when they need it or see that they stay in school and get an education."

"Now wait just a damned minute," Michael protested. "How did we shift from maybe giving those two a male role model to me becoming their father?"

"You got other family obligations?" Harlan inquired tartly, as if that were the only issue to be considered.

"No, but—"

"No buts about it," the old man said, waving off Michael's attempted protest. "A man steps up to the plate in a situation like this. Does what's right. Looks to me as if that woman inside would be happy to take on the lot of you. Oh, she says she's got it all under control, that she doesn't need a lick of help, and maybe she doesn't, but people are meant to go through life sharing good times and bad with someone who'll understand."

Michael swallowed hard. This whole situation was spinning wildly out of control. "Grace and me?" he said as incredulously as if he hadn't known all along that this was where Harlan was heading, as if he hadn't considered the idea himself a time or two.

"Why on earth not? You blind, boy? The woman's beautiful. Smart, too. Had a little talk with her before I came looking for you. She's a keeper, the kind who'll stick by you. You're the one who called her over here at the first sign of trouble, am I right? And she came running."

"Oh, no, you don't," Michael protested, annoyed more by the pressure than by the concept of marriage to Grace. "I know about you and your matchmaking schemes. I am not in the market for a wife or a ready-made family. And when the time comes that I am, I will work out my own arrangements."

Harlan Adams just chuckled at that. "We'll see, son. We'll see." Michael was still thinking about that long after the boys had returned, spent time with Harlan Adams, then gone inside to wash up for dinner. He had been thinking about spending more time with Grace, seeing where that led, but the rest? Marriage? A family? Was he ready to take that plunge?

And even if he suggested it, would Grace agree? He doubted it. She would probably howl with laughter all the way back to Houston. It would ruin the nice, steady courtship he'd had in mind.

Of course, a courtship implied a certain amount of intent, didn't it? Or was he just playing a game of semantics here? What the hell did he really want?

"Something on your mind, bro?" Tyler asked as he joined him, settling into the chair Harlan Adams had occupied earlier.

"Just thinking about something Harlan Adams said."

"Can I wager a guess about what it was?" He studied Michael intently. "He thinks you should marry Grace, adopt Josh and Jamie, and live happily ever after."

Michael stared at him. "How did you know that? I thought you were off riding with the boys. Were you eavesdropping instead?"

"No, but I've spent even more time around him than you have. The man dearly loves to meddle and he thinks everybody ought to be paired off and settled down. He's tried it on me a couple of times, but I always sneak out of town before his schemes can work."

He slanted a look toward Michael. "It's not such a bad idea, you know."

"What isn't?"

"You marrying Grace. You've been in love with her for who knows how long. Stupidity and pride got in the way last time, but there's no reason to let that happen again. I say go for it."

Michael grinned. "You always were her biggest fan."

"No, you were that. I was just an interested bystander who thought you were a damn fool for letting her get away."

"She'll turn me down," Michael said.

"How do you know?"

"I just do. She's not buying that I've changed."

Tyler chuckled. "You haven't."

"You're a help. Be sure to share that with Grace."

"Well, you haven't." He regarded Michael evenly. "You could, though, if it was for something you wanted badly enough. Do you want her that badly, Michael?"

"That's what I've been trying to figure out for the past couple of days."

"And?"

He felt a smile tugging at his lips. "I think I do."

"Now there's a declaration of passion guaranteed to make any woman's heart go pitter-patter."

"You know what I mean."

"No," he said evenly. "I don't. And if I'm not sure, Grace won't be either. Stop hedging your bets. It's time to go for broke or get out of the game."

Tyler was right. He had to make a clear choice, in or out. And he had to do it fast, before Grace created a loving, tight-knit little family that left him out in the cold.

Thirteen

Michael had expected to feel calmer once Harlan Adams left for White Pines, but it wasn't turning out that way. In part that was his own fault. He was the one who'd invited Tyler over here. Now his brother refused to let the matter rest and was almost as interested in Michael's intentions toward Grace as the old man had been.

"Okay, bro," Tyler said as they sat on the deck while dusk settled in around them. "You dragged me over here because you anticipated some sort of problem. I assumed your concern was with Josh and Jamie. That problem hasn't materialized. After our conversation this afternoon and watching the two of you at dinner tonight, I have to wonder if you weren't just hoping I'd provide a buffer between you and your old feelings for Grace."

Irritated by the observation, Michael stared at his brother, cursing the fact that Tyler could read him like a book. "What the hell are you talking about?" he asked, feigning cranky innocence.

"You know exactly what I'm talking about. You've all but admitted it. You're still in love with her. You're scared to death to confess it to her, because then you'd have to risk being rejected for a second time."

"You're here because of Jamie and Josh, nothing else," Michael insisted.

"You did not need me just to get them out from underfoot for an afternoon. I'm sure Kelsey would have been happy to run over and pick them up, but you didn't even consider calling her, did you?"

"This could have gotten complicated," Michael said. "If Justin had gotten a notion to take those boys away today, I wanted backup to help me keep them here."

Tyler uttered a heavy sigh. "Okay, whatever you say, but I've got to tell you, if you let Grace get away again, I'm disowning you. Even a stubborn Delacourt should have enough sense to put pride aside and go for the gold."

"This isn't the blasted Romance Olympics," Michael muttered in disgust.

"You know what I mean."

"Yeah, I suppose I do."

Tyler stood up. "Good, then I can go back to Baton Rouge and face the music."

Michael's gaze shot to Tyler's face, but in the shadows he couldn't read his expression. "Ty, is everything okay? That's the second time you've alluded to a problem."

"Nothing I can't handle," Tyler assured him blithely. "You just worry about Grace."

"And Jamie and Josh," Michael reminded him.

Tyler chuckled. "Whatever. Let me know how things turn out."

"You're sure you don't want to stay the night?"

"Nope. You're on your own. I've got places to go and people to see." Michael heard a worrisome note of dread under his brother's light tone.

"If there's anything I can do to help," he said.

"There isn't," Tyler assured him.

"Then I'll walk you out."

Out front he gave Tyler a hug. "Take care of yourself. Thanks for riding to the rescue."

"Not a problem. It gave me some breathing space."

Again, there was that hint of trouble, but Michael knew Tyler had already said all he intended to on the subject, even though it was precious little. In fact, it was rare that he even let this much leak out about his personal life, which meant whatever it was had to be weighing heavily on him.

For some time Michael had suspected Tyler was involved with a woman he'd met in Louisiana while working on a Delacourt Oil rig in the Gulf of Mexico, but his questions drew only the most cryptic, uninformative responses. It was ironic really. Tyler gave the impression of being the most open of the brothers, yet he could keep his own counsel better than any of them. One topic was absolutely off-limits and that was his relationships. He withstood the teasing the rest of them dished out about his flirting in stoic silence.

After Tyler had gone, Michael returned to the deck. In no time the pressure that had begun building up in his chest earlier felt like it was about to explode. Options chased through his mind at a dizzying speed. He couldn't sort through them quickly enough, so he just counted his lucky stars that he had a few more days here with Grace, Jamie and Josh before they all went their separate ways. Grace and the boys together. Him alone.

The prospect of peace and quiet, of a return to routine, should have been heartening. Instead, the thought depressed him. He'd been going his own way for far too long. What had it really gotten him? His father relied on him, yes, but that would have happened anyway. Tyler had been right when he'd said that Michael was the only one in the family who really wanted an executive position. He would have won by default even if he'd devoted only half of his time and attention to the company.

Of course, that wasn't how he wanted to stay on top. He needed to prove himself, to be the best. For his own peace of mind, he needed to know he'd earned the right to head Delacourt Oil someday.

But hadn't he done that? Did he need to go on doing it forever, sacrificing everything else that really mattered?

Because he had no real answer to that question, he let his thoughts drift back to Grace and the boys. Those three would move on to Grace's apartment. He'd never been there, but he envisioned it as being cozy. The one they'd shared years ago had been, even though she'd furnished it on a shoestring with junk shop finds. She'd had a talent for mixing colors, for creating an atmosphere of warmth every bit as welcoming as what Trish had done with her home here.

He forced himself to face facts. If he didn't want to lose all three of them, he had to take action, do something. Anything. A grand gesture. Whatever.

For the next two days, though, Michael seemed plagued by indecision and inertia. Oddly enough, he had discovered that when the four of them were left alone, there was a certain comfort to be found in having two rambunctious, wise-ass boys underfoot and Grace's company on the front porch at the end of the day. He was even beginning to find a certain soothing delight in those blasted wildflowers.

He realized with a sense of astonishment that he hadn't called his office in several days. He didn't have to fill every empty minute of every quiet hour. He could just sit still, savor a morning cup of coffee on the deck, enjoy the view of Grace as she padded barefoot out to sit beside him, exposing shapely legs as she curled up on the lounge chair.

So, this was what it meant to relax, he concluded one lazy afternoon as he put aside a book and closed his eyes. It wasn't half-bad, especially with the sounds of boyish laughter echoing through the house and the occasional kiss from a woman who could send heat rocketing through him.

Despite the fact that everyone—himself included—seemed to expect something from him where Grace and those boys were concerned, he was surprisingly at ease. Maybe that was because Grace didn't seem to have any expectations at all. She just seemed glad to have company while she awaited further word on her petition to become a foster parent to Jamie and Josh.

He came to enjoy the mind-numbing monotony of the ranch routine, the laughter the four of them shared over cutthroat card games every night after dinner, the nonstop electricity that sparked between him and Grace.

In fact, he couldn't recall the last time he'd been as happy as he was right here, right now, sitting on the deck in the afternoon sun. Maybe this was what people meant when they talked about living in the moment, about not looking ahead or borrowing trouble.

"Michael?"

He opened his eyes and glanced up at Grace's worried expression. "What's wrong?" he asked, sitting up at once, heart thumping with sudden trepidation. He had the oddest sense that his contentment was about to be shattered. "Are Jamie and Josh okay?"

"They're fine, but I've been thinking."

"About?" he asked, when she didn't elaborate.

"Going back to Houston. I think it's time I took them there and got them settled in. I just spoke to the judge's office and got an okay. They'll notify me there when I need to be in court."

"I thought you took the whole week off. It's only Thursday," he protested, aware of a knot of tension forming in his stomach.

"I know, but they need time to adjust. I have to make some arrangements for them for next week, maybe a summer day camp. And I need to look for a bigger place. We can't all crowd into my apartment. There's a pull-out bed in my home office, but they won't be comfortable on that for long." She held up a sheet of paper. "I've been making a list. It's getting longer and longer. I have to get started or I'll panic."

Why had he foolishly thought that they would go on as they had been forever? Why had he counted on having more time? Obviously this living in the moment concept had a serious drawback. It left a person totally unprepared for the intrusion of reality.

"We can take the rental car and drive back," she went on, seemingly oblivious to his dismayed reaction.

"Don't be ridiculous," he said more tartly than he'd intended. At her surprised look, he forced himself to temper his tone. "When the time comes, you can take the corporate jet. I can have the pilot back over here in no time. Jamie and Josh will love it."

She grinned. "To tell you the truth, I was hoping

you'd say that. They'll be thrilled. I imagine they've never flown before."

"You're sure you need to go now?" he asked, trying to buy himself more time to wrestle with the decisions he'd been avoiding.

"Yes. I know they're having a good time here, but I'm just beginning to realize how much needs to be done. I think we should go first thing tomorrow."

He studied her intently. "Second thoughts?"

"About taking them in? Never," she said fiercely.

"Then all the rest will fall into place," he said, offering a solace to her that he wished he could find for himself.

"What makes you so sure of that?"

"Because I know you. When there's a task at hand, you plunge in wholeheartedly. I've seen you accomplish miracles. You're an amazing woman, Grace, professionally and personally."

She regarded him with surprise. "Do you really mean that?"

"Of course. Why would you doubt it?"

"Professionally, at least, you and I almost never see eye-to-eye."

"I called you when I needed help, didn't I? Doesn't that prove how much I respect what you do, even if I'm often on the opposite side of a case from your client?"

"I suppose so," she said. "What about personally, though? I dumped you, remember?"

"I'm not likely to forget." He met her gaze. "I thought we were making progress on getting past that, too. A lot of progress, in fact."

Patches of color stained her cheeks. "Yes, I suppose we have."

"You aren't thinking that will end when we get back to Houston, are you?" He didn't like the heaviness in his chest as he awaited her reply.

"I guess that's up to you," she said. "You're the one with the nonstop schedule."

"If you can make time for Josh and Jamie in your schedule, then I can find time in mine for all of you," he declared emphatically.

"We'll see," she said, sounding blatantly skeptical.

Her tone was as good as a challenge. Michael resolved then and there that he would never give her a moment's doubt. He intended to see to it that he found a way to fit into her life…whether she wanted him there or not.

This wasn't just his second chance, as Tyler had reminded him. It was his last one.

The flight back to Houston the next morning was such an adventure for Josh and Jamie that Grace almost forgot that the moment they landed she and Michael would move back into their old familiar routines. Even though he'd promised to be there for her and the boys, she couldn't help wondering how long that would last once he set foot in the office. She knew what Bryce Delacourt was like. He was a demanding father and an even more demanding boss. He was the reason Michael had spent a lifetime trying to prove himself. He was chintzy with praise and generous with criticism, even though she knew he loved all of his sons. He couldn't seem to stop himself from doing the very things that drove most of them away.

At the airport as they left the plane, she spotted a limo waiting for them.

Josh saw it, too.

"Wow, look at that car." Wide-eyed, he glanced up at Michael. "Do you think it belongs to somebody famous?"

"Not unless you think I'm famous," Michael said, grinning at him. "It's here for us."

"We don't want to take you out of your way," Grace said, not sure why she was resisting the offer. "We can take a taxi."

"The car's here," Michael countered. "And it's not out of my way."

"You don't even know where I live."

"Doesn't matter. I'm in no rush. Besides, I'd like to see where you live."

"Please, Grace," Josh begged. "We've never been in a fancy car like that."

His plea zeroed in on her real fear. With Michael offering them all of these luxuries—riding lessons, a company jet, a limo—would they be content with what she could give them? She made a comfortable living, but it didn't include this kind of perk.

Of course they would be content, she chided herself. They were the least materialistic kids she knew. While they had been grateful for the things they'd received, the opportunities they'd had the last few days, they weren't taking them for granted. What they really wanted was a loving home where they could be together, and she was giving them that. Nothing else mattered.

She lifted her gaze to meet Michael's speculative expression. "Thank you. We'd appreciate the lift."

When she had directed the driver to a high-rise condominium in the heart of downtown Houston, she saw Michael's eyebrows lift. It was definitely a far cry from the tiny apartment that they had once shared in Austin.

That had been a temporary aberration, a blip in his life, a stepping-stone in hers.

This building was more in his league. She knew for a fact that he had once dated a socialite who lived on the penthouse floor. It had driven her crazy when she'd read about it in the paper, knowing that he was in the same building, making love with another woman. And that was during a time when she'd sworn to herself that she hated him. Obviously she'd been deluding herself for years. The past few days had proven that.

The boys were awestruck by the towering sky-scraper, by the lobby and by the swift, silent elevator that whisked them upstairs.

"This is so cool," Josh said. "I could go up and down all day."

"No, you couldn't," Grace admonished. "It's not an amusement park ride."

Josh looked crestfallen. "I just meant it would be fun."

She ruffled his hair. "I know you did. I just want you to remember that there are lots of other people who need to use the elevator. It can't be going up and down just because you like to push the buttons."

"We won't even get on except when we have to," Jamie assured her, shooting a warning look at his brother as if he feared that one little mistake might ruin their chances of staying.

"I think that's enough talk about the elevator," Michael said. "Looks like we're here."

Grace led the way down the hall to her apartment, wondering what they would think of it. "Just remember," she said to the boys, "this will be temporary. We'll hunt for someplace with more room."

"Like a house?" Jamie said wistfully. "With a back-yard?"

A house meant the suburbs, Grace thought, not entirely pleased by the prospect. That meant more driving than she was used to, more chances to get herself tangled up in traffic and thoroughly lost. It was also the way Jamie and Josh thought of home, the way she had once envisioned living.

"We'll look at houses," she agreed impulsively, as she unlocked the door to their current quarters.

When they walked inside, she wasn't sure which of them was more shocked. Jamie and Josh stared at everything, clearly stunned by the view and the very modern decor. She sensed that Michael's amazement was about something else entirely.

"It's not what I expected," he said candidly.

"Oh?"

"All this chrome and black and white," he said with a visible shudder. "It's not you."

"Maybe it is," she said defensively, rather than admitting that she had hated it on sight. She simply hadn't wanted to waste the time it would take to hire another decorator. She had given the woman free rein and refused to back down even when she'd been shaken by the way the woman apparently viewed her. She had consoled herself with the reminder that she was never here, anyway.

"I thought our place in Austin suited you better," he said, capturing her gaze. "I loved that apartment."

She swallowed hard. "You did?" The words were little more than a whisper.

"It made me feel good just walking through the door."

It had felt that way to her, too, but she had told herself

it was because she was young and crazy in love. At that stage, she might even have liked *this* decor.

She glanced around at the sterile environment she rarely paid any attention to and reconsidered. Maybe not.

"Well, it is what it is," she said with a dismissive shrug. "I'm not here a lot."

"When do you plan on going house-hunting?" Michael asked.

"Tomorrow. Maybe the next day. I'll call a Realtor."

"Let me know when you make an appointment."

"Why?"

"I'd like to come along."

If she hadn't had years to school herself never to show a reaction, her jaw might have dropped open. "You want to look at houses with us?"

"Why not? It'll be fun."

"Fine. If you're sure."

"I am," he said firmly. "Somebody has to make sure you don't do anything like this again."

She was certain that when the time came he would be tied up in meetings. Now that he was back in Houston, he wouldn't be able to resist sticking his head into the office, and that would be the end of his so-called vacation. It could be weeks before he surfaced again.

He stepped closer and tilted her chin up. "Everything okay?" he asked, lowering his voice so the boys wouldn't hear. Once they'd been granted permission, they had raced off to explore the rest of the apartment. "You look a little lost. Or maybe that's panic."

"I guess I am feeling a little overwhelmed," she admitted.

"Then why don't I come back around six, and we'll all go to dinner?"

"Won't you be tied up at the office?"

"I'm on vacation, remember?"

"I thought…"

"I know what you thought," he said, brushing a kiss across her lips. "But I'll be back, Grace. You guys discuss what you'd like to eat. I'll go along with anything."

The man who dined out at four-star restaurants was going to let two boys choose where they had dinner? Grace couldn't imagine it. But sure enough, a few hours later when they said they wanted Mexican fast-food, Michael didn't bat an eye. To her added amazement, he actually knew where the closest one was.

Crammed into a booth, the table littered with an assortment of tacos, burritos and nachos, she found herself wedged thigh-to-thigh beside him.

"If your friends could see you now," she teased.

"You think they never come here?" he said. "They have kids, too."

"They probably send them with the servants."

He peered at her intently. "When did you develop this reverse snobbery?"

Taken aback, she replayed what she'd said and sighed. "That is what it sounded like, isn't it? I'm sorry."

"No need. Are you having fun?"

"Actually I am," she admitted. Not that she could stop worrying about whether Michael thought he was slumming in some bizarre way, but beyond that she was enjoying being here with the three males who'd appeared so unexpectedly in her life.

"Good. Then you'll agree to buy some popcorn and rent a video when we leave here," he suggested. "Then after the boys are in bed, you and I can snuggle up on that monstrosity of a sofa."

"It's actually very comfortable," she said.

He winked. "I hope you're right, because I have big plans for that sofa."

"Michael!" she protested, casting a horrified look his way.

"Well, I do."

"Why are you doing this?"

"Doing what?"

"Acting like you're going to stick around?"

"Because I am."

"For how long? Till you go back to work next week?"

"No, darlin'. I thought I told you. I'm in this for the long haul."

Her pulse leaped, despite all the mental warnings that it was nothing more than a turn of phrase. Her gaze narrowed. "How long is that?"

"Five years. Twenty years. Who knows, maybe even fifty years."

"Five days is more like it."

He reached over with a napkin and dabbed at something at the corner of her mouth. Hot sauce probably. That would explain the burning sensation she felt at that exact spot. Surely, it wasn't because of his touch.

"Why don't we tackle this one day at a time," he suggested, "and see how long it adds up to be?"

She could do that. But could it possibly ever add up to enough to erase all these doubts that experience had taught her were totally justified?

Fourteen

"Where have you been?" Bryce Delacourt demanded irritably when Michael poked his head into his father's office the next morning. Even though it was Saturday, he had known his father would be here. His only concession to the day of the week was leaving off his tie and jacket.

"I'm amazed you don't know," Michael retorted. "I thought your spies were better than that."

"Just answer the question."

"Your other children conspired against me."

His father's lips twitched with unexpected amusement. "Did they? That's twice now. They're cleverer than I've given them credit for being. Or you're not that great at learning from your mistakes."

Michael thought of the mistake he'd made in letting Grace get away years ago. He'd learned from that one, all right, but he wasn't ready to discuss it with his father. Instead he said, "Given how they've managed to slip out of your control, I would have thought you'd know better than anyone how inventive they can be."

"Don't remind me." His father pulled a thick pile

of folders off the corner of his desk and held them out. "You need to go over these."

"No can do," Michael said, remembering his promise to Grace. He kept his hands clasped tightly behind his back to prevent himself from instinctively reaching for the work. "I'm still on vacation."

His father regarded him with surprise, then nodded. "Okay, take 'em home with you, then."

Michael grinned ruefully. "You seem to have the same problem with the concept of a vacation that I've had. Fortunately, I've reformed."

"Meaning?"

"Meaning no work, not this week anyway."

"But we've got to make a quick decision on some of these."

"Dad, you were making decisions for this company before I was born. I'm sure you can make a few more. If not, anything you've got there can surely keep until Monday."

His father's gaze narrowed. "You are my son, Michael, aren't you? The real Michael hasn't been kidnapped by aliens, has he?"

"Very funny. You've just proved what everyone else has been telling me. I spend too much time here. You count on me being a workaholic."

"Well, of course I do. Somebody's got to take over this place when I'm gone."

"And you'll probably be sitting right there at that desk when you drop over, won't you?" Michael said, realizing that he'd instinctively followed the example set by his father.

"A man can't ask for more than to die when he's doing something he loves," his father declared.

"What about being with the people he loves? Wouldn't that be better?"

His father studied him with a bemused expression. "What's gotten into you? You aren't thinking of ducking out on me, too, are you?"

"No," Michael assured him. "But I have discovered that there's a lot to be said for getting a little balance into my life."

"You spent too damned much time with your sister," his father grumbled. "You open your mouth and I can hear her talking. Can't imagine where she learned it, since your mother knows that hard work is what puts food on our table."

Michael uttered a harsh laugh. "Food? Dad, you could feed an entire nation with what you take home from here. Maybe we'd all have been a little richer if you spent time with us, instead."

His father sighed heavily. "Now I'm neglectful? That's your sister again. Blast her, isn't it enough that she bailed out on me? Does she need to start influencing you, too?"

"Actually Trish wasn't around all that much. She and Hardy took off to make sure I had lots of free time on my hands. Might have gone crazy if I hadn't had some unexpected company." He gestured toward the stack of bulging folders and grinned at his father. "Remind me to tell you about it one of these days when you don't have so much work piled up."

"Tell me now," his father commanded in a tone that normally would have brought Michael to a halt.

"No time. I'm going house-hunting." He stepped into the outer office and closed the door firmly behind him. Even through the thick mahogany paneling of the door and the top-of-the-line soundproofing, he could hear his father bellowing.

"House-hunting? You already have a house. Michael Delacourt, get back in here this instant and explain what the devil has happened to you."

Michael winked at his father's longtime secretary, who made it a habit to come in on Saturdays as well. She claimed it was for her own good.

Otherwise, her desk was a disorganized mess on Mondays.

"You might want to steer clear of him for the next hour or two," he told her. "I seem to have thrown him off-stride."

She grinned. "It's about time. Whatever you're up to, Michael, have fun. You deserve it."

"I do, don't I?"

If his father had been startled by the changes in his attitude, Grace was positively stunned by his arrival promptly at ten.

"What are you doing here?" she demanded.

"The Realtor's coming at ten, right? That's what you told me on the phone last night."

"Yes, but…"

"I told you I'd be here. Didn't you believe me?"

"Frankly, no. You also said you'd be stopping by the office on your way. I figured your father would have things for you to do."

"He did."

"And?"

"I told him to do them himself."

Her gaze widened. "You didn't."

He chuckled at her reaction. "He was even more

shocked than you are, but he'll get over it." He leaned down and kissed her soundly. "Will you?"

She touched a finger to her lips. "I don't know."

"Where are Josh and Jamie? Surely you haven't locked them in their room for misbehaving already."

"No. They've discovered cable TV. Apparently there is an entire network devoted to cartoons. Thank goodness the Realtor is due any minute. Otherwise, I doubt I'd pry them out of there before school starts in the fall." Michael heard the squeals of laughter echoing down the hall.

"Commandeered your office, too, I see. Until we watched that video last night had that TV ever actually been on before?"

"A couple of times when I was checking the news for reports on cases I had in court," she admitted.

Michael shook his head. "We're quite a pair, aren't we?" He smiled slowly. "Maybe we deserve each other."

Grace's gaze locked with his as if she weren't quite certain how seriously to take him.

Because there wasn't time to get into such a loaded topic right now with Jamie and Josh down the hall and a Realtor on the way, he merely grinned.

He was feeling good today, no doubt about it.

He winked at her. "Something to think about, isn't it?"

Grace had been off-kilter ever since Michael had actually shown up on time. Forget on time. The fact that he'd shown up at all had been shocking. She didn't know what to make of his attitude or his innuendoes. If the man was toying with her, hinting at a future he had no intention of sharing with her, she'd have to strangle him. No doubt about it.

She glanced into the kitchen of the house the Realtor was currently showing them and heard Michael cross-examining her about the age of the appliances, the taxes, the utility bills and a zillion other details she hadn't even thought about discussing. She would have, though. Before she made an offer on a house, she surely would have remembered to ask those same questions, rather than daydreaming about bright color schemes and comfortable sofas.

The only problem was she had hated this house on sight. It was huge and pretentious. Even though the boys obviously loved the big backyard and the pool, she didn't think she could bring herself to live in a showplace like this. It reminded her too much of the Delacourt mansion.

"Grace?" Michael was looking at her curiously. "You okay?"

"Fine."

"What do you think?"

"I hate it," she said candidly, grateful that the Realtor wasn't nearby to hear. Curious about his reaction to a place that so closely resembled his home, she asked, "How about you?"

"Hate it," he agreed. "Maybe we'd better tell her she's on the wrong track or we'll waste an entire day looking at houses that are pumped up versions of a Southern plantation."

She chuckled at the description. "That's exactly what it is, isn't it? You talk to her. If I try, I'm liable to laugh out loud. She might consider that an insult to her taste. To tell you the truth, I doubt she would have shown me this place if she hadn't recognized your name. She probably figures we're trying to outdo your family."

"Heaven forbid," Michael said with a shudder. "Okay, I'll talk to her. You try to keep the boys out of the pool. They're itching to dive in. Any second now one of them is going to give the other a shove, then claim it was an accident."

Grace glanced through the French doors that opened onto the pool deck and saw Josh and Jamie inching ever closer to the side. She bolted for the door.

"Okay, you two, back inside."

"Grace, this is so cool," Josh said. "Are you gonna buy it?"

"No."

"Aw, how come?" Josh asked. "It would be really cool having our very own pool."

Jamie fought to cover his disappointment with disdain for his brother. "Probably 'cause it's too expensive, dummy."

"It's not too expensive," Grace said. "It's just way too fancy."

"We wouldn't mess things up," Josh promised, regarding her hopefully.

"I'm sure you would try very hard not to," she agreed. "I'm not worried about that. I just want someplace that'll be more comfortable."

"You mean like with chairs and stuff?" Jamie asked. "It'd have furniture, Grace. Maybe you'd like it better then."

She ruffled his hair. "I doubt that. Don't look so disappointed. This is only the first house we've seen. The perfect house is out there."

Unfortunately, after two more hours of looking and a break for lunch, they had still seen nothing that fit her idea of a real home.

Michael seemed to agree with her. Once he'd paid for lunch and they were outside waiting for valet parking to return their cars, he turned to the real estate agent. "Thanks for all your help this morning, Mrs. Norton. I think we need some time to fine-tune our needs."

Grace stood up a little straighter. *Our needs?* What the devil did he mean by that? This was her house. She'd let him speak for her earlier, but somehow he'd apparently gotten it into his head that he had a say in what she ultimately chose.

"Michael, could I speak to you for a second?" she said urgently, drawing him aside as the Realtor gave him a speculative look. "What are you doing? It's bad enough that she defers to you on every little detail. She needs to know that I'm the customer. There is no *us*."

"Do you want to look at more houses with her?"

"No, but—"

"Then let me shake her."

"I should be the one to do that."

He shrugged, regarding her with amusement. "Then, by all means, do it."

Grace returned to Mrs. Norton. "Thank you so much for your help this morning," she said graciously.

"You're entirely welcome. Shall we take a look at just one more house. I think I've narrowed down the possibilities, based on your earlier reactions. This could be the one."

Grace doubted it, but the woman was so eager, how could she possibly refuse. "One more," she agreed with a barely contained sigh. She had to try very hard to ignore Michael's *I-told-you-so* look.

Naturally the last house was no better than any of the others. In fact, it could have been a cookie-cutter copy of the first house, except for the color scheme which ran toward burgundy and forest green. Grace actually liked those colors, but not when they were done in heavy velvet and damask fabrics that blocked out every bit of sunlight. It took everything in her to hide her horrified reaction.

This time when she dismissed the Realtor, she had no trouble at all doing it forcefully.

As she, Michael and the boys climbed back into the car, Josh declared, "That place gave me the creeps. It looked like ghosts could live there."

Jamie poked his brother in the ribs. "It's not polite to say stuff like that."

"It is in this case," Michael said. "I expected to find a vampire's coffin in one of the bedrooms."

Grace chuckled. All three males stared at her, then burst into laughter. "It was so awful," she said, choking out the words between giggles.

Then the enormity of what lay ahead of her in finding a dream house sank in. Her laughter died as quickly as it had begun.

"Let's stop by my place," Michael suggested, his expression enigmatic, though it was evident to her that he had guessed she was verging on hysteria. "The boys can go for a swim and you and I can have a tall glass of something cold to drink while we rethink our strategy."

"You're going to keep helping us look?" she asked, surprised and relieved that this wasn't going to be the only day he could dedicate to house-hunting.

"Absolutely. I'm terrified you'll get so worn out that last place will start to look good to you."

"Not a chance of that," she said.

"All the same, I think I'll stick around."

A few minutes later he turned onto a side street in a quiet, older neighborhood where the houses were large, but looked as if real people lived in them. Lawns were mowed, not manicured, and were littered with bicycles and other evidence that there were children on the block.

Grace turned to him in surprise. "You live near here?"

"Just up the street," he confirmed.

"But it's so..." Words failed her.

"Normal?" he suggested. "That's what I wanted. My secretary helped me find it. She lives about a mile from here."

"Are you sure you didn't pick it just so she'd be conveniently located to handle any middle-of-the-night brainstorms you might have?" Grace teased.

"Her husband is an ex-Oiler linebacker. He doesn't permit middle-of-the-night brainstorms." He leveled a look at her. "I bought this place because it reminded me of someplace I used to feel at home."

Could he be talking about their apartment? Grace wondered. That tiny place in what could only be described as a transitional neighborhood wasn't even close to being in the same league as this. Surely she was mistaken about what he meant.

When he turned into a tree-lined driveway, Grace noticed that his house was on a larger lot than most and set well back from the road. A hedge afforded it some privacy. Beyond that, the house itself was much like its neighbors, built of light-colored brick, trimmed in white, with an attached two-car garage on the side. Shrubs and flowers added splashes of color.

"It's lovely," Grace said, something deep inside responding to its welcoming appearance and to the fact that a wealthy, powerful man like Michael had chosen a down-to-earth home like this.

When they walked through the front door, she had to keep herself from gasping in surprise. It was open and airy and filled with the same kind of cozy touches that had made Trish's house so appealing. The same kind he had told her he'd loved about their apartment.

"I had it gutted down here to create a more open feeling. Trish helped me out with the decorating," he said, his gaze intense, maybe even a little worried. "Do you like it?"

"Like it? I love it. The colors, all those windows looking out on the backyard, the trees and flowers. It must feel as if you're living in a garden, just like it does at Trish's."

He regarded her with surprise. "I never thought of it that way, but I suppose it does," Michael said. "I guess I tried to create what we had once along with what she had in Los Piños without even realizing it."

Josh and Jamie had their noses pressed to the glass doors, eyeing the inviting, crystal blue pool.

"Can we really swim while we're here?" Josh asked.

"Sure. There are extra suits in that room off the kitchen. There should be a couple that fit. Don't go in the water, though, until Grace and I get out there."

"How long will that be?" Josh asked impatiently.

"Not long," Grace assured him.

"As soon as I show her the rest of the house," Michael said, then held out his hand. "Come see the upstairs."

Like the downstairs, each room brought the outdoors in with huge windows and complementary bedspreads in the dark greens and splashy florals of the gardens outside. She counted three bedrooms before he led her to the master suite.

"Best for last," he said, stepping aside to let her walk in.

It was, too. She could imagine him in this room with its crisp, clean fabrics and soft sage color. The dresser was littered with framed family photos. Gold cufflinks were tossed carelessly aside next to scattered change.

Then there was the bed. Oh, my, she thought as her eyes widened and her pulse kicked up. It was a huge, thoroughly decadent bed with a thick, puffy comforter and piles of pillows. She could imagine making love in that bed, then snuggling together under those covers for warmth as a chilly breeze stole in from the open doors that led onto a small balcony overlooking the backyard and the forested property beyond.

"What do you think?" Michael asked.

Grace's mouth was dry. Words wouldn't seem to form.

He grinned. "Tempting isn't it?" he asked, stepping up behind her and circling her waist. He linked his fingers loosely in front of her and rested his chin on top of her head. She could feel his breath fanning across her cheek.

"More than you know," she said honestly.

"Gracie?"

He never called her that except when they were alone and intimate. She trembled at the memories of him whispering it at the height of passion.

"Move in here."

She broke free of his embrace to stare. "Here?"

"Why not? You love it. The boys will, too."

"I can't," she said at once. "We can't. The court

would have a cow about me bringing those two boys to live with you."

He had the audacity to chuckle at her indignation. "You mean if we were living here in sin, so to speak."

"Well, of course. And it's nothing to joke about, Michael."

"I'm not joking, Gracie. And I'm not suggesting we set up some sort of informal living arrangement. I want you to marry me. I want us to be a family. This house was made for lots of kids. It was made for us. We can be happy here."

Listening to him, Grace knew the real meaning of temptation. This house. Michael. It was all she'd ever dreamed of, but he'd neglected to mention one thing. He hadn't said anything at all about love. They would need a lot of it if they were going to make it, a lot of it as they learned the art of compromise.

The old Michael had had absolutely no experience with the concept of compromise. She had no reason to believe he'd changed.

"I can't marry you," she said sadly. "I want to, more than you'll ever know, but I can't."

He stiffened at her refusal and his eyes darkened with hurt. "Why is that? I thought we'd made progress the last few days."

"We have," she agreed. "But it hasn't even been a week, Michael, and old habits die hard."

"Which old habit are we talking about? You hating me for letting you down?"

She winced at the direct hit. She wanted to believe the accusation was unfair, but maybe it wasn't. Maybe she hadn't entirely forgiven him for the past. Maybe she needed a whole lot more than a few days worth of evidence before she believed he'd really changed.

"No, you caring about anything more than your job," she said quietly.

"I see."

"Maybe I should get the boys and go," she said, feeling as if something inside had shattered. Her heart, maybe.

"No, stay. Let them have their swim. I'm sure you and I can maintain a polite facade for their sake."

"Dammit, Michael, I don't want to maintain any kind of a facade. This is about facing reality. I won't set those two up for more disappointments. I can't."

He shook his head, regarding her with something that might have been pity. "It isn't about disappointing them, Grace. It's about disappointing you. You're scared to take a chance. The worst part is that on one level I can't really blame you for that. I just don't know how to prove to you that I will never let you down again."

And that, she thought, was the saddest thing of all, because she didn't know how he could, either.

Fifteen

Michael had every intention of fighting for Grace, of doing whatever it took to convince her that they should be a family. He knew she loved him, knew that they could make it work, but he had to find a way to prove it to her. Unfortunately, he didn't have a clue what that proof might be.

And then, just before dawn on Monday morning, his phone rang, waking him from a sound sleep. At first he couldn't grasp what his mother was saying.

"Mother, slow down. You're not making any sense."

"It's your father, Michael. He got out of bed a little while ago and went to the kitchen to make coffee." She choked back a sob. "That's where I found him, in the kitchen, on the floor."

Michael felt his heart slam against his ribs. "Is he okay? What happened?"

"The paramedics say he's had a heart attack. I don't know how serious it is, but he hasn't come to. That can't be good, Michael. They've taken him to the hospital. Can you call the others and meet me there?"

"I'm on my way," Michael said at once. "Mother, get

a neighbor to drive you, okay? Promise me. Don't drive while you're this upset."

"Pauline is here. She'll take me."

Pauline was the housekeeper who had been with them for the past ten years. She was as close as family and she was a rock in a crisis. She would take good care of his mother.

Michael yanked on the first clothes he could grab, then raced to his car. He spent the drive to the hospital making calls on his cell phone. He caught up with Dylan, who'd miraculously returned home to Los Piños, probably five seconds after Michael's departure. Dylan promised to call Trish.

"We'll be over there as fast as we can get there. Call me if you have any news in the meantime."

"I will."

"He's going to be okay, Michael. Dad's tough. He'll outlive us all."

"I pray you're right," Michael said. He had this terrible, gut-deep fear that his behavior on Saturday had been the blow that caused this. Had his father felt Michael slipping away as the others had done? Was he convinced that all his years of hard work to build an empire for his family had been wasted? If so, that would have created unbearable stress for a man like Bryce Delacourt.

Because he couldn't bear to think about that, he concentrated on trying to track down Jeb on his honeymoon. When he finally reached him, Jeb was ready to fly home immediately.

"Wait," Michael advised. "I'll call you back as soon as I get to the hospital. Let's see where we are, before you cut your honeymoon short."

"I need to be there," Jeb protested.

"You won't get here in the next fifteen minutes. Sit tight for that long, at least. Then you can decide."

"Call me the minute you know anything."

"I promise."

That left Tyler, but try as he might, Michael couldn't locate his brother anywhere, not at his apartment in Houston, not at work on the oil rig.

"I'll track him down," the supervisor of operations at the rig said.

"Do you even know where to look?"

"He spends a lot of time in Baton Rouge. If he's there, one of the men will locate him."

"Thanks," Michael said, hanging up just as he turned into the hospital parking lot, tires squealing.

Minutes later, he found his mother in the emergency room waiting area, looking as unkempt as he'd ever seen her in public. It was testament to her panic that she hadn't even combed her hair or changed out of her bathrobe. She was crying silently as Pauline patted her hand and murmured reassurances. The housekeeper spotted him first and stood up to give him a fierce hug.

"It's good you're here, Michael. She's going to make herself sick with worrying."

"Has there been any word yet?"

"Nothing," Pauline said.

He gave his mother a quick kiss, then said to the housekeeper, "Stay with her. I'll see what I can find out."

It turned out to be easier said than done to get a straight answer. Either no one he approached knew anything or they were too busy to stop and explain what was happening.

"Please, Mr. Delacourt, the doctor will be out to talk to you as soon as he has a minute," a nurse told him at the entrance to what was apparently his father's treatment cubicle. "You can't come in here. Let the doctor do his job."

He glanced past her. All he could see amid the cluster of doctors and nurses and machines was a glimpse of ashen skin. "Is he going to make it?"

"This team is the best. They'll give him every chance humanly possible. The rest will be up to God. Maybe you could spend some of this waiting time praying to Him."

Michael knew the suggestion was well-meant, but he'd been praying all the way over here. He wanted answers now. He felt a reassuring touch on his shoulder and turned to find Grace regarding him with a concerned expression.

"Michael, let them work."

Shock at finding her here was rapidly replaced by relief. He desperately needed her right now, needed to hold on to something real and positive. "How did you hear about this?"

"It was on the radio. I was on my way to the courthouse when I heard it. I knew you'd be here and that you'd be causing trouble."

He managed an exhausted grin. "You know me, I hate anything I can't control."

"He'll be okay," she said. "Believe that."

"If only it were that simple."

"I spoke to your mother. She's holding up okay. As soon as we get back there to be with her, Pauline said she was going to go home and get some clothes for her.

Come on, let's go keep her company. The sooner she gets to freshen up a bit, the better she'll feel."

She turned, but when Michael didn't follow at once, she glanced back. "What?"

"You have no idea how glad I am that you're here." He shook his head, hoping to clear it of this fog of disbelief that made everything that had happened this morning seem surreal. "I'm scared, Grace. The only other time I've been this scared was when you walked out on me."

She opened her mouth to respond, but no words came out. Instead, she simply took his hand and squeezed it. The gesture, her presence, provided more comfort than he had any right to expect.

As they waited for what seemed to be an eternity, Grace encouraged his mother to talk, then told her about Josh and Jamie, anything to keep her distracted. Finally, at nine-thirty, a tall man in green scrubs came into the waiting area looking for them. Michael tried to read his expression, but for once his ability to gauge moods failed him.

The doctor took a seat beside Michael's mother. "I won't lie to you," he said. "It was touch and go for a while in there, but we have your husband stabilized for now. I've got an operating room waiting. He needs a triple bypass and he needs it now. I'd like to wait, but, frankly, I don't think that's an option."

"Without it, he'll die?" his mother asked in a hushed whisper.

"Let's just say I don't like the odds if we wait," the doctor said. "I've been trying to get him to come in for a test for months now, but he wouldn't take the time."

So this wasn't as unexpected as Michael had thought.

His father had seen a cardiologist, then ignored his advice. That was typical of him.

"Has he been conscious at all?" his mother asked.

"He's been in and out. Now he's sedated."

His mother looked at him. "Michael, what do you think?"

"There's no choice, Mother. We have to let him perform the surgery. We have to give Dad that chance." He leveled a look straight at the doctor. "Could he die anyway?"

"Yes," the doctor said bluntly. "But the odds of him pulling through go up considerably if he makes it through the operation, makes some lifestyle changes, eats better, gets rid of some of the stress in his life."

Michael nodded. "We'll see to it, doctor. You keep him alive through the surgery and we'll see to the rest."

Tyler's litany of warnings came back to haunt him. Was this the future he faced if he didn't make those same changes? One glance at Grace proved she was thinking the same thing. She didn't need to say a word for him to get the message loud and clear.

The next few hours passed in a complete haze. Dylan and Trish arrived. Michael spoke to Jeb and filled him in. This time Jeb wouldn't be dissuaded from coming home.

"Brianna agrees. We belong there. We've already made reservations. We'll be there tonight. Is everyone else accounted for?"

"Everyone except Tyler," Michael said. "I can't find him. He's not answering his cell phone. His boss is trying to track him down in Baton Rouge."

"Keep trying. He'll never forgive himself if something happens to Dad and he's not there."

"I know."

"You okay, Michael?"

He glanced at Grace, who gave him a quick, reassuring smile. "Yeah, I'm hanging in there, thanks to a little help from an old friend."

"Care to explain that one?"

"You'll see when you get here."

When he'd tucked the cell phone back in his pocket, Grace left the conversation she was having with Trish and his mother to come to him.

"How about some coffee? Something to eat?"

"Nothing." He smacked his fist against the wall. "Damn, I hate this waiting."

"I know."

"Where are Jamie and Josh?"

"I made arrangements for a neighbor to keep them while I was at work today."

"Work?" He stared at her blankly, then shook himself. "Of course, it's Monday, isn't it? Shouldn't you be there?"

"It was more important for me to be here."

She said it matter-of-factly, but Michael heard something else in her voice. She was sending yet another message about her priorities and how she had always put the people in her life first. Unlike him.

As if she sensed his troubled thoughts, she gave his hand another squeeze. "It's okay, Michael. I will have to go soon, though. I promised her I'd pick them up by four."

Michael glanced at his watch, stunned to see that it was after three. "What the hell is taking so long?"

"This isn't something you want them to rush," she reminded him quietly.

"No, no, of course not."

No sooner had he spoken than the doctor came through the swinging doors. Michael introduced him to Dylan and Trish, then asked, "Well, how did it go?"

"He came through the surgery like the stubborn old man he is. He's in recovery now. We'll move him to Cardiac Intensive Care later. He'll be there a few days."

"Then?"

"If all goes well, he'll go into a regular room and be home by the weekend, chomping at the bit to go back to work. I'd suggest you prevent that if humanly possible," he said with a slight grin.

"I'll see that he doesn't," Michael said grimly.

"No, I will," his mother said forcefully. "He will not set foot in the office until I say it's okay. I don't care if that blasted company goes bankrupt in the meantime."

All of them stared at her in shock.

"Well, I don't. It's robbed me of too many years with my husband as it is. I won't let it steal him from me forever. And that's final."

Dylan turned slowly to Michael. "You going to be able to take up the slack?"

"Of course," he said firmly, but even as he spoke he saw Grace's expression of dismay. She whirled around and took off down the hall before he could break away to catch her.

Couldn't she see that he had no choice, that this was an emergency? How could he make her understand that this didn't change his promise to her, that he still intended to do everything in his power to spend time with her and Josh and Jamie?

All the way home Grace told herself she was being unreasonable. Of course Michael had to step in and help out while his father recuperated. But she knew in her heart that this was no temporary measure. Even if Bryce Delacourt recovered fully, his wife would see to it that he didn't go back to working at the same pace he'd set for himself before. She had heard that determination in Mrs. Delacourt's voice. That left the day-to-day operation of the company to Michael. He would immerse himself in it, because that was his nature and because he saw it as his duty.

It didn't help that Josh and Jamie greeted her with a hundred questions about Michael's whereabouts.

"I want to tell him about all the neat stuff we did today," Josh said.

"He can't come over tonight," Grace told them, knowing that unless she put an end to their expectations now, they would go on being disappointed. "His father's in the hospital."

"Is he gonna die?" Jamie asked, looking worried.

"It looks as if he'll make a full recovery," Grace said. "But this means that Michael is going to be very, very busy for quite a while with the family business. I don't think we'll see too much of him."

Josh looked ready to cry, but Jamie just regarded her stoically. "I figured he wouldn't stick around. Who cares? We don't need him."

Grace gathered both boys close and gave them a

fierce hug. The problem was they did need him. All of them did. And maybe she needed Michael most of all.

Everyone else had gone home to get some much-needed sleep, but Michael remained in the waiting area outside of the intensive care unit, slouched down in an uncomfortable chair, drinking coffee the strength of battery acid.

That was where Tyler found him at midnight.

"How is he?" he demanded, his gaze shifting from Michael to the doors of the cardiac unit.

"Where the hell have you been?"

"It doesn't matter," Tyler said, raking his hand through his hair. "How is he?"

"He'll make it."

Tyler sank down on a plastic chair. "Thank God. I was scared to death I wouldn't get here in time."

"Even Jeb and Brianna beat you here," Michael said, not cutting his brother any slack.

"The point is, I came the minute I heard."

"Tyler, where were you? It's not like you to just up and disappear."

"I was living my life," Tyler snapped back. "It's something you should consider." Before Michael could utter a sharp retort, he added, "I suppose you'll bury yourself in work again to take up the slack while Dad's out."

"Of course I will. You might consider coming back for a while, too."

"Not a chance. And if you have an ounce of sense in your head, you won't do it either."

"Dammit, somebody in this family has to be responsible," Michael said.

"And it always has to be you."

"In this instance, yes."

"How does Grace feel about that?"

Michael winced as he thought of the expression on her face when she'd run out earlier.

"Not jazzed about it, is she?" Tyler asked.

"We haven't discussed it."

"But she knows what you intend to do?"

"Yes."

Tyler shook his head. "Look, I know I'm the jokester, the playboy, whatever, but listen to me just this once. Haven't you learned anything from what happened today? Life is short. You've got a woman who's crazy about you, a couple of kids who desperately need a dad. Weigh that against one more merger, one more high-powered negotiation. I know which one Mother would tell you to choose."

Michael knew, too. Her vehement comments earlier had pretty much destroyed any illusion that she'd been content with the way his father had neglected their marriage in favor of the business.

"You know something else?" Tyler said. "I'll bet if you ask Dad the same question right now, he might surprise you with his answer."

Michael wasn't so sure about that. Bryce Delacourt was stubborn, but Michael hoped not to be known for quite the same level of muleheadedness. He stood up.

"Where are you going?" Tyler asked, a faint grin tugging at the corners of his mouth. "Or need I ask?"

"I just hope she'll let me in."

"She might not," Tyler agreed. "But if she does, I

hope you'll have sense enough to go in there, barricade the door and keep asking her to marry you until she says yes."

Michael laughed. "I might have to do just that."

In the end, getting in was even harder than he'd expected. Josh answered the phone when Michael called from the lobby.

"What are you doing up?" he asked.

"Grace is crying," Josh announced. "And it's your fault."

Grace crying? "I'm coming up," he said. "Can you hit the button to buzz me in?"

"I don't know how."

"Get Jamie."

"He's real mad at you."

"Get him anyway."

The phone clattered on the table as Josh went looking for his brother. A minute later, Jamie answered sleepily.

"What do you want?"

"I want to come up and talk to Grace."

"Well, she don't want to see you. None of us do."

"I do," Josh protested.

"Look, Jamie, it's the middle of the night. Just buzz me in."

"Why do you want to see Grace?"

He was explaining himself to a thirteen-year-old, Michael thought wearily. It was worse than going to a disapproving father to ask for a daughter's hand in marriage.

"I need to explain some things to her."

"What things?"

Michael thought he detected a faint click on the line.

He suspected Grace had picked up an extension to see what was going on in the middle of the night.

"That I love her, for starters," he said, praying that he was right about her being on the line. "That I want to marry her and be a father to you guys. And that I am not going to wind up following in my father's footsteps, not into a hospital room, anyway."

There was a buzz on the line. Michael grabbed the door to the lobby and yanked it open. The elevator seemed to take forever, but when it opened upstairs, Grace was standing in the hallway, clutching her robe around her.

"You have a lot of nerve," she said as he came toward her. "It's the middle of the night, for one thing. For another, you woke up the boys. For another, you told them things you've never said to me."

He chuckled. "How do you know that unless you were listening?"

"You knew I was on the line?"

"Of course."

"So you said all of that for my benefit?"

"Yes."

She searched his face. "I want to believe you."

"You can, darlin'. I've learned a lot of lessons today. At the top of the list is the fact that I don't want to go through life without you and I want our life together to be a very long one."

"The company's going to need someone to run it the next few months."

"The company has a very good executive team. It's about time we gave them more to do."

"Do you honestly mean that?"

He brushed a wisp of hair away from her cheek. "I

honestly do." He rubbed the pad of his thumb across her lower lip and felt her tremble. "So, Grace Foster, are you going to marry me and keep me from turning into a workaholic like my father?"

"You're the only one who can do that, buster," she said forcefully, then grinned. "But I guess I'll have to marry you just to make sure you have a really good incentive."

He lowered his head and claimed her mouth. When he finally lifted his head again, he murmured, "That's the best incentive I can think of. I'm still going to want your kisses on my hundredth birthday."

"You'd better."

Michael glanced toward Grace's apartment and spotted two towheaded kids trying not to be seen as they blatantly eavesdropped. He gave a nod in their direction for Grace's benefit, then said, "Think we should have kids right away?"

"As far as I'm concerned, we already do," she said.

"You mean Josh and Jamie?" he inquired innocently.

"Those are the ones. We're a package deal, Delacourt."

"You drive a tough bargain, Ms. Foster. But then you always did."

"Is he saying yes?" Josh whispered.

"Not in plain English," Jamie grumbled.

"Yes," Michael said loudly.

"Oh, wow," Josh breathed, racing into the hall and catching him around the legs in a hug.

Jamie sauntered out more slowly.

"Does this sound okay to you?" Michael asked. "All of us together, a real family?"

"Are you gonna, like, adopt us?"

Michael met Grace's gaze, then nodded. "If we can and only if you both agree."

"Say yes," Josh pleaded. "Come on, Jamie. We'll be together forever and ever. All of us."

Jamie finally released a pent-up sigh and a smile slowly spread from ear to ear. "Yes."

"I guess that makes it official," Michael said, just before he snatched the chance to steal one more long, satisfying kiss.

"Oh, yuck, more mushy stuff," Josh and Jamie declared in unison.

"The mushy stuff is the only thing in life that really counts," Michael told them. "You'll see."

"Hopefully," Grace said. "It certainly took you long enough to catch on."

"But I was worth waiting for, wasn't I?"

She winked at him. "That remains to be seen."

Epilogue

"I ain't never been on a honeymoon before," Josh said as Michael and Grace studied the travel brochures spread out on the dining room table at Michael's house.

"And you're not going on this one," Michael said.

"How come?"

"'Cause it's all about mushy stuff," Jamie said wisely. "They don't want little kids around."

"Where are we gonna stay?"

"With Grandpa Bryce," Michael said.

Grace regarded him worriedly. "I'm not so sure that's such a good idea. He's still recuperating."

"If mother has her way, he'll be recuperating for another year at least, but even she admits he's going stir-crazy. These two ought to keep him occupied and safely at home where she can keep an eye on all of them."

"I like staying with Grandpa Bryce," Josh said. "He lets us play with his computer."

Michael looked stunned. "He does?"

"Uh-huh. Last time, he taught us how to figure out profit and loss figures for the year."

Grace groaned. "The man never gives up. He's already working on the next generation and these two aren't even related to him."

"Not yet," Michael said. "But they're going to be. The court date is next month." He glanced around. "Any second thoughts? Last chance to back out of this adoption business."

"Not me," Josh said fervently.

"Me, either," Grace said.

Michael turned his gaze to the silent thirteen-year-old. "Jamie?"

"Nah. I think it might be pretty cool to finally have a mom who's really around and a dad."

"Not half as cool as I think it's going to be to have two sons to follow in my footsteps," Michael said.

Grace frowned at the comment. "I can still call this wedding off," she said. "It doesn't have to happen."

Three male voices protested in unison.

"Okay, then, no more talk about anybody following in anybody's footsteps. Understood?"

"Yes, ma'am," they all said dutifully, Michael included.

Grace grinned. It was very rewarding that only a few days away from her wedding, they finally knew who was in charge. She wasn't about to delude herself, though. It was three-against-one, if push ever came to shove.

Which was why when she and Michael were finally in the honeymoon suite overlooking the ocean in Hawaii, she slipped out of her negligee and lured him straight into bed, ignoring the food and champagne he'd ordered.

"You seem to be in some sort of a hurry, Mrs. Delacourt. Why is that?"

"I want to make love with you. Surely you knew that

was what we'd be doing on our honeymoon. You know, the mushy stuff."

"Oh, really? I'd hoped to squeeze in a couple of business meetings."

She barely resisted the urge to smack him. "Not in this lifetime," she assured him as she began working on the buttons of his shirt.

"I detect the fact that you have an agenda here. Care to fill me in?"

"I want a baby, Michael."

"We're just about to adopt two hellions. Isn't that enough family for now?"

Grace shook her head. "Nope. I think we need a couple of little girls. Did I ever mention that twins run in my family? On my mother's side. Her mother was a twin. So was my great-great-great-grandmother. It seems to skip every generation or two. I figure we're about due."

His head snapped up at that. "Twins?"

"Just think about it," she murmured, tugging his belt loose. "Won't it be wonderful?"

Michael looked dazed. "Wonderful," he said finally.

Grace shimmied his pants down his legs, then gave him a gentle nudge that had him tumbling backwards onto the bed. She climbed on top of him.

"Have I mentioned that you're going to be a terrific family man, Mr.Delacourt?"

He gave her a wicked grin, then flipped her onto her back. "But first I have to prove what an outstanding husband I can be," he said softly, his mouth moving over her.

Grace felt the familiar rise of heat, the familiar buildup of tension as his wildly clever fingers teased and taunted until her body trembled.

"Michael, please," she murmured when it seemed she was about to be swept away on a tide of delicious sensations.

"Please what?"

"Please show me what an outstanding husband you're going to be," she murmured, reaching for him, sliding her hand over the length of his arousal.

He moaned at her touch, then hesitated above her before slowly sliding deep inside, filling her up, making her whole. The rhythm he set was sweet torment, slow, then fast, then slow again until every nerve ending was on fire, every muscle tense as she strained toward an elusive peak.

And, then, when she was almost there, he stole another one of those devastating kisses, the ones that melted her inside. This time it was just what she needed to hurtle over the edge into spasms of pure ecstasy.

Exhausted, she curled against him. "That was—"

"Outstanding," he suggested, his hand on her breast, already starting something again.

"Better than outstanding," she said and placed one hand on her tummy. "We've made babies, Michael. I just know we have."

He regarded her with tolerant amusement. "Darlin', if we haven't, it will certainly be my pleasure to go on trying."

"I love you, Mr. Delacourt."

"I love you," he whispered solemnly, then added, "More than anything."

Hearing the words meant a lot, but deep in her heart, Grace had already known it was true. She intended to spend the rest of her life making sure that never changed.

* * * * *

Keep reading for a special sneak peek at
The Delacourt Scandal, *part of the 2-in-1 anthology*
Starlit Secrets by #1 New York Times
bestselling author Sherryl Woods.
Coming in March 2024!

One

Tyler couldn't help noticing the woman sitting at the other end of the bar. She had been there for the past week. Petite, with auburn hair cut boyishly short, she had a sweet face with a very kissable mouth—innocence and the promise of sin combined. Tonight she was wearing a prim little white blouse and a bright red skirt that kept creeping up, revealing a very shapely thigh. More of that intriguing innocence-sin contradiction.

She was a plucky little thing, fending off passes with a few words and an engaging smile, nursing what appeared to be ginger ale. What she was doing here in the first place was beyond him. She wasn't looking for a man, that was clear enough. Nor did she drink. And yet here she was at O'Reilly's, night after night, same stool, same bland, disinterested expression, same polite brush-offs.

In times past Tyler would have taken that as a challenge. Harmless flirting with a beautiful woman was second nature to him, as it had been to his brothers. Any one of the Delacourt males would have moved closer and satisfied his curiosity.

At the moment, though, Tyler just wasn't up to his usual casual banter.

He had way too much on his mind. His whole future, for instance.

Until a week ago he'd been out on a rig in the Gulf of Mexico off the Louisiana coast for three straight months, trying to forget the past, trying to lose himself in hard, physical, mind-numbing work. At the end of the day all he cared about was a cold beer, a rare steak and sleep. That was the way he wanted it, the way he *needed* his life to be—clear and uncomplicated.

Women were a definite complication. Family was both a blessing and a curse. He'd intended to steer clear of both for the foreseeable future.

Then the edict had come down that all Delacourts were required to be in Houston for his parents' fortieth anniversary bash. Even Trish, who never came back to Houston if she could avoid it, had been corralled into attending. Only his brother Michael had escaped, because he and Grace were away on their honeymoon.

There was nothing on earth Tyler hated more than being all dressed up in a fancy tux, unless it was being back in an office. In the past week he'd found himself in both these situations.

And if Bryce Delacourt had his way, Tyler would stay in Houston indefinitely. Judging from his father's off-hand comments, Tyler had a hunch that this time it was going to be a whole lot harder to wrangle his way out of the Delacourt Oil corporate headquarters and back onto a rig. He envied Trish and Dylan their escapes to the peace and tranquility of Los Piños all the way across the state. They were back there now, out of their father's reach, while Tyler was still here, still very much under his thumb.

He took a sip of his beer and wondered if the time hadn't finally come to cut the family ties completely—professionally speaking, anyway. He wouldn't be the only one in the family to do it.

His oldest brother, Dylan, had been the first to shun the family business, infuriating their father by setting up shop as a private eye. Then Trish had managed to slip away to another city, have a baby and open her second bookstore—all before their father had caught up with her just in time to see her wed a rancher. Jeb had one foot in Dylan's business, which he'd moved to Los Piños after his marriage to a pediatrician there, and another at corporate headquarters, but he managed to stay out from under Bryce Delacourt's control most of the time.

Only Michael relished being at the helm of a multinational oil company and, ironically, their father couldn't seem to see that he was the only one really suited for the job. Usually Michael provided adequate cover for Tyler, but his current absence had reminded their father that he had one remaining son he could groom for the executive suite.

More than the others, Tyler hated the thought of disappointing his father, but he hated paperwork even more. He shuddered at the prospect of facing a lifetime of it. There were oil companies around the country—around the world, for that matter—that would be happy to hire someone with his lifelong history in the business, with his expertise and willingness to work endless hours, with his daring and fearless approach to oil exploration. Maybe it was time to check into some of them. Maybe it was time to stop worrying so much about being a dutiful Delacourt and worry more about being himself.

His thoughts dark, he barely glanced up when the woman from the other end of the bar slid onto the stool next to him. For once the prospect of an evening's flirtation didn't do a thing to lighten his mood. He just wanted to be left alone to wrestle with the past and with the decision that had to be made about the future.

"Hi," she said, leveling amber eyes straight at him until he finally met her gaze.

"Hi, yourself."

"I've seen you here before."

"Every night this week," he agreed, turning back to the beer he'd been nursing, hoping she would take the hint and go away.

"I thought you'd make a pass by now."

The offhand observation caught his attention. He regarded her with a wry look. "Did you now?"

"You're the only male in this place who hasn't." She made the claim with a surprising lack of conceit and just a hint of puzzlement.

Tyler regarded her with amusement. "Since you turned down every one of them, I figured I'd cut my losses and save myself the trouble."

"Then you were interested?"

"Any male with blood still pumping through his veins is interested in an attractive female."

Suddenly her expression brightened. "You think I'm attractive?"

He shook his head. "Don't be coy. Of course you are."

"*I* know that," she said with a touch of impatience. "I just wasn't sure if *you* did. I wasn't certain you'd even noticed me. You looked kind of lost, as if you were off in another world and not too happy about it. That's why I decided to break my rule."

"What rule is that?"

"I never, ever, talk to men I don't know, not without a proper introduction. I'm Maddie, by the way. Maddie Kent. It's Madison, technically, but whoever heard of a woman named that? I think it was a family name on my mother's side. She was convinced it could be traced back to James Madison, but I never saw any proof of it." She beamed at him. "Who are you?"

"Tyler," he said, deliberately leaving off his last name. Mention of "Delacourt" in this part of Texas tended to stir up all sorts of reactions that had more to do with his father or the family wealth than him. He'd learned to hedge his bets when he first met a woman, see if her reactions were genuine before he laid his full identity on her.

"Why are you here, Maddie?" he asked. He gestured toward the ginger ale. "It's obvious you're not a big drinker."

"I just got to town a couple of weeks ago and moved into this neighborhood. This seems like a nice place. It's definitely better than going back to an empty apartment."

Something about the comment stirred Tyler's suspicions. If she was here to stave off loneliness, then why not accept the attentions of one of the men who'd approached her? Why come here if she had such a hard-and-fast rule about not talking to strangers? And why zero in on the one man who hadn't made a pass at her? Just because she liked a challenge? Or because she knew precisely who he was, after all?

"You've had quite a few admirers the last couple of days. Why have you rejected all of them?" he asked.

"I told you. I have a rule. Besides, they were looking

for more than a little friendly conversation. You can tell, you know, at least if you're a woman."

Tyler definitely knew. On any other night of any other week, he might have been one of them, and chitchat would have been the last thing on his mind. He enjoyed flirting, but the prospect of making the occasional conquest made it more interesting. It kept his mind off another woman—one who'd slipped out of his life when he'd least expected it and now was lost to him forever.

"So you came over here because I looked safe enough?" he asked.

"Exactly."

"Darlin', I wouldn't count on it. The only difference between those men and me is that I've got a lot more than sex on my mind these days."

She didn't bat an eye at that. "Tell me. I'm a good listener. Maybe I can help."

He studied her eager expression and wondered if an impartial outsider could offer a perspective on his life that he hadn't yet considered. The trouble was, he'd made it a rule not to share any of his deepest longings and ambitions with anyone—and especially not a woman. Not since Jen.

From the moment they'd met, he'd told Jennifer Grayson everything.

She'd led a tough life but had come through it with a surprisingly sweet and gentle nature. He'd given her his heart. Hell, he'd even gotten her pregnant and given her a baby, but she'd steadfastly refused his offer of marriage, wouldn't take a penny of support money for their daughter, wouldn't accept the gifts he'd sent. She'd insisted she could make it on her own, without any charity from some rich Texan whose family would only look down on her because she'd come from the wrong side of the tracks.

Talk about reverse snobbery. Jen had had it in spades. Nothing he'd said could persuade her that his offers were motivated by love not pity. He had admired her pride, even as it had exasperated him. He'd accepted her terms, because she'd given him no choice.

Jen and his baby girl, his precious Rachel, had lived in Baton Rouge, conveniently nearby whenever he had time off from his work on the Delacourt rigs in the Gulf of Mexico. Despite her refusal to marry him, Jen had been the best thing in his life.

Even so, he had never shared her existence with his family. She'd accused him of being ashamed of her, but the truth was that at first he'd just wanted something that was his alone, not part of the Delacourt dynasty, not subjected to media scrutiny. Jen had been his secret and his joy.

The time had come, though, after the baby was born, when he'd wanted his family to know everything, wanted them to get to know Jen, even if their relationship was unconventional. Six months ago, after endless arguments, he had finally persuaded her to come to Houston and meet his parents. He had held such high hopes for that trip. He'd been so sure that once she got over that hurdle, Jen would see that she could fit in, that she would be accepted just because he loved her.

In one last surge of stubborn pride, she had insisted on driving, rather than accompanying him in the company jet. He had agreed, to his everlasting regret. En route there had been an accident. The crash had occurred after midnight, and the police suspected Jen had fallen asleep at the wheel, though they would never know for sure. There were no other cars involved, and there had been no witnesses. Jen and Rachel had both died at the scene.

From that moment on Tyler had descended into his own personal hell of guilt and loneliness, made worse because he'd refused to share his torment with anyone. He'd considered the silent suffering to be his penance for pressing her to do something she hadn't really wanted to do.

That was another reason he didn't want to leave Louisiana. All of his memories of Jen and the baby were in Baton Rouge. And when they got to be too much for him, he needed the demanding work on the rig to exhaust him. The waking memories were difficult enough, but the nightmares about that crash were a thousand times worse. At home this last week he'd awakened every single night in a cold, drenching sweat, heart pounding, tears running unchecked down his cheeks.

His family knew something was terribly wrong, but he refused to talk about it. Michael had even made the trip to Baton Rouge to see him before his wedding to Grace. His brother had poked and prodded for two straight days, but Tyler hadn't been ready to reveal a whole part of his life he had kept secret for years. He still wasn't. Someday he would be able to talk about Jen, but not yet, not even to the brother who knew him better than anyone on earth.

He sighed heavily.

"Hey, where'd you go?" Maddie asked, snapping him back to the present.

"Just thinking about someone I used to know," he admitted without meaning to.

Her eyes brightened with curiosity. "Were you in love with her?"

"I was."

"And she loved you?"

"She said she did."

"What happened?"

"Stuff," he said, because talking about the tragedy wouldn't change anything, and he'd already said more than he should have.

"You don't want to talk about it," she concluded.

"Brilliant deduction."

"Then tell me about yourself. What do you do, Tyler with no last name?"

So, he thought, she had caught the deliberate omission. "I work on an oil rig, or at least that's what I did last week. This week it's hard to say."

"Did you lose your job?" she asked, regarding him sympathetically.

"Not the way you mean." This was not a conversation he intended to have, not with a stranger, not tonight. "Look, Maddie Kent, it's been nice talking to you, but I've got to run." He tossed some bills on the bar. "That ought to take care of your drink. Welcome to Houston. Maybe I'll see you again sometime."

"Maybe so," she said cheerfully, showing neither surprise nor hurt that he was walking out on her.

Only after he was outside, sitting in his car and wondering what the heck he was going to do with himself for the rest of the evening, did he regret his impulsive decision. If nothing else, Maddie with the kissable lips might have provided a much-needed distraction from his dark thoughts. He thought of that blend of innocence and sex appeal and sighed. Then again, she might be nothing but trouble.